T/

MW00439513

"Couldn't put the book down ... love the character development in the stories Christopher Valen writes as well as the plots he develops ... a story that grabs your attention and leads the reader through twists and turns that are interesting and entertaining ... awesome continuation of John Santana adventures! ... the best John Santana novel yet! ... an intense, action-packed read ... keeps you on the edge ... the story is first class ... outstanding police procedural."

—*Amazon Reviews*

Speak for the Dead

"In Valen's solid seventh novel featuring St. Paul homicide detective John Santana (after 2015's *The Darkness Hunter*), Santana looks into the stabbing murder of Kim Austin, an accident investigator for the National Transportation Board, whose body was found buried in a cave along the Mississippi River ... The trail eventually takes the dogged detective to Colombia, where he confronts *el Lobo*, a contract killer, in a dramatic showdown ..."

—*Publisher's Weekly*

"Valen slips in a lot of red herrings that keep the reader guessing. In the middle of the plot is beautiful, flirty Reyna Tran, one of the most intriguing characters to walk onto a page in a while. Is she friend or foe, would-be lover or killer? She's unreadable and that makes a lot of fun for readers. Almost as chilling as the murders in *Speak for the Dead* is what Santana learns about the terrors of spoofing, a way for bad guys to hack into and take over phones, airplane navigation systems and other devices. You'll start to look at your cellphone in a new way. As usual, Valen conveys a sense of place, from the damp chill of the river caves to the beauty of nature along the St. Croix River."

—St. Paul Pioneer Press

The Darkness Hunter

"[A] taut story full of mystery and tension . . . with a pertinent message interwoven into a thrilling plot."

—Reader's Favorite

Death's Way

"The tightly wound story moves at a fast pace, with each chapter ending on a cliffhanger so that the audience will want to keep reading . . . this novel represents a gripping offering from an award-winning author."

—Foreword Reviews

Bone Shadows

Midwest Independent Publishers' Association 2012 Best Mystery of The Year

"*Bone Shadows* is guaranteed to hold readers' attention until the last page . . . Valen's highly moral Santana character is golden."

—Library Journal

Bad Weeds Never Die

"The latest John Santana police procedural is an excellent investigative thriller . . ."

—Midwest Book Review

"Christopher Valen's third novel, *Bad Weeds Never Die*, continues the story of John Santana, a homicide detective in St. Paul, Minn., who was introduced in *White Tombs*, and whose story was continued in *The Black Minute*. The three novels are all great police procedural stories . . . I have thoroughly enjoyed reading Valen's novels . . ."

—Bismarck Tribune

The Black Minute

"Santana—an appealing series lead, strong and intelligent . . . Readers who enjoyed *White Tombs* will settle easily into this one; on the other hand, it works fine as a stand-alone, and fans of well-plotted mysteries with a regional flair . . . should be encouraged to give this one a look."

—Booklist

"[A]s in *White Tombs*, Valen writes well about St. Paul and surrounding areas. He gives just enough sense of place to make you feel like you're there, but he never loses track of his story's fast pacing. And he does a super job of keeping the suspense going as the action reaches a crescendo . . ."

—St. Paul Pioneer Press

White Tombs

"Valen's debut police procedural provides enough plot twists to keep readers engrossed and paints a clear picture of the Hispanic community in St. Paul."

—Library Journal

"*White Tombs* is a superb police procedural starring a fascinating lead detective. Santana is a wonderful new addition to the subgenre."

—Midwest Book Review

The John Santana Novels

White Tombs

The Black Minute

Bad Weeds Never Die

Bone Shadows

Death's Way

The Darkness Hunter

Speak for the Dead

The Price of Life

Also By Christopher Valen

All the Fields

City of Stones

For Rebecca Treadway

Thank you so much for all the wonderful book covers

No Way to
DIE

A John Santana Novel

Christopher Valen

Santa Rita Press
Tucson, Arizona

NO WAY TO DIE
Copyright © 2023 By Christopher Valen

SANTA RITA PRESS
1261 W. Camino Urbano
Green Valley, AZ 85622

Cover Design: Rebecca Treadway

Library of Congress Control Number: 2023913147
Valen, Christopher
NO WAY TO DIE: a novel / by Christopher Valen – 1st edition
ISBN: 9781737747116

Santa Rita Press/September 2023
Printed in the United States of America

10 9 8 7 6 5 4 3 2 1

No Way to
DIE

by

Christopher Valen

"Every man must do two things alone; he must do his own believing and his own dying."

— Martin Luther

Chapter 1

Gusts of wind swept across the flat, open landscape like a broom. Snow crystals glinted in the bright light that had broken through the early morning cloud cover. The frozen city looked like something out of an apocalyptic movie. Plows had opened the snow-emergency routes, allowing Homicide Detective John Santana and his new partner, Gabriel Cruz, along with Reiko Tanabe, the Ramsey County ME, Tony Novak and three techs from the Forensic Services Unit, teams from patrol and K-9, and state forensic anthropologist Dr. Kim Solace to reach Como Park—and the skeletal remains uncovered in the snow.

Media uplink vans had parked behind roadblocks a half-block from the bone site. Reporters and camera crews kept the engines and heaters running as they ventured out for a few minutes to yell questions at police officers in the vicinity before retreating back into the warmth of their vans. Despite their efforts, Santana couldn't help but chuckle as the rotor noise generated by the three local television helicopters circling overhead drowned out any chance of asking questions.

Wearing a watch cap with the St. Paul Police patch facing front, gloves, boots, and his Blauer-style fleece jacket over a heavy SPPD sweater, he and Cruz watched as Tanabe and Solace examined and then confirmed that the pelvis, femur, and the six long, flat, curved rib bones belonged to a human.

Santana knew that over ninety percent of men and women had twelve pairs of ribs, refuting the Adam and Eve myth the Catholic priests and nuns had taught him in his catechism classes in which Eve was made from one of Adam's ribs. The exceptions were those few born with a specific genetic anomaly where they either had more or less than the standard twenty-four ribs.

Yellow-and-black crime scene ribbon had been strung among a series of bare sugar maples in the park, though at this early stage of the investigation Santana saw nothing that indicated a homicide.

"Bones could belong to a homeless person," he said. "Animals could've scattered the rest."

"Possible," Tanabe said.

Condensation fogged her wire-rimmed glasses every time she spoke or breathed. Frustrated, she yanked off the scarf covering her nose and mouth and stuffed it in a pocket of her parka.

"We'll need a grid search," she said.

Kim Solace nodded in agreement.

Once the ten uniforms had been gathered together, Santana told them that they would now be under the supervision of Dr. Solace, who would instruct them in the proper techniques of a grid search. The uniforms were all wearing watch caps, black overcoats, gloves and boots, department-approved balaclavas that covered the head and neck, and cold-weather pants.

After turning the search over to Solace, Santana turned to the black, heavy-set uniformed officer standing beside him, whose nameplate identified him as Jefferson.

"Who discovered the bones?"

"Kid named Jadyn Hartley," Jefferson said.

The name sounded familiar to Santana, but he couldn't place where he'd heard it before or if it had any significance.

"Kid said he was looking for the Winter Carnival medallion," Jefferson continued.

The medallion treasure hunt, which began in 1952, was part of the annual ten-day St. Paul Winter Carnival festival celebrating the legend of King Boreas, Queen Aurora, the Vulcans, and the age-old battle between cold and warm. Twelve clues were printed in the *St. Paul Pioneer Press* on twelve consecutive days. The clues indicated the medallion could be found in a local park. Treasure hunters flocked to the park they thought the clues pointed them towards to search for the medallion, worth $10,000. The treasure hunt had started last Sunday. But Jadyn Hartley was the only treasure hunter observable at this hour in Como Park.

"Had him wait in my squad," Jefferson said, handing Santana Hartley's wallet.

According to Hartley's license, he was twenty years old and lived on N. Churchill Street near Como Park.

Santana thought Hartley looked familiar, but he couldn't place him. He handed the wallet and license to Gabriel Cruz. "See if we've got any record on Hartley while I talk to him."

"Gives me an excuse to get out of the cold," Cruz said as he hurried to their ride.

Jadyn Hartley sat in the backseat of Jefferson's squad, his hands stuffed in the pockets of his parka, the hood pulled back on his shoulders. He had a scraggly beard and wore his hair long in a relaxed copper-colored Afro. He had Caucasian features and a complexion that nearly matched his hair.

Sitting on the passenger side of the front seat, his body half-turned so he could look at Hartley, Santana held up his badge wallet and introduced himself. Then he said, "Tell me how you found the bones."

Hartley shrugged. "I was just digging around, searching for the medallion. Didn't know I'd find the bones instead."

Santana noted that Hartley avoided eye contact. He wondered if the kid was lying or if there was another reason.

"Little cold to be out digging. Don't see anyone else out here." Santana gestured toward the park and then realized that Hartley was still not looking at him.

"Not too cold for me," Hartley said. "Got to keep ahead of everyone if you want to win."

"You search every year?"

"Try to."

"Ever won?"

Hartley shook his head.

"You working, Jadyn?"

He shook his head as he continued gazing out the side window, seemingly lost in his own world.

"You live with your parents?"

He shook his head again.

Santana waited for a more complete answer. When he didn't get one, he asked Hartley who he lived with.

"My mother."

Santana stared at him for a time, searching his memory bank. Then it hit him.

"Your father was Steven Hartley."

"Yeah. I'm the one who killed him."

*   *   *

Later that same morning Santana sat at his desk in the Homicide and Robbery Unit at the Law Enforcement Center, reviewing the report on Jadyn Hartley that Gabriel Cruz had prepared.

At the age of fifteen, Hartley had killed his father with a twelve-gauge shotgun that his father had bought him prior to their first deer-hunting trip.

"Hartley's mother said her husband had been abusing her for years," Cruz said.

He was seated at his desk in the cubicle next to Santana, his tie loosened, his sport coat hanging over the back of his swivel chair, the sleeves of his white shirt rolled up to the elbows.

Cruz wore his black hair short, military style. He had a slight scar on his forehead and spoke in low, quiet tones, but the words he uttered were crisp and clear.

Rita Gamboni, Deputy Chief of the Major Crimes Division, had added Cruz to the ten-member unit a month ago after a retirement and right before a hiring freeze had hit the department. Santana had been working solo on cold cases and had argued against training a partner, but Gamboni had insisted.

"Being we're both Latino had nothing to do with your decision," Santana had countered.

"*Nada*," Gamboni had replied with a smile.

Cruz had completed a criminal justice degree at St. Thomas University in St. Paul. After four years as a patrol officer, he'd applied and been promoted to the Gang and Gun Unit and then to Narcotics and Vice. At thirty-two years old, his first murder case had triggered an animated energy and an eagerness to learn.

Cruz pronounced his first name *Gah-BRYEHL* while rolling the R, which was common for his Mexican heritage and in other Latino countries. But cops on the force often used the American pronunciation Gay-Bree-Uhl. Cruz didn't seem to mind how cops pronounced his name, but Santana stuck to the Latino pronunciation.

"Seems Jadyn Hartley's old man had a nightly ritual," Cruz continued. "Come home from the office and start drinking. After dinner, knock Mom around before passing out. When Hartley intervened, his father threatened to kill both of them. Kid got the shotgun out of the gun rack and blew away the old man."

"I remember the shooting," Santana said. "Don't remember much about the father."

"Hartley's mother testified in defense of her son at the trial. Basically, said the kid saved her life. Had the x-rays proving how she'd been battered over the years. Anyway, Hartley was tried in adult court and convicted of voluntary manslaughter. He had a clean record and the mother was convincing. Due to the circumstances and age, the DA recommended Extended Juvenile Jurisdiction."

Extended Juvenile Jurisdiction, known as EJJ, was a program designed to give a young kid like Jadyn Hartley an opportunity to avoid an adult sanction. EJJ applied to teens fourteen and older but younger than eighteen who committed serious felony-level offenses. Normally, the court could only retain jurisdiction over a child until they reached the age of eighteen. EJJ allowed the court to retain jurisdiction until the age of twenty-one. If the kid failed to satisfy conditions of the juvenile court sentence, the court could impose their adult court sentence, sending the juvenile to an adult prison.

"You think Hartley killed someone else?" Cruz asked.

"Easier the second time, but too early to tell if we're looking at a homicide."

"What're the odds he finds human bones in a snowbank?"

"Probably less than finding the Winter Carnival medallion. But that would mean he knew the bones were there in the first place."

"And then he dug them up on purpose and notified the police," Cruz said with a disbelieving shake of his head. "Not real logical."

"Most murders aren't. But Hartley doesn't strike me as an attention seeker. Just the opposite, actually, given his background and EJJ classification."

"Read the last paragraph. Hartley's also mildly autistic."

"No wonder he wouldn't directly look at me."

"You noticed that, too, huh?"

Santana nodded.

"In the meantime?" Cruz said.

Santana's desk phone rang. He answered and listened quietly before hanging up.

"In the meantime we've got a DB," he said, referring to a dead body. "Let's roll."

Chapter 2

Blood had stained her forearms, hands, and legs, and had soaked her white underwear and the green short-sleeved T-shirt she wore with a black ARMY logo across the front. Her head rested against the back edge of the empty bathtub. Her eyes stared blindly into the eternal darkness.

Her name was Tara Easton.

The first officers on the scene reported that a neighbor across the hall, Hannah Thatcher, had come over to watch a Netflix movie and found Tara Easton in the bathtub. After making sure the officers had made no changes to the scene, Santana and Gabriel Cruz had both slipped on a pair of booties and latex gloves and had entered the third-floor apartment. They then worked their way to the bathroom, taking care to avoid disturbing or destroying any evidence.

Reiko Tanabe, the Ramsey County medical examiner, had already arrived on the scene after leaving the bone site, as had Tony Novak and one tech from the Forensic Services Unit, both of them dressed in white Tyvek suits. Novak used a hand-held 3-D high-resolution scanner to document the scene. The Vietnamese tech named Lilly moved in a clockwise pattern, using a digital camera to photograph the scene from all four corners of the bathroom.

Based on the blood spatter on the bathroom wall, Tara Easton had held the knife in her right hand, placed the edge of it against her neck below the left ear, and pulled the handle forward and across, very quickly, severing her carotid artery below the left ear. The rupture caused a projectile blood spatter, leading to hypovolemic shock.

She'd bled to death in a few minutes.

7

The sweet, heavy tang of the bloody death scene hung in the air and lingered in Santana's mouth, filling his throat with the familiar, coppery aftertaste of a licked penny.

He'd seen many deaths in his years in homicide and many ways to die. But deaths by cuts bothered him the most. It wasn't the amount of blood—he had seen plenty of that—but the sheer brutality of a sharp-edged death.

He understood how deep, dark depression sometimes led to suicide. He'd experienced his own darkness, his own demon, especially after his mother's murder. But rather than harm himself, he'd used the darkness to ignite his anger and fuel his revenge toward those responsible for her death.

"Got an estimate of the time of death, Reiko?" he asked the ME.

"Rigor is fixed," Tanabe said, more to herself than to Santana.

Tara Easton's dark purple skin color indicated lividity was fixed as well. Moving the body after eight hours would not alter the discoloration patterns.

"Ambient temp is seventy degrees in the bathroom," Tanabe said. "Rectal temp is eighty-point-seven. I'd say she's been dead about twelve hours."

Santana looked at his watch. 11:00 a.m. That would make the TOD around 11 p.m. last night.

The bathroom had been locked from inside, though it was a push button doorknob lock, meaning someone could have locked the door on their way out. The knife had been recovered from the bathroom floor. All the evidence suggested a suicide.

But two things troubled Santana.

Men often attempted suicide by cutting their throat, while women more commonly chose slower-acting medications. Women also tended to cut their wrists, creating what detectives called "spaghetti wrists" due to the exposed tendons on a red background resembling pasta in tomato sauce.

Also, Santana saw no hesitation marks, no evidence that the young woman had second thoughts about ending her life.

He noted the wedding band and a silver engagement ring with a small diamond on the third finger of Tara Easton's left hand. He made a rough sketch of the scene, and then he and Cruz began a search.

An unframed photo on a small bookshelf in the bedroom of her small, modern apartment off W. 7th Street, near downtown St. Paul and the Mississippi River, pictured the young woman with four men, two on each side.

With her oval face, baby blue eyes, blond hair, and short, choppy shag cut, she reminded Santana of a young Meg Ryan.

Tara Easton wore camo fatigues and no helmet, as did the two men to her left. The three of them were smiling as they held their M4 carbines in a port arms position.

The first bearded man to Easton's right wore a tunic shirt and pants, and a turban on his head. A smile creased his face, but he held no weapon.

The second man to Easton's right was another bearded Afghan, but he wore a tiger-striped uniform with narrow green and brown stripes and broad black strokes printed over lighter olive. He wore a helmet and carried an M4 at port arms. His lips held no smile, and his dark eyes were as depthless as a snake's.

Santana took a picture of the front and back of the photo using his SPPD iPhone.

A second unframed photo on the opposite end of the bookshelf pictured a truck with a narrow wheelbase adorned with colorful stickers and chimes.

"They're called jingle trucks in Afghanistan."

Santana turned and looked at Cruz.

"See the metal tassels hanging from the bottom of the truck frames?" Cruz said.

Santana looked at the photo on Tara Easton's bookshelf again.

"The Army contracted the delivery trucks through Afghan government officials."

Santana knew Cruz had been in the service but didn't know where he'd served. "You served in Afghanistan?"

Cruz nodded. "The NCO responsible for the contracts was called the 'jingle man.' Prices were based on destination and type of truck that were serviceable at best. Same with the Mi-8 birds that shuttled supplies, equipment, and fuel. We nicknamed them 'Jingle Air,' but were forbidden to ride in them because half the pilots reeked of vodka. No way in hell I'd get in one anyway."

Santana had Lilly photograph the front and back of the photo of Easton with the four men and add it to the evidence inventory. Then he peered at the signatures and description on the back of the photo.

Blaine, Angel, and Taimur. KAF.

"Know what KAF means?" Santana asked Cruz, gesturing with the photo.

"Stands for Kandahar Airfield, the main base of operations for southern Afghanistan and the main transportation hub for both helo and fixed wing."

"You were there?"

"Briefly."

Santana had never served but admired those who did. He considered asking Cruz more about his service time and then rejected the idea. Now wasn't the time. And some of the veterans he'd come across were reluctant to talk about their war experiences. He respected those feelings.

Assuming that the names matched the men from left to right, he wrote the three names in his notebook.

Why was the fourth man in the tiger stripes unnamed? he wondered.

Pointing at the man in the photo, Santana said to Cruz, "This guy's name isn't written on the back of the photo."

Cruz peered at the photo for a moment.

"Afghani Special Forces," he said. "Probably asked Easton not to write down his name in case the photo ever got in the wrong hands."

Santana nodded.

A framed color photo of a cute young girl, maybe two years old, sat on the nightstand beside the single bed. She looked much like a younger version of Tara Easton. Probably Easton's daughter.

"Looks like a suicide, huh?" Cruz said.

"Looks like it."

"You don't think so?"

"I don't *know* so. There's a difference."

Cruz nodded.

"Take a look in the closet," Santana said. "I'll search the dresser drawers."

"What're we looking for?"

"Diary, journal, letters, notebook, a suicide note, and a cell phone. Anything that might give us a clue as to why Tara Easton is lying in her bathtub with her throat cut."

Santana made a conscious effort to avoid using the word "suicide," though initial appearances pointed to that conclusion.

"What about drugs?" Cruz asked.

"That, too."

Later, in a dresser drawer containing Tara Easton's undergarments, Santana found a Bronze Star with a capital V Device.

"Gabriel," he called.

Cruz came back into the room.

Santana held out the Bronze Star. "What's the V stand for?"

"Heroism or valor in combat," Cruz said. "She must've been one tough lady."

Two other boxes contained an Army Service Ribbon and the National Defense Service Medal.

"Nothing special," Cruz said. "The ribbon and defense medal are given to anyone who completes boot camp."

In a fourth box was a silver medal with a cross pattée surrounded by a laurel wreath.

"Expert marksmanship award," Cruz said.

"She qualified with a rifle," Santana said, indicating the attached qualification bar underneath the medal.

"Exactly. You're issued four ten-round magazines to engage forty pop-up targets from four shooting positions. Only have eight-to-ten-second intervals to change magazines and positions. She had to hit thirty-six out of forty targets from distances of fifty to three hundred meters. Not easy to do."

Underneath the box containing the medals, Santana found two envelopes addressed to a Matt Easton in St. Paul. He had Lilly photograph the envelopes and letters inside before silently reading the first one.

Dear Matt,

Well, if you're reading this, you know I didn't make it home and never got the chance to tell you again how much I love you. I know we had our differences, especially about my Afghanistan deployment. Unfortunately, it's too late now to tell you that you were right. I should have listened. Take comfort in the fact that I am watching over you and will always be with you in spirit. This last line might surprise you since I've never practiced any religion or expressed any belief in God. But someone once said there are no atheists in foxholes. Take my word for it. He was right.

I want you to know just how important you are to me. I could not ask for a more caring and loving husband. The memories that we've shared over the last few years have been the best of my life. Although it may seem like my life was taken too soon, I lived a life that most women can only dream of. I married the perfect man. I have a beautiful daughter. I couldn't ask for anything more. Whenever you feel sad, just think back to all the wonderful memories that we shared.

I know this time must be hard for you, but I have to believe that this happened for a reason and that someday you will understand. Be strong not only for yourself but for our baby, Jamie. Remind her about her Mommy and tell her that I loved her more than anything else in the world. Her birth was the best day of my life and she was the best thing that ever happened to me. Her smile and laughter represent all that is good and beautiful in this world.

Tell her that Mommy is in heaven now and will watch over her and protect her every minute of every day. I love you Matt, but please do what you need to do to be happy. It's so important that you continue to find happiness in your life. Although you may think this is impossible right now, have faith. Much better times are coming. You and Jamie have a wonderful life ahead of you and I am so happy to have shared some of it with you.

Your loving wife,
Tara

Santana handed the letter to Cruz and read the second.

Dear Jamie,

Although you may not remember me, I want you to know how very much your Mommy loves you. I left for Afghanistan when you were one year old. Leaving you was the hardest thing I've ever had to do. You are so very special to me honey. The best day of my life was the day you were born. Every time I saw you smile my heart would just melt. You will forever be my sweetie. My life was not complete until you were born.

I am so sorry I will not be able to see you grow up. But remember, your Mommy is not gone. I am in heaven now smiling down on you every day. You are so very lucky to have such a wonderful Dad to take care of you. Be good for him and make sure to help him whenever you can. Never forget how important and special you are. We love you so very much.

When you get older and start school, do your best and try to learn as much as you can about the world you live in. Always be nice and caring to others and you will discover that the world will be nice to you. But when things aren't going your way, never forget that your Daddy knows what is best for you and that everything will work out in the end.

You have such a bright and beautiful future ahead of you. Have fun. Enjoy it. And remember, your Mommy will always be proud of you and will always love you. You are and will always be my sweetie.

With all my love,
Your Mommy

Santana exchanged letters with Cruz. When his partner was finished reading Santana said, "Obviously, she never sent them."

"I knew guys that wrote letters like these before they deployed."

"Not you?"

Cruz shook his head. "Always thought it was bad luck. Like you knew you weren't going to make it. Negative thinking can get you killed, you know?"

Maybe there was something to it, Santana thought. He'd always considered himself a survivor even in the darkest of times. He'd had assassins hunting him and criminals looking to take his life. He doubted his experiences were equivalent to a pitched battle in war, but he did know that he suffered from PTSD, as many veterans did, and that he'd learned to live with it. He wondered now if Tara Easton, like many veterans, couldn't live with the trauma that she'd suffered.

"The thing I can't understand," Cruz continued, "if she had a husband and daughter that she loved so much, what is she doing living alone here?" He made a sweeping gesture with his hand indicating the apartment. "And why would she kill herself?"

"Something we need to find out," Santana said.

Cruz pointed his chin at the closet. "Found a cell phone in a purse hanging in the closet," he said.

"Let's see if her husband knows her cell phone password."

He asked Lilly to photograph the iPhone and write it on the evidence inventory log.

Santana knew a warrant wasn't needed for Tara Easton's cell phone found at the crime scene. Courts presumed that any murdered person would want their killer caught. If Tara Easton's husband, Matt, used it frequently, then a warrant was needed after seizing it.

"Anything else in the purse?"

"A set of keys clipped to it. Sixty dollars in twenties. A few credit cards and a driver's license. Tara Easton was twenty-five years old."

Santana asked Lilly to collect the laptop while he and Cruz searched the desk in the bedroom, looking for mail, read or unopened. With many people handling their bills, banking, and credit cards online, they found little in the desk drawers besides a DD Form 214 discharging Tara Easton from military service six months ago.

According to the form, she'd attained the rank of Private First Class, or E3. Her last duty station was Kandahar, Afghanistan. She'd received an honorable discharge. Having dealt with veterans before, Santana knew that MOS stood for Military Occupational Specialty. He wasn't sure what 11B meant. He asked Cruz.

"Means she was in the infantry. Small arms weapons, heavy anti-armor, or crew-served weapons. Standard military jargon."

Santana told Cruz to take a couple uniforms and speak to the neighbors. "Check the lobby security video for the past day or two."

"Will do," Cruz said. "I'll search Tara Easton's vehicle."

"Okay. I'll search the rest of the apartment and then question Hannah Thatcher, the neighbor across the hall who found the body."

In the kitchen Santana saw no recently prepared or partially eaten food. Comparing it with Tara Easton's stomach contents during the autopsy could help determine the time of death. The stove was turned off and there were no signs of clean-up attempts or attempts to burn or wash away evidence.

A large knife was missing from a butcher block on the kitchen counter. Santana figured it was the same knife found in the bathroom. He had Lilly photograph the butcher block.

He observed no signs of a party. No empty bottles, cups, or glasses.

A half-empty pack of Marlboro cigarettes rested on the living room coffee table beside a nearly empty bottle of Johnnie Walker

Black Label Scotch, an empty cocktail glass, and an ashtray containing a crushed cigarette butt and a half-smoked marijuana joint. The butt and joint had no teeth marks or lipstick and were dry.

Lilly photographed the ashtray before collecting the cigarette and joint in separate paper envelopes. She labeled them with exhibit number, initials, date, and location. Then she sealed the glass and bottle of Scotch for evidence.

Santana checked the wastebaskets and trashcans in the kitchen, but saw no indication that someone had been going through them and found nothing of evidentiary value.

The upcoming Friday on the magnetized calendar on the refrigerator door was circled. Doctor's appointment was written in the square box under the date.

The towels in the bathrooms and vanities were dry and had no bloodstains. He saw no signs that someone had cleaned up afterwards or was injured and had bled at the scene. The toilet seat was down, something Santana expected to find in a woman's apartment or house.

After checking the toilet tank for hidden items, he opened the medicine cabinet. It contained bandages, toothpaste and a toothbrush, a bottle of mouthwash, a nail clipper, and a vial of Prozac, a common antidepressant. Martin Conrad was the prescribing doctor.

Santana wrote Conrad's name in his notebook.

He'd found no evidence of forced entry, struggle, or ransacking. No suicide note either, which wasn't surprising since roughly two-thirds of suicides never left notes. Yet Tara Easton had written loving letters to her husband and daughter before her last deployment. Different circumstances to be sure, but it showed that she cared about what her daughter and husband thought of her.

When Santana returned to the living room, a uniform, whose nameplate read MOSHER, waved him over and showed him the Crime Scene log. It logged each person's entry and exit from the scene and would become part of the murder book. The log also kept nonessential people away from the scene.

Mosher said, "Guy down the hall is Wade Crawford." He gestured with the clipboard toward a tall, thickset man in an unbuttoned blue suit, navy blue overcoat, and thick-soled black shoes. He might just as well have been wearing a sign that said "government agent."

"Told me he wants to speak to you," Mosher said.

"About what?"

"Didn't say." Mosher handed Santana a business card.

The business card identified Crawford as an agent in the office of the Special Inspector General for Afghanistan Reconstruction.

"You wanted to see me?" Santana said as he approached Crawford.

Neither man offered to shake hands.

"You Santana?"

"That's right."

Crawford slid his thick hands into his coat pockets. At 6'2" he was as tall as Santana but maybe fifteen pounds heavier. He was bald on the top of his head with a rim of shaved dark hair along the sides and back. His dark brown eyes were nearly black in color, and there was no smile in them.

"I take it Tara Easton is dead," Crawford said.

"You knew her?"

"Not well."

"Yet here you are."

Crawford offered no response.

Santana showed him the iPhone photo of the picture he'd taken in Easton's bedroom.

"Know any of these people?"

Crawford stared silently at the photo. "The jingle man. Taimur Khalil."

"What about Blaine, Angel, and the other unidentified Afghani?"

"Nope."

Santana peered at the business card in his hand. "What exactly is SIGAR?"

"We investigated waste and abuse of dollars in Afghanistan. Looked after all you taxpayers."

"From what I've read, that didn't turn out so well."

"That supposed to be funny?"

"Just the opposite."

Crawford started to say something and then appeared to change his mind. "Was Tara Easton murdered?"

"What's your interest, Crawford?"

"It's government business."

"Really?"

"You have a problem with that?"

"Not at all. But what you're asking about is *my* business."

Crawford placed his hands on his hips, like a drill sergeant about to dress down a new recruit. "Don't make trouble for yourself, Santana."

Santana turned and headed back to Tara Easton's apartment.

"You do the same," he called over his shoulder.

"I'll be seeing you soon, Detective."

"Not if I can help it," Santana said.

Chapter 3

Hannah Thatcher sat ramrod straight in a leather chair while Santana, notebook and pen in hand, faced her in a matching chair.

He always started a new notebook with each case.

He'd expected to see a woman similar in age to Tara Easton. But Thatcher had at least twenty years on Easton and looked like she spent her free time in the gym. She wore faded jeans and a black zippered sweatshirt with GIRL POWER stenciled across the front. She'd cut her dark hair close to the scalp in a buzz cut. A small silver cross hung from the silver chain around her neck.

Framed photos of her in her Army dress and combat uniforms and with her fellow soldiers sat on a tall bookshelf to Santana's right. He noted a signature on one of the framed Army dress photos addressed her as "Major." Another photo taken from the side and slightly behind showed her in civilian clothes aiming an AR-15 at a target in a shooting lane at an indoor gun range. Santana saw nothing indicating the name of the range.

From where he sat in the living room, he could see into the bedroom through the open door. A buffer tube mount attached to the wall near the queen bed held an AR-15 in a vertical position for quick access. The rifle had a distinctive crimson rose and black handguard with two skulls.

The handguard let Thatcher hold the gun by the barrel for more precise aim and prevented her from burning her hands. Wind shifts could cause errant shots otherwise.

In a small enclosed frame with a black velvet background on the bookshelf next to him, Santana saw the same expert marksman silver medal he'd found in a drawer in Tara Easton's bedroom. Both women had qualified as an expert marksman with a rifle.

Santana noted that in the framed photos Thatcher had a large, upturned, scarred nose, possibly from shrapnel. Plastic surgery had reduced the size and removed the curve and scars, changing and enhancing her appearance considerably. Her surgery reminded him of the Chinese belief that if you change your nose, you change your destiny.

Hannah Thatcher wore a silver Army ring on the third finger of her left hand. The unusual-looking opaque green stone in the setting had red inclusions that resembled drops of blood.

She saw Santana looking at it and offered a half smile. "It's a heliotrope made from jasper with inclusions of hematite," she said. She held up the back of her hand to give him a better view. "Sometimes called the 'stone of Babylon.'"

"Never heard of that before," he said.

She admired the ring. "Magicians used it for invisibility, and early Christians believed the red spots were Jesus' blood. Roman soldiers thought it could slow bleeding. Are you a man of faith, Detective?"

Santana had been raised Catholic in Colombia but had lost his faith at sixteen when a drunk driver killed his father and the twin sons of the head of the Cali cartel murdered his mother. Most everything he'd seen since as a homicide detective had only reinforced his belief that there was no higher power, no deity saving the faithful from the daily carnage infecting both believers and non-believers. Surely, Santana thought, if God existed, he or she would never allow the misery and senseless death he'd experienced in his job and in his life.

"A man of justice," he said.

"Then it's justice you seek."

"It's why I'm here."

"You think I can give it to you?"

He shook his head. "But you could give it to Tara Easton."

Thatcher removed a cigarette from the package of Marlboros on the coffee table and lit one with a Bic lighter. She took a long drag and blew a small cloud out her nose.

Thatcher's hazel eyes found his again. "Tara took her own life. At least that's the way I read it."

Santana recalled the package of Marlboro cigarettes and the crushed cigarette butt in the ashtray on the coffee table in Tara Easton's apartment. He wondered if the package and butt belonged to Tara Easton or to Hannah Thatcher.

"Did your friend smoke Marlboros?"

"Sometimes."

"Did she use dope or coke?"

Thatcher hesitated. "She might've tried it."

"How about you?"

She smirked. "That's my business."

"Mine, too."

"Not unless you're accusing me of something, Detective."

"No reason to—at this time."

"That's reassuring."

Santana let it go for now. "Did Tara Easton ever talk to you about committing suicide?"

"Never mentioned it."

"Were you two close?"

"I was in for twenty, but we shared some of the same experiences."

"You both qualified as expert marksmen with a rifle."

"We did."

"Still shoot?"

"I try to get to the range once or twice a month."

"What range is that?"

"The Combat Zone gun shop."

Santana wrote the name in his notebook. "Did you know Tara Easton before?"

"Met her when she first moved in six months ago."

"Spend much time with her?"

"We'd get together occasionally for drinks at a bar or in each other's apartment. We liked to watch sports and movies. Share war stories."

"Ever meet her husband, Matt?"

Her eyes slid off his for a second. "Afraid not."

"She must've talked about him? Told you why they were separated."

"We mostly talked about her daughter, Jamie. How much she missed her. She was excited about getting back together with her husband."

"Were you in Afghanistan, Ms. Thatcher?"

The corner of her mouth curled in a tiny smile. "You always this formal, Detective?"

"It's part of the job."

"Reminds me of the military."

"Similar, I suspect, in many ways."

"Yeah, I spent time in Afghanistan, mostly in and around Shindand Airbase in southwest Afghanistan, about seventy-five miles from the Iranian border, and at Camp Scorpion, just outside of Kabul. Tara spent most of her time in and around Kandahar."

"Did she ever mention anything . . . unusual that happened to her in Kandahar?"

"Lots of unusual shit went down there and everywhere else in Afghanistan. But most days were known as 'groundhog days.'"

"Like the Bill Murray movie?"

She nodded. "Every day rolls out the same way, no matter how you try to change it. Must be sort of like your job, huh? No matter how many psychos you take off the street, there's always another to take their place."

"*Mala yerba no muere*," Santana said.

"Sorry. I don't speak Spanish."

23

"Bad weeds never die," he said. "It's a Colombian saying."

"I detected a slight Latino accent."

Santana wanted to retake control of the questioning. "When I say unusual, I'm not talking about battles or war experiences in Afghanistan."

Thatcher inhaled a mouthful of smoke, tilted her head up, and blew out a small cloud. "Then what?"

Recalling his brief conversation with Agent Wade Crawford from SIGAR, Santana said, "Anything to do with taxpayer dollars or money for the Afghan government."

"Hell, there was tons of waste and corruption by the Afghanis."

"I'm talking about Americans."

"You think Tara was involved in that shit?"

Santana ignored her question and showed her the iPhone photo he'd taken of Tara Easton and the two Americans and two Afghanis.

"This photo was taken at the air base in Kandahar," he said.

"Birthplace of the Taliban."

"Know anyone in the photo besides Easton?"

Hannah Thatcher stared at the photo for a moment as smoke from the cigarette in her left hand spiraled upward. When she lifted her chin, Santana saw the momentary recognition on her face.

"You know them."

"Only this one," she said, pointing to the first soldier standing just to the left of Tara Easton. "Guy's name is Blaine Beckham. The unarmed Afghani is probably a terp. Short for interpreter," she added, anticipating his question.

Santana wrote Blaine Beckham's name in his notebook. "How do you know him?"

"He came by Tara's apartment on a few occasions. He was a meat eater in Afghanistan. What we called special forces."

"Know why Blaine Beckham came by?"

She cocked her head and pursed her lips as her eyes locked on his. "I suppose because he'd served with her."

"Tell me what else you know about him."

"That's it."

"What aren't you telling me?"

She stood. "Time for you to leave."

"Are you currently working, Ms. Thatcher?"

"I waitress at Tinucci's in Newport."

Santana took out a business card and set it on the coffee table. "Call me when you feel like talking more."

"I've said all I'm going to say."

Santana stood. "Think about it, Ms. Thatcher. Better yet, think about your dead friend, Tara Easton."

"You think I don't?"

"Not enough."

"Fuck you, Detective. You don't know shit."

"Then enlighten me."

"Don't let the door hit you in the ass on your way out."

Chapter 4

A gray watery light washed the sky, and a series of mounds hid the rocks that lay underneath the snow-covered ground as Santana and Cruz drove to Matt Easton's house. Santana used the address written on the envelopes he'd found in the dresser drawer in Tara Easton's bedroom.

Cruz sat on the passenger side of the Ford Taurus, his notebook in his lap.

The SPPD had replaced the old Crown Vics with a combination of the Ford Taurus Police Interceptor sedan and a Ford SUV Police Interceptor utility. Santana owned a Ford Explorer for personal use, but would love to have his SUV outfitted like the utility.

He glanced at Cruz. "Neighbors have anything to say?"

Cruz opened his notebook and reviewed his notes before speaking. "No one heard or saw anything unusual," he said after a time. "Everyone I talked to said they either didn't know Tara Easton or said she kept pretty much to herself."

He closed his notebook and said, "You talk to Hannah Thatcher?"

"She's a vet, too," Santana said, "though she and Easton didn't serve together. Met when Easton moved into her apartment six months ago. Thatcher said she had no indication Easton was depressed and wanted to kill herself. In fact, Easton was excited about getting back with her husband and daughter."

"Doesn't sound like a woman planning to kill herself."

"No," Santana said, "it doesn't."

Cruz went quiet, his chestnut brown eyes focused on the road ahead.

Santana was comfortable with silence, like an old married couple still in love. He and his former partner, Kacie Hawkins, had that kind of relationship—he trusted her and she him.

Maybe it was the same with Cruz and the troops he'd served with.

The two of them had watched lobby footage from Tara Easton's apartment building. They saw someone wearing a parka with the hood up and a big man with a Twins ball cap pulled down tight over his face. He'd never looked at the camera. The hood had concealed the other person's identity and gender.

Cruz reported that Tara Easton's blue 2019 Chevy Silverado pickup was parked near her apartment. Inside, it was clean, with nothing suspicious in the glove box or under the seats.

Santana told Cruz about Wade Crawford and his SIGAR background.

"Why is Crawford sniffing around?"

"Something else we need to find out," Santana said.

Since this was Cruz's first death notification, Santana explained that he would do all of the talking. It was easier for a person to follow when only one person spoke. As Santana asked the questions and observed Matt Easton's reaction and body language to the news of his wife's death, Cruz would take notes.

Living in the Internet age, it was common for the next of kin to find out through social media before detectives could even attempt a death notification. Timeliness was more important now than ever before.

Santana understood that nothing he said or did would ease the emotional pain. Still, a direct yet compassionate death notification would aid in the grieving process. He viewed the difficult assignment as both a duty and an honor. Done right, it could ease the pain of the message they were entrusted to deliver.

"How do you deal with it?" Cruz asked.

"You mean homicide?"

"Yeah. I saw my share of death in Afghanistan. But I knew at some point I'd be leaving it all behind, though you never really do."

"Yet you chose to be a cop," Santana said. "And not just a cop. But a homicide cop."

"Quite a contradiction, huh?" Cruz said with a shake of his head.

"Yes, it is."

Cruz looked out the passenger side window. "Instead of killing, I want to find the ones who kill. We didn't make much of a difference in Afghanistan. Didn't change much of anything."

"Except for those Afghanis who got out."

Cruz looked at Santana. "But what about the families left behind?"

"That's how you make this work," Santana said. "Think about the loved ones left behind. Work every case like the victim is the most important person in your life. Never make someone feel victimized twice by your demeanor or lack of attention. They're already hurting and looking for answers or closure. We shouldn't be making it worse for them. Everyone deserves the same level of service and respect going in."

"Sounds like it's personal."

"Any good detective will tell you homicide investigations are always personal. Best you learn to keep it that way."

Matt Easton lived in the Payne-Phalen neighborhood on St. Paul's East Side. Once settled by Irish, Germans, Swedes, and Italian immigrants, the area was now home to the Mexican consulate and many Hispanics, Hmong, and Karen from Myanmar.

Three Southern slave owners had originally purchased the neighborhood in the 1800s, and a number of streets were named after flowers in the South, including Hawthorne, Hyacinth, and Magnolia.

Santana and Cruz stood on the front stoop of the stucco bungalow-style house, their breath forming tiny clouds of condensation in the fifteen-degree temperature as an icy wind freight-trained out of the north. Santana rang the doorbell and waited. He rang it two more times before a twenty-something man in bare feet, gray sweatpants, and a red T-shirt with SPFD FIREFIGHTER stenciled in large letters across the front opened the door.

The man blinked at the bright sunlight and ran a hand through his tousled brown hair, as if he'd just woken up.

"Mr. Easton?"

"Whatever you're selling," he said, "I'm not buying."

As Easton started to close the door, Santana held up his badge. "I'm Detective Santana. This is Detective Cruz."

Easton seemed to snap out of his half-sleep. "What's this about?"

"If we could come in, Mr. Easton."

Easton rubbed his stubbled cheeks as he considered his response. Then he stepped back from the door and made a finger gun gesture toward the living room.

"Have a seat."

Entering, Santana saw the downhill skis, snowboard, and photo of Easton bungee jumping off a bridge. He figured the tall, lanky Easton was a thrill-seeker.

Santana noted an identical framed photo of the young girl that had been on Tara Easton's nightstand on the fireplace mantelpiece.

Santana and Cruz removed their coats, hung one each over an arm of the couch, and sat down.

Easton closed the front door and leaned against it, his cinnamon-brown eyes looking inward. Then he moved across the room and eased himself into the cushioned chair across from the couch, his forearms resting on his thighs, his eyes locked on Santana.

"I'm sorry to have to tell you this, Mr. Easton," Santana said, "but your wife, Tara, has died of an apparent suicide."

Santana made sure his delivery was short and directly to the point. He'd consciously used Easton's name and then stated how he thought she'd died.

Easton held Santana's eyes for a time before his gaze slid over to Cruz, as though looking for confirmation.

Cruz nodded once.

Santana knew from experience that there was no right or wrong way to react to devastating news. Everyone was different. He'd seen reactions ranging from no reaction at all to screaming, crying, and aggression, where a friend or family member had become angry with him as the bearer of bad news.

Easton stared silently into the void for a time.

"Could we get you a glass of water, Mr. Easton, or something stronger?" Santana asked.

Easton shook his head. "No. I just need a minute."

Easton sat still for a few beats before speaking again. "When did this happen?"

"We believe she died in her apartment within the past twenty-four hours."

"How did she do it?"

Santana had anticipated the question, but hoped he wouldn't have to answer it.

"With a knife."

"She cut her wrists?"

"Her throat."

"Jesus," Easton said with shake of his head.

"Was your wife right-handed or left-handed, Mr. Easton?"

"Right-handed. Why?"

Rather than dwell on the brutality of Tara Easton's suicide, Santana wanted to switch topics as quickly as possible.

"Any ideas as to why she would take her life, Mr. Easton?" he asked.

"No. This doesn't make any sense. Who found her body?"

"Woman across the hall. Hannah Thatcher. You know her?"

"I've met her. But I don't really know her."

Thatcher had lied about meeting Matt Easton, Santana thought. He wondered why.

"Are your wife's parents still alive?"

"Tara was an orphan. Spent most of her youth in and out of foster homes. Jamie and I were all the family she had."

"When did you speak to her last?"

"Christmas Eve. She came by to drop off presents for Jamie. She talked about getting back together."

"How did you feel about that?"

"She needed to get her shit together for that to happen."

"And what *shit* would that be?"

Easton shrugged. "If you'd been married to her, you'd get it."

Santana remained silent for a time before asking the next question.

"How long have you two been separated?"

"Since she returned from Afghanistan six months ago."

"Did you notice anything different about her when she came by at Christmas?"

"How do you mean?"

"Did she appear depressed?"

"Why would she be depressed?"

"Well, she'd just returned from a war zone and you two were separated."

Easton clenched his jaw. "That was her decision. Not mine."

"Why did she want to separate?"

"You some kind of marriage counselor?"

"Anything you can tell us about your wife's mental state can help us, Mr. Easton."

Easton paused for a time, his brow knitted in thought. Then he said, "You're homicide detectives, right?"

"We are," Santana said.

"So, it's possible somebody killed her."

"Right now, her death appears to be a suicide."

"*Appears*," he said. "Meaning it could change."

"Meaning everything points to suicide."

"But someone could make it look like suicide, couldn't they?"

"There's no indication of that," Santana said, wondering for a moment if Matt Easton was projecting his own guilt. "But let's get back to why your wife chose to separate."

"She was messed up after her tour of Afghanistan."

"Messed up in what way?"

"She was just . . . different."

"How?"

"She always had a good sense of humor. You know, like she laughed off a lot of stuff. But when she came home, she was a different person. Always had something real serious on her mind."

"Did you ask her about it?"

"Sure. But she wouldn't talk about it."

Santana recalled the short conversation he'd had with Special Agent Wade Crawford from SIGAR and the photo Tara Easton had on her bedroom bookshelf of the two troopers and two Afghanis.

"Did your wife ever mention anyone with the names Blaine, Angel, or Taimur?"

Santana used the American pronunciation of "Angel" rather than "Anhel," the Latino pronunciation.

"Don't believe so."

Santana let Easton think about his response.

Then he said, "Tara had a photo taken with the three of them at the Kandahar Air Field in Afghanistan. Blaine's last name is Beckham."

Easton shrugged. "Don't know who they are."

Santana showed him the photo of Tara and the four men he had on his cell phone.

Easton shook his head. "Don't recognize them."

"How about Wade Crawford?"

"Never heard of him."

Santana had studied body language and facial recognition. He knew detecting deception was imprecise, but he'd also learned that he was one of a small fraction of emotionally intelligent people who could often discern truth from lies.

At the same time, he knew signs of emotion weren't necessarily signs of innocence or guilt. An innocent person might be apprehensive and appear guilty, so he operated under two assumptions: lying was a last interpretation once everything else possible was ruled out, and it was much harder to find the truth than to find a lie.

"You work for the fire department, Mr. Easton?"

"Yeah, at the Engine 17 station at Payne and Hawthorne. I'm off today. Have to work tomorrow, which is why I was sleeping when you rang the doorbell."

"Are you a veteran?" Santana asked.

Easton shook his head. "Never believed in the war."

"Did that cause tension in your marriage?"

"How do you mean?"

"Your wife was a soldier, a very good one based on her service medals. She apparently believed in what she was doing."

"Yeah. But when she got pregnant, the Army gave her the option to leave with an honorable discharge. She was non-deployable for the duration of her pregnancy and had six weeks of convalescent leave. She had another twelve weeks of maternity leave, but still chose to go back after that."

Cruz looked at Santana. "Used to be that married and unmarried women in the military who became pregnant were automatically discharged unless special waivers were granted," he said. "But the new Pentagon policy allows them to stay."

"You're the primary caregiver, Mr. Easton," Santana said.

"Damn right. Thank God my mother is here in town to help me out with Jamie. Don't know what I'd do without her."

"Why did your wife return to active duty?" Santana asked.

"She was an action junkie," Easton said with bitterness in his voice.

Santana glanced at the bungee jumping photo one more time and realized it was Tara Easton under the helmet. Tara Easton was 5'7". The downhill skis were more her size. The snowboard might be hers as well. Though Easton's job as a firefighter wasn't without its inherent danger and adrenaline rush.

"So, you two argued about her decision."

Easton fixed his eyes on Santana. "You trying to make the case that I killed my wife?"

"Not at all."

"Could've fooled me."

"Where were you yesterday and last evening?"

"Then you do think I killed her."

"We have to cover all the bases, Mr. Easton."

"Yeah, right," he said with a dismissive wave. "I was here resting. Like I was sleeping when you rang the doorbell."

Santana knew that St. Paul firefighters typically worked a twenty-four-hour shift and then had two days off.

"Your daughter wasn't here?" he asked.

"She was staying with my mother so I can catch up on some sleep. I'm picking her up later today."

Easy enough to check, Santana thought. "What's your mother's phone number?"

He released a frustrated breath and then gave them her phone number.

Cruz wrote it down.

"Talk to us about your wife's drug use."

Matt Easton sat back on the couch and cocked his head. "What drug use?"

"We found evidence of marijuana in her apartment."

"Well, she might've smoked some dope on occasion."

"You, too?"

"Can't be doing that as a firefighter."

"No other drugs either."

He shook his head but kept his eyes averted. "Nope."

Before leaving Tara Easton's apartment, Santana had used his iPhone to search for the doctor who'd prescribed her Prozac medication. Now he wanted to pursue that line of questioning.

"Did you know your wife was taking Prozac and seeing a psychiatrist named Martin Conrad, Mr. Easton?"

"She never mentioned it."

Santana knew that, under the Minnesota Health Records Act, psychotherapy notes were considered part of a patient's health record. Patients—as well as spouses and parents of deceased patients—had the same rights to access these notes, unless information in them was detrimental.

Santana wanted to see Tara Easton's medical record and Dr. Martin Conrad's psychotherapy notes.

He explained his request to Matt Easton.

"I'd like to see them, too," Easton said. "How soon can I get them?"

"The law states 'upon request.'"

"I'll contact Dr. Conrad today."

Santana looked at Cruz, who was busy writing in his notebook. "You have any questions, Detective?"

The question startled Cruz. His head jerked up. "Ah . . . no. Not at this time."

As long as he didn't coerce Matt Easton, Santana knew he could search the house without a warrant. And he didn't have to tell Easton that he had a right to refuse.

"Mind if I look around, Mr. Easton?"

"What for?"

"See if there's anything that can help us confirm her suicide."

"She hasn't lived here in six months."

Santana gestured toward the downhill skis and snowboard. "Those belong to her."

"The snowboard is mine. Skis are hers. Don't know how they're going to help you, but go ahead and look around. I've got nothing to hide."

Santana stood and nodded at Cruz, signaling that he should keep Easton occupied while he searched.

As Santana headed toward the hallway leading to the rear of the house, he heard Cruz ask Easton if he could have a glass of water.

In the bathroom halfway down the hall, Santana took a pair of latex gloves out of a coat pocket and slipped them on.

He found nothing unusual in the medicine cabinet and no anti-depressive medication like he'd found in the medicine cabinet in Tara Easton's apartment. Two bedrooms flanked the linen closet at the end of the hallway. The closet held bedding and towels and a black hard shell polypropylene pistol case with a handle and two snap latches. There were no padlocks in the holes near the latches. Inside the case was a Glock 19 with an installed trigger cable lock and a detachable magazine.

Santana wondered if Matt Easton had a permit for the Glock or if the gun belonged to Tara Easton.

The master bedroom contained an unmade double bed and a large dresser, on top of which was a small baby monitor receiver. Framed wedding photos and photos of the couple with their daughter, Jamie, hung on the walls and stood on the dresser. The room had all the marks of a loving couple and their beautiful baby daughter. Not the room of a troubled woman and her estranged husband.

In a desk drawer, Santana found Matt Easton's checkbook. He noted the name of the bank and wrote it down in his notebook.

Under the T-shirts and jeans in the bottom dresser drawer Santana discovered a plastic bag containing what smelled like the earthy and woody scent of marijuana. Beside the bag was a small box of Zig Zag brand rolling papers.

Santana recalled the half-smoked joint he'd seen in the ashtray on the coffee table in Tara Easton's apartment. He'd found no pot in her apartment and wondered now if she'd been smoking the joint, or if it belonged to her husband, Matt, or someone else.

Tara Easton still had clothes hung in the large master bedroom closet. There were also two uniforms, one combat camo and one service green, and a pair of combat boots. Santana saw no bloodstained clothes, shoes, or boots.

In the second bedroom, the light pink wall above the crib was decorated with large safari animal decals. The transmitter for the baby monitor sat atop a small pink dresser. There was nothing in the closet or dresser that warranted Santana's attention.

He checked the trash bin in the kitchen and then went out the door to the garage near the alley behind the house. A late model red jeep SUV sat in one bay. The other bay was empty. A tool bench stood against the front wall hung with tools. A lawnmower and snow blower occupied the front corners.

Santana opened the driver's side door of the Jeep and peered inside. He saw no bloodstained clothing or bloodstained seats. He checked the glove box and storage compartment in the center console between the driver's and passenger seats. Then he walked out the side door in the garage to the trash bin in the alley. It was empty, suggesting that the trash had recently been picked up.

He tossed the latex gloves in the trash and headed back to the house.

When he returned to the living room, Santana asked Matt Easton if the Glock in the case in the linen closet was his.

"It's registered in my name. Tara and I used to go target shooting a couple times a month. But I haven't taken the gun out of the case in nearly a year."

"What about the weed?"

Easton let out a heavy sigh. "Don't you need a warrant to go searching around?" he asked in a frustrated voice.

"You gave me permission to look around. I won't bust you for pot possession. But the fire department would if they knew."

Easton's face flushed. "If they *knew*," he repeated. "They don't, unless you tell 'em."

"Don't worry. Did she get the weed from you?"

"No," he said with a shake of his head. "That's an old bag in my dresser. I haven't smoked pot since we had the baby."

"Did your wife have a separate bank account?"

Easton hesitated before answering. "Why?"

"It's important."

"No. We shared a checking and savings account."

"What bank?"

"The All-Citizens Bank in St. Paul."

"How much money did you have in your accounts?"

"A few hundred in each."

"Were there any other accounts she might've had?"

"Not that I know of."

"Mind if we look at the accounts, Mr. Easton?"

His eyes widened for a split second. "What's this about, Detective?"

"Just covering all the bases."

"Yeah," he smirked.

"So how about your accounts?"

"Nothing to see there, Detective."

"I take it that's a no."

"That's exactly what it is."

"If you've got nothing to hide—"

"I don't. Like I said. There's nothing to see."

"Happen to know the password on your wife's cell phone?"

"Sure. It's Jamie one."

Santana took a business card out of his pocket and laid it on the coffee table. "You can reach me at this number."

"What about my wife's body?"

"The medical examiner will contact you after the autopsy."

"Why the autopsy?"

"We need to confirm the cause of death."

"Thought you said it was a suicide."

"As I said, it appears to be. We want to make sure."

Santana removed a second card and set it beside the first. "We work closely with an organization called Survivor Resources. They offer grief support and other services for families of victims of unnatural death. You might want to contact them."

Matt Easton stared at the two cards on the table for a time before he looked up at Santana and Cruz standing in front of him.

"You believe my wife committed suicide?"

"We'll find out one way or another," Santana said.

Chapter 5

Santana called Matt Easton's mother to confirm that she was watching Easton's daughter, Jamie, while he got some shut-eye at the time of his wife's death. That didn't mean Easton couldn't have been with his estranged wife that evening.

"It's a terrible tragedy," Easton's mother said. "Matthew really tried to get back together."

"You're saying Tara didn't want to?"

"I hate to speak badly of her now that she's gone. But that girl was so selfish. Going off to war again after having a baby when she could've stayed home and been a mother. Matthew had to take on all that responsibility, plus hold down a job. It wasn't fair."

"You think your son resented her choice?"

"Well, he certainly wasn't happy about it."

"How did they act when they were together?"

"Happy at first and even happier when Jamie came along. Had Tara made better choices, maybe she'd be alive now."

"You think she killed herself."

"I think she realized too late that she'd ruined her marriage to a wonderful man. That made her a very unhappy young lady."

*   *   *

When they returned to their desks in the Homicide and Robbery unit, Gabriel Cruz used the Jamie 1 password Matt Easton had provided to unlock his wife's iPhone. Clicking on the "Phone" app, Cruz hit the "Recent" button, which listed up to one hundred calls Tara Easton had made in the last sixty days.

"I'm in," Cruz said, holding up the cell phone.

Santana could see the names of the people or organizations Tara Easton had called, and the names or numbers of the people or organizations that had called her. Some calls were listed as "Unknown" and other calls were listed only by a phone number.

"Look at this," Cruz said, pointing at the iPhone.

"Blaine Beckham."

"One of the guys in the photo in Tara Easton's bedroom."

Beckham had called Tara Easton two days ago.

"Make a list of all the calls she made and numbers," Santana said. "And the dates."

Santana spent the rest of the afternoon completing probable cause statements that would be included in the search warrants for Matt and Tara Easton's bank accounts.

Santana knew PC statements were crucial for a judge to approve the search warrant. He followed the "four corners" rule, which only considered information within the pages of the application and affidavit.

The SPPD considered warrants involving bank records as Tier 1 Warrants because they were limited to secure locations with no risks. Homicide detectives could author and execute them under Janet Kendrick's direction, without consulting the SWAT commander or filling out a Search Warrant Threat Assessment form.

Gabriel Cruz swiveled in his chair and looked at Santana in the next cubicle. After completing a list of names, numbers, and dates in Tara Easton's call log, Cruz had been working on compiling information on Blaine Beckham.

"You like Matt Easton for his wife's murder?"

"His alibi is thin."

"But it fits with the ME's TOD."

"Unless she has it wrong."

"You think she does?"

Santana shook his head. "Not likely."

He took the bank records warrant to the Ramsey County Courthouse for a judge's signature and faxed it to Matt Easton's bank. Then he headed to his brick house that sat on two wooded acres of birch and pine in Lake St. Croix Beach, overlooking the St. Croix River.

His golden retriever, Gitana—Gypsy in English—squealed with delight and bounded across the hardwood floor when he entered the house, bushy tail wagging, her mouth open in a smile.

Santana crouched down and let her lick his face as he rubbed her back.

"How's my girl?"

She huffed and gave him another lick of love.

Santana took a strip of chicken filet treats—one of many favorite treats—from a bag in a cupboard. She took it gently from him, ran to the living room, and jumped up on the leather couch, where she quickly devoured it.

Then he went upstairs and opened the small safe in his bedroom. He released the magazine from his Glock 23, racked the slide to eject the cartridge in the chamber, and placed the empty gun and his Kydex holster in the safe. He kept a loaded subcompact Glock 27 in the locked nightstand near his bed. He carried the smaller gun with him whenever he ran with Gitana or went out for the evening.

He kept an additional Glock 27 in a holster attached to the underside of the dining room table. He considered removing it after Ana Soriano had moved in, but felt the move would indicate a lack of trust in her. Plus, unless she made a point to look, she probably didn't even know the gun was there.

The seventeen-year-old from El Salvador had been living with Santana ever since he and a DEA agent named Bobbi Chacon had rescued her from a sex trafficking operation in St. Paul. After she testified against some of the Twin City's wealthiest and most influential men, the court had allowed Santana to act as her guardian until she turned eighteen. Because she'd cooperated, the court had also cleared her record.

When he came down the stairs, followed closely by Gitana, Ana came out of her bedroom on the first floor. She'd braided her waist-length black hair and was dressed casually in jeans and a Minnesota Wild sweatshirt. She wore no makeup, but with her beautiful olive complexion from her Mestizo background, she didn't need any.

"How was your day?" Santana asked in Spanish.

Since Ana had alluded to how much she missed speaking Spanish, they often spoke in their native language when it was just the two of them. Santana had been considering her offer to teach him French, hoping that his genuine interest in learning the language would strengthen the bond of trust he was building with her.

She shrugged. "High school is boring."

At fifteen, Ana had ridden *la Bestia*, "The Beast," also known as *El tren de la muerte*, "The death train," or *El tren de los desconocidos*, "The train of the unknowns," from the Chiapas state in southern Mexico, near the border of Guatemala, north to the Lecherías station on the outskirts of Mexico City. The train then connected with a network of Mexican freight trains heading to different points on the US/Mexican border. Traffickers in Nogales, Arizona had kidnapped her.

Though she hadn't finished high school after having fled the MS-13 gangs in El Salvador, she had an IQ over 130 and was fluent in Spanish, English, and French, having been taught French while working as a high-priced escort in St. Paul. Now she was working on finishing her high school education through a government-approved online program in El Salvador. She wasn't sure what she wanted to be, as long as it had nothing to do with the sex trade.

Santana imagined a high school curriculum wouldn't be challenging for a young woman of her experience and intelligence, which was why he hadn't attempted to enroll her in a local high school.

"The quicker you complete the high school curriculum online," Santana said, "the quicker you can start college."

"And then what?"

"It's up to you."

"Maybe I don't want to go to college."

It was the first time he'd heard that statement from her, and it worried him.

"It's good to have a future plan," he said.

"There's only one thing I'm good at, and it's not covered in a college curriculum."

"You can be anything you want to be."

Ana stroked Gitana's head and leaned her backside against the kitchen counter. "Like a cop?"

"If that's what you want."

Her Caribbean blue eyes grew wide with surprise. "You'd help me?"

"I would."

"Are you working on a new case?"

Homicide investigation was the only thing besides Gitana that Ana seemed interested in lately.

"Might have a new one," he said.

"Might?"

"Not sure yet if it's a suicide or homicide."

"What do your instincts tell you?"

Santana smiled.

In their months together, he'd discovered that she had good instincts and could read people, especially men. No doubt it had something to do with the bullshit detector she'd developed after all the time she'd spent with many high-powered men.

"I think there's more to this case, regardless of how the victim died," he said.

"Want to talk more about it?"

Santana shook his head.

"I'm not a kid."

Santana knew she was mature enough to handle it. Still, he said, "You're seventeen."

"I'm a lot older than that."

Ana reminded Santana of his sister, Natalia. Years ago he'd had to flee Colombia after killing the men who'd murdered his mother. He'd never forgiven himself for it—Natalia could've become a victim like Ana. Now, he was determined to save Ana and make up for leaving his sister. He saw it as part of his mission to do whatever he could for her.

Since she'd entered his life, he'd tried to separate the ugliness associated with his work from the tranquility he sought in his home life. She'd endured many traumas, yet seemed well adjusted. He wondered if this was a mask or if she truly could distance herself from her past.

He recalled the famous Colombian writer Gabriel García Márquez had written in *One Hundred Years of Solitude*: "We all have three lives: public, private, and secret." But Márquez had also written, "What matters in life is not what happens to you, but what you remember and how you remember it."

Santana still carried with him the dark memory of his mother's murder and the revenge he'd sought as a sixteen-year-old. He'd learned over time to control the caged demon that had haunted him for so long, the demon that had eventually led to a career as a homicide detective. He'd never sought therapy, though he'd had sessions with the department's psychologist, Karen Wong, who met with any SPPD officer involved in a shooting.

Santana had encouraged Ana to talk with Wong, but she'd declined. He knew forcing her to see Wong would be futile and might sever the tenuous bonds of trust he'd nurtured.

"Know anything about the bones found in Como Park?" Ana asked. "It's all over the news and Internet."

"Thought you were studying?"

"I can multi-task."

"I'm sure you can."

"So? What about the bones?"

"How about some *pupusas* for dinner?" he said.

She let out a heavy sigh. "Okay. So the bones are off-limits."

"You'll love the *pupusas*," he said.

Made from corn and then stuffed with cheese, pork, beef, shrimp, chicken, or fried beans, *pupusas* were similar to flatbread, a Mexican *tortilla*, or a Colombian *arepa*.

Gesturing toward the cupboard where the spices were kept, Ana said, "You should order some *loroco*."

Loroco was an edible flower common in El Salvador and Guatemala. The plant's buds and flowers were used for cooking in a variety of ways, including in *pupusas*, and had an earthy, vegetal flavor similar to asparagus and artichokes.

"I can do that," Santana said. "I'll get started on the *pupusas* right after my run. Care to come along?"

"No, thanks," she said, heading for her bedroom. "It's too cold."

He'd tried to interest her in exercise to no avail, though occasionally she'd play Frisbee with Gitana when the temperatures were above freezing.

He changed into thermal underwear and a reflective yellow pullover jacket, carbon black stretch pants with neon panels, and a pair of blue Nike reflective running shoes. Then he strapped on a small Kydex kidney holster that held his compact Glock 27, and pulled on a black stretch headband and matching Rothco leather police gloves.

Before leaving the house, he put Qumy dog booties on Gitana's paws to protect them from the ice, salt, and ice melt chemicals. Earlier in the winter he'd tried fitting her with the booties to keep her paws from freezing in the very cold weather, but she'd wanted no part of them. Santana couldn't help laughing at the contortions she went through trying to walk with the booties, flinging her legs back and out to the side as though having some kind of fit.

He'd quickly taken them off.

After a few days he'd started again, one bootie at a time. It had taken some time for her to get comfortable with it, but once she did, he added another and then another till she finally felt comfortable wearing all four booties. Santana liked the anti-slip molded rubber bottoms and water-resistant material that kept her paws warm and dry. With the sun setting at about 5:45, he also liked the adjustable, reflective strips.

As the two of them ran under streetlights and along the plowed, snow-packed roads, columns of supernatural-looking, amber-colored light pillars, caused by freezing temperatures and ice crystals in the air, studded the dark sky.

Regular running and working out in his exercise room in the spare bedroom kept stress to a manageable level.

After his run with Gitana, Santana showered and ate dinner with Ana. Then he cleaned the kitchen while she returned to her bedroom, promising to work on her high school courses.

He checked his email and saw that Gabriel Cruz had sent him a summary of Blaine Beckham's background. Cruz had accessed the information through the US Military Identification Center in St. Louis, one of the nets in AFIS, the Automated Fingerprint Identification System.

According to his enlistment-record brief, Beckham was born in Walker, Minnesota, and had joined the Army after 9/11, when he was eighteen. He transferred to Fort Bragg three years later to attend the JFK Special Warfare School. He first became a Green Beret and later a member of the elite Delta Force, now referred to as Combat Applications Group, or CAG, and the Army Compartmented Elements, or ACE.

Beckham had completed advanced training in weapons handling, hand-to-hand combat, land navigation, professional driving—both offensive and off-road—reconnaissance, surveillance, sniping, infiltration techniques, and high-altitude parachuting. He was taught how to survive behind enemy lines, resist interrogation, and how to escape from POW camps. He'd also learned to read and understand Arabic, but could not speak it.

When he'd finished reading, Santana phoned Cruz. "Got your email on Beckham."

"What we'd consider one badass Delta Force dude," Cruz said. "A real snake eater."

"Lots of acronyms in the service."

"Yeah," Cruz said. "Almost as many as the police department."

"Got me there."

"I'll refer to Beckham as Delta because it's the way I remember it," Cruz continued. "They're part of the first Special Forces Operational Detachment. Primary focus is counterterrorism, aimed at killing or capturing high-value units or dismantling terrorist cells."

"Like the Navy SEALs."

"The Army's counterpart," Cruz said. "Delta Force is known as a Special Missions Unit, like their sister unit, SEAL Team Six. The black ops component of the military. After 9/11 they were permitted to carry out covert actions."

"Such as?"

"Basically, foreign operations where their role wouldn't be apparent or acknowledged publicly, though some of them have been. Like the failed rescue of American hostages held in Tehran, the Black Hawk Down incident in Somalia, and the killing of Osama Bin Ladin."

"Have to live much of your life on the edge," Santana said.

"Got that right. Guys like Beckham are constantly told they're the elite, the best of the best, the ultimate bad asses, and when it comes to killing and capturing people overseas, they are. For a terrorist strike, international hostage situation, or a loose nuclear weapon, the President calls on Delta or SEAL Team Six. They're known as 'quiet professionals.'"

"Meaning?"

"They keep a low profile off the base. Usually aren't flashing their name around."

Cruz went silent for a time.

"Was there something else?" Santana asked.

"You're aware that Delta Force commandos were inserted into Colombia during the hunt for Pablo Escobar."

"I am."

"They came in after the Intelligence Support Activity, or ISA, operatives were in Colombia."

"I had a case involving a former ISA operative," Santana said.

He waited, figuring Cruz would ask for details, but he didn't.

"Interesting," was all he said before continuing. "Anyway, Joint Special Operations Command would rotate Delta and SEAL Team Six detachments in Colombia throughout the hunt. There's some speculation that a Delta Force sniper killed Escobar, but that's never been verified."

"Colombians killed him," Santana said.

"That's my take. Delta Force was also involved in the capture of 'El Chapo,' the Sinaloa Cartel leader, after a firefight in Los Mochis, Sinaloa, Mexico."

"So, we know Beckham is highly trained and skilled," Santana said.

"No question about it."

"And he knew Tara Easton."

"The photo in her bedroom and her call log."

"Where is Beckham now?"

"He mustered out a year ago. Lives in St. Paul. Owns the Combat Zone gun shop in Sibley Plaza."

Where Hannah Thatcher goes to shoot, Santana recalled. She must know Blaine Beckham. Another lie she told.

"We'll pay Beckham a visit tomorrow," Santana said. "See what else he knows."

"What if Tara Easton did commit suicide?"

"Maybe Blaine Beckham knows why."

Chapter 6

Snow had fallen steadily again overnight, blanketing the city and drifting high enough in places to bury a parked car. Santana and Cruz couldn't get to the Ramsey County morgue for Tara Easton's autopsy till late Tuesday morning.

The one-story morgue sat just off University Avenue near Regions Hospital. An additional room had recently been built around a newly purchased piece of technology that conducted a full-body scan—similar to a CAT scan—in thirteen seconds. The machine had replaced an old portable X-ray machine and could quickly find evidence of bullets, bone fractures, and head trauma. In the past technicians had to bring the film next door to Regions Hospital to use their equipment to read the results. The remodel also brought upgrades to the building's security, including adding bulletproof glass in some areas.

The ME's office had ten full-time death investigators and three forensic technicians. In what was once a male-dominated field, half of the employees were women. It was one of only two in the country accredited by both the National Association of Medical Examiners and the International Association of Coroners and Medical Examiners.

Bright lights illuminated the large, cold autopsy suite that smelled strongly of disinfectant. Stainless-steel sinks, cabinets, and countertops spanned the room. Big-screen TV monitors attached to the walls pictured computer information.

Reiko Tanabe, the Ramsey County chief medical examiner, wore a disposable tie-on surgical cap, two pairs of latex gloves, goggles, a long-sleeved light blue surgical gown with sleeve covers the length of old-Hollywood evening gloves, a plastic apron, and booties. A surgical facemask and a clear plastic wrap-around face protector called a "splash shield" covered her face. She wore a wireless headset to record her notes.

Santana viewed the autopsy suite as a scientific space instead of a room of death, which made it easier to process the corpse in front of him that had once been filled with life.

He'd asked Gabriel Cruz if he wanted any eucalyptus oil under his facemask to cut the odor, but the young detective had declined.

Santana recalled how rookie homicide detectives were often introduced to their first autopsy. One detective would get into a clean new body bag and be placed on a gurney. When the new detective came into the autopsy suite, the ME would slowly unzip the body bag and the "dead guy" would jump up, scaring the shit out of the rookie.

Thankfully, Santana's senior partner at the time, Wendell Hudson, had given him a heads-up before his first autopsy, sparing him from making a fool out of himself.

Santana had decided to spare Gabriel Cruz as well.

Tara Easton's naked body lay on the stainless-steel table in front of Tanabe. Easton's head was propped up on a plastic block. A paper tag hung from her right toe. It matched the tag on her left toe that had been attached at the crime scene. The tags maintained the chain-of-evidence and a record of who touched the body.

A large scale for weighing organs hung over the table beside a microphone attached to the ceiling. Forceps, scissors, scalpels, rulers, long, scalloped knives—identical to bread knives—and a bone saw lay on a smaller table next to the autopsy table.

"Victim has a deep, long single incised throat cut injury over the anterior aspect of neck, slightly obliquely placed at the level of laryngeal prominence in midline, extending deep up to the vertebrae," Tanabe said into her headset. "The left end of the injury starts at the upper third of the neck and deepens gradually with severance of the left carotid artery. The right-sided end of the injury is at the mid-third of the neck with a tail abrasion."

Tanabe looked up at Santana.

"Her husband confirmed that she was right-handed," he said.

"That fits. There are no hesitation cuts."

"Isn't that unusual?" Cruz said.

"Somewhat. Suicidal throat cuts are usually—but not always—accompanied by hesitation marks. A fatal suicidal throat cut can sometimes be accompanied by cadaveric spasm, with the knife found firmly clenched in the victim's hand."

"The knife was on the bathroom floor," Santana said.

Tanabe nodded. "Key word there is *sometimes*."

"Any evidence this could be a homicide, Reiko?"

Tanabe peered at Tara Easton's neck once more and then pointed as she explained.

"Suicidal and homicidal throat cut injuries are similar, but a homicidal cut inflicted from behind is usually longer and begins higher on the neck on the side opposite to where it terminates. The cut starts below the ear, runs obliquely downward and medially, then straight across the midline of the neck, and ends on the opposite side of the neck lower than its point of origination. A throat cut extending up to the vertebrae is suggestive of homicidal injury while its absence is indicative of suicidal injury. In this case, the neck incision is compatible with a throat cut from behind by a right-handed person."

Santana felt his heartbeat increase as adrenaline entered his bloodstream. "You're saying Tara Easton was murdered, Reiko?"

"I'm saying the wound is *suggestive* of a homicidal injury. It's noticeable that the deep cut found in this case is a single incision without surrounding injuries. Multiple, parallel, superficial cuts found above and below the deep fatal cut in homicides suggest that the deceased attempted to get away and the head was not sufficiently immobilized by restraint. In this case, there are no such superficial cuts. Presence of single deep cut indicates that the deceased's head would have been restrained firmly. So, yes, it's possibly a homicide. Once I remove the organs, I'll run toxicology tests on the tissues, see if she was drugged or drunk. Might help confirm my initial conclusions and explain why she didn't resist."

Santana had studied the connection between murderer and victim. Paul Kirk's description of Edmund Locard's Exchange Principle—"Physical evidence cannot be wrong, it cannot perjure itself, and it cannot be wholly absent"—stuck with him. He thought of it as the silent witness. Only human failure to find it diminished its value.

Santana knew that Tara Easton's body, like all bodies before hers, would give up its secrets. He just had to keep his mind and his eyes open.

*   *   *

The SPPD Senior Homicide Commander, Janet Kendrick, had requested a meeting with Santana and Cruz after the conclusion of Tara Easton's autopsy. Santana figured he knew what she wanted, but he wasn't sure if he was willing to give it to her.

Gabriel Cruz stared at the yellow brick resting on the corner of Kendrick's desk. She'd completed a ten-week professional course of study at the FBI National Academy. The award was the culmination of a rugged fitness challenge that included a 6.1-mile run through a hilly, wooded trail that was built by Marines. If students completed the endurance test, they received an actual yellow brick to memorialize their achievement.

Santana figured Kendrick was proud of the accomplishment, as she should be, and wanted everyone to know it.

Janet Kendrick's straight black hair contrasted with her fair skin. She wore it parted in the middle and blunt cut a couple inches shorter than she usually wore it.

"Have a seat, Detectives," she said, gesturing at the two chairs placed directly in front of her desk.

Santana and Cruz sat down.

Her midnight blue eyes settled on each of them for a moment before she said, "What did the ME have to say?"

Cruz glanced at Santana, waiting for him to field the question.

"She wants to run toxicology tests before making a determination," Santana said.

"What about the cut throat?"

"Could've been suicide, but I'm betting murder."

Kendrick smiled slightly as she lowered her head and titled it sideways, as if she were peering down at Santana.

"Isn't that the ME's job, Detective?"

"Science isn't perfect."

"But you are?"

There was no sarcasm in Kendrick's voice, only a question.

"Her husband told us they were getting back together. And she loved her kid."

"What makes you think the husband is telling the truth?"

"Experience."

"Ah," Kendrick said, leaning forward in her chair. She looked at Cruz. "What's your take, Detective Cruz?"

"I'm with my partner."

"Of course you are," Kendrick said with a nod.

"She wrote her husband and kid a letter before leaving for her last deployment," Cruz continued, surprising Kendrick with an additional response. "It's the kind of letter you only write if you're thinking about dying in combat. I never wrote one myself, but I knew soldiers who did. Every one of them wanted to live. Wanted to go home to their loved ones. You don't write a letter like that and then kill yourself when you're finally home safe."

Kendrick considered Cruz's response for a time before replying. "Maybe something like PTSD happened to her overseas."

"Something *did* happen to her," Santana said. "And we need to find out what that something was."

"War happened to her, Detective," Kendrick said, her eyes focusing on Cruz again. "Correct me if I'm wrong, but war can mess with your mind, change who you are, or were."

"Sure it can," Cruz said.

"So maybe when she returned home, Tara Easton wasn't the same person as before. The person who wrote lovely letters to her husband and child."

Cruz shrugged. "Could be."

Kendrick's gaze slid back to Santana. "I just spoke to Forensics. Only prints found on the knife belonged to Tara Easton. You have no proof she was murdered."

"We need more time."

"Don't we all," Kendrick said. "In the meantime, I want you to focus on the bones found in Como Park. The media is all over it, and people are hunting for more bones instead of the medallion. That's hurting attendance at Winter Carnival events."

"We wouldn't want that."

"Are you being sarcastic, Detective?"

"Not at all," Santana lied. "But I don't want to lose the momentum we have with the Easton case."

"There is no momentum until the ME rules Easton's death a homicide."

Santana let out a frustrated breath. "Give the bones to someone else."

"We have a backlog of carjackings and robberies. We're getting pressure from the mayor and city council. I've got two teams working those cases. That means you and Detective Cruz catch the bones."

Chapter 7

The state's previous board-certified forensic anthropologist, Rob Wallace, had moved to Hollywood, where he now worked as a consultant for movies and television.

Dr. Kim Solace had taken his place.

Along with consulting on possible homicide cases, Solace had been asked by the legislature to identify buried human remains in the state's possession. The remains had been found over the years in unmarked graves as commercial and residential land was developed around the state. By law, any remains identified as belonging to Native Americans were sent to the Minnesota Indian Affairs Council, while all non-Indian remains more than fifty years old were transferred to the state archaeologist.

Santana and Cruz dropped off the interstate at Riverside Avenue and left their department ride in the circular drive in front of the Humphrey Center at the University of Minnesota. They took the elevator to a lab on the third floor in the Department of Anthropology.

The lab itself resembled a classroom filled with long tables and large drawers containing human bones. Anatomical charts covered the walls. Most of the bones in her lab had been donated over the years and used to train the next generation of forensic investigators. Others were a part of the legislature's Human Remains Project.

Kim Solace came forward as the detectives entered the room, her right hand outstretched, her white lab coat shiny and crisp, as though it had just come from the dry cleaner.

"Thanks for taking the time to see us," Santana said, shaking her hand. Cruz did the same.

She smiled. "Of course."

Solace was a petite woman with bright hazel eyes and short, dark hair that was starting to gray.

She gestured toward a lab table in the center of the room, where she'd spread the pelvis, rib bones, and femur found in Como Park across the surface.

Santana stepped close to the table. "What can you tell us?"

"Well, if we could get only one bone from an entire skeleton, I'd want the pelvic bone. That and the skull are the gold standards."

"Nothing else turned up in the grid search?"

She shook her head.

Santana had hoped the search teams could find the other six pairs of ribs and the rest of the skeleton.

"Doesn't mean there aren't more bones out there," Solace continued. "But they're tough to find in the snow cover. Might've been more bones near where we found these at one time, but scavengers could've taken them."

"Male or female?" Santana asked, nodding at the bones on the table.

"Definitely male." She pointed to the pelvic bone. "The male pelvis is shorter and narrower, with heavier and thicker bones. Female pelvis is larger and wider, with dense and light bones. Also, the male pelvis inlet is heart-shaped, as you can see here, while the female pelvic inlet, or brim, is in a slight oval shape."

Cruz wrote in his notebook. "Any idea of the age?" he asked.

"Patterns of morphological change can be very subtle. That's why we use broad age categories for adult skeletal remains. I'm confident this was a middle-aged adult somewhere between thirty-five and fifty years old."

"What about TOD?" Santana asked.

"Time of death is harder to pin down. So much of decomp depends on the environment. You know bodies decompose fastest in hot, moist environments. A cool, boggy environment could take months to reach the same state."

"We had a humid, hot summer," Cruz said. "Could be when the body was dumped."

"Except the whole body wasn't dumped," Solace said. "Take a look at the femur."

Santana and Cruz leaned closer.

"Careful," Solace said.

Cruz smiled. "I won't touch them."

"Sorry for the warning. It's just that these bones are brittle. They also exhibit smooth cut surfaces and straight edges, commonly found in bones cut during dismemberment."

"You think this body was dismembered?" Santana said.

"I do. Likely with a chain saw."

Given the lack of contamination at the bone site, Santana figured it was a disposal site and not the actual crime scene.

"How do you know?" Cruz asked.

Solace pointed to the femur bone on the table. "We look at the striation patterns within the cut marks, or kerfs, they produce. These patterns yield information on all the key class characteristics of the saw in question. I'll show you."

She gestured for the two detectives to follow her to the computer on a metal desk. Sitting down in the desk chair, she woke the computer with a keystroke.

"Axes, knives and saws—the three tools most commonly used in dismemberment—each leave distinctive marks in bone. So do machetes, meat cleavers, and hatchets. But chainsaws have a completely different type of tooth shape than your rip or cross-cut saw and are designed to cut soft material at high speeds. Marks produced by power saws are often easier to interpret than those produced by handsaws. One of the telltale signs is the consistency of the cut. Cuts made by power saws also show a uniform direction of blade progress, with none of the variation seen in handsaws."

She turned the monitor toward the detectives. "I examined the kerf walls from each cut on the femur found in Como Park under a stereoscopic light microscope. This is a photo." Tracing a cut mark with an index finger, Solace said, "You can see the deep false starts here that are most likely to be products of a powered chainsaw. False-start kerfs also are more frequent and have greater depths. Once the blade skips out of the kerf with a power saw, it's easier to start a new cut rather than try to resume the old one, as one would do when using a handsaw."

"You think he was alive when he was dismembered?" Cruz asked.

"No way to tell for sure."

"In either case," Santana said, "it's no way to die."

Solace nodded and said, "Three motives for postmortem dismemberment. Prevents positive identification. Makes storage, transportation, and disposal of the remains more manageable. And it sends a message that the perpetrator has no regard for human life or for the victim."

She'd ticked each motive off on her fingertips.

"Could be more than one motive," Santana said.

"Yes. If the perp is trying to hide the identity of the victim, the dismemberment usually involves removal of the victim's head and hands, and removal or mutilation of other areas of the body that might have distinguishing features, like tattoos.

"The other two motives usually result in a more generalized pattern of dismemberment. If the perpetrator's intent was to make the remains of the victim easier to maneuver and dispose of, then the dismemberment involves removal and further sectioning of the limbs. If the third motive was at play, there might be no logical pattern to the cuts."

"I've worked a few dismemberment cases," Santana said. "They're usually committed by someone in close relationship with the vic, like a family member or friend. And the dismemberment is almost always performed in the same place as the murder, generally the home of the perpetrator."

Solace looked up at Santana, her face clouded with thought.

"Is there something else?" Santana asked.

"Few perpetrators think to dismember a body at the joints, which are just as conveniently located, anatomically speaking, but which have far less tissue and almost no bone to cut through. In nearly every case I've seen, bodies aren't separated at the joints. In the rare case where a body is dismembered at the joints, as in this case, it suggests that the perpetrator had prior experience with butchering techniques or human anatomy."

Santana considered what Solace had said before he spoke to her again. "You said the bones were brittle. What if bacteria didn't cause decomposition?"

"As in maceration."

"Possible."

"Definitely is," she said.

"That could change the time frame," Cruz said.

"It could."

"How would someone go about that?" Santana asked.

Solace sat back in her chair. "Well, if you want to chemically dissolve a body, you don't dump it in a bathtub full of acid. You'd use an alkaline, like potassium hydroxide. Alkalines have a higher pH, and catalyze with water to attack chemical bonds much more quickly, especially if you add heat, which speeds up decomp."

"Like bio cremation."

"Yes. In the end, just bones remain—plus any pacemakers, orthopedic implants, and detritus from plastic surgery, all that stuff can be recycled. The bones themselves are pristine, if a bit brittle. These get passed along to a machine called a cremulator that pulverizes the bone into an ashy powder, which gets passed along to the dead's family."

"Bone shadows," Santana said.

"Sorry?"

"The small pieces of bones left after a flame cremation that need to be pulverized."

"Not many people know that."

"I worked a case once where I learned the term."

She nodded. "Alkaline hydrolysis is similar to how cremation by fire works, except the bony remains are quite charred by the time they come out of the kiln. Plus, the fire doesn't make them quite as brittle, so they don't pulverize to as fine a powder as they do with the chemical method."

Cruz released a long breath.

Solace's gaze settled on him. "You don't approve?"

"Give me an old-fashioned dirt burial," he said.

"Lots of people feel that way when it comes to burning Grandma. I always tell them bio cremation is like putting Grandma in a warm bath." She focused her eyes on Santana. "But someone would need to have access to a machine."

"But they could achieve similar results with alkaline without one."

"Certainly," Solace said. "It would just take more time. I'll send a bone sample to the BCA. See if they can get a DNA match in NamUs."

In the past, Santana had used the National Missing and Unidentified Persons System—a national clearinghouse and resource center for missing, unidentified, and unclaimed person cases across the United States—to help match missing persons with unidentified remains. The Bureau of Criminal Apprehension in St. Paul had used NamUs as well.

"I'll keep you informed," Solace said.

Santana nodded. "We'll do the same."

Chapter 8

Taimur Khalil, the "jingle man" in the photo in Tara Easton's bedroom, lived in a renovated apartment building in the Dayton's Bluff neighborhood in St. Paul. Many of the mansions on the bright white cliffs overlooking the city no longer stood, though much of the bluff, cut by the Mississippi River, remained the same. The Dakota Indians, the first inhabitants of the bluff, had called the area *Ionize Ska,* meaning white cliff. Their burial mounds could still be found on the sacred site.

As he and Cruz pulled up to the curb in front of the apartment building, Santana recalled a case he'd investigated near the burial mounds. He hoped this current case turned out as well as that one had, but without the deaths.

"Kendrick wanted us to focus on the bones," Cruz said.

Santana shut off the ignition and looked at Cruz. "We know the man the bones belonged to was likely murdered and his body dismembered. But that's all we know right now. Let's see if Solace and the BCA can ID the remains. For now, we'll work the Tara Easton case."

"Even if she committed suicide?"

"Tanabe has her doubts. That's good enough for me."

Cruz let the silence sit awhile. Then he said, "You wondering how Wade Crawford, the SIGAR agent, knew Taimur Khalil?"

"Yeah. I am."

"Khalil probably speaks Dari," Cruz said. "Used to be known as Farsi in Afghanistan till some dumb shit politicians, who were mostly not mother-tongue Persian speakers, decided to rename it."

"Like if Congress decided it'd be more patriotic if the majority language in the USA was known as 'American' rather than 'English,'" Santana said.

"Like that," Cruz said.

"You speak any Dari?"

"Some. Whatever I picked up over there."

Inside the vestibule, Santana noted the camera mounted high above the inner door. Cruz located Khalil's name and apartment number and quickly pressed a call button.

A woman's voice answered. "Yes?"

"Detective Cruz and Detective Santana from the St. Paul Police Department. We're here to talk to Taimur Khalil. Is he in?"

"I am sorry, he is not."

"Are you related to Taimur?"

"I am his daughter."

Cruz looked at Santana.

"Tell her we'd like to talk with her," Santana said quietly.

Cruz repeated Santana's request.

She hesitated a moment before replying. "Okay."

When the inner door buzzed, they entered the lobby.

"Let's walk up," Santana said. "I can use the exercise."

They took the stairs to the third floor, where Santana noted the pairs of slippers, shoes, and boots in the hallway outside of Taimur Khalil's apartment.

"Afghans wear different shoes in different rooms," Cruz said. "Bathroom shoes, kitchen shoes, you name it."

"This the usual custom?"

Cruz shrugged. "Yeah."

"If it builds trust, then we'll do it."

Santana knocked on the apartment door.

The attractive twenty-something woman that opened the door had olive skin and a small but sturdy-looking frame. She wore a leopard-print scarf over her head and wrapped loosely around her neck. It allowed her long, wavy black hair to hang unfettered over a copper-colored sweater. Her tight jeans were faded blue. Santana was surprised to see she also wore rose-colored lipstick.

"Yes?" she said, focusing her green eyes at Cruz and then at Santana.

Santana showed her his badge.

She stared at it for a time.

Santana said, "And your name is?"

She hesitated and looked over the two detectives, as if taking their measure.

"I take it you speak English."

She nodded.

"Your father has done nothing wrong," Santana assured her. "We just want to talk to him."

"My name is Nasrin Khalil," she said proudly.

"Is your mother here?"

"She was killed in Afghanistan."

"I'm sorry."

Nasrin looked into Santana's eyes but offered no response.

"When will your father return?"

"He has been gone a long time."

"How long?"

"Months," she said. "Something has happened to him."

Santana glanced at Cruz. Then he said, "If we could come in and talk, perhaps we can help locate your father."

"I have to work later this afternoon."

"We won't be long."

She hesitated a few moments before she stepped back and held the door open.

After they'd slipped off their shoes and entered the apartment, Nasrin Khalil positioned their shoes facing outwards.

"So we can put them on more easily when we leave," Cruz whispered to Santana.

They sat on traditional Afghan floor cushions on a large red rug with an octagonal elephant's foot pattern in the middle. An Afghan flag hung on one wall. An American flag hung on the opposite wall. In a corner two parakeets in a cage sitting on a stand chirped.

Santana noted the unusual but pleasant earthen scent of petrichor in the apartment. It reminded him of the first rain after a long period of warm, dry weather.

"I will serve some chai tea," she said, heading for the kitchen.

"No need to—"

"That would be fine," Cruz said, interrupting Santana.

After Nasrin had gone into the kitchen, Cruz said quietly, "Guests in an Afghan home are always offered tea. It's a sign of the host's respect for you. Your acceptance of the offer is a sign of your respect for your host. Not offering tea is a social affront unless the host does it on purpose to make a point."

"Got it," Santana said.

"Once she brings the tea out, she'll keep refilling our cups as long as we're here. If you've had enough, you can turn your cup upside down, or you can cover it with your hand and thank her."

"I'll keep that in mind."

Ten minutes later Nasrin reentered the living room carrying a silver tray filled with bowls of almonds, sugar cubes, three teacups, and a steaming pot of tea.

She filled each cup and passed one to Santana and another to Cruz.

"It's called *Kahwah* in Afghanistan," Cruz said. "A combination of green tea, cardamom, cinnamon, and saffron."

Nasrin cocked her head. "You are familiar with *Kahwah*."

"Drank quite a bit in your country."

She peered at him a moment longer. "You were a soldier."

"I was."

Cruz held up a lump of sugar. "Afghans usually put the sugar in their mouths rather than in their tea," he said to Santana. "Lumps are called *qand*." He placed the lump of sugar in his mouth and sipped some tea.

"It is our custom that the first cup of tea offered to a guest should be sweetened," Nasrin said. "We call sweet chai tea *shireen*. You can use honey instead of sugar. Each family has its own recipe."

"The more sugar the cup contains, the greater the honor shown to the guest," Cruz added.

"I did not want to offend you by making the tea too sweet," Nasrin said to Santana. "You may add as much sugar as you like."

"Take a handful," Cruz said. "Sweeten you up some."

Santana gave him a look. "Thanks."

He normally didn't drink tea, but to honor Nasrin Khalil, he put two lumps of sugar in his mouth and drank the tea, which he found flavorful.

"Perfect for a cold winter day," he said.

Nasrin smiled.

"Who arranged for the apartment?" Santana said.

"The Afghan Cultural Society together with ZACAH."

"What's ZACAH?"

"An aid and charity organization here in Minnesota," she said. "Comes from the word *Zakat*. It means to purify."

"One of the five pillars of Islam," Cruz said.

"Yes. We purify our wealth by donating a portion of it to those in need. Wealth is a gift, a blessing from Allah. It does not belong to those who have it."

"It's called *sadaqah*, or voluntary charity," Cruz said.

Nasrin's eyes opened wide and her jaw dropped in surprise as she stared at Cruz. "You know much about my culture."

"I tried to learn something while I was there," Cruz said, looking away in embarrassment.

Nasrin held her eyes on him a moment longer as a slight smile creased her lips.

Santana wasn't sure if they were flirting with each other, but he wanted to redirect the conversation.

"Did your father say where he was going when he left?"

"No. He did not."

"Did you contact the police when your father went missing?"

Nasrin shook her head and let her eyes linger on him. Unusual, he thought, for an Afghani woman, though, in spite of her loose headscarf, her clothing and lipstick suggested she was more Western.

"My father is just another Afghan refugee," she said.

"We're looking for him," Cruz said. "We could use your help."

"You are looking for my father not because he is missing. For another reason."

Santana showed her the iPhone photo of Tara Easton with the four men. "Do you know any of these people in the photo with your father?"

As Nasrin stared at the photo, tears welled in her green eyes.

"It was taken at the airbase in Kandahar," Santana said.

She wiped away the tears with the back of a hand and shook her head.

"Maybe you heard your father speak of Tara Easton, Blaine Beckham, or Angel Duran?"

"Angel I remember," she said. "I remember because the name is so unusual. But I never met him or any of the others."

Santana was about to ask another question when his gaze settled on a pair of framed 5" x 7" photographs sitting on a small round table. One photo showed a dozen Afghani women dressed in camo fatigues with their M-4 rifles carried at port arms. In the second photo, Nasrin Khalil, still dressed in camo but not carrying a weapon, stood next to a woman also dressed in camo.

The woman was Hannah Thatcher.

"These two photos," Santana said, gesturing toward them. "They were taken in Afghanistan?"

She nodded.

"You were a soldier?"

"Yes, with the Female Tactical Platoon."

Santana looked at Cruz.

"There were rumors," Cruz said. "But I never met anyone belonging to the platoon."

In a country where most women didn't leave home without a male escort, Santana found it astonishing that a group of women had operated virtually undetected for a large part of the Afghan war. And to look at the small young woman before him, he could only admire the courage and determination it must've taken to join this platoon.

"The woman alone with you in the photo. Hannah Thatcher."

"She was one of our trainers," Nasrin said.

"Have you spoken to her recently?"

"We talk often. I visit her apartment sometimes."

"You drive?"

"I use my father's car."

Santana knew that Afghanis had legal status when they arrived in the US and could obtain a driver's license.

"Hannah and other veterans are helping us apply for Special Immigrant Visas," she said.

Having come from Colombia to the States at the age of sixteen, Santana was familiar with his immigration process. He looked to Cruz for an explanation about Afghani immigration.

"SIVs were available to Afghan nationals who worked as translators or interpreters with our Armed Forces or under Chief of Mission authority. If they worked for a period of at least twelve months, they applied under one category. Afghan nationals employed by our government or International Security Assistance Force for at least two years applied through a different category."

"How easy was it?"

"Well, translators or interpreters had to also obtain a favorable written recommendation from a general or flag officer in the chain of command of the US Armed Forces unit that was supported by the individual, or from the COM at the US Embassy in Kabul."

"Is that how your father gained admission to the US?" Santana asked Nasrin.

"Yes. He was given a packet to bring to the US to present to Customs and Border Protection."

"SIVs automatically became Lawful Permanent Residents, or LPRs, for humanitarian reasons after being admitted to the US," Cruz said. "They were eligible for the same benefits as refugees. SIVs provided a direct pathway to a green card, which was mailed after admittance to the United States."

"You have your green card?" Santana asked.

She nodded.

"How many others came with you?"

"Thirty-nine of us from the platoon were flown out of the country to Qatar just before the Taliban captured Kabul. A few hours later, another plane flew us to Ramstein Air Base in Germany. I was there for seven days. Then I was flown to Fort McCoy in Wisconsin. I stayed there for three months before I was brought here to be with my father."

"What made you want to be a soldier?"

"When I was a little girl, I was always told that girls and women could not join the military," she said. "And that upset me. So, I wanted to be the first to do those things. It is the only thing I know, the only thing I am good at. But I don't want to be a soldier anymore."

From the tone of her voice, it sounded as if Nasrin was seeking a new purpose in life. But finding a purpose that matched her old one—fighting the Taliban—would be difficult.

"You mentioned you had to go to work."

She nodded her head. "I work for a janitorial services company. I clean offices." She said it as though any work was meaningful.

"Do you have other family members still in Afghanistan?"

"Two sisters and a brother. And I have left my country in the hands of the enemy I spent years fighting. My family is now in hiding, targeted by the Taliban because of my service."

"You're safe here," Santana said.

She smiled crookedly. "Like my father?"

Santana left her question unanswered.

*   *   *

Late that night, Gabriel Cruz dreamt again of Camp Keating and the battle that often raged in his mind whenever he slept.

Fourteen miles from the Pakistan border, located in the deepest valley of Nuristan's Kamdesh District, surrounded by steep mountains with peaks as high as twelve thousand feet, the camp's defenseless location allowed three hundred Taliban to fire directly into the compound while remaining concealed behind trees and boulders along the ridgeline.

Gabriel sees the smoke signatures from incoming RPGs now and the orange-colored muzzle flashes from the AK-47s, raining mortars and bullets into the camp from all directions, the rounds kicking up dirt and small stones, coming so fast they overwhelm his senses. From the camp, a cacophony of thunderous sounds erupts, the cracks and thumps of M4 rifle fire, the sharp piercing sound of the M240s and the low growl of the .50 caliber machine guns, the chug, chug of the Mark 19 as it launches 40mm grenades instead of bullets, nearly three hundred rounds per minute.

Then he hears a deafening bolt of sound as a B-1 bomber drops a five-hundred-pound smart bomb at the base of the mountains, only two hundred feet from the compound. The concussion that follows is like a huge, pulsating wave slamming into his solar plexus, pushing through tissue and bone.

The air is so thick with dust he can taste it. Black smoke rises from the burning buildings behind him.

Now he sees three Taliban coming through the wire, wearing brown robes, tennis shoes, and chest racks loaded with bullets and hand grenades. One is balancing an RPG on his shoulder. A second carries a PKM machine gun. The third, an AK-47.

He takes aim, sighting the first Taliban, but when he presses the trigger on his M4, nothing happens. He futilely presses it again and again.

The Taliban with the AK-47 has a wolfish grin as he raises his weapon, ready to take the shot.

Gabriel Cruz woke up with a scream stuck in his throat, his body shaking and bathed in sweat. He put his hands under his thighs for a time to stop them from shaking. Then he threw back the covers, launched himself out of bed, and hurried to the bathroom, where he vomited into the toilet.

Chapter 9

Low, thick clouds grayed the sky, and a gusty north wind shook bare branches and unsettled hard patches of snow as Santana headed for the LEC the following morning. He had received a call on his SPPD cell phone from a public defender named Megan McKenna. She had represented Jadyn Hartley when he was charged with killing his father. She worked out of the Ramsey County Public Defender's Office in the Town Square Complex in downtown St. Paul, and she wanted to speak to him. Santana said go ahead, but she insisted he come by her office. He knew what she wanted. He also knew that if he didn't stop by, she would continue hassling him till he did.

Thick file folders from the cases she worked and the defendants she represented covered the front corners of the desk in Megan McKenna's office.

To the right of the stack of files sat a stained white coffee cup. The phrase written on the cup read:

PLEASE DON'T CONFUSE YOUR GOOGLE SEARCH
WITH MY LAW DEGREE

"Hang your jacket on the coat rack and have a seat, Detective," she said in a weary voice. She offered a small smile, which revealed the gap between her front teeth. Then she gestured at the hardback chair in front of the desk with one hand while she signed a document with the other.

Her straight brown hair was parted in the middle and hung limply to her shoulders. She wore thick tortoiseshell glasses and a worn gray sweater.

When she finished signing the document, she tossed the pen on the desktop and leaned back in the swivel chair with a heavy sigh.

"You called about Jadyn Hartley," Santana said.

"I'm assuming you've researched his background."

"I have."

"Then you understand how tenuous the young man's situation is."

"He hasn't been accused of anything."

"You're not understanding what's actually occurring."

"What we see depends mainly on what we're looking for," he said.

"And what are *you* looking for, Detective?"

"Justice."

"Then we're looking for the same thing."

Pointing to the thick files on her desk, she said, "I work mainly with juvenile clients. Most, like Jadyn Hartley, are children of color. Gaining their trust is even tougher given the time constraints I face working through a backlog of cases and dealing with staff turnover. Jadyn and others like him are the ones who suffer when I can't adequately do my job."

"Yet, you were able to secure an Extended Juvenile Jurisdiction for Hartley."

"Despite the obstacles, I'm good at what I do."

"We have that in common as well," Santana said.

"What a shock. A detective who thinks he has all the answers."

"Not now. But eventually."

She raised her eyebrows and tilted her head in a skeptical look. "The EJJ ruling was the right decision. Jadyn's father was an abuser and had threatened to kill him and his mother. Jadyn is a wonderful writer and a talented young man with a bright future."

"Tell me about his father."

"I only know what I learned during the hearing. His father worked as a mechanic at the Ford dealership in White Bear Lake."

"What about the mother?"

"She died two years ago. Ovarian cancer."

"Jadyn told me he lived with his mother."

A slight smile graced McKenna's lip. "He lives with me."

"Did you adopt him?"

"I took him in."

Santana peered at his notes for a moment. "He found the bones. That doesn't mean he's a suspect in what we assume is an evolving murder case. He needed to be questioned."

She leaned forward and rested her forearms on the desk. "Given his background, I'm worried the media will focus on him."

"I can't guarantee anything."

"Well, I can. If you continue pursuing Jadyn, I'll do everything in my power to stop you."

"Even if he's guilty."

"He isn't."

"You're pretty sure of yourself."

"No more than you, Detective."

* * *

Back at his desk in the Homicide and Robbery Unit, Santana logged into his SPPD computer, where he found an email and zip file attachment from the All-Citizens Bank containing the records for Tara and Matt Easton's shared checking and savings accounts.

After downloading and running off copies of each account, he handed Cruz copies of their savings account.

"Take a look at these and let me know if anything jumps out."

Santana sat down in his cubicle next to Cruz's and scanned their monthly checking account statements for the past two years. The bank had collated them from oldest to newest, so he started with the oldest statement and worked forward.

As a private first class, with two years of experience, Tara Easton had a monthly salary of $2160. Matt Easton earned nearly $5000 per month as a St. Paul firefighter. Doing a quick calculation, Santana estimated their yearly combined salary of about $86,000, an above average income for a young married couple in St. Paul.

Based on expenditures, they spent much of their income on ski trips and Mexican vacations whenever Tara had a leave. But the birth of their child had changed their spending habits and the number of vacation trips. In fact, Santana saw no trips taken in the past year. However, he did notice that monthly amounts of cash ranging from $250 to $500 had been withdrawn beginning nine months ago. Could be for miscellaneous expenses, Santana thought, if he could define "miscellaneous." Still, he wondered which one of them had been withdrawing the money and for what purpose.

Then, six months ago, one of them had deposited three separate $5,000 deposits into their checking account over the span of two weeks.

Where had that money come from?

Cruz stood up and leaned on the divider between their two desks. "*Nada*," he said. "Not much going in or out of their savings account in the last two years. What about you?"

Santana pointed to the three deposits he'd marked with a yellow highlighter. "Look at these."

Cruz peered over Santana's shoulder. "Lot of cash."

Tara Easton had mustered out of the service about the time of the deposit. Could she have been involved in the theft of money while in Afghanistan? Or, if her husband, Matt, had deposited the money, where had it come from?

"I need to talk to Matt Easton again," Santana said. "What about Tara Easton's cell phone call logs?"

Cruz took half the call log pages out of a manila file folder and handed Santana four two-sided pages.

"The last three months of call logs," he said.

They spent the next twenty minutes looking through them.

Cruz stood up and showed Santana the name and number he'd highlighted in orange.

"Blaine Beckham," Santana said.

Cruz nodded. "They called each other a dozen times."

* * *

Santana was seated at the dining room table in Matt Easton's house. Easton, wearing a sweatshirt and baggy green sweatpants, sat across from him. A half-eaten tuna sandwich and a few chips remained on the plastic plate in front of him.

"We need to be quiet," Easton said. "My daughter, Jamie, is taking a nap."

Santana removed a copy of a page from the Eastons' checking statements from his briefcase and pushed it across the table. "Tell me about the three five-thousand-dollar deposits."

Easton stared at the checking statement for a time, as if he had never seen it before.

Maybe trying to come up with a response.

When Easton looked up from the paper, his gaze drifted from the wall to Santana. "I won the money gambling."

"Where?"

"Mystic Lake Casino. Blackjack. I had a good run."

Santana recalled the regular $250 to $500 checking account withdrawals beginning nine months ago.

"How often you visit the casino?" he asked.

Easton shrugged. "Maybe a couple times a month."

"This start about nine months ago?"

"Around that time, yeah. What does this have to do with anything?"

Santana knew that casinos preferred to pay winners in cash whenever possible, since it increased the chances that the customer would keep playing—and maybe give it all back in losses. Still, state law required Easton and the casino to report all gambling winnings.

"You have a W-2G form from the casino?" he asked.

"Probably around somewhere."

"I need to see it."

"What the hell is this all about?"

"I need to see it," Santana repeated.

Easton raised his hands in a gesture of surrender. "All right. I'll look for it. But not right now while Jamie is sleeping."

"Text a photo of it to me," Santana said. "Soon."

When Santana returned to his unmarked, he called Gabriel Cruz and updated him on his conversation with Matt Easton.

"You believe Easton is telling the truth?"

"He's hiding something."

"You're pretty sure of it."

"You've been doing this as long as I have, you start trusting your instincts."

Chapter 10

The Combat Zone gun shop occupied space between a smoke shop and liquor store in the Sibley Plaza, a small strip mall with single-story shops on W. 7th and Davern Streets.

Santana pulled his slickback into the plowed lot and drove past an Aldi grocery store, a Caribou Coffee, and Planet Fitness before parking in an open space in front of the gun shop.

With the temperature in the low twenties, Santana felt a chill run through him as he and Cruz exited their ride and entered the shop to the sound of entry chimes. Although the man behind the counter had a Van Dyke beard and a shaved head, Santana recognized him as Blaine Beckham. He looked like he'd gained ten pounds since the photo Santana had found in Tara Easton's bedroom had been taken. His muscular arms were clearly visible in the tight T-shirt. The white lettering on the front of it read:

THERE'S NO SUCH THING AS TOO MUCH AMMO UNLESS YOUR HOUSE IS ON FIRE

A row of AK-47s and AR-15s hung along the wall behind the counter. Boxes of ammo filled the shelves underneath the assault rifles. Various handguns were mounted in glass cases under the counter. Mounted shotguns and rifles covered the surrounding walls. Targets, hunting gear, holsters, and Combat Zone caps filled the display stands on the floor.

Enough firepower, Santana thought, to outfit a small army.

A CCTV, or closed-circuit television, camera hung high on the wall behind the counter and cash register, enabling Beckham to keep a watchful eye around his business, as well as record and archive footage for later use.

A partially open door with an OFFICE sign attached to it was located just to the right of the counter and cash register.

A posted sign on the wall to the right of the door warned:

IT IS UNLAWFUL TO STORE OR LEAVE A LOADED FIREARM WHERE A CHILD CAN OBTAIN ACCESS.

Minnesota law required federally licensed firearms dealers to post these warning signs conspicuously on their premises.

A different sign with a red arrow on the staircase to Santana's left pointed down to the RANGE.

Santana saw no other customers or employees. He wondered if any employees were downstairs, but he heard no shooting from the gun range.

The slide, take down pin, guide rod, spring, barrel, and frame for a compact/carry Ruger LC9s lay on a long towel beside a magazine insert, punch, cleaning kit, and two rags on top of the glass counter.

"What can I do for you fellas?" Beckham said with a welcoming grin.

The grin vanished the moment Santana showed Beckham his shield.

"I'm Detective Santana. This is my partner, Detective Cruz."

"There a problem?" Beckham said, his lifeless eyes darting between the two men.

"We're here about Tara Easton."

Santana could see the recognition in Beckham's dark, shifting eyes.

"What about her?"

"She's dead."

Beckham's face was as blank as an empty canvas. "Well, ain't that a kick in the ass."

"Damn right it is," Cruz said.

That Beckham had shown no emotion when informed of Tara Easton's death had surprised Santana. Maybe Beckham already knew she was dead. But the more Santana thought about it, the more he wondered if Beckham had seen so much killing that another death held no meaning for him now.

Beckham fixed his stare on Cruz for a time, as if taking the measure of the man. Then he said, "You a vet?"

"Afghanistan."

"Where?"

"Nuristan Province in Eastern Afghanistan near the Pakistan border."

Beckham placed his hands on the counter and leaned forward. "Were you at COP Keating near Kamdesh?"

Cruz nodded.

Santana hadn't heard of Kamdesh and wasn't sure what COP stood for.

Beckham held out his right hand. "Well, brother, let me shake your hand."

Cruz reluctantly took it.

"That was one clusterfuck," Beckham continued. "Couple of Medals of Honor came out of it. Good to see you survived."

"Tell us what you know about Tara Easton," Santana said, steering the conversation back on track.

Cruz took out his notebook and pen.

"She was a damn fine soldier." Beckham shook his head in frustration. "Survived two tours and then dies at home. Doesn't make sense, huh, Detective."

"Not yet," Santana said.

Beckham offered a half-smile. "I like your attitude."

Santana knew the answer to the next question he was about to ask, but he wanted to know if Beckham would lie about it.

"Had you seen Tara Easton since you both returned home?"

Beckham considered the question for a time as he brushed solvent through the Ruger's barrel.

"Yeah," he said at last. "A couple times."

"Where did you see her?"

"At her apartment."

"When was the last time?"

"Don't know. Maybe a couple weeks ago."

"Talk to her on the phone recently?"

Beckham hesitated, as if he suspected Santana already knew the answer to his question.

"Yeah."

"What about?"

"She'd mentioned wanting to visit the range here. I called to see about setting up an appointment."

"What did she say?"

"She'd get back to me."

"Then you two were close."

Beckham shrugged as he picked up a clean white patch, squirted it with solvent, and wiped the outside of the gun barrel.

"How 'bout focusing on my questions rather than the handgun," Santana said.

Beckham offered a dismissive shake of his head as he set the brush and barrel on the towel. "I can multi-task, Detective."

"How close were you with Tara Easton?"

"We were friends."

"Did she seem depressed?"

"Only when she talked about missing her kid."

"Where did you meet her?"

Beckham used the long brush to push a solvent-soaked patch through the barrel. "She was at the Kandahar base when I was there."

Santana pulled out his cell phone and showed Beckham the picture of the photo he'd found in Tara Easton's bedroom. "You must've known Angel and Taimur, too."

Beckham flinched for a millisecond as he peered at the photo. "Yeah, I knew 'em."

"What about this man on the end?" Santana pointed to the Afghani in the tiger-striped uniform.

"Nope," Beckham said.

"Funny he'd be in a photo with other friends of yours."

"He was Tara's friend. Not mine."

"Who took the photo?"

Beckham shrugged. "Don't recall."

"Know where Duran is now?"

"Last I heard, out near Afton."

"Got an address?"

Beckham shook his head.

"Have you seen either of them since you got out?"

"Nope."

"Yet you saw Tara Easton."

"She's prettier than Duran or Khalil," Beckham said with a sly smile.

"And now she's dead."

"Hey," Beckham said, holding his hands palms out in a stopping gesture. "I don't know anything about that."

"You smoke dope with her?"

Beckham let out a short laugh. "Like you're going to arrest me for it?"

"Did you?"

"I don't touch that shit. Screws up your mind."

"You knew she was married."

"Separated."

"That makes a difference?" Santana said.

"We weren't balling each other, if that's what you're getting at."

"Ever meet her husband, Matt?"

Beckham shook his head.

"Hannah Thatcher?"

"Couple times."

"What about Wade Crawford?"

Beckham's eyes flitted like shadows in dark corners. Then he said, "Know what the difference is between animals and humans, Detective?"

Santana sometimes thought there was no difference, but he shook his head.

"Animals would never allow the dumbest ones to lead the pack."

"So, Crawford is dumb."

"As a fencepost."

"How do you know him?"

"I'd see him around the base in Kandahar. Always looking to jam someone up. Not a popular guy."

Santana nodded at Cruz to make sure he got the details in his notebook. Then he turned his attention back to Beckham. "You never asked how Tara Easton died."

"Dead is dead."

"Little cold for someone you called your friend."

"I'm used to death, Detective. Maybe you are, too. Don't mean it as an excuse. Just a matter of fact."

"You a Twins fan?"

"What's that got to do with anything?"

"Maybe have a Twins hat?"

Beckham's face colored. "I'm a Vikings fan."

"I take it that's a no."

Beckham nodded.

The entry chimes rang as two young men entered the shop.

Santana took out a business card and placed it on the countertop. "You think of anything else that might be important, give me a call."

"You know when the funeral is?" Beckham asked.

"I don't. But I'm sure there'll be an announcement."

"Tara deserved better."

"We all do," Santana said.

Chapter 11

Santana and Cruz stopped for lunch at My Burger on the corner of Snelling and Grand Avenue, a small fast-food restaurant in the Macalester/Groveland neighborhood. They each ordered a California burger with sweet potato fries and a chocolate milkshake.

As they sat down at a table for two underneath an "Oh, my" wall logo, waiting for their food, Santana's cell phoned pinged.

Matt Easton had texted Santana a photo of the W-2G form he'd received from the casino indicating his winnings.

"Easton's fifteen-thousand-dollar checking deposit is legitimate," he told Cruz.

"Guess I can scratch him off our list of suspects."

"Not just yet," Santana said.

"You see how Beckham reacted when you asked him about the Twins hat?" Cruz asked.

"I did."

"I'd like to look through his closet."

"Maybe we'll get the chance."

A balding, middle-aged, slightly overweight man wearing a brown synthetic leather jacket, matching slacks, heavy boots with red laces, and a rumpled white shirt with the top button opened approached the table. The Windsor knot on his striped tie was loose at the neck, his semi-rimless glasses were perched above his forehead, and his walrus mustache was in need of a trim.

He held a spiral notebook and pen in his hands. "Pat Grainger. *Pioneer Press*," he said in a gravelly voice, offering a hand.

When neither Santana nor Cruz shook it or replied, Grainger flipped over the front cover of his notebook and continued. "What does Jadyn Hartley have to do with the bones found in the snowbank in Como Park?"

"We're eating," Santana said.

Grainger looked at the table and then glanced toward the kitchen in back. "Not yet."

"Hartley found the bones," Cruz said.

Santana gave Cruz a look and shook his head slightly, indicating he shouldn't respond to Grainger's questions.

Grainger peered at Cruz. "But Hartley killed his father. Couldn't he be responsible for this victim as well?"

A young woman working behind the counter brought out their milkshakes. She paused by the table, not wanting to interrupt.

Santana waved her in.

She set the drinks and straws on the table and said their burgers and fries would be ready shortly.

When she left, Santana stood and looked down at Grainger. "*Now* we're eating."

"Hey," Grainger said, backing up a step. "I'm just doing my job."

"Not here and not now."

Grainger dug into a jacket pocket and produced a business card. "I'd appreciate a call when you want to talk to the press."

Santana looked at the card but didn't take it.

Grainger set the card on the table. "Thanks for your time. Stay in touch," he said, heading for the entrance.

Santana sat down at the table again.

"He's pushy," Cruz said.

"Some reporters are. Most know it's more productive to call and set up a meeting than to ambush us at lunch."

Santana waited a few beats before he said, "Yesterday, I noticed an unusual scent in Nasrin Khalil's apartment. Know what it is?"

"Attar," Cruz said. "Afghani women wear perfume oils that don't contain alcohol. Comes from flowers, herbs, and spices. Mitti attar is the most special. Smells like the scent of the earth.

Reminds me of washed *khullads*, or clay cups, they use to hold steaming chai tea."

Santana sipped his chocolate malt before speaking again. "Blaine Beckham mentioned something about COP Keating?"

"Stands for Command Outpost Keating."

"Near Kamdesh?"

Cruz nodded as the young woman set their burgers and fries on the table and departed.

Santana noted the inward gaze of Cruz's eyes and suspected the battle was playing out again in his partner's mind. He wondered if Cruz suffered from PTSD, as he'd suffered after his mother's murder and the revenge he'd sought against the men who'd killed her.

"I could look it up," Santana said, "but I'd rather you told me what happened there."

"Why?"

"Insight," Santana said. "We're partners."

"You want to know if you can trust me."

"Investigating a major case can sometimes feel like you are putting a puzzle together without the picture on the box to use as a reference. We need to rely on each other, especially in violent situations. It's important that I know you'll have my back."

"And that you'll have mine."

"Two-way street," Santana said.

They ate some of their burgers before Cruz said, "I know all about violence."

"I'm sure you do."

The gruesome damage Santana had seen during his years as a homicide detective led him to believe that as a society, we don't hate violence. We hate the wrong kind of violence. When it's the right kind of violence, like the war Cruz had fought in, we reinforce it and reward it.

Cruz took another bite of his burger and a sip of his shake. Then he wiped his mouth with a napkin. A moment later he nearly jumped out of his chair when a plate shattered on the floor in the kitchen.

"You want to be effective, you need to let the anger go, Gabriel."

"And you know this because?"

"Because I carried it for a long time after my mother was murdered."

Cruz looked away for a moment. "I didn't know."

"Now you do."

His eyes found Santana's again. "So how did you lose the anger?"

"I never did."

Cruz shook his head. "I don't get it."

"You focus on the mission."

"I'll think about it."

"Better do more than that."

They ate quietly for a time before Santana said, "You ever have nightmares or flashbacks?"

"No point in talking about it," Cruz said.

"Sure there is. Remember, it's not about what's wrong with you but what happened to you."

"You're not a vet."

"Don't have to be one to experience PTSD."

Cruz's eyes narrowed as he thought about what Santana had just said.

"Nightmares are less now. No flashbacks or paranoia. I'm not depressed. Appetite is fine, as you can see," he said, gesturing at the empty paper wrap and glass of chocolate malt.

"You want to talk more about it, let me know."

"That works both ways," Cruz said. "So, what're your thoughts about Beckham?"

"What're yours?" Santana countered.

"He's hiding something," Cruz said, tossing the crumpled napkin on the table.

"We need to figure out what."

"I take it you have another move."

"Always," Santana said.

*   *   *

The city of Afton is located approximately fifteen miles east of downtown St. Paul, south of I-94 on the eastern border of Minnesota, along the banks of the St. Croix River.

The small city wasn't far from Santana's home. He'd instructed Gabriel Cruz to search for information on Taimur Khalil's possible whereabouts, while he'd stop by Angel Duran's place on his way home.

Snow flurries fell like confetti in the ten-degree air. Ice slicked the road. Santana kept the manual transmission on his Ford SUV in low gear. As he approached the turn-off to Duran's place, Siri cautioned him that a right turn was just ahead. Santana recalled an old saying his defensive driving instructor had once told him about driving in the snow. "Don't do anything to scare the car, and the car won't do anything to scare you."

On an isolated, heavily-wooded lot set far back from the road outside Afton, Angel Duran's timber frame cabin sat on a slight rise under the gray sky. A plowed driveway on the far right wound past a metal Quonset hut to a stand-alone double garage.

Santana noted the dark green Range Rover parked in front of one of the garage stalls.

Thankful that he'd worn his Blauer-style fleece jacket, he exited his SUV and walked toward the cabin, his boots crunching the ice crystals. The still air smelled of pine and woodsmoke. The woods were as silent as a grave.

Stepping up to the front door, Santana pressed the doorbell and waited. He pressed it again a half-minute later. Then he cupped his hands and peered into the sidelight to the right of the door. It was dark inside and looked as if no one was home.

Santana stepped back and looked for a security camera but saw none.

Halfway back to his SUV, the roar of a chainsaw shattered the tranquil silence. The saw whined through wood as he headed in that direction.

As he came around the back of the cabin, Santana saw a heavily bearded man clothed in thick brown coveralls, heavy boots, and a red ski hat and gloves. A pair of thick goggles covered his eyes and yellow and black earmuff safety protectors his ears. A six-foot-high stack of firewood stood behind him.

Santana's thoughts turned to the meeting he and Cruz had had with Kim Solace. How the forensic anthropologist had shown them that the recovered bones from Como Park had been cut with a chainsaw. Santana wondered if he was looking at that same chainsaw now.

Not wanting to startle him, Santana retraced his steps and walked to the opposite side of the cabin, where he could approach from the front rather than from behind.

Coming around the corner of the cabin, Santana made a wide arc to avoid the high stack of wood and held up his badge wallet as he advanced.

It took a few seconds before the man looked up and saw Santana coming toward him. He stood still for a moment, holding the chainsaw with both hands, staring at Santana and the badge wallet, before he switched off the machine.

Santana's ears were still ringing as he gestured for the man to remove his goggles and ear protectors. When he did, Santana said, "Angel Duran?"

The man with the steely gray eyes nodded. "What's up?"

"I'm here about Tara Easton."

Duran leaned over and set the chainsaw, ear protectors, and goggles on a tree stump. He paused for a time and then gestured toward the badge wallet Santana still held in his hand. "Mind if I take a look at that?" He held out his hand.

Santana held up his badge wallet again for Duran to see—but didn't give it to him.

Duran shrugged and dropped his hand. As he peered at the badge wallet, he said, "Santana. You Mexican?"

"Colombian."

Duran chuckled. "Came here for the weather, huh?"

"You get used to it."

Duran shrugged. "Never have. Anyway, I heard Tara committed suicide."

Even though Reiko Tanabe hadn't yet ruled on the cause of death, the media had indicated a possible suicide.

"Media talk," Santana said.

"Then you must be from homicide."

"Why is that?" Santana said, returning his badge wallet to the inner pocket in his jacket.

"Why else would you be here asking me about Tara?"

Santana preferred to leave the possibility of homicide on the table to see how Duran would react.

"What can you tell me about her?" he asked.

"I didn't know her that well."

Santana pulled his iPhone from a coat pocket, clicked on the photo app, and showed Duran the picture of the four men with Easton at the Kandahar base in Afghanistan.

"Doesn't mean I knew her that well."

"Doesn't mean you didn't either."

"I haven't seen or talked to Tara Easton since I left Afghanistan. That was nearly a year ago."

Santana held up his phone again. "What about Blaine Beckham?"

"Haven't talked to him in a while."

"Taimur Khalil?"

Duran's eyes shifted back and forth as he composed his answer. "Why would I keep in touch with a raghead?"

"That what you called them?"

90

"That's what they are."

"Heard Khalil was a 'jingle man.'"

"Know what that is, Detective?"

Santana recalled Gabriel Cruz's explanation. "Basically, a delivery truck driver."

"Yeah. But Khalil ran his own company. Had some sideline operations going with the Taliban as well."

"Could you prove that?"

He snickered. "Everyone knew it."

"But nobody did anything about it?"

"Lotta people had their hands in the till, if you get my drift."

"What about this guy?" Santana said, pointing to the unnamed Afghani in the photo.

"Don't recall his name."

"So how did he end up in this photo?"

"Got me."

Flakes of snow fell more heavily now.

"Look, Detective, as part of our counterinsurgency operations, we were supposed to form relationships with civilians, consult with locals, and train and co-operate with the Afghani troops. But we were trained to fight, not be fuckin' community organizers, for chrissake. Besides, I never trusted Khalil. Never trusted any of the ragheads."

"Not even their special forces?" Santana said, pointing to the unnamed Afghani again.

"Especially those assholes."

Santana silently noted that when Duran talked about Afghanis, he exhibited contempt or anger towards them. No doubt based on his wartime experiences. Yet, Santana saw no anger or recriminations when Gabriel Cruz spoke about the Afghanis, though he still refused to discuss his wartime experiences. Knowing that anger could limit thinking and end discussion, Santana appreciated Cruz's attitude toward the Afghanis. He wanted answers, not recriminations.

"That how Blaine Beckham felt?" he asked.

"Damn right."

"And Tara Easton?"

"Never expressed her feelings on the subject."

"Hard to believe she'd keep a photo of Khalil and this man in her bedroom if she felt like you did."

"Too bad you can't ask her about it."

"It is."

Duran picked up the goggles and ear protectors. "I need to finish up here, Detective, before we get another foot of snow."

"One more question. Do you know Wade Crawford?"

"That fucker."

Santana was about to ask Duran why he had such a low opinion of Crawford when he caught a slight movement in the woods behind Duran. In the heavily falling snow, he thought at first it might be an animal.

Duran followed Santana's gaze and half-turned, as if he wanted to see as well.

As he did, Santana realized what he thought was an animal was actually someone crouching behind a tree, aiming a rifle at them.

He grabbed Duran by the front of his jacket, pulling him toward cover behind the firewood pile.

"Get down!" he yelled.

Santana heard the whip-like snap of a bullet as the first shot rocketed past, followed a split-second later by the crack of the rifle.

A second bullet clipped Duran in the thigh. He winced and cried out in pain as Santana pulled him down and dragged him behind the stack of firewood.

As Santana dropped to his knees a third bullet splintered wood in the six-foot-high stack, creating a cracking sound like tree branches snapping in a gale.

With his heart thudding in his chest and adrenaline coursing through his body, Santana crouched behind the woodpile and drew his Glock. Staying low, he peered around the corner of the woodpile, ready to shoot.

Whoever had fired the shots had disappeared.

Behind him, Angel Duran clutched his leg, trying to staunch the blood flow.

"God dammit!" he screamed. "Fucker shot me."

Santana kept his eyes and gun focused on the near corner of the woodpile as he squatted beside Duran and called 911.

"Who shot you?"

"The hell I know!"

The wound just above and on the outside of Duran's left knee had torn away a chunk of skin and fabric. Judging by the amount of blood, Santana wondered if the bullet had caught the femoral artery. The average time for first responders to arrive at a scene was seven to ten minutes. Might be longer way out here, Santana thought. Duran could bleed out and die within five minutes.

Santana removed Duran's belt and tightened it two inches above the wound. Using a stick as a torsion device, he twisted it to tighten the hold and to apply pressure to the wound.

He needed answers, and the only way to get them was to make certain Angel Duran stayed alive.

Chapter 12

Since Afton didn't have its own police department, deputies and two detectives from the Special Investigations Division of the Washington County Sheriff's Department, along with forensic techs from the sheriff's department and the Bureau of Criminal Apprehension in St. Paul, worked the crime scene where Angel Duran had been shot. He'd been rushed to the emergency room at Lakeview Hospital in Stillwater.

Santana wished Duran had been brought to Regions Hospital in St. Paul, where he might have had more control over the situation. But Lakeview was a Level III Trauma Hospital and the best equipped in the area. It was also much closer to the crime scene. Doctors worked closely with the team at Regions Hospital, and many of them treated patients at both hospitals.

Falling snow had gradually obscured the large footprints Santana had found in the woods, but one footprint beside the tree where the shooter had crouched took longer to fill, giving Santana time to snap a few photos and to note the tread pattern and the octagon shape in the middle of the tread.

He'd also recovered the three shell casings before they were lost under a blanket of snow. The Federal Cartridge Company had made the cartridge, as indicated by the FC on its headstamp. The .223 signified the caliber, and REM stood for Remington.

Having fired both AK-47s and AR-15s during his training exercises, Santana knew that AR-15s were designed with tighter accuracy than the AKs. The headstamp and effective range led Santana to the conclusion that the shooter had used an AR-15 to try and kill Angel Duran.

"Every gun tells a story," he said to Del Taggart, one of the two Washington County investigators on the scene. "Make sure the BCA sends the casings through NIBIN."

The National Integrated Ballistic Information Network database stored 2-D and 3-D images of cartridge cases from crime scenes, as well as pictures of shell casings test fired by law enforcement. Its software searched each image for similar topographical characteristics to generate a list of possible matches.

"I know how to do my job," Taggart said, looking up from the notebook he held in his hand.

The heavyset investigator with the ruddy complexion wore a thick brown department jacket and black knit hat with SHERIFF stenciled in gold across the front.

"Speaking of doing your job," Taggart said, "good of you to notify us that you were on our turf talking to Duran."

"Would that have made a difference?"

"If I'd been with you, maybe the ME would've been bagging the shooter."

"Have the BCA lab look for prints on the shell casings," Santana said, ignoring Taggart's comment.

Taggart released a heavy sigh. "You know as well as I do, Santana, we got a snowball's chance in hell of imaging fingerprints from expended shell casings. Firing temperature alone is enough to vaporize the skin oils from a fingerprint on a brass nine-millimeter casing. Any good latent print expert will tell you that. And what if the shooter wore gloves?"

Santana knew that obtaining a usable print from whatever remained on a shell casing was challenging, made even more so by the fact that the casings were cylindrical. If they were flat, it would be easier to lift non-distorted prints from them. Still, he figured it was worth a shot.

He pointed to the BCA van in the driveway. "You've got the equipment right here."

The BCA had recently purchased two additional NIBIN machines to boost capacity, along with a new mobile NIBIN van from the ATF that could process gun crime evidence more efficiently and close shooting cases faster.

The software compared ballistic evidence from shooting scenes to what was already in the system, aiming to link multiple crimes back to one weapon. NIBIN leads were meant to be turned around in twenty-four to forty-eight hours. Santana saw every firearm as an individual thumbprint, since no two guns were identical. A hit would indicate the gun had been used at another crime scene, giving him something new to go on.

"Why spend time doing DNA testing at the expense of inputting data into NIBIN immediately?" Taggart said. "Could delay getting a hit."

"And if we don't get a NIBIN hit, then we have *nada*."

"Tell you what, you find the weapon used in the shooting, we can match it with the shell casings."

"I'll be looking for it."

"That makes two of us," Taggart said.

Santana left Taggart standing in the swirling flurries and trudged through the snow to the back of the BCA van and opened one of the two side-by-side doors.

Dennis Crane, wearing a gray reflective windbreaker and matching pants, sat at a fold-down bench and small table, looking at a computer screen. A small, thin man with dark-framed, Coke-bottle glasses, a bowl haircut, and a wisp of a dark mustache, he greeted Santana with a wide-eyed expression of surprise.

Santana stepped up and into the van and closed the door behind him.

Stainless-steel lockers, drawers, and overhead units stored photography, fingerprint, and personal protection equipment, evidence collection containers and measuring devices, flashlights, crime scene tape, and laptops for communication and research. Heating and A/C units kept the inside comfortable in any weather.

"Do me a favor," Santana said.

Crane's eyes blinked rapidly, indicating anxiety. "Let me guess. Does your request involve something I shouldn't do?"

"I wouldn't ask you to."

Crane shook his head in disbelief. "You are John Santana, right?"

Santana ignored the dig. "Shell casings from the shooting are coming your way from the Washington County Sheriff's Department. Test them for prints."

"That's a long shot."

"Better than no shot at all."

"Shouldn't Taggart be asking me to do this?" Crane said.

"Yes. He should. But he probably won't."

"That'll delay getting them into the NIBIN database."

"We're not linking this gun to another shooting and an owner. Best chance of solving this might be through fingerprints."

Crane stared at his computer screen as if his next response was written there. "You gonna be my umbrella if it starts raining shit?"

"Always have before."

He looked at Santana again. "I'm having a hard time remembering that."

"Kim Solace sent the BCA a sample of the bones found in Como Park."

"You think this shooting is related?" Crane said, his eyebrows rising in anticipation.

Santana had no indication that the Duran shooting and the bones found in the park were related. But by piquing Dennis Crane's interest, he figured he'd get a faster turnaround on the fingerprints.

"It's setting up to be a big case," he said. "Lots of media attention."

"That big, huh?"

"Very big."

Crane held up an evidence envelope containing the three shells Santana had found. "You know these are steel casings."

"Cheaper than brass," Santana said.

"It's the sixty-percent copper in brass that's expensive. Steel lowers the price. But they can cause problems with extraction."

"How so?"

"They expand during ignition but fail to contract afterward. Makes them unsuitable for hand loading. Some manufacturers coat their steel cases in lacquer or polymer to help reduce metal-on-metal friction. Treatments still don't make steel cases as reliable as brass ones. And they can damage range equipment, too, including the backstop. Lotta commercial ranges issue blanket bans on all steel-cased ammo."

"Your point is?"

"Might want to use steel-cased ammo in a cheap weapon. Wouldn't recommend using it in a more expensive one."

"Or in a weapon you were using to murder someone," Santana said.

"Why take the chance?"

"I'll keep that in mind. Let me know if you find a print," Santana said, heading toward the rear van doors.

"Never said I'd do it," Crane said in a weak voice.

Santana stopped and turned toward Crane, giving him his best cop glare.

Crane shrugged. "Never said I wouldn't either."

Santana nodded and opened the door and stepped out of the van, giving Crane one more practiced look before he slammed the door shut and headed back to his detective ride to call Janet Kendrick and Gabriel Cruz.

"You need to talk to OIS," she said when she answered, referencing the Officer-Involved Shooting Team, "even if you never fired a shot."

He assured Kendrick that he'd file a report in the morning before calling Cruz to let him know he was okay. Then he drove slowly to Lakeview Hospital, thankful for the four-wheel drive and the wiper blades that worked overtime to keep snow from clumping on the windshield.

While waiting alone in the visitor's lounge outside the emergency room, where surgeons were working on Angel Duran, he looked out a window at the heavily falling snow and wondered if Duran had any relatives that the Washington County Sheriff's Department had notified.

His cell phone rang, drawing him out of his reverie.

He recognized the SPPD deputy chief's number.

"I was in a meeting when I got word on the shooting," Rita Gamboni said when Santana answered.

"I'm at the hospital now."

"Were you shot?" Gamboni said, her voice rising with concern.

"No. Angel Duran was. I'm here waiting to talk to him."

"Then he'll survive?"

"That's my impression. But I'm not a doctor."

Gamboni released a long breath. "You scared the hell out of me, John. I don't want to lose you."

"I don't want to be lost," he said.

They'd been surreptitiously seeing each other again since Rita had returned to the SPPD after a stint with the FBI. They'd dated years before when they were partners, but Santana had ended the relationship when Rita became the SPPD's first female senior homicide commander—and his boss. Technically, as deputy chief of the Major Crimes Division, she was his boss again, though Janet Kendrick commanded the Homicide and Robbery Unit.

Given the SPPD's grapevine, Santana knew their relationship was common knowledge. But since they were not flaunting it, the rest of the brass, led by the chief, had chosen to look the other way. Santana figured they would continue to look the other way till he rattled the wrong cage. Something he often did.

"Are you alone there?" Rita asked.

"For the time being."

Since the Washington County Sheriff's Department was leading the investigation and was responsible for contacting Duran's family members, someone from the department would be at the hospital soon.

"Tell me about Duran," Rita said.

Santana reviewed the case with her, beginning with Tara Easton's apparent suicide and the fact that Angel Duran was in the photo he saw in her apartment.

"And you don't believe Easton killed herself," Rita said when he'd finished bringing her up to speed.

"No. Especially not after someone tried to take out Angel Duran."

"What does Kendrick think?"

"Until the ME concludes Tara Easton was murdered, Kendrick has us working the bones found in Como Park."

"And you'd rather pursue whoever tried to kill Duran."

"I believe there's a connection between Duran and Easton. You could talk to Kendrick."

"I won't do that, John."

"It's the right way to go."

"You can discuss the shooting first thing tomorrow morning with Kendrick and the chief. And how you believe the two cases are linked."

"Will you be there?"

"No."

Santana preferred to have Rita in his corner, but he understood her position.

"What time?"

"Kendrick will let you know," she said. "How's Gabriel Cruz working out?"

"His military background is a plus."

"Thought it would be," Gamboni said.

Santana saw a doctor dressed in surgical greens coming out of the emergency room, holding his surgical cap in one hand.

"I've got to run, Rita."

"Let me know what happens."

"Will do," he said, breaking off the connection.

The doctor stopped and looked around till his eyes found Santana.

"I'm Dr. Hoffman," he said, approaching Santana.

He looked to be in his mid-forties, slender, with dark curly hair.

"Are you a family member?"

Santana showed Hoffman his badge. "Family members are being contacted. I'm investigating the shooting."

Duran's shooting had to be connected to Easton's death, Santana thought. So, in his mind, he hadn't lied to the doctor. He *was* still investigating.

"Mr. Duran is in recovery now."

"Is he going to make it?"

"Well, he's a lucky man. Bullet just nicked him. Left no fragments in the leg."

Hoffman paused a moment, as if reflecting on his last statement, before continuing.

"Was this a high velocity round?" he asked.

"It was."

"Unfortunately, I've seen too many gunshot wounds from high-powered rifles recently. Like we're living in a war zone."

"Seems that way," Santana said.

"This type of bullet tends to yaw widely after entering the body while breaking off at the cannelure with the tip remaining intact. The lead core and rest of the jacket shred, resulting in a lead snowstorm."

Santana understood that Hoffman was referring to the small bullet fragments scattered along the wound track.

"Much more difficult to treat and recover from," Hoffman continued. "But I've learned to treat the wound, not the weapon."

"So he'll fully recover?"

"Right now I'm worried about infection. We'll treat him with one gram of intravenous cefazolin every eight hours for a couple days."

"I'd like to speak to Duran."

"He's sedated. That's not possible right now."

Santana knew he'd bigfooted Taggart and the Washington County Sheriff's Department by extracting and taking the bullet he'd found lodged in the woodpile. But he wanted to keep momentum going. If forensics had the bullet, a comparison could quickly be made with the shell casings and perhaps with the particular AR-15—when he found it.

He'd placed the bullet in an evidence envelope annotated with the date, time, and location. Since the first bullet had missed and the second had only clipped Duran and kept going, they would likely never be found, at least not till the snow melted in the spring.

"What's the prognosis?" he asked Hoffman.

"He's sustained significant tissue damage. But there is no damage to the femur. His foot was cyanotic and cool, but he has intact sensation and movement of his toes. Blood pressure and EEG look good. If his luck continues to hold, he should be able to ambulate independently with full sensation in his foot."

"Thanks for the update, Doctor."

"Did you apprehend the shooter?"

"Not yet."

"Well, good luck to you, Detective," Hoffman said.

Santana hoped he wouldn't need it.

* * *

After returning home Santana typed a BCA analysis request form specifying the essential case details and the type of forensic testing he'd like done on the steel-case bullets. Since it was after hours, he'd drop off the evidence envelope first thing tomorrow morning.

He sent copies of the footprint photos he'd taken in the woods behind Duran's place to Tony Novak, the SPPD forensic specialist, and asked if Novak could ID the boot type.

Then he placed his Glock 23 in the safe, took a shower, and changed clothes.

His department cell phone rang as he was about to head downstairs.

"What the hell did you do with the bullet in the woodpile?"

"Deputy Taggart."

"Damn right it is."

"I'm taking the bullet to the BCA tomorrow morning, where you would've taken it."

"This isn't your case, Santana."

"You're wrong. Angel Duran is involved in a case I'm working."

"Then how about sharing instead of acting like the Feds."

"Be happy to. Let me know where and when."

"Damn sure I will."

Santana disconnected. In the absence of the rifle used to shoot Duran, the BCA had nothing to compare the bullet to, which left him unable to identify the possible shooter. Yet.

He went downstairs, where Ana Soriano sat on the leather couch in the living room, watching live reports from the Afton crime scene on a local TV station. Gitana lay beside her. Rather than have her find out later that he'd been involved in the shooting, he sat down and told her what had happened.

Having experienced so much violence in her young life, she didn't appear shocked by what she'd heard, but Santana saw the concern register in her eyes.

"Are you all right?"

"Fine," he said. "The shooter wasn't after me."

"Why would someone want to kill this man Duran?"

"I need to find out."

Her gaze looked inward as a thought formed behind her eyes. "You shouldn't risk your life for these people, John."

"What people?"

"The gangbangers, the addicts, the dealers, the pimps, the . . ." she stopped.

"Whores?" Santana said.

"I wasn't going to use that term." Her eyes locked on his for a second before she looked away. "I suppose you were about to say *I* was one of those people."

"It doesn't matter."

Her eyes found his again. "Doesn't it?"

He shook his head. "You know who Justitia was?"

"One of the four Virtues in Roman mythology. Lady Justice in your legal system. Blindfolded, holding scales and a sword, with the snake representing evil at her feet, and a book representing the Constitution."

Ana always surprised him with her knowledge and intelligence, despite having had limited educational opportunities.

"Then you understand everyone is entitled to justice," he said.

"Under the law."

"That's what I operate under."

"All the time?"

When he didn't respond, Ana stood, walked to the small bar beside the fireplace, and poured Santana a shot of Cristal *aguardiente* from the Caldas region in Colombia. In Colombia and South America, *aguardiente* was produced differently depending on the region. Colombian *aguardiente* was an anise-flavored liquor made from sugar cane. Santana purchased Cristal through a local liquor chain that stocked it.

Returning to the couch, Ana handed him the full shot glass and said, "I will fix dinner this evening. You have a drink and rest."

"No need for you to—"

She held up a hand in a stopping gesture. "Don't argue. I'm a good cook. You've said so yourself."

Santana shrugged and drank, the black licorice flavor creating a slow burn in his throat and chest.

*   *   *

That night Santana dreams he's walking through a maze of tangled roots and scattered bones. Around him, other bones shaped like snares have trapped small animals and birds with a rope or wire that tightens around them. But one snare is bigger and can trap a much larger prey —such as a man. Wary of being caught in the trap, Santana takes care to avoid it. Soon he comes to a T in the maze. Right or left? He turns right and is soon drawn toward a field of red flowers in the near distance.

When he enters the field, he sees that the flowers are growing out of skeletons. Dark clouds are gathering overhead, dimming the light. The temperature has dropped. Condensation forms as he breathes. His body shivers in response.

He comes upon a slim tree that is growing out of a brainless skull. A gold beetle crawls out of it. Struggling to make sense of his environment and the meaning of what he sees, he looks behind him. The maze is much taller and thicker now. He understands he cannot go back the way he came. He must go forward. When he turns to continue his journey, he glimpses something on the far horizon that appears to be a polygon-shaped sign, but he cannot read what it says. Suddenly, pitch darkness surrounds him, as if he'd been hooded. There is nowhere to turn now and nothing to guide him.

He is alone.

Chapter 13

Before rising the following morning, Santana wrote in the dream journal he kept in the nightstand beside his bed. He had been taught the meaning and importance of many dreams as a young boy from Ofir, the maid who worked for his parents in the house that sat on a steep hill in the Chipre neighborhood overlooking the city of Manizales, Colombia, 7,000 feet high in the Andes, in the shadow of the Nevada del Ruiz volcano.

He recalled that dreaming about human bones outside the body represented issues from his past that were difficult to forget or let go of. But he also knew that seeing a human skull in a dream was a warning that trouble would come, that he might do something he should not do.

In his journal he described the images he'd seen and the feelings that he'd experienced. As with many of his dreams, he wasn't sure why he'd had this particular dream. But past encounters had taught him that his dreams were important, particularly when working a new case. He believed the answers to this mystery might well lay somewhere amongst the tangled roots, scattered bones, and skulls of the dead.

The SPPD's Homicide Commander, Janet Kendrick, and the new chief, Thomas Murdoch, wanted to meet with him at 9:00 a.m. Murdoch had been one of five finalists for the position. St. Paul's police chiefs had traditionally risen through the department's ranks, and four of the five finalists had been internal candidates. Santana figured this time wouldn't be any different since it was no secret that only two candidates from outside of the department had been hired as chief in the past century.

Born in St. Paul, Murdoch had graduated from Central High School and the University of St. Thomas with a bachelor of science degree and a master's degree in criminal justice. He'd spent twenty-four years as a police officer and sergeant and had command experience in every division. He'd also served as a trainer and use of force expert. He'd last commanded the SPPD's narcotics and human trafficking divisions before his appointment as chief.

From his cushioned chair in front of the chief's large desk, Santana could see the blue pennant with the gold fringe bottom and the gold logo of the chief's SPPD badge hanging from the wall behind Murdoch's desk. Mementos, photos, awards, and a few books on policing and management style lined the shelves of the floor-to-ceiling bookcase covering the long wall to Santana's right.

Thanks to a $10 million federal grant, the mayor expected Murdoch to quickly address the wave of violent crime that had swept the city. Rumors had already spread that Murdoch had an advantage coming in as the mayor's preferred candidate.

The chief concentrated on the large plastic cube with pictures of his wife and his two college-age children on the corner of his walnut desk. Then he removed his thick-framed glasses and placed one temple in his mouth for dramatic effect. His dark brown eyes were hard and alert.

Those in positions of power, or who wanted to make a statement of power, Santana knew, often wore thicker-framed glasses.

"I've read the report you submitted to Commander Kendrick detailing your reasons for being in Afton," he said, gesturing toward Kendrick seated in the chair to Santana's right. "Good report." Murdoch smiled in a practiced way, his teeth shiny and white under a dark mustache.

Santana nodded, waiting for the other shoe to drop.

Murdoch held his smile for a time, though Santana saw no warmth in it.

"The city and the media are focused on the bones that are showing up. We've got hundreds of citizens looking for bones instead of the Winter Carnival medallion and attending events.

Don't get me started on the revenue the city is losing. The city council and mayor are breathing down my neck. They want this mess solved. I'm assigning Detective Art Tatum to work with you and Detective Cruz."

Santana bristled at having to share the case with a third detective. "Didn't Tatum just return from a five-day suspension?"

Murdoch nodded.

Santana thought Murdoch might provide more details. Still, he recalled the case.

Two SPPD officers had found a man down at an intersection after two a.m. He was transferred to Regions Hospital and died an hour later. The doctor found hair clenched in the victim's fists and trauma to the head, but no other injuries.

At around four a.m., the first officer contacted Homicide Detective Art Tatum about the deceased male. Twenty minutes later, the second officer informed him of blood and brain matter at the scene with a broken van window, a stick with blood splatter, and a notebook on the ground. Tatum directed them to clear the scene without detectives responding.

Ultimately, it was determined that the decedent was a victim of a homicide and a suspect confessed, was arrested, and charged with murder.

Internal Affairs received a complaint memorandum advising that Detective Tatum may have failed to properly have a crime scene processed. The internal complaint requested that IA initiate an administrative investigation to determine if Tatum committed any violation of departmental policy.

IA concluded that Tatum should have immediately sent the on-call homicide detectives and the Forensic Services Unit to the scene to look for and secure any potential evidence. IA also concluded that Tatum released the crime scene without having the scene properly processed, which could have impacted the prosecution of the case.

Santana liked Tatum, but this wasn't the first time he'd known the man to be careless.

"Detective Cruz and I don't need any help," Santana said, hoping one last plea might change the chief's mind.

"I'm afraid you do. Didn't your commander order you to investigate the bones found in Como Park?"

Santana could feel Kendrick's eyes on him.

"I think the bones are related to Tara Easton's murder and Angel Duran's attempted murder," he said.

"The ME is leaning toward suicide," Kendrick said, her eyes flitting back and forth between Santana and Murdoch.

"That was my understanding as well," Murdoch said, looking directly at Santana.

Santana didn't believe the ME wanted to rule it a suicide— at least not yet. But disagreeing with Kendrick and Murdoch would lead nowhere.

"Do you have evidence to the contrary, Detective?" Murdoch said.

"I believe I will."

Murdoch took a clean white handkerchief out of his coat pocket and wiped the lenses on his glasses. "Care to enlighten us?"

"As soon as I have the evidence linking the crimes, I'll let you know."

"In the meantime," Murdoch said, "we want you focusing on the bones and not getting shot at in other counties."

"Tells us something, though, doesn't it?" Santana said.

Murdoch slipped on his glasses. "What's that?"

"Someone thinks I'm closing in."

Kendrick said, "According to your report, Detective, Duran was the target. Not you."

"Let's hope it stays that way," Santana said.

* * *

Cirrus clouds that looked like wispy strands of blowing hair crystallized the blue sky. Warming temperatures left mushy, melting clumps of sand and snow, blackened by exhaust and dirt. Grimy water splashed Santana's door panels as his tires tracked through slush on the way to Hannah Thatcher's apartment.

Santana knew he'd have to bring Art Tatum up to speed, but it could wait for now.

He'd met with IA investigators after his meeting with Kendrick and Murdoch. It was a perfunctory meeting because he'd never fired a shot.

Now, as he parked in the visitor's lot of Thatcher's apartment and exited the Taurus detective sedan, he saw her jogging on the paved trail that ran along the Mississippi River shoreline.

She wore a pair of gray running shoes, a black ski hat, and a running suit with the Under Armour logo on the front.

Stopping near a bench along the trail—and with her body facing away from him—she placed both hands on the back of the bench, planted her feet, arched her back, and stretched her hamstrings and calves.

Santana followed a paved, wet path toward the river. Not wanting to startle Thatcher, he stopped five yards from her and cleared his throat.

She whirled toward him and assumed a defensive karate stance, fists up, protecting her head.

"Didn't mean to startle you," he said, showing her his palms in a calming gesture.

She let out a heavy breath and relaxed her posture. "Well, you did startle me, dipshit. Lucky I didn't kick your ass."

"We need to talk."

She placed her hands on her hips. "About what?"

"Nasrin Khalil."

Thatcher's cheeks, ruddy from the run and cold, seemed to lose their color.

Gesturing toward the bench, Santana said, "Nice day. Let's talk here."

Thatcher considered his offer.

"We will talk somewhere and soon," Santana continued. "Until I get answers."

"What does Nasrin have to do with anything?"

"Is 'idiot' written across my forehead, Ms. Thatcher?"

Her eyes looked down as she shook her head.

"Then don't treat me like one. You know damn well that her father, Taimur, knew Tara Easton and that he's missing."

Thatcher hesitated a moment before sitting down on the bench and tapping the slats beside her, indicating he should sit as well.

"What do you want to know?" she asked, not looking at him as he sat down.

"You never told me about your relationship with Nasrin Khalil."

"Didn't see it as important. You think her father had something to do with Tara's death?"

"I'll ask the questions."

She let out a long breath and nodded.

"Tell me about the female platoon you trained."

"Aren't you supposed to be investigating Tara's death?"

"I'm doing it."

"I don't see how."

"That's why I'm the detective and you're not."

She gave him a sidelong glance, a suppressed smile at the corner of her mouth. "Okay, hotshot. The platoon was a covert unit of female Afghan soldiers created and trained by US Special Operations."

"That would be you."

"Not me alone. But the platoon stayed under the radar, even within the US military."

"Why the secrecy?"

"Because they did the work that male soldiers couldn't do in a Muslim country, like searching and questioning women and children on high-risk nighttime missions."

"This went on throughout the war?"

"For a decade before the war ended. Never lost anyone in combat in over two thousand missions, though two of the women were seriously injured."

"All the platoon members in the States now?"

She nodded. "Scattered around the country. Some are with family members. Besides her father, Nasrin is the only member of her family who made it out."

"She said her mother had been killed."

"I'd heard that, but we had no solid verification."

"Where did you train the platoon?"

"At Camp Scorpion outside Kabul. US Special Forces once used it as a staging area for operations around the country."

"Was Tara Easton involved in the training?"

Thatcher shook her head. "I didn't want to be either."

"Why not?"

She let out a long sigh. "Look, I was part of a newly formed unit called the Cultural Support Team. We were highly trained American women who were embedded with US Special Operations forces on their missions. Our job was to interact with women and children. In any tribal community, women know where the men and weapons are. But if male soldiers talked to or searched women, local Afghan men might punish or even kill the woman who'd been interviewed, along with her children. That often led to a spike in hatred for the US military."

"Sounds like a no-win situation."

"In many ways it was. Our Cultural Support Team was controversial enough. Some men resented that we were given precious seats on helicopters flying into combat zones. And if they didn't trust American women, wrap your head around Afghan women as elite fighters sent into the worst parts of

Taliban-held Afghanistan. Dangerous at best. A disaster at worst."

Thatcher paused and let her eyes focus upward, as though recalling past memories.

Behind the bench, drops of melting snow splattered the pavement as they fell from barren trees.

"We were planning to withdraw from Afghanistan one day, so the brass wanted to create a parallel Afghan unit," Thatcher continued. "Women who didn't have to use an interpreter. But how could we possibly recruit Afghan women? They're traditionally not supposed to work or be out of the house at night."

"They don't go running or lifting weights either," Santana said.

"Hell, no. Most couldn't do a single sit-up or push-up. A hundred women would show up at recruiting sessions. After hearing the job requirements, only ten would return. But the platoon members had to be fit enough to keep up with the male commandos on raids, which could mean sprinting out of a helicopter under fire or walking up a mountain wearing body armor.

"We selected women who passed psychological and character screenings, could get permission from their families, and were willing to maintain a cover story. They had to do twelve-mile walks carrying thirty-five pounds of gear in the heat while wearing hijabs. We brought them to Camp Scorpion and taught them to shoot, lift weights, search rooms, question suspects, and run with night-vision goggles.

"Anytime they were off base, they had to wear civilian clothing and operate undercover, lying to their neighbors about where they were going each day. On base, they needed their own spaces, separate from men, to work out, train, eat, and pray. It was, logistically, a mess."

"Yet they did it."

"Well, they'd always been taught to be silent in their country. I think in a setting where they were together and encouraged to be a badass, it just brought up so much happiness."

"How is Nasrin's transition going?"

Thatcher chuckled. "A year ago, she was running off Chinook helicopters into remote compounds in the middle of the night, carrying an M4 assault rifle and searching for Taliban and ISIS targets. She was part of some fifty midnight raids, alongside Green Berets, Navy SEALs, and Army Rangers. Then, six months ago, she boarded a C-17 military cargo plane out of Kabul, sitting on the floor with hundreds of her countrymen, heading toward an American life she hadn't really asked for. She went from elite soldier to refugee, literally overnight. How do you think her transition is going?"

Santana recalled his own transition from Colombia to the US when he was sixteen and alone. Though he wasn't a soldier, he knew what it was like to take a life—and to save his own.

"We were supposed to offer safe haven to Afghanis who had worked for the US government," Thatcher said. "But we created the platoon, so they weren't formally under the employment of the Afghan National Army, which meant the women didn't have a letter from a US employer, as required for the visa."

"Nasrin alluded to the fact that she didn't feel safe here. Why would she say that?"

"In the chaos of the country's collapse, all of the Afghan military documents and records related to the platoon weren't destroyed and likely fell into the hands of the Taliban. These women are an insult to everything the Taliban stands for. The platoon was one of the few groups who were kill-on-sight for the Taliban. If any of the women were captured, they'd be killed."

"But the women are here now."

"Yeah. No way anyone could get to them," she said with a sarcastic laugh.

"You think the Taliban are here in the States, looking for the women?"

"The Taliban had a saying when we were over there, Detective. 'You have the watches, we have the time.'"

Santana paused a moment to collect his thoughts. "You told me you'd never met Matt Easton. He said he did meet you."

"Okay. Maybe I did meet him briefly."

"Lies make me suspicious, Ms. Thatcher."

"Try oversight."

"Semantics."

She shrugged. "Whatever you say."

"You look like you stay in good shape."

"Try to."

"You told me earlier that you shoot once or twice a month at the Combat Zone gun range."

"Yeah. So what?"

"That's Blaine Beckham's gun shop. Thought you didn't know Beckham."

"I don't. Other than to say 'Hi' when I visit the range or when I saw him at Tara's."

"Saw a photo in your apartment of you shooting an AR-15. Yours?"

"Yeah."

"Good to keep in practice."

Thatcher stared at him for a moment and then stood. "I'm cooling down. Don't want to stiffen up," she said, heading for her apartment building.

"You never answered my question about the Taliban possibly being here in the States."

"You're the detective, remember?" Thatcher said over her shoulder. "Figure it out for yourself."

Chapter 14

Dr. Martin Conrad was board-certified in general pediatrics, adult psychiatry, and child/adolescent psychiatry. According to his website, he counseled patients with depression, schizophrenia, attention-deficit/hyperactivity disorder (ADHD), attention deficit disorder (ADD), sleep disorders, bipolar disorder, binge eating and mood disorders, personality disorder, and manic-depressive disorder.

Santana wondered what disorder, if any, the doctor couldn't treat.

Conrad had completed his medical degree at the University of Minnesota and held a post as assistant professor of psychiatry there. Santana located Conrad's psychiatric office in a large, modern, four-story brick and glass building on University Avenue in the Midway neighborhood.

"Thanks for seeing me on such short notice," Santana said as he sat on a comfortable padded chair facing Martin Conrad's cherry wood desk.

A white noise machine in the waiting room outside the office on the top floor made sure no one could hear what was happening inside. A clock rested on top of a bookshelf near the entrance to Conrad's office, where he could see it. A second clock sat on one corner of his desk so the clients could also see the time. A banker's lamp stood on the opposite corner of his desk. Drawn blinds masked the daylight in the office suite. A second taller bookshelf in the far corner of the office contained games and drawing and coloring supplies for his younger clients.

An eight-foot, caramel leather couch with roll arms, two large pillows, and a comforter took up space behind Santana. A big, soft-looking matching chair sat in front of the couch.

NO WAY TO DIE

"Fortunately, I had a cancellation," Conrad said, sitting in a high, wing-backed leather chair behind his desk, elbows resting on the arms, his manicured fingers laced across his stomach, his eyes focused steadily on Santana's face. His degrees and certifications were framed in glass on the wall behind him.

A bulky, imposing man with a good tan, Conrad had black hair, except at the temples, where it was gray. He wore it slicked back and longer in back, so it curled over his shirt collar. His neatly trimmed beard made him appear older and wiser. A look, Santana figured, Conrad cultivated. It reminded him of the photos he'd seen of a younger Ernest Hemingway. Santana wondered if Conrad deliberately cultivated that look as well.

Conrad's casual dress included a button-down shirt, open at the collar, and a blue blazer. The blazer nearly matched his dark blue eyes. He wore a thick gold band on the third finger of his left hand.

The graduation dates on his degrees indicated he was around forty-five. The tan suggested he'd recently been in a warm climate for a winter vacation.

"You were counseling Tara Easton," Santana said.

"Briefly. But as I'm sure you're aware, I can't discuss details."

"Her husband came to see you."

"Yes. Did you put him up to it?"

"I told him he was entitled to her records."

Conrad sat silently for a time, motionless, his eyes still focused on Santana.

"I'm sure you're aware, Detective, that meeting with the surviving spouse is often more difficult in situations where the patient has committed suicide. The surviving spouse may be seeking information that will ultimately be used against the therapist in a lawsuit or claim for damages. They blame the therapist for failing to recognize the risk to the patient, or for failing to take appropriate action to prevent, or to try to prevent, the suicide."

Santana nodded.

"So, I have to balance the risks and benefits of meeting with or giving information to the surviving spouse."

"You do understand that, legally, you have no choice."

"Of course. It's why Mrs. Easton's information is not truly confidential. Not in the same way as it would be with a lawyer. But I firmly believe that a deceased patient continues to be entitled to confidentiality, and I'm under a continuing duty to protect the confidentiality of their records and information. My first instinct upon receiving a request for information about a deceased patient is to resist disclosure."

"You've had other patients who have committed suicide?"

"Unfortunately, in my profession, I've had to deal with unexpected death. I'll wager you have as well, Detective."

Santana opened the file folder he was carrying and pulled out a thin stack of papers. "Tara Easton's husband provided me with your notes and after-visit summaries."

"Then you know what I know." Conrad leaned back with his fingertips pressed together, satisfied with himself.

"There's always something else."

"Perhaps in your line of work. Not so much in mine."

Santana ignored the deflection. "You prescribed medication."

"Prozac."

"To help her cope with PTSD?"

"SSRIs are one of the first types of medication used to treat patients with anxiety disorder."

"SSRIs?"

"Selective serotonin reuptake inhibitors," he said with a thin smile. "Increases serotonin in the brain to help regulate mood and other functions. Low levels can lead to depression, anxiety, and suicidal behavior. It's often used to treat anxiety and other disorders."

"Your notes indicated that you believed Tara Easton was suicidal."

"Based on the news articles I've read, that seemed to be the ME's conclusion as well. Your appearance here seems to contradict that assumption."

"Wouldn't want to make a mistake."

"I'm sure you wouldn't."

"You wouldn't either, Doctor."

"Wouldn't be good for my patients or my reputation."

"Besides the Prozac," Santana said, moving on, "Tara Easton was receiving cognitive behavioral therapy and exposure therapy."

"Are you familiar with the terms?"

"Vaguely."

"CBT addresses how a patient's thoughts and behavior calm or exacerbate the symptoms of anxiety. Exposure therapy creates a safe environment where the patient is exposed to the things they fear and avoid in order to weaken negative associations and manage feelings of anxiety."

"According to your notes, she feared losing her family and her freedom."

"Yes."

"Why?"

"Unfortunately, I was never able to identify the cause."

"Could it be something that happened during the war?"

"Certainly. It could also stem from a childhood trauma. She was, after all, an orphan."

"Again, I saw nothing in your notes indicating a childhood trauma."

"For therapy to be optimally effective, a patient must be able to disclose their thoughts, feelings, experiences, and behaviors without fear of judgment. They must also be confident that their therapist will not share this information with third parties. The ability to be vulnerable in therapy can help a person recover more quickly."

"And you don't believe that Tara Easton felt secure enough to be honest with you."

"All my clients are people with broken wings. If I can't mend them, I feel I must've missed something, especially if the client chooses death over hope. Regrettably, in Mrs. Easton's case, I didn't have enough information to know what kind of help she needed."

* * *

When Santana arrived to the Homicide and Robbery Unit later that morning, Gabriel Cruz stood next to Santana's desk, looking intently at sheet of paper beside a manila envelope on the desktop.

Art Tatum stood beside Cruz, his striped tie loosened at his thick neck, his sport coat looking a size too small on his heavy-set frame.

Tatum looked at him. "You didn't call me and let me know about the shooting at Angel Duran's place. Had to hear it on the news this morning."

"I meant to."

"Sure you did," Tatum said, his dark brown eyes glaring at Santana.

"I haven't worked with two partners for a long time. Have to get used to it."

Santana knew it was a lame excuse, but it was all he had.

"You'd be pissed off if the situation were reversed," Tatum said.

"I would."

Tatum nodded as the fire in his eyes dimmed.

"Cruz get you up to speed?"

"He has."

Turning to Cruz, Santana said, "See what information you can dig up on Angel Duran."

Cruz nodded. "Take a look at this," he said, lifting his chin for a moment before pointing to the sheet of paper.

Santana hung his overcoat on a coat rack and set his brief-case on top his desk. When he was beside Cruz, the young detective pointed to the 8 ½" by 11" white sheet of paper.

If you're looking for more bones,
You detectives are not alone.
Check down by old sandy
And find something quite dandy.
Look near the stream
To find the answers to your dream.

"This a take on the medallion hunt?" Cruz said.

"Has to be."

Santana tried to connect his dream, the bones in Como Park, and the rhyme.

He looked at Cruz. "You talk to anyone about this?"

"No one. It came in this," Cruz said, pointing to the PRIOR-ITY envelope.

"You touch it?"

"It was addressed to us. When I pulled the letter out of the envelope, I didn't know what it was."

In comparison to typewriters, Santana knew it was rarely possible to link a particular document back to the specific computer on which it was written. Forensics might be able to determine the type of printer used. And if there were some mechanical deficiencies unique to a particular printer, that defect might allow the printout to be traced back to the specific machine. It was much easier to determine the typeface, the type of paper, and class of ink used.

"Glove up," Santana said. "Let's talk to Kendrick."

The three of them waited outside Kendrick's door till she was off the phone and had waved them in.

Looking at Tatum, Kendrick said, "Good to have you back, Detective."

"Good to be back," Tatum said.

Santana and Cruz sat in the two chairs in front of her desk. Tatum pulled up a third chair that was against the wall. Santana set the letter on Kendrick's desk so that she could read it.

"Don't touch it," he said.

Kendrick frowned. "I know what I'm doing."

Perhaps thinking that Santana might respond inappropriately, Cruz said, "It came in a priority envelope in the morning mail."

Kendrick peered down at the letter. A few moments later she looked up at Santana again. "Any idea what it means?"

Santana shook his head. "We should contact the *Pioneer Press*. See if the clue writer can help us out."

"No one knows who the medallion clue writer is," she said.

"Someone at the paper does."

"You think someone at the paper wrote this?"

"Only if that someone committed murder and then cut up the body."

"The paper keeps the current medallion writer and hider a secret for a reason," Kendrick said. "The prize is ten thousand dollars. If someone knew who it was, he or she could be stalked. The better the secret, the better for everybody. Someone who really needed or wanted the money badly enough could make a bad decision."

"I get the integrity of the hunt," Santana said. "But we're not asking to reveal the source of the clues. We're just asking for help to interpret this clue," he said, pointing to the letter on Kendrick's desk.

"All right," she said. "I'll make a call. In the meantime, take the letter and envelope to Tony Novak. See if forensics can get some prints."

"I touched the envelope and letter," Cruz said. "I didn't know what was in it."

"Probably won't make a difference," Kendrick said. "I'm betting whoever sent it wore gloves."

As they stood to leave, Kendrick said to Santana, "What about this Hartley kid?"

"What about him?"

"He murdered his father. Seems to me you might want to look into him further."

"He's on our radar."

"Good," Kendrick said. "Make sure he stays there."

When they left Kendrick's office, Santana said to Tatum, "Take the letter and envelope to forensics. See if they can get a print."

"We're probably not first in line," Tatum said. "They won't do it right away."

"Talk to Novak. Tell him I sent you. He knows how important this case is and the pressure the department is facing."

Tatum ran a hand through his slicked-back graying dark hair. "What're you two gonna do?"

"Talk to someone at the *Pioneer Press*. See if we can get some help on the poem."

"I'd like to go along."

"Look, Art, if we're going to make this partnership work, we all have to do our part. Makes no sense for all three of us to go to the paper."

Tatum offered a reluctant nod.

"Good. We'll keep in touch."

"You do that," Tatum said.

When Santana returned to his desk, Cruz was putting on his jacket. "Kendrick got a name at the *Pioneer Press*. Pat Grainger. He's written medallion clues before. Thinks he can help us."

Santana raised his eyebrows. "The guy who interrupted our lunch?"

"The same."

*   *   *

The *Pioneer Press* occupied the seventh floor of the eight-story Comcast Regional Headquarters located in the River Plaza, a glass-paneled building on the west bank of the Mississippi River facing downtown, and a five-minute drive from the LEC.

A stiff wind blew out of the north, lowering the temperature to 15° and buffeting their detective ride as they crossed the Robert Street Bridge. Thin sheets of ice had formed on sidewalks and main streets that had been plowed from curb to curb after the latest snowstorm.

After checking through security, Santana and Cruz took an elevator up to the seventh floor.

Pat Grainger met them with a smug smile and what looked like the same clothes he'd worn yesterday.

"Well, well," he said. "The worm turns."

"And it could turn again," Santana said. "What have you got for us?"

Caught off guard by Santana's comment, Grainger lost the smug look and nodded. "Our relationship should be a symbiotic one, Detective."

"You ever worked the crime beat?"

"Other cities."

"Then you should know this 'symbiotic relationship' doesn't happen overnight."

Grainger nodded and led them to a meeting room, where the three of them sat at one end of a long rectangular table Santana figured was used for staff meetings.

He said, "You used to write the medallion clues for the paper."

"Did it for a few years. Had some fun."

"But you don't write the clues now."

"I do not."

"But you're knowledgeable about the city and its sites."

"I'd say I know it pretty well."

Santana showed him a photo of the mysterious poem he'd taken with his iPhone.

"Well, I can't tell you anything about the bones." He looked up at the detectives. "That would be your purview. But I believe 'old sandy' refers to Como Lake."

"How do you know?"

"Research," he said. "It was called Sandy Lake in the 1840s when Charles Perry owned and farmed the land. Perry named it after his birthplace in the Swiss-Italian Alps. When he sold the land, a real estate developer named Henry McKenty changed the name to Como Lake after the lake in Italy."

"Anything else you can tell us about the poem?"

"'Fraid not. But if you get another clue, I'd be glad to help."

Santana glanced at Cruz and then looked at Grainger again. "What makes you think we'll receive another poem?"

"From what I understand, you only found some partial bones. Seems to me whoever killed this poor bastard is making a game of it. Probably going to lead you all over the city."

"That what you would do, Grainger?"

He offered a half-smile. "Maybe if I was some kind of psychopath. But I'm not."

*　　*　　*

They were driving back to the LEC when Cruz said, "What do you make of Grainger?"

"Seems on the level."

"You think he might be the one who wrote the bone clues?"

"Check out his background. First, though, get forensics and a dive team to Lake Como. If more bones are there, we need to find them. Keep Tatum in the loop. And see if forensics found any prints on the letter."

"Where are you going?"

"To see Wade Crawford. Something happened between Blaine Beckham, Angel Duran, Taimur Khalil, and Tara Easton in Afghanistan. We're going to find out what."

Chapter 15

Santana contacted Wade Crawford using the cell phone number on the SIGAR business card Crawford had given him in the hallway outside Tara Easton's apartment.

They met in the Station 81 restaurant in the remodeled neoclassical Union Depot in Lowertown. An 80-foot arch spanned the depot's football-field-sized waiting room and concourse, which featured skylights, restored tile flooring, and paint colors that matched the original 1920s Jazz-Age gold tinge.

From his seat at a restaurant table, Santana could see the banded maroon blossoms across the ceiling and the detailed terra cotta frieze depicting the history of transportation in Minnesota.

"You a fan of history, Santana?" Crawford asked.

"I'm more interested in the here and now."

Crawford made a sweeping gesture with an open hand, indicating the depot. "Lots of history here. Thought I'd like to see this place before I left town."

"Leaving soon?"

"Soon as I get what I've come for."

"And what's that?"

"Answers."

"So maybe we can help each other," Santana said.

"I don't need your help."

"Then book a seat on the next Amtrak out of town."

Crawford chuckled. "That supposed to intimidate me?"

Santana's gaze settled on Crawford. "We're not talking about intimidation. We're talking about jurisdiction. I did some checking before our little *tête-à-tête* this afternoon. Seems Wade Crawford no longer works for SIGAR. Hasn't for the last six months. I'm guessing your former bosses wouldn't be happy knowing you're impersonating a federal agent. So, you can shred those worthless business cards you've been handing out. And if you get in the way of my investigation, I'll throw your ass in jail."

"Think you've got me over a barrel, huh, Detective?"

"I know I do."

Santana let Crawford mull it over.

After a short time, Crawford offered a high-wattage smile and patted his stomach. "Well, if we're gonna talk, then let's eat. I'm starving."

Both men selected a burger with seasoned fries. Crawford ordered coffee, Santana a Coke.

When the waitress left the table, Santana said, "A man named Angel Duran got shot yesterday in Afton."

"All over the news. Any leads as to who shot him?"

"I'm working on it."

"Since when does the SPPD investigate murders in Washington County?"

"Tara Easton, Angel Duran, Blaine Beckham, and Taimur Khalil knew each other in Afghanistan. Now Easton is dead, Khalil is missing and someone tried to take out Angel Duran. Something went on in Afghanistan that might be connected to their deaths."

"I thought Easton was a suicide."

"The ME hasn't made a determination regarding cause of death."

"What do you think?"

"I think you need to tell me what went on over there and why you're here in town."

Crawford nodded his head slowly, as if making up his mind. "I'm trying to locate Taimur Khalil."

"Why?"

"Kahlil worked as an interpreter for the US military before working as a defense contractor delivering fuel and supplies to the American base in Kandahar. Unlike the Iraq war, where international companies brought in supplies, in Afghanistan the military outsourced its overland-logistics chain to local contractors. They hauled cargo to bases across the country in something called 'jingle trucks.'"

"Tell me something I don't know."

Crawford cocked his head.

"My partner, Gabriel Cruz, is a vet who spent time in Afghanistan."

"Oh. Well, contractors outnumbered our troops three to one in Afghanistan."

"How come?"

"Moving around on the ground was basically a shitstorm. So, the US military paid local people to risk their lives by driving trucks and transporting materials. In the beginning, the military paid contractors in cash after missions were completed."

"Something changed?"

"Yeah. Khalil quickly built a network of truckers and subcontractors who were known for their reliability. But later in the war, many defense contractors either hired Taliban guards directly or hired subcontractors who made payments to the Taliban. Instead of investing in security, contractors bribed the Taliban to refrain from launching attacks that could disrupt their services. They viewed protection payments made to terrorists and enemy forces as a cost of doing business. Trouble was, the Taliban now had money to organize attacks on non-protected contractors and American troops."

"You're saying Khalil paid the Taliban."

"Damn right. And he inflated his costs and billed the Defense Department for work that was never done. You have to understand, Santana, we didn't lose in Afghanistan because of an insurgency. We lost because of systemic corruption."

"But you're not working for SIGAR anymore. Why keep chasing the case?"

"I did a little checking on you, too, Detective. You're a hard charger. Like a dog that doesn't let go of a bone once you get your teeth into it. Same here. I don't like walking away from a case till it's solved."

"No other reason?"

"Like what?"

"I don't know. Why I'm asking."

"Suspicious son of a bitch, aren't you?"

"Comes naturally working in homicide."

"Bet it does."

"What's your financial situation, Crawford?"

"How 'bout sticking that fork on the table where the sun doesn't shine. I've got no ulterior motive. Just doing my job."

Santana wasn't convinced, but he let this line of questioning go.

The waitress appeared with their meals and drinks. They ate quietly for a time till Santana said, "Were Duran, Easton, and Beckham involved in kickbacks?"

"That's my thinking."

"But you have no proof."

"I was working on it before . . ." he paused.

"Before you were let go."

"I stepped on some large shoes. That's a mistake when you work in government."

"Whose shoes?"

"Doesn't matter."

"Maybe not to you."

"Look, Santana, I'm not looking at top military brass."

"Maybe you should."

"Whatever went down happened at Kandahar."

After they finished their meals, Santana showed Crawford a copy of the photo of Easton, Duran, Beckham, Khalil, and the unidentified Afghani in the tiger-striped uniform.

Pointing at the unidentified man, Santana said, "You know who this is?"

Crawford's eyebrows lifted and his jaw went slack. It was only for a microsecond, but Santana saw the recognition in his eyes.

"You do know him."

Crawford shook his head as his gaze shifted from Santana. "Never seen him before."

"Tell me the truth."

"I told you."

"Why is it I don't believe you?"

Crawford gave a little shrug. "Job like yours makes you skeptical, Santana. That's a good thing. Till it bleeds into everything and everyone you know."

"We have a saying in Colombia. *Las mentiras tienen patas cortas.* Lies have short legs."

"Well, here's an American saying. 'Fuck you.'"

Santana smiled to himself.

"Something funny?"

"That's pretty universal, Crawford. What about this guy, Blaine Beckham?"

"Same answer as before."

Santana figured he wouldn't get any more out of Crawford, so he moved on. "Ever hear of a platoon made up of Afghan women?"

Crawford's face was shrouded in thought. "I looked into it once. But when I asked Special Operations Command about the platoon, he told me he'd never heard of it. Neither had his counterparts at US Central Command. The only information the Special Operations historian had on the program was classified."

Santana nodded but offered no comment.

An inquisitive gleam lit Crawford's brown eyes. "You know something about this platoon, now's the time to tell me."

Santana wasn't sure if he should let Crawford know what he'd discovered. But he'd already opened the door.

"You wouldn't have asked about this platoon unless you knew something, Santana. Let's hear it."

"Taimur Khalil's daughter was a member of the platoon."

Crawford sat back in his chair. "No shit."

"Don't know if it's the reason her father is missing, or if it's connected to Tara Easton's death and the attack on Duran."

"Has to be one or the other," Crawford said.

"Maybe both."

"I want in on this."

"We've shared info, Crawford. That's as far as this relationship goes." Santana stood. "Where are you staying?"

"Holiday Inn downtown. That mean you'll stay in touch?"

"If I need to."

Santana's department cell phone rang as he was walking out of the restaurant. He recognized Gabriel Cruz's number.

"What's up?" he asked.

"A skull was found near Lake Como. Probably belongs to the bones found earlier."

"You at the lake now?"

"Yeah. With Tatum."

"I'm on my way."

"One other thing," Cruz said.

Santana waited.

"Jadyn Hartley found the skull."

"Bring him to the LEC. I'll meet you there."

"Roger that."

"And write up a warrant to search his residence," Santana added.

*   *   *

Gabriel Cruz sat in a chair at his desk in his cubicle, typing on his computer, when Santana arrived.

"Working on the warrant?"

Cruz nodded. "Just about finished."

"Where's Hartley?"

"Interview room," Cruz said, continuing to type.

"How about Tatum?"

"Went to the lab to see if forensics got any prints off the letter."

Santana hung his overcoat on the rack beside his desk and waited.

Five minutes later, Cruz pushed a computer key and the warrant template was printed.

Santana read it. "Looks good. Run it by Kendrick and then take it to a judge while I talk with Hartley. Give me a call when it's signed."

Santana figured they would have no problem with Kendrick since she had Hartley in her sights as the prime suspect. He hoped they wouldn't have a problem with the judge either.

He let Jadyn Hartley sit alone in the interview room for another thirty minutes before he entered, giving Cruz more time to get a judge's signature on the search warrant he'd typed.

Hartley sat in a hardback chair in an interview room. He wore a bright orange turtleneck, jeans, and a pair of leather boots with orange laces. His gray parka hung on the back of his chair. His bright orange watch cap and black mittens lay on the table in front of him.

As he sat down across the table from Hartley, Santana noted that Hartley's fingernails were bitten down to the quick.

"Am I under arrest?" Hartley asked, his gaze flitting around the room, never truly settling on Santana.

"Not at this time."

Santana knew his probable cause for arresting Hartley and charging him with murder was thin. And if he did arrest Hartley, he could hold him for only forty-eight hours from the time of arrest—with a judge's approval. Santana would have to submit the facts pertaining to the crime to a judge under oath, either orally or in writing. He and Cruz were not that far down the road yet with Hartley. At best, he hoped a judge would sign off on a warrant to search Hartley's residence.

"Then I'm free to go," Hartley said, sliding his chair back and standing.

"That would be a mistake."

"Wouldn't be the first one I've made."

"Might be your last as a free man."

Hartley's eyes jittered as he processed Santana's statement. "You said I wasn't arrested."

"Doesn't mean you can't be."

"You think I killed whoever the bones belong to."

"If you didn't put them in the ground, how come you keep finding them?"

"With all the cops around Lake Como, it wasn't hard to figure out."

"Still, you found the bones and the skull."

"I was gonna say 'just lucky,' but, looking at my surroundings, I guess I'm not so lucky."

Santana's cell phone vibrated. He looked at the number and said, "Excuse me a minute."

Stepping into the hallway, he answered the call.

"Judge signed off on the warrant," Cruz said.

"All right."

"One thing, though."

"Go ahead."

"The address he gave us belongs to Hartley's public defender, Megan McKenna."

During his meeting with McKenna, Santana had learned that she was now acting as Jadyn's mother. But he'd neglected to inform Cruz.

"Meet me there," he said.

"What about Hartley?"

"Don't think he'll admit to anything if he is guilty. And we need more evidence to charge him. I'll drive him home."

*   *   *

Gabriel Cruz stood beside his ride in front of the Craftsman on Churchill Street when Santana arrived with Jadyn Hartley.

When Hartley, Cruz, and Santana entered the house, Megan McKenna was seated on the couch, reading the newspaper.

"What's going on here?" she said, standing.

"They want to look around," Jadyn said, making a hitch-hiking motion toward the detectives.

She dropped the paper on the coffee table and crossed her arms over her chest. "For what?"

Cruz handed her the warrant.

"For God's sake," she said. Slipping on her glasses, she looked it over.

"Where's your room?" Santana asked Jadyn.

"You have no business in there," McKenna said, glaring at Santana.

"Warrant says we do."

"This is harassment. Jadyn has done nothing wrong."

"Then he has nothing to worry about."

Jadyn gestured toward the hallway. "This way."

"You don't need to help them," McKenna said.

Santana gave Cruz a look.

The younger detective nodded that he understood. "I have some questions for you, Ms. McKenna," he said. "Have a seat."

Hartley led Santana down a narrow hallway to his bedroom in the back of the house.

The tidy, but small bedroom had a neatly made single bed, a dresser, a small bookcase, and a wooden chair and desk. An Apple laptop computer sat on the desk. One wall featured a poster of William Blake, the English poet, painter, and printmaker. On another wall hung a second Blake poster depicting a giant red dragon descending from a dark sky upon a woman.

The *Red Dragon* poster reminded Santana of the movie based on the novel by Thomas Harris.

"You're a fan of William Blake," Santana said, initiating the conversation.

"You familiar with his work?" Hartley asked, sitting on the edge of the bed, his feet flat on the floor, his hands resting flat on his thighs.

Santana heard the excitement in Hartley's voice. He nodded. Focusing on the kid's interests might get him to open up.

"Surrealists were inspired by Blake's art," he said.

"You're into surrealism, huh?"

"Grew up with it in Colombia."

"Have to read André Breton. Learn more about the surrealists."

"You study Blake in school?"

Hartley shook his head. "Blake and I think alike when it comes to school."

"How's that?"

"Blake said, 'Thank God I never was sent to school. To be flogged into following the style of a fool!'"

"Not everything you learn in school is useful," Santana said.

"That's for sure."

Santana's gaze was drawn to a book on the desktop entitled *The Complete Poetry & Prose of William Blake*. The book was open to a poem.

The Voice of the Ancient Bard

Youth of delight! come hither
And see the opening morn,
Image of Truth new-born.
Doubt is fled, and clouds of reason,
Dark disputes and artful teazing.
Folly is an endless maze;

Tangled roots perplex her ways;
How many have fallen there!
They stumble all night over bones of the dead;
And feel — they know not what but care;
And wish to lead others, when they should be led.

Santana wasn't familiar with the poem, but the line "they stumble all night over bones of the dead" reminded him of his recent dream. He wondered now if the poem was somehow connected to the murders and to Jadyn Hartley finding the bones.

"Interested in Blake's poetry?" Hartley asked.

"Maybe," Santana said.

"Go ahead and search. I've got nothing to hide."

"How long have you lived with McKenna?"

"Since my mother died."

Santana kept his gaze on Hartley even though the young man's eyes rarely held steady.

"Cervical cancer," Hartley said. "Deadly."

"You like living with McKenna?"

"She's okay."

Santana let his eyes wander the room before they came back to Hartley. "Tell me about your father."

"I don't wanna talk about him."

"Why not?"

"He was an asshole."

"Why didn't you and your mother leave?"

Hartley snickered. "What were we gonna live on? Food stamps?"

"Your mother didn't work?"

"Always had health issues. The old man resented it."

"Anything else you can tell me about your father?"

"Thought you were gonna search my room?"

Santana took that as a "No."

After he finished searching the bedroom, Santana asked Hartley if he and McKenna shared the same bathroom.

"No way. Mine is across the hall. Hers is upstairs."

In the neat and tidy bathroom, Santana first searched the medicine cabinet. Among the usual box of bandages, mouthwash, toothpaste, and brush, he found a plastic vial of Prozac anti-depressant pills. Martin Conrad had prescribed them, the same psychiatrist who had prescribed Tara Easton's medication.

Chapter 16

Jadyn Hartley's fascination with William Blake led Santana to Professor Xavier Dyer, who taught 18th and 19th century British literature and history at the University of Minnesota. A Google search had revealed that Dyer was an expert on the Romantic poets, especially William Blake.

Xavier Dyer maintained a small, cluttered office in Johnson Hall.

With white hair that hung over his ears and pale blue-veined cheeks, Dyer's complexion reminded Santana of a sheet of lined notebook paper. He wore dark brown slacks, hush puppies, and a tweed sport coat over a burgundy sweater vest and tie. A neck chain held a pair of horn-rimmed glasses that dangled on his chest.

Santana figured the professor had to be in his late fifties or early sixties, but his hazel eyes twinkled with an amused, youthful light as he sat in his high-back banker's chair.

Surrounded by floor-to-ceiling shelves filled with hardback and tattered paperback books, Santana sat in an old cane-back swivel chair and handed Dyer his cell phone with a photo of the William Blake poem he'd seen in Jadyn Hartley's room.

"Ah, Mr. Blake," Dyer said with a sly smile and a British accent. He slipped on his glasses and peered at the poem. His thick white eyebrows rose and lowered as he silently read the lines.

"What can you tell me about Blake?" Santana asked when Dyer returned the cell phone.

The professor removed his glasses and gazed at Santana. "Blake the revolutionary, opposed to what we often refer to as the establishment, though it could be any organization that tries to rule or control human behavior."

Dyer took an oval-shaped billiard pipe from an inner pocket of his sport coat and a pouch of cherry blend tobacco and wooden match from another pocket.

"Care if I smoke?"

"I don't. Maybe the university does."

"I'm too old to care," Dyer said with a wink. "Mind closing the door?"

Santana rolled his chair back and shut the office door. As he rolled forward again, Dyer cracked a window open and switched on a small electric fan perched on the windowsill.

Dryer filled the pipe, tamping the tobacco in with a forefinger, and lit the match by scratching it with a thumbnail. He gave the flame a moment for the sulfur to burn off, so it wouldn't ruin the tobacco flavor, and then applied the flame to the bowl in a circular motion, drawing gently on the pipe. He paused to let the "false light" burn out and then repeated the process till the pipe had "true light."

The sweet cherry blend scent triggered Santana's olfactory senses and a boyhood memory of his father smoking one of the pipes from his collection in the living room of their home in Manizales, Colombia.

He held the memory close till Dyer's voice broke the spell.

"Our inhibitions lie primarily within the mind, Detective, rather than in external factors," Dyer said, pointing the pipe at Santana for emphasis. "Society makes its fears, guilt, and shame into rules and laws. Then enshrines them in social institutions such as the church and state."

"So how does Blake's view relate to the poem?"

"He believed humans were spiritual beings. Most people in his time didn't believe the same."

"Not sure they believe it now."

"I concur."

"Tell me about the maze," Santana said.

Dryer took a small puff on his pipe, turned his head, and blew out a geyser of smoke. Santana watched as the smoke drifted like a spirit out the window.

"Blake believed that social restrictions and religious institutions destroyed spontaneity and stunted imagination," Dryer said. "Like a maze, such folly gets people lost in any number of dead ends. Nevertheless, many fools still desire to be our leaders, when *they* need to be led and enlightened themselves."

"What about the tangled roots, Professor?"

"They symbolize the twisted pathways that the soul must follow to return to the Edenic state. But the maze and the tangled roots can snare the unwary, stopping them from walking freely in the light."

"'How many have fallen there,'" Santana said, quoting a line from the poem.

"Exactly."

"And the bones?"

"Are you a religious man, Detective?"

"Not for a long time."

Dryer nodded as if he understood. "Mark Twain once said, 'If Christ were here now there is one thing he would not be—a Christian.'"

"Twain also said, 'People are lucky because entry to heaven goes by favor. If it went by merit, we'd all stay out while our dogs got in.'"

Dyer smiled. "A literate detective. I take it you have a dog."

"Golden retriever."

"Ah, yes. Wonderful dogs. I have an old Lab, myself. Been with me for years." Dyer's gaze drifted upward for a moment, as if remembering. "But you're here to discuss William Blake, not Mark Twain." He took another puff from his pipe and said, "The bones in Blake's poem are an allusion to the valley of dry bones seen by the prophet Ezekiel in the Old Testament. It's a recurring image in his poetry."

The professor held his pipe between his teeth, pulled a King James Bible off the shelf, and paged through it till he found the passage he was searching for. Handing the Bible to Santana, he removed the pipe from his mouth, pointed the stem at the page, and said, "Ezekiel 37, 1-2."

37 The hand of the Lord was upon me, and carried me out in the spirit of the Lord, and set me down in the midst of the valley which was full of bones,
² And caused me to pass by them round about: and, behold, there were very many in the open valley; and, lo, they were very dry.

Santana looked at Dyer for an explanation.

"In ancient Israel, an unburied corpse with exposed remains was a disgrace to the dead," he said. "The bones Ezekiel is referring to were obviously denied proper burial and were likely from a defeated army. In Biblical times the victorious soldiers would often strip the valuables from the slain and then leave their enemies' bodies unburied. In remote places where battles often took place, skeletons sometimes remained for years afterward, till animals scattered the bones or the elements destroyed them. Ezekiel lived at a time when one could literally find valleys of bones."

"That's the literal translation."

"I'm not a Biblical scholar."

"But you *are* a scholar."

Dryer nodded. "Someone once said that intelligence is like underwear. It's important that you have it, but not necessary that you show it off."

"You can show off all you want, Professor. Intelligence doesn't threaten me."

He smiled mischievously. "No, I suspect it doesn't."

"Then what's the figurative translation?"

"Please read passages nine and ten."
Santana read them silently.

⁹Then said he unto me, Prophesy unto the wind, prophesy, son of man, and say to the wind, Thus saith the Lord God; Come from the four winds, O breath, and breathe upon these slain, that they may live.
¹⁰So I prophesied as he commanded me, and the breath came into them, and they lived, and stood up upon their feet, an exceeding great army.

Dyer puffed on his pipe till Santana finished. Then he said, "Ezekiel was Hebrew from the tribe of Levi. He was among the elite of Judah who were captured by Nebuchadnezzar and carried away to Babylon. I believe he's saying to his fellow captives that God gives them life to fight. They become an army. In the same way, He gives us spiritual life so we can become soldiers in His army. He breathes into us the breath of life."

Santana considered Dyer's response for a time before replying. "Isn't Afghanistan called the graveyard of empires?"

"Yes, it is. The British Empire fought three wars there. Got our ass handed to us in two of them. That was before the Soviet Union's and the US's debacles."

Recalling the poster in Jadyn Hartley's bedroom, Santana said, "Ever see the *Red Dragon* movie or read Thomas Harris' book?"

"Saw the movie. Did not read the book."

"Know what the dragon stands for?"

"Satan. Taken from the book of Revelation. All about exacting revenge on the woman who gave birth to a follower of God and would spread the Christian faith. Represented Blake's belief that good and evil were a duality, like the dark and light sides of the moon. Neither was completely independent from the other. All men were capable of good and evil. Blake warned about the fallen condition of humanity, the pervasiveness of evil, and states of spiritual and moral crisis."

Not much has changed since the 18th century, Santana thought.

He stood. "Thank you for your help, Professor."

"Does this have something to do with the bones found around Lake Como?" he asked as Santana reached the door.

"That—and something else," Santana said.

Chapter 17

Light snow fell as Santana drove to the LEC the next morning. The temperature had dropped to 12° as an arctic blast blew down from Canada. He'd just taken off his overcoat when the phone in his cubicle in the Homicide and Robbery Unit rang.

"Pat Grainger from the *Pioneer Press*. Jadyn Hartley is the prime suspect in the bones case. Care to comment?"

A sidebar article in the *Pioneer Press* this morning, written by Grainger, was headlined: FATHER'S KILLER SUSPECTED OF BURYING BONES. The article included Hartley's photo.

"No," Santana said and hung up.

Neither Gabriel Cruz nor Art Tatum had arrived yet.

While Santana waited, he opened his thermos and poured himself a cup of hot chocolate. He'd never developed a taste for coffee, though his father grew coffee on the *finca*, or farm, the family owned.

As a child in Colombia, Santana loved the Jet chocolate bars and the hot cocoa made from dark, unsweetened chocolate produced by the Luker Company. His mother would mix the chocolate in an aluminum pitcher called a *chocolatera* and stir it with a wooden mixer called a *molinillo*. He'd eat *queso* Colombiano, a white cheese, while he drank hot chocolate. Now he often shopped at the Centromex Supermercado on 7th Street in St. Paul, where he could buy Colombian products.

He took a couple of sips of the delicious chocolate. Then he dialed the number for Kim Solace, the forensic anthropologist he and Cruz had spoken to three days ago.

She picked up on the third ring.

"What can I do for you, Detective?" she said after he identified himself.

"There's a woman in town who works with skulls."

145

"Dana Monroe," she said.

"Do you have her number?"

Santana waited.

"Dana is not a detective or a forensic anthropologist. She doesn't work for any university or government agency. She's technically a self-taught amateur working for free at the asking."

"I understand."

"She also belongs to Websleuths."

"What's that?"

"A network of hobbyists who work on mysteries police departments can't crack."

Though Santana had never used Dana Monroe as a source before, he'd become familiar with the growing field of investigative genetic genealogy, where citizen-scientists used DNA databases and genealogical research to help identify John and Jane Does by connecting them to potential living relatives.

Each year about forty-four hundred unidentified bodies were recovered in the US. About a thousand or so remained unidentified a year later. It was a long shot that could cause trouble for him if the department discovered he had sought out Monroe, an unlicensed researcher whom the press might characterize as a quack. Still, he was willing to take the chance if she could help him identify the remains.

Kim Solace gave him Monroe's number. "Dana has a special gift and is a wonderful person—once you get to know her."

"But..."

"But you have to tread lightly at first. She's a bit ... eccentric."

"Thanks for the warning," he said.

*　　*　　*

Dana Monroe was a large woman with a beautiful, unmarked complexion that looked like it had never been exposed to the sun. Her gray-blond hair was twisted into a single braid that hung down her back to her waist. Black lipstick shaded her full lips. She wore open-toed sandals, a white cotton zip sweater over a pretty blue, purple, and pink ankle-length tie-dye dress, and a matching headband.

A great summer look, Santana thought, but impractical in the dead of winter. Maybe that was why she had logs burning in the living room fireplace.

Kilim pillows and rugs, tapestries, macramé wall hangings, candles, and lots of green plants decorated the room.

Santana imagined this was what a typical room might have looked like had he grown up in the sixties in San Francisco.

He saw no photos of children or family. The lack of photos reminded him that he had only two photos of what remained of his family. His sister, Natalia, the frame gracing the fireplace mantel in his living room, and a crinkled photo of his dead mother that he kept in his wallet.

Dana Monroe took his overcoat and directed him to sit on the small rattan loveseat with green print cushions.

"Would you care for some tea, Detective?"

"No, thank you."

"Sorry I don't drink coffee."

"I don't either," he said.

She sat in a rocker facing him, her hands flat on her thighs. "You have a slight accent. South American?"

"Colombia."

"And you don't drink coffee."

"I get that a lot."

"I'll bet you do."

A calico cat appeared out of nowhere and rubbed her head and body against Santana's pants leg.

"That's Bella. She doesn't like everybody."

"Me neither."

The corners of Dana Monroe's mouth twitched in a hint of a smile. "Are you a cat lover, Detective?"

"I have a dog. Nothing against cats, though." *Except the hair left on my pants.*

Dana Monroe's eyes were the color of fireplace ash. They met his eyes in a long look.

He let the uncomfortable silence hang in the air.

"Forgive me for staring, Detective," she said at last. "I view the living the way I view the dead."

"Sort of the opposite for me."

"Yes, I suppose it is." She sat perfectly still for a few beats longer. Then she said, "Your pupils are a bit larger."

"Meaning?"

"It has something to do with the locus coeruleus."

She had a quiet voice with smoky undertones, which made everything she said sound sensuous.

"Not sure what the locus coeruleus does."

"Releases norepinephrine, also known as noradrenaline, in response to pain or stress. What we often call the fight-or-flight response. Something I suspect comes in handy in your line of work."

"Occasionally." *Like the shooting at Angel Duran's cabin.*

Her eyes remained locked on his for a time before she said, "Are you familiar with T.S. Eliot's poem 'The Wasteland'?"

"Vaguely."

"There's a stanza that has always fascinated me. So much so that I committed it to memory." She paused for a moment before speaking again.

"Who is the third who walks always beside you?
When I count, there are only you and I together
But when I look ahead up the white road
There is always another one walking beside you
Gliding wrapt in a brown mantle, hooded
I do not know whether a man or a woman
—But who is that on the other side of you?"

"Isn't Eliot making a Biblical reference?"

Monroe nodded her head slowly as her eyebrows lifted in surprise. "It's an allusion to Jesus on the road to Emmaus. But what I'm speaking about is your aura, Detective. Like Eliot's allusion, your aura, the glow around your body, is always with you."

Born in the land of Gabriel García Márquez and magical realism, where dreams and reality are often conflated, Santana saw no humor or foolishness in what Dana Monroe had suggested. Rather, he chose to understand her beliefs in order to better understand her.

"And what color is my aura?"

She smiled as her gaze held steadily on him. "You have an open mind."

"Best to have one in my line of work."

"I have a neurological condition called synesthesia," she said. "Comes from the Greek words 'synth,' which means 'together,' and 'ethesia,' which means 'perception.' Information meant to stimulate one of my senses stimulates several of them." She pointed to her head, as if for emphasis. "Researchers call me a synesthete."

"What researchers are those?"

"From the University of Granada in Spain."

"Didn't know researchers had studied auras."

"Science is evolving, as are we. My brain is cross-wired, allowing me to establish associations between brain areas not normally interconnected. I can see or taste a sound, feel a taste, or associate people or letters with a particular color. It's the same phenomenon often found among painters and artists, more synaptic connections than normal people."

"So, what's my aura?"

"Primarily blue and purple. Like most people, your aura is a combination of colors, with one being more dominant than others."

"What do those colors mean?"

"Blue is a sign of a powerful mind. You are very insightful, which would help you in your job. Blue is also the color of the throat chakra governing expression and truth. It is what you seek."

"And purple?"

"It is your primary color and is associated with strong intuition and sensitivity. Purple is the color of the third-eye chakra, which deals with intuition. You also have some psychic, empathic, or intuitive abilities."

Santana nodded as his gaze shifted momentarily to the three gleaming skulls on a wall shelf beside a small gold-plated statue of the Buddha.

Her eyes followed his. "Those aren't real, Detective."

He shrugged. "Just wondering."

"I named them Francis, Edmund, and Calvin," she said, admiring the skulls for a time before her eyes met his again.

"Oh," Santana said, not knowing what else to say.

"I hope you don't think I'm crazy."

"Not at all," he said, thinking maybe he had made a mistake coming here.

"Francis Galton, a cousin of Charles Darwin, published the first detailed model of fingerprint analysis and advocated for their use in forensic science. You're familiar with Edmund Locard's Exchange Principle."

"I am."

"And then there's Calvin Goddard. Headed the first Bureau of Forensic Ballistics and the first lab devoted to criminology. All three men are an inspiration for me." Pointing to the gym bag he had set on the floor, she said, "Let me see it."

Santana took out the skull he'd signed out from the Evidence and Property room and handed it to her.

She closed her eyes and gently rubbed the skull with her long fingers, as if trying to get a sense of the person it once belonged to.

Still cradling the skull in her hands, she opened her eyes and said, "Please pass me the bag."

Santana gave it to her.

She carefully placed the skull in the bag, zipped it, and set it gently on the floor beside her.

"I use a computer program to create 3-D reconstructions, Detective. They're more effective than sculptures or 2-D reconstructions since they don't appear too artificial. The National Center for Missing and Exploited Children uses this method when it releases an unidentified decedent to the public."

"I'm familiar with NCMEC."

"I'm sure you also know that reconstructions of any kind are not considered a legally recognized technique for positive identification, and aren't admissible as expert testimony. Reconstructions can only aid the process of positive identification."

"Of course."

"Families have a right to know what happened to a loved one."

"And if someone was responsible for their death," Santana said.

"Absolutely. We have this vast population of possible missing persons that remains could match. We need to narrow down that universe."

Santana's cell phone buzzed. "Excuse me," he said, removing the phone from his sport coat pocket.

He recognized Gabriel Cruz, no doubt wondering where he was. He clicked off the sound and returned the phone to his pocket.

"Can you tell the race of the victim?" he asked Monroe.

She inhaled and let out a long, slow breath, as if controlling her anger.

"Forensic anthropologists call that ancestry estimation, a nineteenth-century procedure of measuring skulls to determine race—originally used to prove Caucasian intellectual superiority.

Though still used, the practice remains entangled with its racist roots."

Santana was reminded of the tangled roots in his dream.

"It's not one hundred percent accurate either," she said. "Imagine if someone had his mother's African jaw and his father's light skin. As an investigator, you'd be searching for the wrong person, if his neighbors considered him white. Translating skeletal data into race—a socially determined category—still reinforces the erroneous notion that race is biological."

She waved the idea away as she would an insect.

"There's no checklist of skeletal, physical, or genetic traits shared by all people of a certain race," she continued. "In fact, there's far more variation within racial categories than between them. No," she said with an adamant shake of her head. "I don't believe in race science or practice it. And then we have the problem with the criminal justice system."

Her complexion was suddenly flushed.

"What problem is that?"

"Surely, as a minority, you know that when remains are classified as members of marginalized groups, they often receive less attention."

"Not with me."

"Then you're the exception, not the rule, Detective."

"Race is included in missing persons' reports, police case files, and in almost every other description of a person," he said. "It's part of how people identify. That follows them in death."

"In your world, Detective. Not in mine."

She leaned forward in the chair and rested her elbows on her knees.

"People from Latin America and the US are all 'Hispanic,' but this is biologically meaningless. Traditional racial categories don't reveal specific social or biological differences; rather, they obscure them. I refuse to make definitive ancestry statements, saying instead that a bone is 'consistent with' or 'likely of' a certain ancestry."

"That's good enough for me."

"It will have to be, Detective Santana."

*   *   *

When Santana returned to the Homicide and Robbery Unit at the LEC, he saw Gabriel Cruz sitting in the cubicle next to his.

"Where you been?" Cruz asked.

Santana started to explain when he saw Janet Kendrick standing in the open door of her office, waving him in.

"You have a lint roller?" Santana asked.

"What the heck for?"

Santana pointed to his pants leg. "Cat hair."

"Detective," Kendrick called.

Santana headed for her office. "See what you can dig up on Martin Conrad, the psychologist Jadyn Hartley is seeing, including his finances," he said to Cruz.

"How come?"

"I'll update you later."

"Got to have a warrant for the finances."

"Get creative," Santana said, heading for Kendrick's office.

As Santana entered, his eyes were drawn to Chief Thomas Murdoch seated in one of the two chairs facing Kendrick's desk.

"Have a seat," Murdoch said, gesturing toward the vacant chair beside him.

Santana's heartbeat kicked up a notch as he sat down. His mind raced through the possible reasons for the sudden sit-down with Kendrick and Murdoch, but he came up empty.

Kendrick settled herself in the chair behind her desk and fixed her gaze on him. "We're scheduling a press conference for later this morning."

"A press conference? For what?"

Murdoch maneuvered his chair so that he faced Santana. "I understand you have a suspect in the bones case."

Santana shook his head. "That's not exactly correct."

Murdoch raised his eyebrows as his eyes shifted to Kendrick.

"What the chief is referencing is your search of Jadyn Hartley's residence. I received a call from Megan McKenna complaining about the search."

Santana nearly cursed out loud. "After the phone call, you're holding a press conference accusing Jadyn Hartley of the crime?"

"We're not accusing anyone, Detective," Murdoch said. "But the media is all over this. They're gathering like a pack of jackals. And I'm getting heat from the Winter Carnival Committee. Attendance at events has dropped off because everyone is searching for more damn bones. We need to give the media something. And we need to reassure the people of this city that we're going to find out whomever that skull belongs to. If someone committed a crime, we're going to arrest and prosecute that person as well. It's reached a point where we believe a press conference is needed."

"So let the media gather. That's what they do."

Murdoch cleared his throat. "We're holding the press conference whether you agree with it or not, Detective."

"What're we going to say?"

"That's why you're here," Kendrick said. "The chief and I want both you and Detective Cruz at the press conference."

Santana hated press conferences and thought they were a waste of time. They could also cause embarrassment for the department and lead to confusion and accusations. Something said in front of a microphone and a pack of reporters could not easily be retracted.

"What about Tatum?"

Murdoch shook his head.

Santana figured the department still saw Tatum as a liability after his suspension.

"I don't want to speak," he said.

"You're the lead detective. Tell them we're reviewing the case and could use the help of the community."

That's all we need. More bone seekers and unfounded tips clogging the phone lines.

"This is premature," he said. "We don't have anything concrete yet."

Kendrick released a frustrated breath. "The press conference is this afternoon."

"Tara Easton's funeral is this afternoon."

"The press conference will be held after the funeral."

Santana knew that anger would cloud his thinking. He had to give them something. "Kim Solace believes the bones were cut with a chainsaw."

"I read that in your report," Kendrick said. "Then we're definitely talking murder."

"But we shouldn't share that information with the media at this time," Murdoch said.

Santana nodded in agreement.

"What else have you found?" Kendrick asked.

"We're working on identifying the skull that was found."

"And how are you doing that?" Murdoch asked.

"I've given the skull to a person in the forensic anthropological field familiar with this type of identification."

"You mean Kim Solace?" Kendrick said.

Santana had shaded the truth, hoping his answer would be sufficient. If he had to be more specific, he knew he would be in trouble.

"Not Solace," he said.

"Then who?"

"A woman named Dana Monroe."

"Who the hell is Monroe?" Murdoch asked.

"A woman who has considerable experience in this field."

"I've never heard of her."

"I haven't either," Kendrick added.

"Monroe works in the field of genetic genealogy."

Kendrick's eyes grew large in surprise. She leaned forward, her hands clamped on the armrests as if she was about to spring out of the chair. "You took the skull to a civilian?"

"We need to know who that skull belongs to. I believe Monroe can tell us."

"By just looking at the skull?"

"She can create an accurate computerized drawing."

"Of whom?"

"I believe the skull belongs to Taimur Khalil."

"I read that name in your report on Tara Easton's suicide," Kendrick said. "What do the bones have to do with Easton's suicide and this man Khalil?"

Santana wanted to correct Kendrick about her use of the word 'suicide' but thought it would only cause him more grief.

"You know from my report that Cruz and I interviewed Khalil's daughter, Nasrin. Her father has been missing for nearly six months. There's a good possibility that the skull is his."

"Well," Murdoch said, "you will not mention anything about this Monroe woman at the press conference. Is that clear, Detective?"

"Yes."

"We've got enough crazies wanting to offer help as it is."

"Then maybe we shouldn't ask the community for help."

Murdoch gave him a hard stare.

Kendrick said, "Let's stick with a description of the deceased. We know from your reports that the bones belong to a middle-aged male somewhere between thirty-five and fifty years old. Although Solace couldn't clearly establish TOD, we're probably looking at months, not years."

"I like it," Murdoch said. "Gives the media and the community enough information to get the ball rolling. Someone might have a relative or significant other that has gone missing in this time frame."

"Nasrin Khalil's father has been missing for six months," Santana said.

"We heard you the first time," Kendrick said. "But as of now, we have no clear evidence that the bones belong to him. His name will not be mentioned at the press conference."

"Okay."

Kendrick looked at Murdoch. "Anything else, Chief?"

Murdoch shook his head.

"That will be all for now, Detective," Kendrick said. "Make sure you and your partner are prepared for the press conference this afternoon."

Santana stood.

"And make sure you stick to the agreed-upon script," Kendrick added.

Chapter 18

Burial in Fort Snelling National Cemetery is open to all members of the Armed Forces who have met a minimum active-duty service requirement and are honorably discharged. Tara Easton's final resting place would be here with the 180,000-plus men and women veterans and their spouses.

Given Matt Easton's feelings about his wife's military service and war in general, his choice of a burial site surprised Santana. Perhaps, he thought, she'd expressed her desire to be buried here.

Heading for one of the six outdoor pergola-like committal shelters, where the short military ceremony would be held, Santana saw Gabriel Cruz and Art Tatum approaching. Both men wore stocking hats and overcoats.

"Where you been?" Cruz said, his voice rising with frustration.

Santana told them about his visit with Dana Monroe and his meeting with Janet Kendrick and Thomas Murdoch.

"We could've gone with you to meet Monroe, maybe learned something," Cruz said, the water vapor from his breath fogging the air.

"I dropped off the skull. Not much to learn, other than Dana Monroe isn't a racist."

"I don't want any part of a press conference," Tatum said.

"It's just Cruz and I."

"Fine with me," Tatum said.

Cruz tapped his feet on the ground in an effort to keep them warm. "What're we supposed to say?"

"We'll discuss it after the funeral."

"Well," Cruz said with a shrug, "you would've learned something had you bothered to call us."

"What's that?"

"I called Lakeview Hospital. Duran has an infection, but we can talk to him. Find out what he knows."

"Or what he's willing to tell us," Santana said. "Any word from the lab on the fingerprints?" he asked Tatum.

"Nothing except Detective Cruz's prints on the anonymous letter."

The way Tatum emphasized *Cruz* suggested the detective should've known better than to touch the letter without gloves.

Cruz's complexion reddened.

Wanting to get him off the hook, Santana said to Tatum, "You write the info in the chrono?" referencing the chronological record in the murder book.

"Not yet."

"How about the report from the crime lab on the prints?"

Tatum shook his head.

"That needs to be done—soon."

"Right after the ceremony," Tatum said.

Santana sat on a wood-slatted bench in the committal shelter between Cruz and Tatum.

Matt Easton, Blaine Beckham, and Hannah Thatcher sat on the bench in front of him. Beckham and Thatcher were dressed in their Class-A dress uniform. Beckham had neatly trimmed his beard.

Mourners included members of the St. Paul Fire Department, most of whom, Santana figured, worked with Matt Easton. Before sitting down, Santana had spotted Wade Crawford lingering near the back of the structure. Recalling that Tara Easton was an orphan, and that her daughter was a toddler, Santana hadn't expected to see any family members besides her husband.

The morning's confetti-like flurries had ceased, the wind had died, and the early afternoon sun had broken through the cloud cover, warming the temperature to a balmy 25°.

From his vantage point, Santana could see the precisely-aligned and seemingly never-ending rows of headstones and their slight color variations against the snow. Some were pale yellow, some light gray, some silver, some winter white, and some bright white.

Because of the frigid winters, the labor-intensive efforts of digging roughly 1,000 graves to use for burials throughout the winter had been completed in the fall. The stones would be inscribed where they stood when the grave became occupied. Current burial rates helped forecast how many urn and casketed graves would be needed in each respective interment section.

Santana watched as the color guard, carrying five flags—the US as well as the colors of four branches of military service—lined up outside the shelter. Ceremonial guards were posted to either side of the colors. The squad commander gave the orders, and five members of the Fort Snelling Memorial Rifle Squad, the oldest all-volunteer group for national cemeteries in the US, fired a three-rifle volley.

Standing among the rows of headstones, two buglers created a haunting echo effect while playing taps. The color guard lowered the four military flags, and rifles were presented. The squad commander stepped forward and presented a folded US flag to Matt Easton.

"On behalf of the President of the United States, the Armed Forces of the United States and a grateful nation, I present you this flag, a symbol of our great republic which our departed comrade has honorably served."

The color guard retired, then the rifle squad. Several of the Memorial Rifle Squad members picked up the spent casings, placed three in a small purple sack, and handed it over to Matt Easton.

Santana had heard that the squad picked up roughly 8,000 spent casings in a year.

The squad commander asked Matt Easton if he'd like to say a few words to the attendees.

Easton hesitated. Then he rose slowly, turned toward the mourners, and quickly thanked everyone for coming.

*   *   *

Santana and Cruz grabbed a quick bite to eat at the Tavial Mexican Grill on W. 7th Street. Santana chose the taco with *carne asada*, or steak, and fries. Cruz ate a *birria*, or shredded beef burrito, along with fries. They both ordered *horchata*, a popular Mexican drink made from white rice soaked in water, and flavored with cinnamon and sweetened with granulated sugar.

"Love the food at this place," Cruz said as they drove away.

Santana drove to Lakeview Hospital while Cruz sat in the passenger seat.

"What time is the press conference?" Cruz asked.

"We've got a couple hours."

"Better come up with something."

"We will. I imagine you've been to military funerals before," Santana said.

"A few. You?"

"A couple."

"But you're not a vet."

"Same situation as today."

"Homicide deaths?"

Santana nodded.

"I thought Matt Easton might say more than a few words about his wife."

"Maybe he wasn't happy about the choice of burial sites."

"I got the impression he wasn't a fan of war."

"Not many are," Santana said. "Got any background on Pat Grainger and Martin Conrad?"

Cruz nodded. "Tell me again why I'm looking at Conrad?"

"He treated both Tara Easton and Jadyn Hartley."

Cruz paused for a time after Santana's reply before he spoke.

"Grainger was born in Minot, North Dakota. Served in the Navy for four years. Honorable discharge. Then earned a bachelor's degree in communications from the University of Illinois.

Started his career as a reporter for the *Minot Daily News*. Later worked for *Sun-Times* in Chicago and for newspapers in Florida and South Carolina before joining the *Pioneer Press* as an investigative reporter. Was nominated for a Pulitzer a few years back for coverage of child abuse stories. Never married. Owns a home in St. Paul. No history of scandal."

"Know how long he wrote clues for the medallion hunt?"

"No."

"What about Martin Conrad?"

"Conrad filed for bankruptcy a couple years ago. Piled up a ton of credit card debt, mostly from travel outside the US. Trips to Europe and to Africa."

"What was he doing in Africa?"

"Big game hunting."

Santana felt his heart rate kick up a notch.

"Conrad goes hunting in Namibia and South Africa. Only two countries in Africa where you can hunt all the big five: lion, leopard, Cape buffalo, elephant, and rhino, both black and white. And once you've killed the animal, you can export your *trophy* home."

Cruz had emphasized the word "trophy" to indicate his disgust.

"It's trophy hunting and not canned hunting," Santana said.

"You mean where captive bred animals are released into small enclosures and hunted in a no-kill no-fee arrangement?"

"Yeah. Like that. You hunt as a kid?"

"Mostly mule deer and bighorn sheep in Sonora. I get the pro-hunting argument. Hunting provides revenue that funds conservation. Still, once you've hunted men, the idea of . . ." Cruz's voice trailed off as his eyes glazed over.

"Then Conrad knows how to shoot a .30-06."

"You could take plains animals with the .30-06," Cruz said. "Need something like a .450 caliber for elephants and rhinos.

Probably get by with a .375 H&H Magnum for lions and Cape buffalo."

"In any case, Conrad knows how to shoot a rifle," Santana said. "What else you got?"

"Conrad married his third wife a few months ago. Gloria Welch, the daughter of Gordon Welch, a very successful investment banker. Welch and his wife were killed in an auto accident in Europe two years ago. Left the daughter with a load of cash."

"Only child?"

"One and only. Not long after the funeral she met a swindler she thought loved her. He scammed her out of a large chunk of her inheritance. She had a breakdown and sought therapy."

"With Martin Conrad."

"Bingo. They married and he moved in with her."

"Ever catch the swindler?"

"Skipped the country and disappeared."

"Were you able to look at Conrad's finances?"

"Nope. Couldn't convince the judge."

"Dig up anything on Angel Duran?"

"Plenty." Cruz turned the page in his notebook. "Duran grew up in the border town of McAllen, Texas, after his family migrated from Jalisco, Mexico, when he was six years old. Moved with his mother to St. Paul when he was thirteen. Along the way, he got dual citizenship. Enlisted in the Army when he turned eighteen. Followed the same military track as Blaine Beckham. Pretty sure that's how they connected."

"Anything else?"

"Yeah. Get this. Duran has an older brother, Enrique. First arrested at sixteen in Texas while trying to cross the border with a load of marijuana. He pleaded guilty and spent thirteen months in federal prison. After his release, he moved to Mexico and connected with cartels. He bribed Mexican lawmakers and law enforcement and became the leader of La Empresa, a network that transports drugs into the US and launders money for rival drug cartels including Sinaloa Cartel, Cartel de Jalisco, Nueva Generación, and Los Zetas. Mexicans eventually arrested him and sent him to prison."

"Let me guess," Santana said. "Enrique didn't stay there long."

"You got it. Mexico is notorious for prison escapes. Enrique only spent ten months in prison before he broke out. DEA figures La Empresa smuggles, on average, ten tons of cocaine into the States per month while laundering at least ten million of drug proceeds back into Mexico. Wonder if Angel Duran is still in contact with his brother Enrique?"

"We'll ask him," Santana said.

They rode in silence before Cruz spoke again. "Tatum wasn't happy about not coming along to the hospital."

"We don't need three detectives interviewing Angel Duran."

Santana took out his cell phone and called the Washington County Sheriff's Office and asked to speak to Del Taggart, the Washington County investigator assigned to the case. Because they had not hit it off at the crime scene, he wanted to offer the courtesy of notifying Taggart of his intentions.

"I've already been up to the hospital, Santana," Taggart said in a dismissive tone. "Duran had nothing to say. No sense in wasting your time."

"I don't see it as a waste."

"Oh, you don't."

"Duran might be involved in a case we're working. I need to talk to him."

"Your case the reason he got shot?"

"Could be."

"But you haven't shared shit with me."

"I said 'could be,' Taggart. Doesn't mean Duran is involved. No sense in wasting your time."

"You're a funny guy, Santana."

"Hilarious. You have a deputy watching Duran's room?"

"We're not a bunch of hicks."

"Let him know we're coming."

"You bet. Anything else I can do for you, Detective?"

"I'll let you know if I find out anything."

"Make damn sure you do."

Santana disconnected.

"Sounds like a real friendly guy," Cruz said.

"Yeah. We're already best buddies."

Angel Duran had a private room at Lakeview Hospital. A Washington County deputy sat in a chair in the corridor outside of Duran's room.

A doctor at the nursing station on the floor had informed them that if the infection cleared up soon, Duran could be released by Wednesday of next week.

"Heard you were coming," the young officer outside Duran's door said as Santana and Cruz badged him.

Duran was half-sitting up in the hospital bed behind a tray table that held a plastic cup and straw and an empty dinner plate. He wore a standard hospital gown and had an IV snaking from a drip trolley in his left forearm. A heart monitor tracked his blood pressure, heart rate, and body temperature.

A TV attached to the wall broadcasted one of the many talk shows Santana wasn't familiar with.

He stood on one side of the bed, Cruz the other.

Duran still had his full beard, but someone had groomed it and cut it a little shorter. A rubber band held his long, black hair in a ponytail.

"Remember me?" Santana asked, showing Duran his badge. He saw no confusion behind the man's eyes.

"Yeah, I remember you," Duran said in a weak voice. "We were talking just before I got shot."

"This is my partner, Detective Cruz," Santana said, gesturing toward him. "You remember what we were talking about?"

"Can't say I do."

Santana opened his cell phone, found the photo he was searching for, and showed it to Duran. "This is you with Blaine Beckham, Tara Easton, Taimur Khalil, and an unknown Afghani soldier in a tiger-striped uniform. We were talking about your connection to these people just before you were shot."

"What did I tell you?"

Santana wondered if Duran was being cagey or if he'd actually forgotten.

"I know that you, Beckham, and Tara Easton served together. I know that Taimur Khalil was what you called a 'jingle man.' But I'm more interested in this man."

Santana pointed to the Afghan in the tiger-striped uniform.

Duran shrugged. "Didn't know him."

"What was he doing in the photo?"

"Maybe Tara or Blaine knew him."

Santana recalled that Beckham had said that Tara knew him.

"Guy in the tiger-striped uniform likely belonged to the Zero Unit," Duran said.

Santana looked at Cruz to see if he could offer clarification.

"Heard of 'em," Cruz said.

Duran turned his gaze on Cruz, his eyebrows raised in surprise. "You a vet?"

Cruz nodded. "Tell me what you know about them."

"Afghan paramilitary commandos sponsored and controlled by the CIA are what I heard. We called them 'ghost units.' Fuckers had a scary reputation."

"You ever fight alongside them?"

Duran shook his head. "Never had the opportunity. Would've been interesting."

Cruz's glance let Santana know he was finished with his questions.

"Speaking of 'fuckers,'" Santana said. "That's what you called Wade Crawford when I asked if you knew him."

Duran's gaze shifted to Santana. "Yeah? What did I tell you?"

"You didn't. Someone shot you."

"You doing anything about that?"

"Why we're here."

"Well, Tara is dead. Blaine and I were friends. So that eliminates them."

"*Were* friends?"

"Haven't seen Blaine in a while. But far as I know, nothing has changed."

"Khalil have any reason to want you dead?"

Duran shrugged, but the darting of his eyes said something else.

"Lots of money changed hands over there," Cruz said.

"So I heard."

"Some end up in your pocket?"

He shook his head.

"Why is Wade Crawford nosing around?" Santana said.

"Ask him."

"I did."

"And?"

"He seems to think Khalil stole money."

"No surprise there. We spent two hundred ninety million dollars every day in Afghanistan for twenty years. Yet it took only nine days for the Taliban to seize every provincial capital, dissolve the army, and overthrow the US-backed government. And they did it without firing a single shot. We left behind abandoned air bases, half-finished construction projects, and tens of thousands of untraceable guns, all purchased with American tax dollars. You ask me, that whole war effort was pretty fucked up. And Kahlil was part of it. Transferred funds to a known Taliban 'money man.' Should ask him about it."

"I would, if we could find him."

"He off the grid?"

"Might be terminally off."

What little color Duran had in his pale face drained away. Santana paused for a moment. "How's your brother Enrique doing?"

Duran's body twitched, as if he'd experienced a myoclonic jerk before falling asleep.

"My brother is fine."

"And on the run from the Mexican authorities."

"I wouldn't know."

"When's the last time you talked to him?"

"Long time. Before he went to jail."

When Duran spoke, he avoided eye contact.

"I think someone is taking everyone in the photo off the board," Santana said. "You might not be so lucky next time."

Duran's gray eyes stared off into the distance. "Don't know what you're talking about, Detective."

"I think you do."

"Think what you want. But I'm done talking."

Chapter 19

The St. Paul City Hall and Ramsey County Courthouse are located on Kellogg Boulevard in a twenty-one-story Art Deco skyscraper built out of limestone during the Great Depression. The press conference was scheduled to take place at 4:00 p.m. inside the building in Memorial Hall, with its white marble floors and three-story black marble pillars leading to a gold-leaf ceiling.

The names of men and women who gave their lives in military service to the country from World War I through the Iraq and Afghan conflicts were engraved alphabetically on the marble pillars on the first, second, and third floors.

An onyx Vision of Peace statue stood thirty-eight feet tall in Memorial Hall in the center of the building. Ramsey County's war veterans were honored with the hall and statue in 1936.

A podium with an SPPD emblem had been set up in front of the statue. Reporters and camera crews from the major media outlets had gathered in front of the podium, waiting to ask questions.

Santana recognized a few press members, including Pat Grainger from the *Pioneer Press*.

He and Cruz, along with Janet Kendrick and the chief, Thomas Murdoch, stood in a row behind the mayor as he approached the microphone on the podium. Cruz's gaze had shifted to the names of the dead war vets on the pillars. Santana wondered what thoughts were running through his partner's mind. Did Cruz feel guilty because he'd avoided the Grim Reaper's scythe while so many others had perished?

The mayor, a handsome forty-four-year-old African-American man in his first term, thanked everyone for being here. He told the attendees that Chief Murdoch would speak first, followed by the lead detective in the bone investigation, John Santana. Questions would be answered after the short presentations.

The mayor stepped back and Murdoch took his place.

"Good afternoon. The department is well aware that you and members of the community have many questions concerning the bones recently discovered in Como Park. I'm here to assure all of you that we are working twenty-four seven to determine whose bones they are and the exact cause of death. We will not stop till we have answers to those questions.

"A promise I made to you when I became chief of this wonderful city was my intention to lower the crime rate and to significantly reduce the incidents of gun violence plaguing some of our fine neighborhoods. I believe solving crimes and incarcerating offenders will go a long way in helping me fulfill that promise. Of course, I can't do it alone. I need help from the community and from the members of this department. I'd like to introduce you to one of those outstanding and experienced members now, Detective John Santana, the lead detective assigned to the case."

Murdoch half-turned, and with a big smile, gestured for Santana to come forward.

The chief's glowing introduction had embarrassed him. Since Murdoch had recently been chosen for the position, Santana doubted the authenticity of his praise. Murdoch had said it primarily to appease the media and the citizens and to, hopefully, put a stop to the growing conspiracy theories suggesting that an insane serial killer like Michael Myers from the *Friday the 13th* movies was strewing bones of his victims across city parks.

Santana cleared his throat as he stepped up to the microphone. He had spoken with many individual reporters over the years and to small groups of media, usually at crime scenes. But this was a more formal situation given the mayor and chief's attendance. And unlike the mayor and chief, he and Cruz had written down a few notes to make sure he covered the key points.

"We believe the bones discovered in Como Park are those of a male, between the ages of thirty-five and fifty years old. We're pursuing all avenues of investigation. Anyone with information is asked to please contact the department. The call can be anonymous. If you provide information that leads to an arrest, you may be eligible for a reward through Crime Stoppers of Minnesota." Santana gave the number and reminded everyone, "You can leave information with Crime Stoppers and also remain anonymous."

Murdoch moved up next to Santana and asked if there were any questions. When many of the reporters called out at once, the chief chose Pat Grainger from the *Pioneer Press*.

"Detective Santana. What makes you so sure this is a homicide?"

Before Santana could respond, Murdoch said, "We're not going to provide details at this time."

In a quick follow-up, Grainger said, "But you're certain it's a homicide."

"At this time, yes," Murdoch said.

Reporters began calling out questions again as Murdoch selected a woman reporter from one of the local television stations.

"Do you believe the bones belong to one individual?" she asked.

"We do."

An unidentified reporter shouted out, "Is this the work of a serial killer, Detective Santana, and are you searching for more bones?"

"No, I don't think this is the work—"

Before Santana could complete his response, Murdoch said, "That's all the questions for now. Thank you for coming."

*   *   *

Gabriel Cruz invited Santana to join him for a drink after the press conference. They met at the Groveland Tap, located in a brick building with a wall of floor-to-ceiling windows near the intersection of St. Clair and Fairview Avenues in the Macalester/ Groveland neighborhood. Santana hadn't been in the bar since the recent renovation that had expanded the entryway and seating while separating the beer and wine bar from the restaurant. A museum-like array of hundreds of beer spigot handles hung on the walls above the tables and high-backed wooden booths.

The after-work crowd drifted in as Santana and Cruz sat at one of the tables. They both ordered Blue Moons from a menu of forty beers. Santana found it more difficult to find a Sam Adams in city restaurants and bars, especially with all the local craft beers entering the market.

Cruz drank half his glass of beer and said, "What's your take on the press conference?"

"Waste of time."

"Wouldn't want to be chief. Way too much ass-kissing."

"Not a job I'm interested in either." He sipped his beer and said, "You getting enough sleep?"

Cruz set his beer on the table. "Yeah. You?"

"Not always."

"How come?"

"I have PTSD."

"You told me." Cruz shrugged. "Who sleeps well every night?"

"My father did. Used to tell my mother he had a 'clear conscience.'"

"You saying I don't?"

"I read about the Battle of Kamdesh and Outpost Keating. You went through hell."

"Part of the mission," Cruz said, finishing off his drink and ordering another.

"Everyone needs one."

Cruz nodded. "You told Duran that Taimur Khalil might be terminally off the grid."

"Just a hunch."

"You think the skull might be his?"

"Possible."

"So why is everyone in the photo being killed?"

"My guess is money. But tell me about this 'Zero Unit' Duran mentioned."

The waitress arrived with a fresh Blue Moon. Cruz drank some before he responded.

"Used to be called Mohawks before the name change," he said. "Started as an irregular commando force controlled by the CIA. Trained as guerrilla fighters out of small US outposts, mainly in the north and east of Afghanistan, near the Pakistan border. CIA used them to conduct cross-border raids into Pakistan. Something US personnel weren't approved to do."

"Gave us deniability," Santana said.

"Exactly. Program was similar to the CIA's Phoenix program during the Vietnam War.

"The Zero Units were also known as 01, or Khost Protection Forces. Pretty much operated without guardrails under Afghanistan's intelligence agency, the National Security Directorate. Lots of night raids that killed civilians, many at close range, execution-style. During the time I was there, these guys were virtually invisible. Most Zero missions were led by a small number of CIA advisers, or US Special Forces, borrowed from the Pentagon's Joint Special Operations Command."

"Wasn't Blaine Beckham connected with JSOC?"

"Yeah. He was a Delta Ranger. Once we started pulling out of Afghanistan and the Taliban took control of Kabul," Cruz continued, "the Zero units helped control the crowds of Afghans and foreigners trying to enter Hamid Karzai International Airport to board evacuation flights. Taliban fighters maintained control at other airport entrances around the same time."

"Did members of the Zero Unit get out?"

"Not only did they get out. They were given priority for evacuation to the States. Heard at least seven thousand former commanders and their family members were flown out of Afghanistan."

Santana wondered if the man in the tiger-striped uniform was among those who got out of Afghanistan, and if he was now in St. Paul.

When they left the bar, Cruz's late model Chevy Tahoe wouldn't start. While they waited inside the bar for the service station tow truck to arrive, Cruz drank another Blue Moon.

Santana wondered if Cruz was self-medicating because of his PTSD.

They continued waiting inside while the tow truck driver, wearing a hooded parka, thick, greasy gloves, and knee-high boots, determined the problem was either the alternator or starter.

"Battery's good," he said. "We'll get it towed in and looked at first thing in the morning."

Given the amount of alcohol Cruz had consumed in a short amount of time, Santana hoped the Tahoe wouldn't start so he could give his partner a ride home. He knew if he suggested Cruz had had too much to drink and shouldn't drive, Cruz wouldn't accept the offer.

*   *   *

Gabriel Cruz lived in the Mac-Groveland area on the western edge of St. Paul, not far from the Groveland Tap and Macalester College. Santana had noted in past visits that streets were named after colleges like Amherst, Wellesley, and Princeton. Cruz lived in a bungalow on Stanford Avenue.

"Come on in for a drink," Cruz said, exiting Santana's Ford Explorer.

Santana knew little about his partner's private life. This could be a chance to get more of a sense of Cruz. He followed Cruz up a series of shoveled steps to a front door that looked as thick and heavy as a coffin lid. As he waited in the cold night air for Cruz to unlock it, he noted the bars on the stained-glass windows and, as they entered, the deadbolt lock on the front door and the keypad Cruz used to turn off the alarm system.

Santana had heavy security on his home because the Cali cartel had, for years, threatened to kill him. He wondered what were Cruz's reasons for the high-level security in a relatively safe neighborhood.

After hanging their coats in the front closet, Cruz went to the kitchen. "I'm having a Jack Daniel's. Only beer I have is Modelo *Especial.*"

Santana didn't want another beer, but if it kept Cruz talking, he would take it. "Beer is fine," he said.

"Want a glass?"

"Not necessary."

While he waited for Cruz to return, Santana scoped the living room: a white brick fireplace to his right, a large-screen TV built into the wall above the mantel, a wide arch dividing the living room from an open kitchen and dining area to his left. The stainless-steel appliances, light oak hardwood floors, and fresh white paint looked new.

Santana saw no dust, nothing out of place, and no indication that Cruz lived here with someone else.

He walked to the bookshelf that covered half the wall facing him for a closer look. Bookends held trade paperbacks by Mexican authors such as Octavio Paz and Carlos Fuentes, but framed photos filled most of the space on the three shelves.

Some of the photos were taken in what Santana assumed was Afghanistan. Another photo labeled Fort Knox, Kentucky, showed a smiling Cruz with three of his Army buddies, all wearing aviator sunglasses and dressed in camo, their arms around each other's shoulders.

Latinos liked family photos and Cruz was no exception. Six frames held color photos of a younger Cruz with his parents and two sisters.

"Like the house?" Cruz said, returning to the living room. "I do."

Cruz handed Santana a can of Modelo. "Place was built back in nineteen twenty-six. Constructed with cordwood."

"Like firewood?"

"Similar. Walls are over eight inches thick. Built out of cedar logs set into mortar. They're called cordwood because they resemble firewood."

"Lots of security for a relatively safe neighborhood."

Cruz offered a half grin. "One thing I learned overseas. Never can have too much security."

Santana wondered if paranoia or practicality drove Cruz's security decisions.

"House needed to be renovated," Cruz said. "Did the basement, too." He gestured toward the leather chair opposite the couch. "Have a seat."

Santana sat down and sipped his beer.

Cruz sat on the couch opposite him.

"No lady in your life?" Santana said.

Cruz's eyes jittered as if he were considering how to answer. "You know how it is."

"How is it?"

"Tough being in Homicide and having much of a love life."

"Sometimes."

Cruz started to respond and then seemed to think better of it.

A familiar scent of petrichor triggered Santana's memory. Now he recalled the same scent when they first visited Nasrin Khalil's apartment.

"You're seeing Nasrin Khalil."

As Cruz's face colored with embarrassment, Santana knew his assumption was accurate. "How long?"

"Hey, John, I'm not—"

"I can't trust you if you lie to me," Santana said in an even tone. "How long?"

"Recently." Cruz paused for a time, waiting for a response. When he got none, he said, "After our first visit with her."

"Not a good idea."

"Why not?"

"I shouldn't have to explain it to you."

Cruz shrugged. "It's her father we're looking for. Nothing sinister about that."

When working a murder case a few years ago, Santana had become involved with a woman whose brother later turned out to be the killer. His relationship with the woman hadn't ended well. Because Cruz had experienced so many traumas, Santana hoped that Taimur Khalil was innocent and that Cruz's relationship with Taimur's daughter would not suffer the same fate.

"You shouldn't be talking about the case with her."

"Don't worry. I'm not."

Santana wanted to ask what the two of them talked about, but he figured belaboring the subject might shut down further communication. To change the subject and to keep Cruz talking, he pointed to one of the framed photos on the bookshelf.

"That a photo of Camp Keating?"

Cruz didn't bother turning around to look at the bookshelf behind him. "Sure is."

"In a valley with mountains on three sides. Not a smart place to build an outpost."

"Like being in a fishbowl."

"Why build an outpost there?"

"We were supposed to be stopping the flow of weapons and insurgents from Pakistan."

"Obviously didn't work out."

Cruz gave a derisive laugh and drank more Jack Daniel's. He sat perfectly still for a time before he abruptly stood up. "Want another beer?"

"I'm good."

Cruz went into the kitchen and returned to the living room with a cocktail glass full of Jack Daniel's. He stood for a moment staring at the photos on the bookshelves. Then he sat down and drank.

"Blaine Beckham said a couple Medals of Honor were awarded," Santana said.

Cruz lifted his head and looked at Santana. "Medals awarded usually means others have died."

Santana wondered if Cruz had been awarded a medal but was hesitant to ask.

Cruz read the look of curiosity on Santana's face and said, "Silver Star."

Santana hadn't seen the medal displayed on one of the bookshelves. It didn't surprise him. Many veterans he'd met over the years were reluctant to talk about their war experiences or the medals they had received.

"Never could understand why I survived while others didn't," Cruz said softly.

Santana understood survivor's guilt. As a homicide detective he'd dealt with twisted, psychologically damaged killers and survived where others had not. He felt certain that the same question that lingered in his subconscious lingered in Cruz's. Could he have done more to save the lives of others?

In his past meetings with Karen Wong, the psychologist attached to the department, Santana had come to understand that survivor's guilt is a symptom of post-traumatic stress disorder. Having distorted feelings of guilt and negative thoughts and regrets was common among those who survived traumatic situations.

Ruminating over the events that took place and thinking about things he could have or should have done that would have altered the outcome only exacerbated feelings of guilt, particularly if he felt that his own actions or inactions may have worsened the consequences.

Wong had called this rumination "hindsight bias." Survivors look back and overestimate their ability to have known the outcome of an event. Because they feel like they should have predicted what happened, survivors become convinced that they should also have been able to change the outcome.

"We were told it was a just war," Cruz said. "But there aren't two different kinds of killing. There isn't murder and killing. Killing is killing. I was good at killing. Not much call for that now."

"You should see Karen Wong."

"The department shrink?"

"She's good."

"No way. I'm fine."

"Might have to do some killing in this job."

"Hope not."

"Can you pull the trigger if necessary?"

"Not gonna hang you out to dry, partner."

Santana wasn't so sure. "How many did you lose at Camp Keating?"

"Eight soldiers. Twenty-seven wounded. Eight Afghan soldiers were wounded, along with two Afghan private security guards."

"And the Taliban?"

"Estimates were that one hundred fifty Taliban were killed."

"Everything I've heard and read said that they're tough fighters."

"Better than most of the Afghans." Cruz finished his drink and set the empty cocktail glass on the coffee table. "Wars aren't just fought by soldiers. A country and its people and institutions fight them. The Taliban believed in their cause; the Afghan army didn't. Armies lose the will to fight when they lose faith in their leaders."

"I sometimes disagree with Kendrick and the rest of the brass."

Cruz chuckled and peered at Santana. "From what I heard, you disagree quite a bit."

"But I haven't lost faith in their leadership."

Cruz let out a long sigh and leaned his head against the backrest. His eyes had a blank, unfocused gaze often called a "thousand-yard stare." Santana had seen it before in post-combat vets and others who had become emotionally detached from the horrors around them.

"You're Colombian, I'm Mexican," Cruz said, refocusing on Santana. "Afghans are here now. Before that the Vietnamese came and then the Hmong from Laos and Karen from Myanmar. And a couple hundred years before that, the blacks, and later the Chinese came or were brought here."

"Your point being?"

"The more things change, the more they stay the same. Reality doesn't change. Neither does the status quo." Cruz leaned forward and pointed toward his heart. "Has to change in here before we get lasting change. Doubt I'll ever see it in my lifetime."

"That's why the mission is so important," Santana said. "Everyone gets our best no matter what their status or ethnicity."

"You really believe that?"

"If I didn't, I'd find another line of work."

Chapter 20

On Saturday morning, with the temperature rising into the low forties, Santana took Gitana for a run outdoors. Now, with the warmer weather, he didn't have to worry about booties and freezing her paws.

A half-mile into their run Santana saw a large yellow Lab vigorously wagging its tail as it trotted toward them. A tall woman in a bright green ski jacket, jeans, and knee-high boots held onto a leash as she jogged beside the Lab. Wisps of straw blond hair peeked out of a stocking hat that matched her jacket.

She waved as she and the Lab drew closer.

"Is your dog friendly?"

"Always," Santana said.

"Can they play?"

"Sure."

The woman stopped about a foot in front of Gitana, and the dogs looked at each other. They sniffed each other. They circled each other, sniffling as they went. Santana stayed close. Gitana stretched her front paws out and dropped her chest and raised her hind end. The Lab did the same. Santana unhooked her leash. The woman unhooked the Lab.

Then Gitana rose up and tore around in a circle. The Lab chased her. The circle widened and soon the two dogs were racing around a large, snowy yard near the road. Occasionally, they would stop to put their heads down and tails up. Then they would race around some more. Finally, the two of them stood still, panting, tongues lolling, tails wagging, looking at each other.

Santana and the woman walked over to their dogs and clipped the leashes onto their collars.

"What's your dog's name?" she asked.

"Gitana. Spanish for Gypsy."

She smiled and gestured toward the Lab. "Her name is Lexie. Thanks for the playtime."

"You're welcome."

As Santana watched the woman jog away, he realized he hadn't gotten her name. But that's the way it was with most dog owners he'd met on his runs with Gitana. Like him, they were dog people and only interested in meeting his golden girl.

Santana remembered hearing that once someone has had the good fortune to share a true love affair with a golden retriever, one's life and one's outlook are never quite the same.

As she sat in front of him now, her golden eyes focused only on him, a smile on her face, he thought of her loyalty, her unconditional love, her sense of wonder, and all the joy that she'd brought to his life, a life he'd mostly spent alone.

His mother's murder and the years he'd spent in Homicide had contributed to his loss of faith in the goodness of humans. In Gitana's jubilance, in her excitement of life, he saw all the innocence that he'd lost.

She had literally saved his life by warning him of an impending bullet. Without her senses, her awareness of impending danger, he would likely be pushing up daisies now.

He believed he'd saved her life as well after her first owner had been killed. Though he'd had dogs growing up in Colombia, he'd struggled with the idea of having a dog given his work schedule. But deciding to adopt her had been the best decision he'd ever made.

He'd been told that dogs did not feel emotions in the same way humans do, and that what he'd observed in Gitana was instinctual and nothing more than a wishful interpretation of what he saw.

He believed none of it. Instincts were different than intuition.

The instincts he'd honed in his training as a police officer were automatic responses to certain environmental stimuli. In contrast, his intuition was a feeling of knowing that arose subconsciously. His judgments or evaluations of something derived from his intuition. He couldn't pinpoint how he came to the judgment. It just felt right.

He often received good or bad vibes from people based on their facial expressions and body language gestures, which he processed subconsciously. Bangers called it "street-smarts."

Gitana constantly read his body language and emotions.

Santana had learned through experience to trust his intuition. Years ago, he'd read Gavin de Becker's book *The Gift of Fear*. In it de Becker wrote that intuition was the key to self-protection. But Santana knew his intuition paled in comparison to Gitana's.

He squatted, took her face in his hands, and kissed her head. "Ready to go, girl."

She responded with a little "woof."

* * *

Later that morning Santana drove to the LEC and ran Martin Conrad's DMV information. According to his driver's license, he lived in the private exurban community of North Oaks.

Santana shut down the computer and headed for his SUV.

Driving along the winding roads in North Oaks, Santana noted the absence of sidewalks, limited streetlights, and private access signage posted around the secluded and once-gated community of rolling hills, woods, open meadows, lakes, and wetlands.

Martin Conrad lived in a brick and stucco storybook home with a steeply sloped shingled roof and a mix of arched and tall leaded glass windows and eyebrow dormers.

The house had a whimsical feel, a characteristic Santana hadn't associated with Martin Conrad.

He parked his SUV in the cobblestone driveway near the double garage and rechecked the address he'd typed in his iPhone, making certain he had the right place. Then he recalled that

Conrad had moved into his third wife's house. Reassured, Santana exited his vehicle and rang the doorbell, which elicited a chime that sounded like a magic wand being waved.

A small woman with short, dull brown hair, deep-set olive-green eyes, and rounded cheeks and chin answered the door. She wore a brown cardigan sweater and plaid skirt, white leggings, and brown flats. Santana wasn't sure of her age, but given the crow's feet at the corners of her eyes and creases at the corners of her mouth, he made her for mid- forties.

The woman smiled shyly. "Yes?" she said in a voice just above a whisper.

Santana badged her. "I'm looking for Martin Conrad."

She held her hands folded in front of her skirt while she leaned slightly forward and peered at his badge, her eyes widened in surprise. "You're a detective."

"And you are?" Santana asked, ignoring her statement.

"I'm Gloria." After a momentary pause she said, "Doctor Conrad's wife." She said it as if to convince Santana she'd spoken the truth.

"Is the doctor home?"

"Yes. Excuse my manners. Please. Come in."

Santana stepped inside and wiped his shoes on the rug in the entryway. "Would you like me to remove my shoes?"

"Oh, no. You're fine. Martin is in the study. Please. Follow me."

She led Santana to a set of mahogany four-panel pocket doors at the back of the house and knocked lightly.

"What is it?"

Gloria slid the doors open a crack and said, "A Detective Santana is here to see you, Martin."

"Tell him I'm busy."

Gloria glanced at Santana, her pale face reddening with embarrassment.

Santana stepped forward and opened the doors wider.

Wearing a burgundy smoking jacket and silk pajamas, Conrad sat on a Chesterfield sofa with his stocking feet resting on a coffee table and a Dean Koontz paperback in his hand titled *False Memory.*

"We're all busy," Santana said.

Conrad scrambled to his feet as Santana entered the study.

"Could I get you something?" Gloria called after him.

"The detective won't be staying long," Conrad said.

"That depends, Doctor."

Santana heard the pocket doors close behind him.

Without being invited he removed his overcoat, laid it on the back of one of the two leather club chairs opposite the couch, and sat down in the other.

With its mahogany wall panels, floor-to-ceiling bookcase, and stag's head hanging on the wall over the crackling fireplace, the room reminded Santana of an English manor. He figured Conrad viewed himself as lord of the manor.

A portrait over the mantel pictured Conrad in full camo with a rifle and a Tilley hat, resting on one knee beside a dead lion with a massive head and thick mane.

He saw no gun rack or guns in the study.

Conrad sat down on the couch again, his body partially obscured by the large globe on the coffee table. He set the paperback on the coffee table beside four crystal glass tumblers and matching decanter filled with what Santana assumed was Scotch whiskey based on the half-empty bottle of Johnnie Walker Blue Label next to it.

Santana recalled that he'd seen a similar bottle in Tara Easton's apartment.

"You're a hunter," he said.

"Nothing better."

Santana wondered if Conrad hunted anything besides animals.

"That a problem for you, Detective?"

"Everyone has his hobbies."

"Big game hunting is not a hobby. It's a sport."

Santana noted the framed photo on the bookshelf of Ernest Hemingway posing with a dead Cape buffalo.

He stood, walked over to the bookshelf, and picked up the photo, noting the eerie resemblance between the famous author as a younger man and Martin Conrad.

"You read much Hemingway?" Santana asked.

"I have."

"Then you know that Hemingway said, 'There are only three sports: bullfighting, motor racing, and mountaineering; all the rest are merely games.'"

"I'm betting if he were asked today, Hemingway would agree that big game hunting is not a game."

"Guess we'll never know," Santana said.

Returning the photo of Hemingway to the shelf, he noted that many of the antique-looking books filling the shelves were nothing but panels formed by attaching phony pasteboard book spines side by side onto a flat board. The sideboards supporting the panels looked like hardcover books and left the appearance that the visible side of the panel was the first book on the shelf.

Santana wondered if anyone had noticed this before, and if Conrad had ever been embarrassed when asked about it.

"Don't suppose you'd care for a drink, Detective?"

"Little early for me."

"Yes. For me as well."

"Nice smoking jacket."

Conrad lifted an arm and peered at the sleeve as if seeing it for the first time.

"Yes, it is."

Santana recalled the Marlboro cigarette butts left in Tara Easton's ashtray.

"What type of cigarette do you smoke, Doctor?"

"Oh, I don't. Smoking ruins my sense of smell, and that's indispensable for hunting. I can smell lion, Cape buffalo, rhino."

Not knowing what to say, Santana let the comment go.

"You hunt?" Conrad said.

"In a way."

"Hunting humans is not the same as hunting animals."

"No," Santana said, staring at Conrad. "It isn't. I'm not looking for a kill."

"But you have killed, haven't you?"

"Sometimes you're left with no choice."

Conrad nodded as if he understood. "Ever read Hemingway's *The Green Hills of Africa*?"

Santana shook his head.

"Hemingway wrote that he didn't mind killing any animal if he killed it cleanly. They all had to die anyway, and his interference with the nightly and seasonal killing that went on all the time was very small."

Conrad rested an arm on the back of the sofa as he half-turned toward Santana. Casual. Confident. "My parents used to take me to the zoo when I was a kid. But I quit going when I reached my teens. I don't like to see the people making fun of the animals, when it should be the other way around."

"Yet you're a therapist."

"My job is to help people overcome their problems."

"Who helps you overcome your problems, Doctor?"

Conrad smiled. "*Touché*, Detective. But answer me this. Did you feel guilt after your first kill?"

"I didn't come here for a therapy session."

"Perhaps you should have."

Santana sat down in the club chair once again.

"Then what brings you here, Detective?"

"I wanted to get a better sense of you."

"And why would you want to do that?"

"I think you know the answer to that question, Doctor."

Conrad tented his hands and placed his fingers against his lips. Then he let out a long breath. "If you truly believe I murdered

Tara Easton—for God knows what reason—then you definitely need to make an appointment so we can work through your break with reality."

"Only one thing I'm sure of," Santana said.

"What's that?"

"You're fully capable of it."

*   *   *

That evening for Ana Soriano's eighteenth birthday, Santana and Rita Gamboni took her to Mañana, a Salvadoran restaurant on E. 7th Street in St. Paul. A colorful mural depicting three older women making *pupusas* adorned the side of the popular neighborhood restaurant that had been in business for nearly twenty years.

Knowing that the SPPD's top brass frowned on their relationship, Santana and Rita had limited their times out together in public. But this was a special occasion, and Santana doubted that they'd run into any command staff in the restaurant, despite its popularity and good reviews.

Ana and Rita ordered *pupusas* with *queso*, rice, beans, and handmade *tortillas*. Santana chose the *churrasco* with grilled *ranchera*, shrimp, and *chorizo*, rice, beans, and handmade corn *tortillas*.

Because Minnesota's legal drinking age was twenty-one, Santana and Rita declined the waitress's offer of a cocktail and ordered a *hortchada*.

"I have had alcohol before," Ana said in mild protest.

With her sophisticated look, Santana had little doubt that she could easily pass for a woman in her mid-twenties, as she once had as an expensively dressed, high-priced escort.

Tonight she was wearing a black, three-quarter length, belted, faux fur coat, white turtleneck, designer jeans, and knee-high black leather boots. She wore just the right touch of makeup and eye shadow to accentuate her striking blue eyes. A blue butterfly clasp held her waist-length black hair in place.

"We're cops," Santana said with a smile. "Cut us some slack."

Ana shrugged and ordered a *hortchada* as well.

Rita said, "I understand you've completed your high school credits."

"The courses were easy and boring."

Rita's eyes were a slightly darker blue than Ana's Caribbean blue eyes, and they were focused intensely on Ana, giving the young woman her full attention. It was one of the qualities that had first attracted Santana to Rita. When they were talking about something important, he knew he had her full attention.

"What are your plans?" Rita asked, brushing a strand of her white blond hair off her cheek.

Her hair was parted in the middle and cut shoulder-length and waved. Her makeup was, like Ana's, understated, as was her navy-blue pants suit and two-button blazer over a white crewneck sweater.

"I am not sure at the moment," Ana said.

"John tells me you're thinking of college."

"Perhaps John is the one who is thinking of college."

Ana shifted her gaze to Santana, as if waiting for a reply.

Santana would have to notify the court that his guardianship had ended on Ana's eighteenth birthday. He would have liked to have had more time with her, more time to help her find her way, her mission, her purpose.

"You need to make your own choices," he said. "Make sure they're wise ones."

"I am not sure I can be in college with all the young people," Ana said.

"They're mostly your age," Rita said.

Ana shook her head. "Only chronologically."

Santana tried to imagine Ana in a college setting. His emotional side thought it would be a wonderful new experience for her, being around students her age, enjoying the college life. But his rational side understood that Ana was, in many ways, well beyond the college years and the young men and women on campus.

He'd missed out on those years as well, taking undergraduate criminal justice courses on off-site campuses in the evenings, while he worked a variety of jobs and enrolled in the SPPD Internship Program. Later, when he'd become a police officer, he'd completed his master's degree.

The waitress appeared with their *hortchadas*.

"*Feliz cumpleaños*," Santana said as they toasted and then drank.

"John tells me you're fluent in three languages," Rita said. "Why not work as a translator?"

Ana dabbed her lips with a napkin and thought for a moment. "I want to bring my mother and younger sister here," she said.

Rita offered an understanding nod. "What's your sister's name?"

"Maria. She's ten."

"Have you been in contact with them recently?"

Ana shook her head and looked at Santana with furrowed brows. "I have not been able to contact them for two weeks."

"You never told me."

She shrugged. "I thought I could reach them."

"You've never talked about your father," Santana said.

"He was a farmer. The Mara Salvatrucha came and took him one day when I was fourteen. I never saw him again."

Rita leaned forward and placed a hand over Ana's. "How do you usually contact your mother and sister?"

"By phone or email. They have never been out of touch for this long. Something has happened. I need to go back and find them."

Santana's heartbeat kicked up a notch. "You're here illegally, Ana. I'm working on getting your papers. If you go back to El Salvador, you might not be able to return."

"I have to know," she said. "They are my only family."

"Let me look into it. See what I can find out."

"Okay. But I need to know soon. Before the MS-13 harms my sister."

Chapter 21

Early Sunday morning the sun shone brightly in the icy blue sky, and ice crystals coated the bare tree branches. Santana took Gitana for a run and then played Frisbee with her in the backyard. She loved bounding through the deep piles of snow and hunting voles that hid under it, though she never seemed to know what to do with them once she dug them up.

Ana Soriano, bundled up in a down jacket, tall leather boots, gloves, and a ski hat with a Lutsen logo Santana had given her, joined them. She laughed as she held the Frisbee and encouraged Gitana to chase her around in the deep snow. Santana noted that playing with Gitana was one of the few things that made Ana happy.

When they finished playing, Santana collected the copy of the *Pioneer Press* from his doorstep, showered, and fixed a cheese, bacon and egg *tortilla*, and cups of hot chocolate for the two of them. He gave Gitana part of his *tortilla* and two strips of bacon, which she always looked forward to on Sundays.

Ana had used a towel and hair dryer on Gitana, who loved the warm dryer, and then had added a refreshing spray to keep her smelling fresh and clean.

After breakfast Santana lit the logs in the living room fireplace and retrieved his SPPD cell phone from a jacket pocket in the downstairs closet. As Gitana curled up in front of the fire, he sat down on the couch to read the Sunday *Pioneer Press*.

The front-page headline read: "SEARCH FOR SKELETAL REMAINS REPLACES HUNT FOR MEDALLION." The city had descended into chaos. Teens were burying fake bones in municipal parks, and the police were bombarded with an avalanche of phone calls from frantic citizens who had discovered them. Patrol cars were being sent out on wild goose chases to answer

192

reports about bone-finders. Kids had turned up in skeleton costumes and masks, running around as if it were Halloween.

I told you so, Santana thought, recalling the ill-advised press conference the chief and mayor had called.

Santana took out his department cell phone and listened to a voicemail the watch commander had left. Jadyn Hartley had attempted suicide by overdosing on Prozac. He'd been taken by ambulance to Regions Hospital.

"Thought you'd want to know," the watch commander said as the voicemail ended.

Santana called Gabriel Cruz, but his phone went straight to voicemail. He left Cruz a message regarding Jadyn Hartley's attempted suicide.

Thirty minutes later Santana arrived at Regions Hospital. Jadyn Hartley had been moved from the emergency room Trauma 1 center in the south wing of the eleven-story building.

Santana took an elevator up to the eighth floor.

A middle-aged nurse with a kind face and a nametag identifying her as Cathy sat behind the counter. "Can I help you?"

"I'm looking for Jadyn Hartley's room."

Cathy gave him the room number.

As he turned to leave she said, "He was in the newspaper. The young man who found the bones."

"Yes."

She gently bit her lower lip as she considered another question. Finally, she said, "He's the one who . . ." She paused, apparently reconsidering her question. "Have a good day, Detective."

"You, too," he said.

When Santana entered the hospital room, he saw Megan McKenna seated in a chair by the young man's bed.

She glared at him and said, "What are *you* doing here?"

"How's he's doing?"

"Why do you care? You're the one who put him here."

No use arguing the point, Santana thought.

"He'll be fine, no thanks to you! But he had to have his stomach pumped, and now he has to stay here overnight for observation. Get out," she said in a threatening voice. "I don't want you here."

"Fair enough." He turned, walked into the hallway, and headed for the elevator, trying to shake off Megan McKenna's stinging rebuke.

When the elevator doors slid open, Santana came face-to-face with Martin Conrad, Jadyn's psychiatrist. Conrad wore a white lab coat over a white shirt and red and gray striped tie. His tan offered a stark contrast to the lab coat.

"Detective," Conrad said with a thin smile. He stepped off the elevator as the doors closed behind him. "Here checking on Jadyn's condition?"

"I am."

"I'll get him back in therapy as soon as he recovers. My job is to unearth whatever is troubling him."

"Might be the fact that he killed his father."

"Are you being facetious, Detective?"

"Not at all."

Conrad shrugged. "Of course his father's brutal death has greatly affected Jadyn's psyche. But in these situations I have to consider secondary factors as well."

"What might they be?"

Conrad offered another thin smile. "I had no choice in discussing Tara Easton's records with you. In Jadyn's case I do have a choice." He turned to leave.

"Consider this," Santana said.

Conrad stopped and looked at him again.

"One of your patients, Tara Easton, is suspected of committing suicide. Another of your patients, Jadyn Hartley, attempted suicide."

"It's unfortunate."

"Might be more than that."

"What are you getting at?"

"Could be a connection."

"Like what?"

"I'm working on it."

"You do that, Detective. In the meantime, I'll focus on getting Jadyn well."

Conrad did a quick 180° and marched away.

* * *

That evening Santana drove to Rita Gamboni's house for dinner. She'd invited Ana as well, but Ana had declined. "You two need some alone time. I'll cook something for myself and look after Gitana."

Rita Gamboni lived in a modest split-level house in Saint Anthony Park, which bordered southeast Minneapolis and the St. Paul University of Minnesota campus. Many university students and faculty lived in the larger, historic single-family homes among the hills and curving streets of the picturesque neighborhood.

An eight-foot redwood fence around Rita's backyard kept the neighborhood children from falling into the pool and gave her some privacy while she lounged on the patio on warm summer days. Now a safety cover and snow blanketed the pool.

Having been single for a number of years since her divorce, Rita rarely cooked for herself, preferring to dine out or to grab something on the run. But based on past experience, Santana knew she was an excellent cook. Tonight was no exception.

She fixed chicken piccata coated in a sauce mix of white wine, capers, and lemon juice, along with farfalle pasta and ciabatta bread dipped in olive oil. They drank a bottle of sauvignon blanc with the meal.

After dinner they sat on a couch in front of the fireplace drinking snifters of Remy Martin XO cognac.

"Expensive, isn't it?" Santana said, raising his snifter.

Rita grinned. "Only the best for you."

Santana glanced at the half-empty bottle on the coffee table and beside it a paperback book of T.S. Eliot's poems. Santana knew that Rita had graduated college but had not known her to be interested in Eliot.

"Either you've been drinking on your own, or you've shared the cognac with someone besides me."

She looked into his eyes. "Not recently. And not for a long time."

When it came to their relationship, Rita had always been truthful. No reason to doubt her now. But he had his doubts about Jadyn Hartley's psychiatrist, Martin Conrad.

They sat silently for a few more beats before Rita said, "What are you thinking about?"

"You."

"That's nice."

"It is."

She held his gaze and cocked her head. "That all?"

Santana shrugged. "And Jadyn Hartley."

"Hard to think about anything but the case you're working. Even me," she said with a little smile.

He hated to admit it, but obsessiveness came with the job. At least it did, he thought, if you were a dedicated cop.

"You remember," he said.

"All the time."

"We always had that in common."

"Made us good partners."

"It did."

"Suicides, or attempted suicides, are always an ugly business," she said.

"We only get one shot at life, Rita. Shame to waste it."

She nodded her head slowly. "It wasn't your fault."

"Easy for you to say."

"Because it's true." As Rita sipped her cognac, her blue eyes never left his. "There are times, John, when guilt may be legitimate, like causing an accident that leads to another person's death or injury. But in a lot of cases, there's little or nothing you can do to prevent or change the outcome."

Santana understood. Blaming himself for something out of his control could be devastating. Still, he wondered if he'd pushed Hartley too hard and too far.

"Do you think Hartley is responsible for the bones?" she said.

"Awful lucky or coincidental that he keeps finding them."

"Maybe he's smart."

"He is that."

"You think he's good for the murder?"

"Kendrick is leaning in that direction. But Hartley's psychiatrist, Martin Conrad, bothers me."

"How so?"

"He treated both Tara Easton and Jadyn Hartley."

"Another coincidence."

"Could be. Cruz checked into Conrad's background. Guy is a big game hunter. Good with a rifle. He could've tried to take out Angel Duran."

"Why would he do that?"

"He was treating Tara Easton. Maybe she told him about money she, Duran, Blaine Beckham, and Taimur Khalil smuggled out of Afghanistan."

"You have proof?"

Santana shook his head. "Something connects all of them. Not sure what it is yet. But Martin Conrad has had money problems. Could be he saw a way out of it."

Rita sipped some cognac before speaking again. "How is Cruz working out?"

"He's suffering from PTSD."

"Is that affecting his work?"

"Probably is, but he hides it well."

"Does Kendrick know?"

"Haven't told her anything."

"You have to be able to trust your partner, John. You know that."

"Cruz hasn't given me any reason not to trust him."

"But it's bothering you."

"Lots of things do."

Rita smiled and drank some cognac. "I trust your judgment."

"Not sure Kendrick does."

"She's caught between a high closure rate and the public's focus on solving the case. Media is adding pressure as well."

"You're familiar with all that."

"I am. But Kendrick knows you're a damn good detective, even if you two butt heads now and then. Cut her some slack. She'll support you."

"You sure of that?"

"Trust me."

"I do."

Rita leaned forward and kissed him gently on the lips.

He kissed her back.

Keeping her face close to his, she said, "I never kiss people I don't trust."

"Me neither."

The powdery scent of vanilla, amber and jasmine in her perfume reminded him of Jordan.

She saw the look of reflection on his face.

"Grief never ends, John, but it's a passage, not a place to stay."

Rita reached for the book of T.S. Eliot's poems on the coffee table and opened to a page she'd bookmarked. "I think this is appropriate," she said, handing him the book in which she'd highlighted a passage:

Time present and time past

Are both perhaps present in time future
And time future contained in time past.

"The past is always with us, John," she said. "It's irreversible, no matter what we wish for."

Intuitively, he knew she was right. But finally coming to grips with Jordan's death was another matter.

Chapter 22

On Monday morning Santana and Cruz met with Ramsey County medical examiner Reiko Tanabe in her office. Because she often met with the victim's family to discuss autopsy results, she had gone out of her way to make her office warm and inviting. Whitewashed furniture and light gray carpet brightened the room. The lampshades over the brass lamps on the end tables flanking the print couch matched the dark green walls, as did the two cushioned chairs in front of her desk and the wicker basket that held a tall silk plant standing in one corner.

She sat in a high-back chair behind her desk and laptop computer. It was unusual to see her in a dark blue sport coat and button-down light blue shirt rather than a white lab coat. She wore no makeup or jewelry except for a thin gold wedding band.

With her youthful complexion, most people would have guessed that she was in her late twenties or early thirties. But the graduation dates on her bachelor's and medical degree from the University of Minnesota and her license from the American Board of Pathology hanging in frames on the wall behind her indicated she was actually in her forties.

Santana and Cruz sat in the two cushioned chairs.

Before entering Tanabe's office, Santana had filled Cruz in on Jadyn Hartley's condition.

"You wanted to see us about Tara Easton's manner of death," Santana said.

Tanabe nodded, adjusted her wire-frame glasses, and peered at the computer screen on the corner of her desk.

"Tara Easton had eaten pasta with chicken two hours prior to her death along with some red wine." Tanabe looked at Santana. "She'd also had sex with someone prior to her death."

Santana sat forward in his chair. "You have a DNA swab?"

The ME nodded. "Need to run it through CODIS. See if we can get a hit."

"Any indication the sex was forced?"

"Small fissure in her posterior fourchette. It's a thin tissue fold that stretches during sexual intercourse. Located at bottom of the vaginal entrance. It's the most common location of injury from rape."

"Could she have been injured during consensual sex?"

"Only about a ten percent chance of that. Usually occurs in a female with a history of dry or painful intercourse."

"Tara Easton was estranged from her husband," Cruz said, looking at Santana.

"We need a DNA sample from him."

"You think he killed his wife?"

"Like to make sure he didn't."

"Will he voluntarily give us a sample?"

"We'll get his DNA one way or another," Santana said.

"All we have to do is get him to admit he had sex with her the night of her death."

"From what Reiko is telling us, the sex wasn't consensual."

Tanabe looked at her computer screen before speaking again. "Toxicology tests showed that Tara Easton had high concentrations of THC in her blood and urine."

"Meaning?" Santana said.

"THC could've caused her to be high at the time of her death."

"Doesn't mean she killed herself."

"No, it doesn't."

"You said 'could've been high,' Reiko.'"

"The level of THC in the blood and the degree of impairment don't appear to be closely related. Unlike alcohol, someone can show little or no impairment at a THC level while someone else might show a greater degree of impairment. But it's not the THC I'm concerned about. It's the morphine."

Santana fixed his eyes on her. "Morphine?"

"Probably from heroin use."

"Maybe she ate poppy seeds," Cruz said.

Tanabe shook her head. "A false positive test wouldn't occur in hair analysis after eating poppy seed pastries. The opioid in poppy seeds doesn't stay in the bloodstream long enough or in high enough concentrations to be trapped inside hair follicles in measurable quantities."

"We found no indication of heroin use in her apartment," Santana said.

Tanabe explained that heroin has a short half-life and can't be detected in autopsy samples. But evidence of heroin use could be found by testing for six-acetylmorphine, which has its own short half-life that may not be detectable in postmortem samples. However, codeine is often present in heroin, and a ratio of morphine to codeine greater than one indicates heroin use.

"I also found a puncture wound on the right inner forearm," she said. "Couldn't see it without my head visor magnifying lens."

"Was that the only puncture you found?" Santana asked.

"It was."

"Maybe she took all the heroin she had," Cruz said.

Santana glanced at Cruz. "Then where's the syringe and other drug paraphernalia?"

"Would've made suicide easier and less painful," Tanabe said.

Santana turned his attention to her. "But you don't think it was suicide, do you? I thought you were leaning toward homicide."

"I was considering undetermined."

"What changed your mind?"

"Not what. Who."

"Let me guess. Kendrick."

She nodded.

"Why would she do that?" Cruz asked.

Tanabe shifted her gaze to him. "You'd have to ask her."

"I've got a good idea why," Santana said. He looked at Tanabe again. "What's your gut feeling, Reiko?"

She sat back in her chair, thinking. "It's a tough call. Could go either way."

"Then why not leave it as undetermined?"

"You know why."

"Yeah," Santana said. "I do."

*   *   *

Art Tatum stood waiting near Santana's cubicle in the Homicide and Robbery Unit when Santana and Cruz returned.

"Need to see you for a moment, John," Tatum said.

"Go ahead."

Tatum glanced at Cruz. "Alone."

"Okay."

They walked to a vacant interview room. Santana closed the door behind him as Tatum leaned against the far wall with his arms crossed.

"Why you shutting me out?" Tatum said.

"It's not intentional."

"The hell it isn't. I feel like a dog trailing behind the pack."

"I'm just trying to bring you up to speed."

"Yeah. I've read the murder book. I get what this is all about."

"Then you're ahead of me. Because I'm still trying to figure it out."

Tatum paused for a time, his eyes focused on Santana. "Does this have something to do with my recent suspension?"

"You were sloppy, Art."

"I made a mistake. You never made one?"

"Not because of carelessness."

Tatum blew out a breath and shook his head. "I've been doing this job for fifteen years. No one ever accused me of being careless."

"Till now," Santana said.

"You gonna cut me in on the action or not?"

"This wasn't my call, Art."

"I get that. But here I am. Give me something to do."

"Or?"

"Or I go to Kendrick and let her straighten this out. And Gamboni won't protect you."

"What the hell does that mean?"

"You know damn well what it means. So does everyone in the department. Gamboni is watching your six."

Santana could feel the heat of anger building. He took a deep breath and let it out slowly, trying to control his temper. "Look, Art, despite what you and others might believe, no one is protecting me. I go my own way, as always."

Tatum gave a reluctant nod. "I know that. You get yourself in hot water despite the support."

"I do, don't I."

"Wouldn't know you if you didn't."

Santana thought about his options, none of them good ones. "All right. Go see Blaine Beckham."

"The guy who owns the gun shop."

"Right. Get his reaction to the attempted murder of his pal, Angel Duran. He might be more open to talking after Tara Easton's funeral."

Santana took out his iPhone and showed Tatum the photo of Beckham, Easton, Duran, Khalil, and the unknown Afghani from the ghost unit. "I'll air drop this photo to you. Ask Beckham about the guy in the tiger striped uniform again. See if he's willing to cooperate."

"You think this Afghani guy killed Easton and tried to kill Duran?"

"I'd like to know who and where he is."

"You got it, John. And thanks. You won't regret it."

Santana hoped not.

*   *   *

Later that morning, Santana and Cruz were seated in two chairs in front of Janet Kendrick's desk. The formal ambiance couldn't have been more different than Reiko Tanabe's office.

"You've spoken to the ME," Kendrick said.

"We have."

Seated behind her neat desk, her hands clasped together on the desktop, Kendrick's eyes shifted from Santana to Cruz and then back to Santana again.

"Then it's time to move on. How's the bones case coming?"

"I believe the bones are related to Tara Easton's death," Santana said.

Kendrick picked up a manila file folder. "This is the ME's autopsy report. I was under the impression that she determined Tara Easton's death was a suicide."

Santana shook his head. "I don't think so."

"Why not?"

"Whether she killed herself or was murdered, Tara Easton's death has something to do with the bones. I know it."

"Perhaps you could share your evidence?"

"We're working on it."

Cruz shifted uncomfortably in his chair.

Kendrick gave a little shake of her head. "It's possible we're dealing with a serial killer who is purposely causing chaos during the Winter Carnival. Citizens are fearful. It's costing the city money and resources we need. The bones are your focus now, Detectives. Don't get distracted."

Santana knew it was futile to argue. Kendrick was getting heavy pressure from above to solve the bones case. He figured if his assumptions were correct, solving it would also lead to a satisfactory explanation for Tara Easton's death. Besides, he had a favor to ask of Kendrick. Now wasn't the time to upset her.

"We'll focus on the bones," he said.

Cruz met Santana's eyes for a second and then looked away in an attempt to hide his surprise at Santana's sudden capitulation.

"Good," Kendrick said. "Hit the streets and find this bastard."

Santana remained seated when Cruz stood.

"Is there something else, Detective?" she asked.

"There is." He looked at Cruz. "It won't take long."

Cruz gave a nod and left the office.

"So?" Kendrick said.

"You remember Ana Soriano."

"Of course. How's she doing?"

"She just completed her high school credits."

Kendrick smiled. "Good for her."

"And she turned eighteen."

"Your guardianship has ended."

"Yes. But I need a favor."

Kendrick raised her eyebrows. "Oh?"

"From the DEA."

"Good luck with that."

"That's where you can help."

"How?"

"Joel Ryker, the DEA agent who was shot and killed, was crooked. You buried that investigation as a courtesy to Special Agent in Charge Scott Weston. As I recall you saying, he's in your pocket. Weston owes you."

Kendrick leaned back and placed her hands on the armrests. "Where are you going with this?"

"Ana hasn't been able to contact her mother and sister in El Salvador for the past two weeks. Something might've happened to them. Ana wants to go back and search for them. I don't want that to happen."

"What's this got to do with the DEA and Weston?"

"The DEA has agents in San Salvador. They could find out if something has happened to Ana's mother and sister."

"You can't be serious."

"Oh, yes, I am. She's like a daughter to me. I'm not letting that young woman return to El Salvador. That's a death sentence. I'll do anything to prevent it."

"You can't expect me to ask Weston to use his limited resources searching for a mother and her child in San Salvador."

"You forget. We kept the DEA out of the news when their agent went rogue, killed two people, and stole a half million dollars in drug money. That's your bargaining chip."

"And it's the only one I have. I can't waste it on something like this."

Santana stood. "You could be saving two lives. That's worth something."

Chapter 23

"What was that all about?" Cruz asked after Santana left Kendrick's office and returned to his desk.

Santana sat down and told him about his request while saying nothing about the DEA agent and the case against Joel Ryker Kendrick had buried.

"Will Kendrick talk with Weston?"

"If she doesn't, I've got another angle."

Cruz looked at him for a time without speaking.

"Something else on your mind?" Santana said.

Cruz waited a moment before responding, his eyes looking inward, as if he were rehearsing his reply. "How come you didn't talk with Kendrick about the morphine in Tara Easton's system?"

"Because I'm not sure if she injected it herself."

"Isn't that the point? Seems Easton would've resisted if someone else injected it."

"Unless she was unconscious."

"But Tanabe found no evidence of a struggle or assault."

"Other ways of rendering someone unconscious," Santana said.

"Like a sleeper hold?"

"If you've been trained how to use it."

Cruz thought for a moment. "Army has a combative course at Fort Benning that trains special operatives in hand-to-hand techniques based on Brazilian Jiu-Jitsu. Started back in ninety-five, I believe, with the second Ranger Battalion."

"Chokeholds part of the course?"

"Yeah. The rear naked chokehold, the cross-collar choke, and sleeve choke. Lots of close-quarter, hand-to-hand combat training."

"Beckham would've taken the training."

"Definitely. I remember after 9/11, vets returning from Afghanistan helped refine the training by learning what worked or didn't work in real combat."

"Someone familiar with this training could render Tara Easton momentarily unconscious before injecting heroin into her."

"But why?"

"Make sure she doesn't resist when her throat was cut and when he was raping her. And maybe the ME doesn't find traces when the autopsy is done."

"That's why we found no syringe or heroin in Easton's apartment," Cruz said.

"Fits with my scenario."

"Tanabe is good."

"She is. But maybe we've been looking in the wrong place. Maybe this isn't just about money. Maybe it's about heroin."

"Because Tara Easton had it in her system?"

"And because Angel Duran's brother is mixed up with Narcos."

Santana took out his department cell phone.

"Who are you calling?"

"CRI I know," Santana said, using the familiar cop acronym for a confidential reliable informant.

When Santana finished the call, his eyes shifted from Cruz to a manila envelope on his desk.

"You've got mail," Cruz said.

Santana slipped on a pair of latex gloves, opened the envelope, and pulled out a half-sheet of paper on which was typed:

Together they will sleep
Where their beds are dark and deep,
Forgetting the evil they have done
And the lives they have taken with a gun

His history is written in stone
As are all who die alone,
Murdered by an explosive blast,
We still remember his gangster past

Sightless and soundless he lies
As the world now passes him by,
On a bluff overlooking the city
For him there will never be pity.

Cruz stood behind Santana, reading the poem over Santana's shoulder. When he sat down in his chair he said, "What do you make of it?"

"What beds are dark and deep?"

"Graves?"

"On a bluff overlooking the city."

Cruz shrugged. "Don't know the city well enough."

"I do," Santana said. "Cemetery on a bluff would be Calvary." He stood and used his iPhone to snap a photo of the poem.

"What about the guy who died in an explosive blast?" Cruz asked.

"We'll drop the poem at the lab and then talk with Grainger at the *Pioneer Press*. See if he can help us."

*   *   *

They located Pat Grainger at Frank's Levee Tavern, on the second floor of the Cossetta's complex on W. 7th Street in downtown St. Paul. The pub was named in honor of Frank Cossetta, the past patriarch of the Italian eatery, and "The Levee," which was once considered St. Paul's Little Italy.

Grainger was eating a porchetta sandwich and drinking a beer in a chilled glass at one of the tables across from the hand-carved bar that ran the length of the dark paneled room.

"You called about more clues?" Grainger said, wiping his mouth with a napkin.

Santana showed Grainger the photo of the poem he had taken with his iPhone.

"We think Calvary is the cemetery. We're interested in the specific grave."

Grainger put on a pair of reading glasses and looked at the poem, nodding as he read.

"Well, I believe the gangster the poem refers to is 'Dapper Dan' Hogan, the Irish Godfather, a mob boss during the height of St. Paul's organized crime in the city. Owned the Green Lantern Saloon on Wabasha. Place catered to crooks, bootleggers, and shady characters associated with organized crime. Operated as a speakeasy and an illegal gambling casino, as well as a front for laundering stolen property and money."

"Wasn't that when the city let gangsters R&R here as long as they didn't cause trouble?" Cruz said.

"You got it." He took a big bite of his sandwich and washed it down with a slug of beer.

"Place was known as 'Crooks' Haven' at the time," he said, chewing as he spoke. "Chief of Police John O'Connor worked out a layover agreement. Dillinger and his girlfriend, Evelyn Frechette, stayed here. Capone, Bonnie and Clyde, Ma Barker, and Alvin Karpis all spent time here. Hogan acted as a liaison between the police and the crooks, collecting bribes and delivering the money to the police. Hell of a time it was."

"What about the 'explosive blast' in the poem?" Santana asked.

Grainger thought for a moment while he picked at a piece of food caught in his teeth. "If my memory serves me, someone planted a bomb under the floorboards of Dan Hogan's car in December of nineteen twenty-eight. Doctors amputated a leg, but he died anyway."

"And Hogan is buried in Calvary Cemetery," Santana said.

Grainger had his notebook out and was taking notes. "Yeah. Not sure where. But you can check for his plot."

Grainger stood and grabbed his overcoat off the back of the chair.

"Where you going?" Santana asked.

"To the cemetery."

"Not with us."

"Figured I wouldn't," Grainger said. "But I won't be far behind."

* * *

Calvary Cemetery is spread across a 100-acre bluff along Front Avenue in St. Paul. Known for its unusual monument styles and architectural features, including angels of all sizes, a number of the Archdiocese's early bishops and archbishops, including Cretin, Dowling, Grace, and Ireland, are all buried at Calvary.

A simple gravestone labeled HOGAN in section 59, Block 6, Lot A, marked Daniel Hogan's resting place.

Slate gray clouds veiled the sun. Snow around the marker had been shoveled clean as Santana and Cruz cautiously approached. Behind him, Santana could hear Pat Grainger breathing hard as he trudged through the knee-deep snow to catch up.

Six pairs of rib cage bones were arranged in front of the headstone.

"Jesus," Grainger said in a heavy breath as he lumbered up behind them.

"Stay back," Santana said.

His eyes searched for recent footprints in the snow, where forensics could take impressions, but snowfall and melting had obliterated any footprints besides their own.

"Figure the bones are from the same body?" Cruz asked.

"We'll find out. Get forensics on the phone. And we'll need additional officers out here for a grid search."

An hour later, as darkness began to settle, three high-intensity LED tripod floods lit the scene around the Hogan headstone. Small clouds of condensation fogged the air as patrol officers searched the grounds around the site in a grid pattern. Forensics took photos, and Kim Solace arrived to supervise the bone collection.

Santana wasn't confident any evidence beyond the rib cage bones would be found, given the lack of trace evidence at the previous crime scenes. And while every crime scene had its unique features, outdoor scenes challenged forensics because they had to work against the clock, as the elements changed the nature of evidence over time.

"How long you figure the clues will keep appearing?" Cruz asked.

"Two hundred six bones in the human body," Santana said.

Trying to get warm, they sat side-by-side in the front seat of the department ride. Santana kept the engine running as they finished cups of hot chocolate from his thermos. Routine SPPD radio chatter on the tactical frequencies provided familiar background music.

"He'll keep this up," Cruz said.

"Unless we catch him."

"What's our next move?"

Santana thought for a moment. "Are Afghan refugees being fingerprinted?"

"Sure. Probably going through a biometric scan. Why?"

Santana ignored the question. "How do you know?"

"Sometimes, when we went into villages," Cruz said, "we'd have someone from the Special Operations Command with us. They came along to enroll Afghanis into a biometric data system using this device called a HIIDE, military speak for Handheld Interagency Identity Detection Equipment, about twelve inches by six inches wide."

Cruz spread his hands to indicate the size. "The device would scan their fingerprints, their retina, and take a picture of them. Helped us identify bomb-makers and to confirm the identities of contractors and locals working with us. Military hoped to enroll eighty percent of the population, or about twenty-five million people, in the system, but I doubt they came close."

"Any HIIDE devices fall into Taliban hands?"

"Be surprised if they didn't. But data from HIIDE devices is stored in the Pentagon's Automated Biometrics Identification System, not in Afghanistan. We never shared data with Afghan partners. Helped keep corrupt officials from tipping off the Taliban. Pentagon calls PABIS a 'system of systems' because of its complexity. So even if the Taliban got hold of a HIIDE device, they probably wouldn't have the technical know-how to exploit it. Taliban likely sources more information off social media."

"But we don't know that for sure."

"Nothing is for sure," Cruz said. "Taliban are still hunting for people who collaborated with us."

"You're saying the biometric data collected by both the US military and the Afghan government could pose a risk to those facing reprisals."

Cruz nodded. "Where you going with this?"

"Not sure at the moment," he said, wondering if Wade Crawford had access to information.

They both startled when Santana's department cell phone rang. It was the watch commander. He listened and then clicked off.

"Shooting at Beckham's gun shop," he said.

Cruz's eyes grew wide with shock and excitement. "Why didn't we hear it on the radio through dispatch?"

Santana shoved the Taurus in gear and stomped on the gas pedal. "Want to keep media out of it."

"Tatum!" Cruz said.

Santana nodded and hoped he hadn't made a mistake sending Tatum to the gun shop.

Chapter 24

As they neared the Combat Zone gun shop, Santana could see the flashing blue and yellow lights of the patrol cars and the bright strobes of the media cameras creating a false dawn against the surrounding darkness. A Fed Ex truck had angle parked at the curb, one door down from the gun shop. Two uniforms were stringing yellow crime scene tape from one stanchion to another across the front of the building. A third held a clipboard containing the Crime Scene Attendance Log.

Santana parked in the lot and removed a Bootie Box from the trunk.

As he approached the building, Santana recognized the older of two uniforms whose nametag ID'd him as Wilson. "You first on the scene?"

Wilson nodded. "Two vics. I'd met Tatum and the owner, Blaine Beckham, before. Bought a couple of guns from him in the past."

"Who discovered the bodies?"

"Fed Ex driver. Sitting in the back of my squad. Figured detectives would want to talk to him."

Santana turned to Cruz. "Get a statement from the Fed Ex driver. Then find out where Beckham's parents live. We'll need to do a death notification. Get Beckham's address as well."

"Will do," Cruz said.

With an officer down, Santana knew the brass would soon be converging on the scene, along with forensics and the ME. He wanted to get a look at everything before they arrived.

He signed the attendance log and slipped under the yellow tape.

Before entering the gun shop, Santana set the Bootie Box by the entrance. It worked by placing a sheet of adhesive plastic film on the bottom of a shoe or boot to avoid tracking dirt and debris into a crime scene. Santana simply had to step, pull, and tear. No need to bend over and struggle to apply like traditional shoe covers. Santana stepped into the box and then gloved up.

Art Tatum lay on his back, a foot to the left of the counter, his Glock 17 close to his right hand, his feet facing toward the counter. A 9mm shell casing lay on the floor to the right and rear of the gun.

Santana felt the heat of anger and frustration. He'd been reluctant to give Tatum a separate assignment but had relented against his better judgment. Now Tatum lay dead on the floor, and Santana felt responsible for his death. His rational side argued that he couldn't have predicted or even anticipated this outcome. Still, doubts about his decision lingered like the stench of death. To reach any sense of closure, he needed to understand exactly how and why Tatum had died. Anything less, and he'd never quell the heavy burden of guilt.

In his experience, shell casings from his Glock 17 typically ejected to the right and back. But the single greatest influence on where spent shell casings landed when ejected from a semiautomatic handgun depended more on how the shooter physically manipulated the gun.

Santana squatted beside the body.

Tatum's eyes were closed, but his stretched mouth indicated apprehension or fear.

Santana could see an entry wound through Tatum's shirt into his chest. He knew that close-range wounds inside of three feet had a small central entry wound, an abrasion collar, and charring around the wound from hot gases. Shots often led to tattooing around the entry point too. The spread depended on how close the muzzle was. Little blood had been spilled, indicating the bullet had stopped the heart almost immediately.

Santana's initial reading suggested Tatum had been shot from a distance of more than three feet.

He stood and observed Blaine Beckham, sitting with his back to the wall behind the counter, his mouth open wide, his eyes staring blankly at the ceiling, a bullet hole in his black T-shirt near the heart. A shell casing lay on the floor in front of the counter. A Ruger LC9 rested beside Beckham's right hand. Santana wondered if it was the same gun Beckham was cleaning the day he and Cruz first interviewed him.

Initial indications suggested the two men had shot each other. But Santana went behind the counter and squatted to look more closely at Beckham's body.

Drops of blood blotted Beckham's parted lips, cheek, and chin, indicating he'd coughed it up as he died. The bullet entry point had likely ripped through Beckham's chest, causing massive damage to the heart and lungs. He'd collapsed on the spot where he'd been standing when shot. His wide-open eyes and open jaw suggested the gunshot had surprised him.

Both wounds were near or directly into the heart, indicating the men had gotten off excellent shots, despite the pressure of facing a loaded gun. Santana knew Tatum to be a good shot. Given his military training, Beckham likely was as well.

Santana wondered what had triggered the confrontation. He'd asked Tatum, an experienced detective, to observe Beckham's reaction to the attempted murder of his pal, Angel Duran. He figured Beckham might be more open to talking after Tara Easton's funeral. He'd also told Tatum to ask Beckham once more about the unidentified, bearded Afghani wearing the tiger-striped uniform in the photo found in Easton's bedroom.

Neither of these questions should have caused a violent confrontation between the two men. Beckham could have easily deflected or denied knowing the Afghani or anything about the attempt on Duran's life.

Santana peered at the security camera mounted high on the wall behind the counter. Seeing no cord, he figured Beckham had installed a wireless system he could operate using his iPhone.

Digital video recorders were an essential part of CCTV security systems. Every time a CCTV security camera captured something of interest, a recorder archived the footage, allowing viewing after the fact.

Santana stood and entered Beckham's open office door to the right of the counter.

The 10' x 10' room contained a small metal desk, file cabinet, a desk chair and a canvas director's chair. A framed ATF gun license hung on the wall just above the desk. A poster hanging above the license depicted an American flag on a black background with two black AR-15's in the foreground. The lettering underneath the flag read:

BLACK
GUNS
MATTER

Photos of Blaine Beckham and his fellow soldiers in their combat uniforms hung on the other three office walls.

Looking at each of the faces under the helmets, Santana recognized Angel Duran in two of the photos, but no one else.

A DVR and a black-and-white TV monitor took up half of the desktop. Invoices and manila file folders covered the remaining space.

CCTV security cameras could record everything they captured. But archiving everything quickly filled up internal storage space and could be costly. For this reason, most retailers programmed their security cameras to only record footage during a particular time of day, or when movement was detected. Doing so saved them the hassle of constantly buying more storage space to archive the constant stream of footage.

Forensics would add the computer and DVR to the Evidence Log and look at the computer drive and footage in the lab. If a third party had shot Beckham and Tatum, it should be archived.

When Santana walked out of Beckham's office, he saw Tony Novak and his forensic crew setting up to process the crime scene. Squatting beside Art Tatum, Reiko Tanabe, the ME, placed breathable preservation bags over Tatum's hands to prevent any loss of gunshot residue and secured the bags with the fitted drawstring. The bags, marked LEFT and RIGHT, were much more effective than the old method of using a paper bag secured with tape.

Santana knew that gunshot residue could stay from four to eight hours on a live and mobile individual's hands if steps were taken to preserve this evidence, such as bagging the hands. Washing or wiping the hands on anything, even putting them in and pulling them out of pockets, could transfer GSR off the hands. It could remain for longer periods of time on deceased hands and clothing if precautions, like bagging, were taken. But current technology couldn't link GSR with a particular firearm or ammunition since nearly all ammunition, regardless of type or manufacturer, contained the same basic materials.

Later, in the autopsy suite, Tanabe would collect primer GSR with adhesive lifters, also called dabs, or stubs, from Tatum's hands and clothes. The adhesive contained carbon that colored the lifters black in order to conduct electrons in the scanning electron microscope, or SEM.

Tanabe peered up at Santana. "I'll test the vic behind the counter in a minute."

"We'll need a sample of Beckham's DNA, Reiko. See if he's the one who had sex with Tara Easton prior to her death."

Gabriel Cruz came in the door. "Gamboni and Kendrick are in the MCCV in the parking lot," he said, referring to the Mobile Command and Communications Vehicle. "They want to see you."

"What did the Fed Ex driver have to say?"

"Just dropping off a delivery. Entered the shop and saw the bodies. Stepped out and called nine-one-one."

"Didn't touch anything?"

Cruz shook his head. "Didn't see anyone leaving. Said he watched the shop till patrol arrived. Never saw anyone come out."

"You find an address for Beckham and his parents?"

"Same place in St. Paul," Cruz said, holding up his notebook as if offering proof.

"Beckham lived with his parents?"

"Mother lives with him. Name is Renee."

"No father?"

"Not that I could find."

"Make sure we get his cell phone." Santana glanced at his watch. "Then get a search warrant for Beckham's house. We'll go there once I'm finished with the brass."

Santana exited the gun shop and buttoned up his overcoat.

Yellow crime scene tape had been stretched across the parking lot, south of the MCCV, to hold the gathering media at bay. Despite the SPPD's efforts to keep the shooting under wraps, the media had gotten wind of it, and their vans and reporters were arriving as Santana entered the Mobile Command and Communications Vehicle.

Rita Gamboni, Janet Kendrick, and Gina Luttrell, the district supervisor, sat in three of the four chairs on one side of the six-foot conference table. All three of them wore Blauer-style jackets.

Nearer the front of the vehicle, Santana could see two tactical dispatchers seated in front of their computers connected to the communications center at the LEC. Three large video screens were attached to the walls on each side of the vehicle.

Gamboni gestured at Santana to take a seat in one of the four vacant chairs on the opposite side of the table.

"How you feeling?" Gamboni asked.

Responsible was the word that came to mind. Then again, Janet Kendrick had stuck Tatum with him and Cruz over Santana's objections. But blame got him nowhere. Given his years of experience, Tatum should have been more cautious, though the scene bothered Santana. Something didn't seem right.

"I'll be okay."

"You'll need to attend a Critical Incident Stress Debriefing," Kendrick said.

The SPPD's Line-of-Duty Death Policy & Protocol Manual held that police witnesses and other officers and police employees, both sworn and civilian, who may have been emotionally affected by the serious injury or death of another officer had to attend a Critical Incident Stress Debriefing conducted by SPPD Employee Assistance Program staff members or other trained mental health professionals. Having been involved in shootings before, Santana was familiar with the EAP and also with Karen Wong, the psychologist attached to the department.

"I believe that's unnecessary," he said.

"But Tatum was your partner."

Santana gave Kendrick his best cop stare, hoping that she'd receive his message loud and clear.

She leaned back in her chair, no doubt recalling that she'd forced Santana to take him.

"How did it go down?" Gamboni asked, abruptly changing the subject.

"Appears they shot each other."

"Appears?"

"Each of them has a wound in or near the heart."

"One wound?"

"That's right."

"Well, this is a major clusterfuck," Luttrell said. "Wait till the media gets ahold of this."

"Shouldn't be an issue," Kendrick said. "Art Tatum died defending himself."

Santana knew Gamboni was in his corner and had wanted him to speak his mind in front of Kendrick and Luttrell. If Kendrick forced him to look in another direction—or suggested a vet possibly suffering from PTSD had killed Tatum—it would end the investigation and clear the case. But if it turned out Santana was right, and the deaths involved cash or drugs from Afghanistan, Kendrick and Luttrell couldn't deny ever hearing Santana's theory. Of course, he thought, if they were right and he was wrong, then . . .

"We don't know that yet," Santana said.

Kendrick glared at him. "Are you suggesting Tatum shot Beckham first?"

Santana shook his head. "In all my years in homicide, I've never seen two perfect shots through the heart, especially in a shootout. And since they died quickly, the shots had to be nearly simultaneous."

"How else would you explain it?"

"What if a third person killed both of them?"

Kendrick let out a frustrated breath. "What are you talking about, Detective?"

"Suppose a guy walks into the gun shop while Tatum and Beckham are talking. They figure it's a customer. Guy walks around and checks the range downstairs. Makes sure no one else is in the shop. When he comes back upstairs, Tatum is still there. So he gets the drop on both of them. He pats down Tatum and gets his Glock. Uses it to kill Beckham and then Beckham's Ruger to kill Tatum. Happens fast. The perp is a professional and knows how to handle guns and how to shoot."

"I don't believe that scenario for a minute," Kendrick said.

"Then tell me what prompted Tatum and Beckham to shoot each other."

"What was Tatum doing at the gun shop?" Gamboni asked before Kendrick could answer.

Santana told her.

"You sent him there?" Kendrick said. "Alone?"

"No reason to believe he was in any danger."

"You'd spoken to Beckham before," Gamboni said.

"Cruz and I had."

"Novak will do GSR testing," Kendrick said. "See if they each fired a shot. And why would a third party want to kill Tatum and Beckham? Was there evidence of a robbery?"

"No," Santana said. "But we have the DVR from the security camera. That should show us something."

"Let's go back to this third party, John . . . Detective Santana," Gamboni said, quickly correcting herself.

Santana caught Luttrell's slight smile. Kendrick acted as if she hadn't heard it.

Gamboni said, "Why do you think there might be a third party involved, Detective?"

"Tara Easton, Blaine Beckham, and Angel Duran all knew each other in Afghanistan. Easton and Beckham are dead. Someone tried to kill Duran. I believe the murders and attempted murder are connected."

"Do you have a suspect?"

Santana scrolled through the photo app on his cell phone till he found the photo he'd taken in Tara Easton's bedroom. Then he handed the phone to Gamboni. She looked at it for a short time and then handed it to Kendrick, who then passed it on to Luttrell.

Santana said, "The people with Tara Easton in that photo taken at a base in Kandahar, Afghanistan, are Blaine Beckham, Angel Duran, Taimur Khalil, and an unidentified Afghani from their special forces. I believe he may be responsible for the deaths of Easton and Beckham, and the near death of Angel Duran. Taimur Khalil has been missing for six months and is likely dead as well."

"Have you been able to locate the suspect?" Luttrell asked, handing the phone back to him.

Santana shook his head.

"What makes you believe this suspect is here in the country?" Kendrick asked.

"Wade Crawford, a retired Special Inspector General for Afghanistan Reconstruction, told me as much."

"And you trust Crawford?"

"Not entirely."

"Then why would you believe him?"

"Because Crawford has as much interest in finding the truth as we do."

Kendrick smiled without any humor. "The ME has ruled Easton's death a suicide."

Because of the pressure you're exerting, Santana thought.

"The chief is on his way here," Kendrick said. "He'll want a debriefing."

"Tell him what I just told you."

"Better to hear it from you."

"I need to keep moving. If I'm right, the shooter is still out there. And Duran is still alive."

Gamboni leaned forward. "What's your next move?"

"We need to talk to Beckham's mother, let her know about her son's death. Someone needs to give the news to Tatum's wife."

"We'll send a notification officer to Tatum's house and make sure his name isn't released to the press till his wife has been notified," Gamboni said. "You concentrate on Beckham."

"The chief will need to assign a family liaison officer, a department liaison officer, and a benefits coordinator," Luttrell said.

Gamboni nodded and looked at Kendrick. "I want the news media handled by Mike Murphy, the public information officer. If the family decides to accept an interview, Murphy should screen the questions presented to the family. I don't want to jeopardize any subsequent legal proceedings."

"I'll take care of it," Kendrick said.

"I'll need a search warrant for Beckham's house," Santana said.

"Of course," Kendrick said, glancing at Gamboni. "You have my full backing."

Chapter 25

The ranch-style home Blaine Beckham had lived in sat at the end of a cul-de-sac that backed up to the woods near Lake Phalen in St. Paul. Lights gleamed in the windows. Snow covering the ground glistened in the reflective light.

Gabriel Cruz had typed up an affidavit and had emailed it with an application for a search warrant to an after-hours judge, who'd signed it. A search warrant could be served in Minnesota only between the hours of 7:00 a.m. and 8:00 p.m. unless a nighttime search outside those hours was authorized. Cruz had assured the judge that they'd meet the timeline.

As the two detectives exited their unmarked, Santana's ears felt the sting of the 8° temperature. The quarter moon looked like a fragment of ice against the black stare of the endless dead sky. His breath condensed in the air as he and Cruz made their way along the partly shoveled sidewalk. He caught the smoky scent of logs burning in a neighborhood fireplace.

A wall sconce above the front door lit the entrance. Standing on the steps, Santana could hear a siren originating from a television program as he pressed the doorbell.

Someone muted the sound and a woman's voice yelled, "Who is it?"

"St. Paul Police Department," Santana said.

"Yeah, sure it is. Go away!"

Santana looked at Cruz, who shrugged his shoulders. Figuring the woman must be Beckham's mother, Santana took a chance.

"I'm Detective John Santana. My partner is Detective Gabriel Cruz. It's about your son, Blaine."

Silence.

Santana waited a few more seconds before he said, "Ms. Beckham?"

"I'm coming."

When the latch clicked and the door swung open, Santana saw the gun in the tall woman's hand, pointed in their direction.

"Gun!" Santana yelled as he jumped quickly to the side and away from the line of fire. He pressed his back against the cold siding and drew his Glock. Cruz did the same.

"Show me your badges," the woman said.

Santana and Cruz pulled them out of their coat pockets and, at arm's length, held them open in front of the screen door.

"Put the gun away, ma'am," Santana said.

She hesitated a moment before speaking again. "Okay. You're cops. Has something happened to Blaine?"

"Cold out here," Santana said. "How 'bout we talk inside?"

She thought about it for a few beats and then said, "Come in."

"As soon as you put away the gun."

"All right."

Santana peeked through the corner of the screen and saw the woman placing the gun in an end table drawer. Nodding at Cruz, they holstered their Glocks and stepped inside.

"Wipe your feet," she said, her hands planted on her shapely hips. "And close the damn door."

Santana shut the door behind him.

"You could've gotten shot," he said.

"So could you, banging on someone's door at night. Sit," she said, nodding toward the leather couch in the living room.

Both men took off their overcoats and laid them over the back of the couch.

Knotty pine wood paneling covered the living room walls, giving the room a rustic, cabin-like feel.

As Santana sat down he noted the large framed photo over the fireplace of Blaine Beckham, along with his mother, squatting beside a dead buck with their .30-06 rifles.

Then he turned his attention to Renee Beckham.

Her thick mane of midnight hair hung loose on her shoulders. She had high cheekbones and smooth light brown skin, suggesting she might have Native American blood. He recalled that Blaine Beckham had grown up in Walker, Minnesota, which was on the shores of Leech Lake and near a large Ojibwa reservation.

She sat in a soft cushioned chair across from the detectives and used a remote to turn off the television. Then she picked up the cigarette burning in the ashtray on the table beside her and took a long puff. Her dark brown eyes never left Santana's as smoke leaked out her nostrils. A light blue cable knit sweater, black leggings, and gray, knee-high mukluks added a youthful look to her appearance. Santana made her for mid-forties.

"Tell me," she said.

"Your son, Blaine, was killed in a shooting at his gun shop. We're very sorry."

Her eyes glistened as she took another long drag on her cigarette and blew the smoke out slowly.

"Who did it?"

Santana couldn't sugarcoat what looked to be obvious, though he had his doubts. And the media would be all over the television and newspapers with their take on the story.

"It looks like he died in a shootout with a detective from our department. They both were killed."

She crushed out her cigarette in the ashtray and shook her head. "No way Blaine killed a police officer. He had too much respect for the law."

Santana had doubts about that observation as well but held his tongue.

"We're still investigating."

"You damn well better."

She stood and walked slowly to the small knotty pine bar with two matching stools sitting to the right of the fireplace. She went behind it, took a cocktail glass and half-empty bottle of Maker's Mark off a lower shelf, and poured herself a stiff drink.

"Don't suppose you two would like one?"

Cruz looked at Santana.

"No, thank you," Santana said.

She downed the drink in one swallow and poured another, carrying the drink with her as she returned to her chair.

Santana waited till she settled before asking the next question. "Is there a Mr. Beckham?"

"Once was," she said.

"Do you know where he is now?"

"Tim died of lung cancer years ago. Blaine took it hard."

"Any other children?"

She shook her head.

"Did Blaine ever get in trouble as a child?"

"What child didn't?"

"I mean serious trouble."

"Oh, no. Just small stuff."

"Like what?"

"Kid's stuff. Pranks. Blaine loved fishing and hunting. More of a loner."

"Did he always want to join the military?"

"His father was in the Army for four years. Never saw any combat. But Blaine idolized him."

"What did your husband do for a living?"

"He was a butcher."

Santana watched Cruz write the information in his notebook and circle it.

"I never wanted Blaine to enlist, but I couldn't stop him when he turned eighteen," she said.

"Have you lived with your son for some time?"

"Moved in three months ago. Was planning on getting my own apartment, but Blaine insisted I wait."

"Know why?"

"Said he had some money coming. Would help me pay for my place."

"He ever mention where the money was coming from?"

"I guess from his business or his military service."

"Are you working?"

"I bartended and waitressed back in Walker before I sold the house. Haven't applied for anything here."

She finished off her second drink, set the glass on the table beside her, and lit another cigarette.

"We're aware of your son's military background and training."

"Lot of good that did my boy, huh?"

"Not sure I understand," Santana said.

"After fighting in a war, he comes home and is shot dead in his own gun shop. And by a cop." Holding the cigarette between her index and middle finger, she leaned forward and said, "What's the cop's name?"

"Art Tatum. He was a detective and experienced officer."

"Doesn't make sense. Why would Blaine shoot him? And why would the detective shoot my son?"

Santana didn't understand it either. But he couldn't respond with that answer.

"It's why we're still investigating."

She sat back in the chair, her eyes drifting from Santana to Cruz and then back again. "There's something you're not telling me."

"I'm telling you what we found."

"But not what you know."

"I didn't say that."

"You don't have to."

She took a long drag on her cigarette and exhaled a small cloud of smoke, her eyes never leaving Santana's.

He removed a copy of the search warrant from his sport coat pocket and handed it to her.

"What's this?"

"Search warrant."

"What for?"

"Did Blaine ever talk with you about his experiences in Afghanistan?" he asked, changing the subject.

She shook her head. "He was always pretty tight-lipped about that. Why?"

"No reason."

"Like hell," she said with a sarcastic laugh. She iced Cruz with a glare. "What're you two looking for?"

"The reason why your son is dead," Cruz said.

She nodded as if convincing herself. "All right. Go ahead and look."

"That's your copy of the search warrant," Cruz said. "We'll leave a receipt if we take anything."

"You don't take anything 'less I see it first."

Santana checked Beckham's bathroom and found nothing of evidentiary value.

When he entered the bedroom, Cruz stepped out of a walk-in closet and said, "Look at this."

He held a Twins cap in his hand.

"On the apartment security video where Tara Easton lived, we saw a man wearing a Twins cap," Cruz continued.

"Lots of Twins caps around. We'll need to collect the computer and printer on the desk. See if forensics can get a match with the letters sent to the LEC."

Santana knew that any smartphone is constantly communicating with cell phone towers in order to find the strongest signal. But the tower that communicates with the cell phone has a limited range. If records showed that Beckham's cell phone was communicating with a specific cell phone tower, then Santana would know that the cell phone was in the geographical limits of the tower. That information could place Beckham near the location of Tara Easton's apartment on the night of her murder.

While searching the drawers in the small desk in the bedroom, Cruz found an AT&T cell phone bill and a journal. He paged through the journal and then handed it to Santana.

Beckham had cut out clues and articles about the medallion hunt.

"Could've sent you the anonymous letters," Cruz said.

"Possibly. Forensics needs to take a look at his hard drive and online chatter."

"Could be responsible for the bones, too."

"Let's see what else we find."

When they found nothing more in the bedroom, they went to the door that led down to the basement.

"Nothing to see down there," Renee Beckham said.

Santana met her gaze. "Then you won't mind if we look."

He opened the door, flicked on the light switch on the wall to his right, and descended the stairs to the unfinished basement. Cruz followed close behind.

A large furnace took up half the basement to the right of the stairs.

Mounted white skulls of antlered deer, antelope, and elk hung on the wall to Santana's left. A tall, red oak octagonal gun display cabinet with LED lighting and glass etching stood in the far corner. Inside the cabinet Santana identified an AR-15, .30-06, 12-gauge pump shotgun, and six handguns.

"Looks like Beckham was ready for the apocalypse," Cruz said as he walked to the gun case and then let out a low whistle.

"What's up?"

"Beckham owns a Daniel Defense DDM4 V7."

"High-end?"

"Sells for nineteen hundred, give or take. Double your low-end AR-15."

"List it on the evidence log. See if Crane can match the shell casings I found at Duran's cabin with the bullets fired from Beckham's AR."

To the right of the gun cabinet a long workbench sat against the wall below a small window. A pegboard underneath the window held scalpel blades, scissors, knives, and fleshing tools.

A large stainless-steel pot stood in front of the bench beside a 50-pound plastic container of potassium hydroxide, a propane tank, and attached hose. Heavy gloves, goggles, and a thick rubber butcher apron hung on a hook beside the workbench. A chainsaw lay on the floor beneath the apron.

As he walked toward the workbench, Santana could see a large stainless-steel pan and plastic containers of Oxiclean and gallon jugs of hydrogen peroxide.

The chemicals and paraphernalia triggered a painful memory of Jordan Parrish's death. Santana grabbed the edge of the workbench for support and took a few deep breaths to calm his racing heart.

"You okay, John?" Cruz said, coming up beside him.

"I'm fine."

"You don't look it. You feeling all right?"

"Give me a minute."

Santana took two more breaths and waited till his heartbeat slowed. He hadn't experienced such an extreme physical reaction since Jordan's death.

"Something about this place?" Cruz said.

"Reminds me of a similar place where someone close to me died."

"Yeah," Cruz said. "I heard."

Santana gestured toward the animal skulls on the wall. "Beckham used Oxiclean and hydrogen peroxide to boil the fat and flesh off the skulls. Had to be careful not to boil the skulls for too long, otherwise the bones start falling apart."

"Which could be why the bones found in the parks were so brittle after thawing."

"I think so. Boiling time varies depending on the animal and size of the skull. Turns very white after cooling and sitting in the hydrogen peroxide overnight. But this," he said, pointing to the propane tank, stainless steel pot, and plastic bag of sodium hydroxide, "is a bone bath for larger species."

"You're talking humans," Cruz said.

"I am. Potassium hydroxide is the same as lye. Mix it with water and heat it to boiling. Human tissue can be dissolved in a matter of hours. Leave it in for too long, you're left with nothing but sludge and some small, brittle bones. They're called bone shadows."

"I remember you telling that to Kim Solace."

"Yeah. Lye is used to remove clogs in drains, so the sludge can be poured into a bathtub and rinsed away."

Cruz looked at the chainsaw and then back at Santana. "You think Beckham cut up the body belonging to the bones we're finding?"

"His father was a butcher. Bet Beckham learned from him how and where to cut bones. He cleans and mounts animal skulls as a hobby. I'm betting we can find some DNA on the chainsaw. Get a match from the bones we've found."

"But we still don't know who the bones belong to."

"My guess is still Taimur Khalil."

Chapter 26

The following morning at his desk in the Homicide and Robbery Unit, Santana called the Cass County Sheriff's Office in Walker, Minnesota, where Blaine Beckham had grown up, identified himself, and asked to speak to the sheriff, Tom Blackburn.

A minute later Blackburn came on the line. "What can I do for you, Detective?"

He spoke in a gravelly voice that suggested he'd been around awhile. Probably seen things he wished he hadn't.

"I'm looking for information on a man named Blaine Beckham," Santana said. "He grew up in Walker."

"Sure did," Blackburn said. "Want to tell me what this is about?"

"Beckham was killed last evening in an apparent shootout with one of our detectives. Detective was killed, too."

"I'll be damned." Blackburn paused a moment, digesting the information. "You said *apparent*. I assume you used that word intentionally."

Like any good cop, Blackburn was a good listener.

"I did," Santana said. "Not sure yet if there was a third shooter involved."

"Well, I figured Beckham would more likely be killed overseas in the Army."

"Any childhood run-ins with the police?"

"Wouldn't say that. I was a patrol officer when Beckham was younger. I remember the kid had a temper. Probably got that from his old man. Always thought the kid, like his old man, was a little off."

"How so?"

"Got himself into a few fights when he was young. Won most of 'em, as I recall. Came home on leave one time and got into a barroom scuffle with three locals. Kicked their asses."

"You said he was 'a little off like his father.'"

"Hard to put a finger on it. Just the way the kid looked at you. Dead eyes. Like he was listening to you, but thought you were full of shit."

Santana recalled the first time he looked into Beckham's eyes.

"Any arrests?"

"Not when he was young. No one willing to press charges in the barroom fight."

"You mentioned Beckham's dad. I heard he passed away."

"Oh, yeah. Tim was a character. One of these survivalists you might've heard of. Loved to hunt and fish. Taught the kid how to fend for himself. Thought the world was about to end. Built a bomb shelter and fully stocked it. Heavy drinker who had a temper, especially when he had too much liquor. Tim died of lung cancer from heavy smoking in his forties. Maybe the loss of his father contributed to Blaine's temper."

"How about the mother?"

"Good looking woman," Blackburn said with a chuckle. "Found out a few years back Renee was a second cousin of mine, though you couldn't tell by looking at my face." He chuckled again. "She worked off and on in one of the bars in town. Moved out of here three months ago, I believe. Went to live with Blaine."

"You think Beckham was capable of shooting a cop?"

"Hell, I couldn't venture a guess. Father taught him respect for guns. But war can twist your mind and your soul."

Blackburn sounded like he spoke from experience.

"You never said what this shooting was all about, Detective."

"Might involve drugs and money."

"Lot of that goin' around."

"No matter where you live."

"Damn sure. But if Beckham didn't do it, I'd appreciate it if you'd find that third party you mentioned. Pretty sure my cousin, Renee, would appreciate it as well."

"I'll do my best."

"Can't do better than that," Blackburn said.

* * *

Tony Novak, the head of the SPPD's Forensic Services Unit, worked in the FSU lab in the Griffin Building at the LEC. Santana had sent Gabriel Cruz to the BCA lab. Then Cruz needed to get a DNA swab from Matt Easton. Santana needed to know if Easton had had sex with his estranged wife on the day of her death.

Novak sat on a stool at one of the long tables in the lab, peering at a large computer monitor attached to a scanning electron microscope. About the size of four computer towers pushed together, the SEM looked nothing like a traditional microscope, yet it was the most reliable laboratory method for GSR identification and analysis.

"What do you have for me, Tony?" Santana asked.

Novak swiveled on the stool and looked at Santana with a wry smile. "No money, that's for sure."

"How 'bout information?"

"Might be able to help you with that."

Novak's mustache and short hair were gray and his nose a little flat, courtesy of the punches he'd taken as a middleweight Golden Gloves fighter years ago. The bald spot on the crown of his head had expanded over the years and had given him the moniker of "Monk" around the department. He wore a black T-shirt under his white lab coat. The white lettering on the front of the T-shirt read:

HATE COPS?
THE NEXT TIME YOU NEED HELP
CALL A CRACKHEAD

"The particles on both Tatum's and Beckham's gun hands are lead, antimony, and barium," Novak said. "Similar to fireworks, but unique to cartridge primers and microscopically different."

"Doesn't mean Beckham and Tatum fired a weapon," Santana said.

"No, it does not."

"It's possible a third party could've deliberately wiped GSR on their hands after shooting Tatum and Beckham."

Novak gave a nod. "Or it could indicate that both men were in the vicinity of the discharging firearm or made contact with a surface where GSR had previously been deposited."

"It's a gun shop. Has a range. Lot of GSR around."

"Could be secondary transfer. Any evidence a third party was there?"

"Not yet," Santana said.

"Before you go, take a look at this."

Novak pulled an enlarged black-and-white photo of a boot print out of a file folder on the lab table and handed it to Santana.

"This is from the photo you took after the Duran shooting."

Santana could clearly see the Vibram logo.

Novak pulled a color photo from the same file folder and set it on the table. "Got this off the Internet. Note the yellow Vibram logo. Comes from the inventor, Italian named Vitale Bramani, who developed the first rubber lug soles in the late thirties. Lots of his soles on footwear for outdoor and workwear activities. Military uses these soles, too. I believe some of the patrol guys have them as well."

"I might've had a pair or two when I was on patrol."

"One of the most recognizable shoe logos in the world," Novak said.

*　　*　　*

Santana took the stairs to the Computer/Digital Forensics Lab on the third floor to see Lynn Pierce. She spent the majority of her time processing the backlog of evidence in Internet Crimes against Children (ICAC) cases, which made up half of her caseload. But Santana knew that investigating Art Tatum's death would now be priority number one.

Lynn Pierce was tall and statuesque. She had shoulder-length raven hair like her Mdewakanton Sioux ancestors and had tied it in a ponytail.

"I downloaded the data from Tara Easton's computer," she said. "Not much on it. Like she didn't use it much."

"You have a chance to look at Blaine Beckham's computer?"

"Still running the program."

"How about his cell phone?"

Beckham's cell phone had been transported in a specialized Faraday bag. Despite its standard security features, a cell phone could still be hacked by an outside source to alter, delete, or even add evidence. The Faraday bag ensured that the phone couldn't be tampered with.

Lynn Pierce used Cellebrite technology, developed by an Israeli digital intelligence company, to unlock cell phone data.

"Well," she said, "a typical smartphone has sixty-four gigabytes of internal storage, which amounts to approximately thirty-three thousand reams of paper. I need to know what you want me to look for."

"I need to know Beckham's location on Sunday, January twenty-ninth."

Santana knew that GPS, or the Global Positioning System, worked best in open areas, with an unobstructed view of the sky. When a user was in a building, surrounded by buildings, clouds, or trees, GPS accuracy was limited. Pierce would likely use wi-fi, or cellular tracking networks. The location of a user within a building could also be pinpointed within a few feet.

"I'll see what I can find," she said.

"What about the digital evidence from the gun shop security camera?" Santana asked.

"New equipment has helped." Pierce pointed to the two-foot-tall device on the lab counter. "I used to have stacks of CDs needing to be processed. Had to manually upload each individual disc onto a hard drive and then analyze it to determine if there was any incriminating evidence. Now I can load up to fifty CDs, DVDs, or Blu-ray Discs into the two bins to automatically analyze each disc. Saves me a ton of time. I'm in hog heaven."

"What about the security camera data?"

She gestured toward a chair in front of a computer monitor. "Have a seat and take a look."

Santana sat down as Pierce clicked on a link on the screen. Immediately, he saw the counter and front entrance to Beckham's gun shop.

"I've got it set up to the approximate time we believe the shooting occurred," Pierce said, standing to his right.

Santana could see Blaine Beckham behind the counter. Moments later Art Tatum entered the shop. Santana watched as Tatum showed Beckham his badge. He could see the two men talking, but since Beckham had no audio system, he could hear nothing that was said.

Then the image on the screen suddenly turned to snow.

"What the hell happened?" Santana asked.

"Signal interruption. Picture comes back on in a few minutes . . . after the shooting."

"Convenient."

"Very."

"How could that happen?"

Pierce crossed her arms and leaned her backside against the counter. "Wireless security cameras like the ones in the gun shop are more vulnerable to being jammed because they transmit a signal that can easily be disrupted. All someone would need is a radio frequency interference device, like an RF transmitter or receiver. Works on the same gigahertz frequency bands as wi-fi. As long as the jamming device's signal is stronger, it overpowers the other. The result is the loss of video and audio from the camera."

"Where would someone get a jammer?"

"Internet, where they get everything else."

"That easy."

"Sure. People use them to stop location tracking by phones or planted devices. Businesses who don't want their meetings recorded use them. Some wireless jammers are small enough to fit in the palm of your hand or in a pocket. Usually have a built-in rechargeable battery and a universal charging adapter."

"Then we have no way of knowing who else might've been in the gun shop or how the shooting went down?"

Pierce shook her head. "Sorry," she said.

Santana had another thought. "How long is video footage stored?"

"Usually lasts from three months to one year. Old footage is deleted automatically to create space for new recordings. But each security camera is different, and storage space too. Larger businesses and financial institutions have a large amount of storage capacity."

"I'd like to run the video back a few days."

"What are you looking for?"

"Might recognize a face in the store prior to the killing. Might've been casing the place."

"Use the mouse to select the date and time in the right sidebar," she said, showing Santana how to access it. "Once you choose the date and time, click the link below it to start viewing."

Santana thanked Pierce and chose a date and time six days before the shooting at the gun shop. He figured if someone had planned to interfere with the security video feed, they would need enough time to case the store and then purchase the needed equipment. He figured his odds were no better than hoping for a specific number with a roll of dice. Then again, sometimes he got lucky.

He also knew that the store closed on Sundays, and he could quickly skim through the minutes and hours when no customers were in the store, saving him considerable time.

He spent the next two hours reviewing the footage from Saturday, Monday, Tuesday, and Wednesday of the previous week before he got a recognizable hit on Thursday afternoon.

It was Jadyn Hartley.

*　　*　　*

When Santana returned to his desk in the Homicide and Robbery Unit, he saw Gabriel Cruz hanging his overcoat on the coat rack beside his cubicle.

"Got a buccal cheek swab from Matt Easton," Cruz said with a smile. "Gave it to Dennis Crane at the BCA."

"You tell Easton why we needed the swab?"

Cruz shook his head. "Told him we wanted to eliminate him as a suspect from the DNA collected at the crime scene."

Santana considered telling Cruz about finding Jadyn Hartley on the gun shop security footage but decided to wait till he had a chance to talk to the kid. Instead, he used his department cell phone to call Dennis Crane at the BCA.

"What's up, Santana?"

"That sample of Blaine Beckham's DNA Tanabe sent you."

"Yeah?"

"Compare it to the vaginal sperm swab Tanabe took from Tara Easton."

"Got a full plate now, Detective," Crane said. "Have to get in line."

"I'll tell that to my commander the next time I update her on Art Tatum's death. Talk to you later."

"Wait a minute!" Crane said. "Don't hang up! I didn't know Easton's death had anything to do with Tatum's."

Santana didn't know if the two deaths were related either. But hinting they were would get a faster DNA comparison from Crane.

"Call me when you know," Santana said before disconnecting.

"Think Crane will get right on it?" Cruz said.

"I know he will."

Cruz nodded in understanding. "What did I miss?" he said, changing the subject.

Santana told him that forensics had found GSR on both Tatum's and Beckham's hands. Then he told Cruz what he and Lynn Pierce had seen on the video.

"Any thoughts as to who erased the video from the gun shop?"

"Not sure."

Cruz opened the murder book on Santana's desk and turned to a page with the photo of Easton, Beckham, Duran, Khalil, and the unnamed Afghani.

"Him," he said, pointing to the unnamed Afghani. "I think he killed Easton, Beckham, and Tatum. Probably tried to kill Angel Duran, too. Help if we knew where he was or if he was even in the country."

"I've got an idea who might know. But let's talk to my CRI first."

*　　*　　*

Luis Garcia worked construction in summer and in winter as a bartender at La Costa Mexican Sports Bar and Grill on Caesar Chavez Avenue on St. Paul's West Side. As Santana's primary confidential reliable informant, Garcia might know of any heroin deal going down.

The restaurant where Luis Garcia worked had wooden ceiling beams, a wood wall and bar, and an open floor plan that featured three glass-paneled doors that opened vertically, like garage doors, in the warmer months. Most tables were filled, but all the high-top chairs at the bar were open.

"*Hola*, Santana," Garcia said with a big grin.

Luis Garcia had once been a member of the Latin Kings, but had gone straight after helping Santana solve a murder case involving forged visas. The department used a number of CIs for information. But CRIs like Garcia had proven their reliability over time and were better compensated for the information they provided.

When both detectives were seated at the bar, Santana introduced Gabriel Cruz.

"Working with another *Latino*, huh?" Garcia asked, the grin remaining on his face.

He was a stocky young man in his early twenties, about five foot seven, with a flat nose and darker complexion in keeping with his Mixtec Mexican heritage. He wore his black hair in a side swept cut, short on the sides and longer on top with a deep side part.

Garcia finished mixing three margaritas and set them at the end of the bar for the waitress. Then he came back to Santana and said, "What can I get you?"

"A *Jarritos guava*," Santana said, ordering the naturally-flavored, non-alcoholic Mexican drink. Made in a variety of fruit flavors, the popular drink was less carbonated than traditional American soft drinks. *Jarrito* meant "little jug" in Spanish and referred to the Mexican tradition of drinking water and other drinks in clay pottery jugs.

Cruz asked for a strawberry flavor.

When Garcia brought them the glass bottles, Santana said, "Any info on the heroin I called you about?"

"Been meaning to get back to you," Garcia said, leaning over the bar. In a low voice, he said, "Word on the street is that a gringo has four kilos of China White for sale."

"You get the name of the gringo?"

Garcia shook his head.

"Why haven't the kilos been sold?"

Garcia shrugged.

"Know where the kilos came from?"

Garcia shook his head again. "Sorry, *amigo.*"

As they were leaving, Cruz said, "Maybe Narco/Vice knows about this."

"I know someone I can talk to. But Tanabe is cutting Tatum and Beckham."

Chapter 27

At the Ramsey County morgue, Reiko Tanabe, dressed in her autopsy clothes, hunched over Blaine Beckham's body. Lifting her face shield, she said, "Scanned both bodies with the new CAT scanner. Believe it or not, the bullets in Tatum and Beckham were lodged in almost the same spot."

"Almost perfect shots under stress," Santana said.

Tanabe pulled down her face shield and described the exact location of the entrance gunshot wound in the left pectoral region of the chest, including the measurement and description of the abrasion collar. She found no soot deposition or gunpowder stippling on the skin or in the soft tissues around the wound, indicating a non-contact shot.

After she cut open Beckham's chest, she traced the direction of the wound path left to right, front to back, and downward through the heart till she located the bullet.

Santana noted the direction of the wound path. *Downward through the heart.*

Tanabe used a bullet extractor—a standard curved Kelly forceps fitted with two-centimeter lengths of standard-gauge rubber urinary catheter as protective tips—to recover the moderately deformed 9mm round. Using a standard forceps could scratch the jacket or lead of the bullet, producing marks that could hamper or prevent analysis of bullet striations and firearm identification.

Tanabe took the bullet to the counter, where she photographed it and let it air dry before wrapping it in paper. She then placed the bullet inside a small, labeled paper evidence bag and sealed it.

Santana knew cleaning or washing a recovered bullet might destroy evidence, as might a plastic bag. He marked the paper bag with their initials, the case number, contents, and date of recovery to begin the chain-of-custody.

While Cruz waited for the ME to retrieve the bullet from Art Tatum's chest, Santana called Wade Crawford, the SIGAR agent.

"You calling because you need my help?"

"You need to come see me," Santana said.

"That an invitation?"

"I'd call it more of an order."

"I'm not one of your lackeys, Santana. You can't order me around."

"Maybe not. But I can make your life a living hell."

"What happened to the spirit of cooperation?"

"Why I'm calling."

Crawford went silent for a time before he said, "What's this all about?"

"Cooperation," Santana said.

Wade Crawford showed up thirty minutes after Santana's phone call. He and Santana settled in chairs in an interview room.

"This an interrogation?" Crawford said, his eyes locked on Santana.

"We need a private place to talk."

Crawford shrugged. "About what?"

Santana slid the photo of Tara Easton and the four men across the table. "The Afghani in special forces. I need his name. Now."

Crawford snickered. "What makes you think I know it?"

Santana leaned forward. "Don't bullshit me, Crawford. You've known from the very beginning. You had access to the finger-print biometric data collected in Afghanistan. You know this Afghani came here."

Crawford's gaze shifted from Santana to the camera in a corner. "The video on?"

Santana shook his head. "Whatever you say is between the two of us."

Crawford thought about it. "Okay, Santana. I'll play ball. Tell me what *you* know."

"I know that Easton, Beckham, and probably Taimur Khalil are dead. I know that someone tried to kill Angel Duran. I know that special forces operatives like this unidentified Afghani were airlifted out of Afghanistan after the government collapsed. Over twelve hundred Afghanis were sent to Minnesota. I'm betting this guy is one of them."

"Abdul Rahim."

Santana wrote down the name in his notebook. "Where is he?"

"Who do you think I've been looking for?"

"And you haven't found him?"

"Look, the deal was that Afghan refugees had to find a job and pay rent after their first six months in the country. That was the state's resettlement plan. Resettlement agencies secured six-month leases for refugees to coincide with the federal rent support, expecting that families' primary earners would find employment in time. But it wasn't that simple. Job searches have been all but impossible for Afghan refugees to navigate since many have limited to no English proficiency, no access to a car, no driver's license, and no familiarity with the process. The one advantage Rahim has is that he speaks English."

"And he's a valuable asset."

"That, too."

"He just fell off the radar."

"On purpose," Crawford said. "You have access to all the tracking databases like AutoTrack, DMV, LexisNexis. I don't have access anymore. You could help me out."

"What's Abdul Rahim after?"

"What is everyone after?"

"Money."

"Bingo."

"You think the five of them stole money from Afghanistan?"

Crawford nodded.

"What if they didn't?"

Crawford's eyes narrowed. "You know something I don't?"

"Most likely."

"That's cute, Santana. How 'bout sharing."

"Heroin."

Crawford straightened up in his chair. "You're sure?"

"Not till we have it in our hands. But it's likely."

"Who has it?"

"We searched Easton's apartment and the house she lived in with her husband. Searched Beckham's house as well except for the mother's bedroom. Might have to get another warrant to search there. But my guess is that Angel Duran has the heroin, if he hasn't already sold it. Abdul Rahim likely shot Duran and would've searched his house if I hadn't been there."

"Got any idea who he might've sold it to?"

Santana shook his head. "But I have an idea who might know."

"Keep me informed."

"All in the spirit of cooperation," Santana said.

*　　*　　*

When Cruz returned to the LEC, Santana told him what Wade Crawford had told him about Abdul Rahim.

"Run Abdul Rahim's name through all the search engines. AutoTrack, DMV, LexisNexis, utilities, cable companies. You know the drill. See if you can find any information about him."

Santana took the two 9mm bullets recovered from Beckham and Tatum to the crime lab for comparison with Tatum's Glock 17 and Beckham's Ruger LC9 recovered at the scene.

Tony Novak fired a round from Tatum's Glock into a bullet tank in the lab, fished it out with a net, and then used a comparison microscope that allowed him to look at the round from

Tatum's Glock with the round removed from Beckham side-by-side simultaneously.

Novak repeated the process with the bullet removed from Tatum.

It took Novak only a few minutes to state the comparisons a match.

Chapter 28

Luke Thornton had a solid reputation working Narco/Vice. Santana had worked with Thornton's brother on a previous case. Santana met the undercover narc in his apartment in the sixteen-story Pioneer building in Lowertown. Once called the "Wall Street of St. Paul" because of the many prominent businesses located here, the building with the Romanesque facade was the city's first skyscraper. It had once housed the *Pioneer Press* before being renovated for apartments.

Designated as a historic site, the building had a wide fourteen-floor light court atrium that ran straight up through the middle of the building. Santana took one of the modernized elevators that had retained the original cab and glass window panels. The spring-loaded crank had been left in the elevator for decoration, and automatic doors had replaced the sliding gate. The hallway on the tenth floor had a chime and a double globe lamp above the elevator doors that reminded Santana of the vintage globes outside old police departments.

Thornton looked as if he'd just gotten out of bed when he opened the door to his apartment. A tall, muscular man with a thick dark beard, he wore faded jeans, flip-flops, and a long-sleeve denim shirt. A rubber band held his long dark hair in a ponytail. The aroma of perking coffee filled the apartment.

"Get you a coffee?"

Santana declined Thornton's offer. He loved the smell but not the taste.

The apartment had an open floor plan with a counter separating the kitchen from the dining room and living room. A floor-to-ceiling bookshelf covered one living room wall. A large screen TV hung on another. Santana sat in one of the four wingback leather chairs encircling a rustic wood rectangular coffee table.

Santana noted the small gold-framed photo of a pretty woman and two young girls on one of the bookshelves. Like many undercover narco/vice detectives, Thornton was probably separated or divorced.

Some of the book spine titles that caught Santana's eye were *The Best and The Brightest* by David Halberstam, *The Innovators* by Walter Isaacson, *War and Peace* by Leo Tolstoy, and *Gravity's Rainbow* by Thomas Pynchon.

Thornton brought a cup of coffee into the living room. He sat down in a chair opposite Santana and lit a cigarette from the package of Camels on the coffee table.

"Rough night?" Santana said.

"Lots of 'em. What brings you here?"

"I need information."

"Doesn't everyone?"

"Heard any talk about four kilos of China White?"

"From where?"

"I don't know for sure. Might be Afghanistan."

Thornton sipped his coffee as he considered Santana's question. "Did hear some rumors about the kilos."

"What would four kilos be worth?"

"Well, if it's pure China White and not the cheaper brown powder or black tar, we're talking between three thousand to four thousand an ounce. You figure a kilo is a little over thirty-five ounces. So now we're talking approximately one hundred forty thousand per kilo, or over a half-million dollars for all four kilos. But one kilo of nearly pure heroin can be divided into thirty thousand glassine bags. By the time you get your hands on a bag, which is about a tenth of a gram, it'll only cost fifteen to twenty dollars because dealers cut it with fentanyl. Why today's China White is so deadly."

Thornton paused, took a drag on his cigarette, and exhaled the smoke through his nostrils. "Now we're talking one hundred twenty thousand bags of heroin at twenty dollars a bag.

Works out to a cool two point four million if my math is correct."

"Lot of money."

"Sure is. Want to share how the heroin got here?"

"I think a small group of soldiers who served in Afghanistan smuggled it in."

"Afghanistan is the world's biggest opium producer. Last year's crop was the most profitable in years. They've also started to produce cheap methamphetamine. The Taliban have become the world's biggest drug cartel and use drugs as a way to keep their country running since they are cut off from the West."

"Who could afford to buy four kilos of heroin?"

"Only one banger I know might have that amount of cash. Montez Dixon, former Gangster Disciple. Did three years for possession in his teens. Big boxing promoter now. Claims he's out of the business, but I don't buy it. Been trying to bust him since he's been out. Still trying."

"I've heard Dixon's name mentioned on fight card promotions," Santana said. "You ever use a snitch to try and get him?"

"A snitch can paint a picture for me. Figure out whatever we think will get me with a particular dealer. But dealers know that the surest way to get arrested is selling to somebody new. Number one thing you don't do if you're a dealer."

Thornton finished his coffee and set the cup on the coffee table. "But sometimes greed gets to 'em and you can build your way up the ladder. After two or three buys, and the cops don't crash the door, he figures you're OK. Problem is, you need enough buy money to work your way up to the large dealers. To get to a dealer who's selling or buying kilos, the department has to make a large number of buys of increasing weight. We can't afford to buy up like that. Means guys like Montez Dixon are still in business. Even if he claims he's clean. Wish I could help you, Detective."

"I wish you could, too."

"You got any other ideas?"

"Got to find the heroin first, if it even exists."

Thornton rested his elbows on his thighs. "You don't know for sure?"

"Not yet," Santana said.

*   *   *

Crepuscular beams of light radiated from the late afternoon sun as it sat just above the horizon. The beams appeared to converge toward the sun but Santana knew it was an illusion, similar to the impression that the rails on train tracks appear to come together in the distance. He wondered now, as he drove toward Angel Duran's cabin, if this case was an illusion. If what he'd observed and heard were designed to mislead him.

Duran was scheduled for release from Lakeview Hospital in Stillwater tomorrow. Santana doubted a judge would approve a search warrant for Duran's cabin based on a belief that Duran might be hiding four kilos of heroin that he and Tara Easton, Blaine Beckham, and Taimur Khalil had smuggled out of Afghanistan. Santana would have to use other means to search the cabin, and he didn't want to jeopardize Gabriel Cruz's career by getting him involved.

Snowplows had cleared the main two-lane road leading to Duran's heavily wooded lot, but untouched drifts of wind-blown snow covered the asphalt driveway. Not wanting to leave tire tracks, Santana parked at the end of the driveway on the plowed road and scoped the two-stall garage and Quonset hut. Blanketed by snow, Duran's Range Rover remained parked in front of one garage door. Santana figured it hadn't been moved since the shooting and Duran's subsequent hospitalization.

Before leaving the LEC, Santana had changed his shoes for a pair of Blauer waterproof boots and his sport coat and overcoat for a heavy SPPD sweater and his Blauer fleece jacket.

As he exited his Ford Explorer, he once again smelled the heavy scent of pine and woodsmoke wafting in the cold air. In the distance he heard the sound of what he thought was a snowmobile engine.

He broke off a two-foot branch from a birch tree on the opposite side of the road. The branch had plenty of twigs to help sweep away his trail to and from the house. Falling snow and a stiff wind should do the rest. Then he trudged through the ankle-deep, hard-packed snow, staying in a straight line, one foot in front of the other, toward the front door of the timber frame cabin.

Santana didn't see any home alarm system sign, but it might be buried under all the snow. Still, even if Duran had an alarm system, he likely had not set it while he was on the property cutting logs. And after being shot, he'd immediately been taken to the hospital.

Duran likely knew that unbranded yard signs and window decals were the best way to protect an alarm system. That way, he could still deter a potential burglar without revealing his system.

Upon reaching the front door, Santana pressed the doorbell and waited. Then he peered through the sidelight window to the left of the door. Seeing no one inside, he removed his gloves and took out a leather case that held his lock pick set.

Duran had installed a lever lock on the front door. Most lever locks featured either three or five levers. The more levers a lock had, the greater the security. Five lever locks were also more difficult to pick than three lever locks.

Instead of using his standard tension wrench and rake, which worked on a typical and common tumbler lock, Santana removed a special curtain pick and tension wrench from his lock pick set and inserted the wrench into the keyhole. He applied pressure to the curtain pick till he was able to move each of the levers into the appropriate position.

It took him a little over a minute before the lock gave way.

He left his boots on the mat outside the front door, slipped on a pair of latex gloves, and entered the cabin, closing the door behind him.

Someone had ransacked the cabin.

Dishes and cans and tins pulled from the open kitchen cabinets were scattered on the counter. A garbage can and recycle bin were dumped on the floor. The cushions on the leather couch and chairs in the dining and living rooms were cut open.

Santana doubted it would have been the Washington County Sheriff's Department looking for clues as to why someone would want to kill Angel Duran. He figured someone had been looking for the heroin. He wondered if it had been found and searching for it now would be a waste of his time. But experience had taught him how to search. This slash-and- toss method led him to believe that the previous search had been random and possibly unsuccessful.

He stood in the entryway as his eyes scanned the cabin, trying to get a sense of where he could start searching.

A green light on the alarm panel attached to the wall assured him that the system was off. The wood blinds on the windows were closed.

The Douglas fir post and beam cabin had an open floor plan, ceramic tile made to look like light oak wood, tall windows, and no attic, which allowed for the ceiling to extend twenty feet all the way to the roof, giving the cabin a much larger feel.

The kitchen and counter with two bar stools made of western saddles mounted on a horseshoe base lay directly ahead. A wood stove fireplace sat on a rectangular bed of tile at the far end of the room to Santana's right, beside a stack of birch and oak logs. A red leather couch and rustic coffee table faced the fireplace. The three-place gun rack attached to the wall on the opposite side of the living room held a Winchester Model 70 bolt action, a Mossberg 590 tactical pump-action 12-gauge shotgun, and a Colt AR-15.

Santana saw no cameras.

A round rustic dining table with a distressed finish and four chairs sat under a wagon wheel chandelier with six glass cylinder shades. Suspended by lengths of natural rope wrapped rods, the chandelier hung from a heavy wooden beam.

On the counter separating the kitchen from the living room, Santana saw a coffee grinder, rubber gloves, an air purifier, and a scale. Equipment typically used for packaging narcotics, though one could argue they had other uses.

He knew that a kilo of heroin weighed about 2.2 pounds. If Duran did have the heroin, he would need to hide about nine pounds or four glassine-wrapped blocks of the drug. One kilo of compressed heroin would be about 4" x 8" x 1.5" thick, or 48 cubic inches, an inch longer than a large paperback book.

Santana checked under the dining room chairs first, looking to see if any kilos were taped underneath. Then he searched the only bathroom in the cabin. Dealers often wrapped drugs in plastic and placed them in or underneath toilet tanks to avoid detection. Finding no drugs in either location, he searched the medicine cabinet and then moved on to the master bedroom.

On one wall Duran had framed a poster of a soldier standing in a field of red flowers, holding his rifle at a forty-five-degree angle. Ahead and above the soldier a bald eagle held a large fluttering American flag in its talons. An image of God, or Jesus, extending a hand through the heavens appeared above and to the left of the flag. The heading at the top of the poster read:

HONOR THE FALLEN

Written at the bottom of the poster were the words:

THANK THE LIVING

The flowers in the poster reminded Santana of those he had seen in his dream. He felt the rush of adrenaline. Maybe he was on the right track after all, he thought.

The mattress and box spring had been yanked off the bed and cut open, and stuffing covered the floor. Dresser drawers were pulled out and the contents dumped. The intruder had likely checked the back and undersides of drawers, knowing it was possible to tape a small bag of drugs to the flat back and underside of a drawer. But Santana also checked the space between the bottom drawer of the dresser and its frame, a spot that was easy to overlook. He'd once found a small handgun used in a drive-by shooting taped to the frame. Finding the gun had sent a homicide suspect to prison.

The room had no desk, so he looked through the books and magazines that had been moved around on a small bookshelf. He knew there were companies that sold home safes made to look like reading material. They weren't meant to conceal drugs and paraphernalia, but a dealer or addict could use the safes to conceal them. A creative and very patient dealer could also take the time to hollow out a book to stash drugs inside its pages, though it would have to be a thick hardcover to fit a kilo of heroin.

When he came up empty, he went through the clothes, shoes, and boots in the bedroom closet. Given that some of the clothes had been pulled off their hangers and thrown on the floor, Santana figured the intruder had also searched the closet.

In the open nightstand drawer, he found a thick hardbound edition of *The Greatest Works of Edgar Allen Poe*. Santana lifted the heavy book and turned it over. The quote on the back cover read:

"The boundaries, which divide Life
from Death, are at best shadowy and vague.
Who shall say where the one ends
And where the other begins?"

He opened the book and carefully turned the thin pages till he came to a story entitled "The Gold-Bug." He wasn't familiar with the story, but the title gave him pause as adrenaline rushed into his bloodstream. He had seen a gold bug in his dream of the bones in the field of red flowers and skeletons.

Three-quarters of the way through the book, a kilo of what he believed to be China White had been placed in a hollowed-out space. If someone had seen the thick book and hurriedly turned a few pages, he would not have found the bag of heroin.

One kilo down, Santana thought. Three more to go.

Two folding doors opened into a laundry closet between the bedroom and kitchen. Santana looked behind the side-by-side washer and dryer and searched the two overhead cabinets containing laundry soap and dryer sheets. Then he moved on to the kitchen.

Dusk had fallen, dimming the interior light in the cabin. Santana switched on a kitchen light and looked through the cupboards and larger tin cans on the counter, making sure none had been opened and emptied for use as a hiding place.

Behind a door in the kitchen, he found a large pantry. A plastic bin of cat litter sat on the floor beside a vacuum cleaner. He had seen no litter box indicating Duran had a cat. Given the freezing temperatures, he doubted the animal would be outside, though he'd come across enough idiots and dead cats and dogs in his time as an officer and detective to know that not everyone properly cared for their pets.

Popping open the cover of the plastic bin, Santana stuck his hand into the litter all the way to the bottom of the bin. No kilos.

Next, he unclipped the vacuum cleaner bag and opened it.

Inside he found kilo number two.

He reattached the vacuum cleaner bag and closed the pantry door. Then he snapped off the grilles in front of the refrigerator and dishwasher. Underneath the refrigerator he located kilo number three. He reattached the grilles and stood up.

Interestingly, he thought, he had seen no photos of Duran with his parents, his brother, Enrique, or sisters, if he had any, or with his fellow soldiers.

Feeling the heat on the bottom of his stocking feet, Santana figured Duran had installed an in-floor radiant heating system, which used fluid-filled piping below the floor to heat living areas.

Had Duran installed a traditional heating system, Santana would have looked for the last kilo inside the baseboard vents and cold air return ducts by removing the screws using the small screwdriver he kept in his leather lock pick case. A wood floor would have made it possible to hide drugs underneath the boards. So would a ceiling made of ceiling tiles.

Since the cabin sat on a slab with no basement, he was running out of places to check.

It could be that Duran had hidden the rest of the China White in his Range Rover or in the garage or Quonset hut. Or, he might not have it at all. Perhaps Abdul Rahim had it. Then again, if Duran was trying to sell the kilos, he might want one close to show perspective buyers, despite the risk of possibly being stopped and searched.

Santana made one final pass through the cabin, looking for something that he'd missed.

A five-foot-tall yucca tree with two stalks and spiky green leaves stood in a large pot in the far corner of the room to the left of the stove fireplace. He had seen no other plants in the house, and, though Duran had placed soil in the planter to make it look real, this tree proved to be artificial upon touch.

He squatted and dug into the soil. He'd only reached down a few inches when his fingers hit something that felt like cardboard. Sweeping the soil to the side, he saw that Duran had cut out a ring of cardboard and placed it inside the planter. A hole had been cut in the middle of the cardboard to allow the two stalks to protrude through.

Returning to the pantry, Santana retrieved two paper bags. He laid them beside the plant and, placing two fingers in the hole, he lifted up the cardboard, which had stuffed newspaper underneath it to hold it up. Duran had hidden the last kilo of heroin with the newspaper.

Santana lowered the cardboard and dumped the little bit of spilled dirt on the paper bags back into the planter. Then he wiped off the bags in the kitchen sink, ran the water to remove any traces of dirt in the sink, returned the bags to the pantry, and turned off the kitchen light.

After locking the door on his way out, he put on the ice-cold boots he'd left on the mat on the porch and tied the laces. Then he changed his latex gloves for the pair of leather ones in his coat pocket.

It would be obvious to Duran that his cabin had been searched. Santana saw no reason to conceal his tracks now. And given the amount of falling snow, he felt certain that no trace of his visit would be left by tomorrow when Angel Duran returned from the hospital. He tossed the broken tree branch he'd left on the porch and then paused for a moment, looking at the Quonset hut beside the double garage.

Recalling the equipment used for packing drugs on the kitchen counter, Santana decided to take a look inside the hut. He made his way through the snow to the door of the hut.

The padlock securing the door was broken. He figured whoever had ransacked the cabin had also broken the lock.

Removing the busted padlock, he opened the door. His mini-Maglite provided enough light till he located the switch and turned it on. While scanning the 12' x 12' room, he noted that it reeked of vinegar.

He hadn't been inside a Quonset hut since Jordan's death, and he felt a queasiness in his stomach now and lightness in his head as the memory came rushing in like a stiff gust of wind. He placed his right hand against the metal surface to steady himself till the feeling passed and he straightened up again.

He saw four empty eighteen-liter jugs stacked against the wall to his right. A workbench stood along the back wall and beside it a five-gallon drum of acetic anhydride. From where he stood, he could see a large red triangle on the drum warning that the liquid and vapor were highly flammable.

A propane stove stood underneath a window.

He took out his iPhone and called Luke Thornton.

Thornton answered on the second ring.

"You busy?" Santana asked.

"Not at the moment."

"I need you to look at something. Switch to FaceTime."

When Santana could see Thornton's bearded face, he turned his iPhone so that it faced the drum of acetic anhydride. "What's this used for?"

Thornton gave a low whistle. "Where are you?"

"Can't say right now."

"You wouldn't be breaking the law now, would you?"

"'Course not."

"That's what I thought."

"What about the acetic anhydride?"

"Used to make heroin," Thornton said. "Without it, all you have is crude opium and no heroin. And it doesn't take much of the stuff to do the job."

"Is acetic anhydride legal?"

"It is, but primarily for use in laboratories and factories. Most common use is in the production of cigarette filters. But acetic anhydride is a schedule one chemical as of two thousand one. Even if you acquired the acetic anhydride, you'd also need to purchase ammonium chloride, some calcium oxide, or quicklime, and sodium carbonate to solidify the heroin. Then you'd have to purify it using filters and activated carbon. Add hydrochloric acid to the acetone solution, which converts the heroin base to heroin hydroxide. Let it sit while the acid changes the heroin base to heroin hydrochloride. Filter the solution again to retain the heroin hydrochloride and dry it. Now you've got yourself a batch of China White with a purity of eighty to ninety-five percent."

"Take a look at this," Santana said.

He slowly swept the camera along the workbench on the back wall.

"Shit," Thornton said. "All the ingredients are there, except for the sap drained from opium flowers. Even have the stove to heat the water you'd need."

"What if you smuggled the sap here from Afghanistan?"

"You wouldn't smuggle the sap as is. Takes about three months after poppy seeds are planted before you get a brightly-colored flower and an egg-shaped seed pod. Sumerians called it Hul Gil, the 'flower of joy.' Gotta love that," Thornton said with a chuckle.

"Then what?"

"The milky sap is inside the seed pod. You extract the sap by slitting the pod with a special curved knife. Sap turns into a brownish-black gum. You bundle the gum into bricks and wrap them in plastic. A broker buys the packages. Traffickers refine it into morphine."

"Why morphine?"

"Morphine bricks are easier to smuggle than bundles of smelly, jelly-like opium."

Santana focused his iPhone on the eighteen-liter jugs.

"Takes only two to two-and-a-half liters to make a kilogram, or two point two pounds, of China White," Thornton said. "Just one liter can yield a kilogram of lower-grade heroin. When full, those four eighteen-liter jugs could produce eighty pounds of high-quality China White. That's a street value in the US of at least three point six million. Those jugs are big enough to make lucrative quantities of heroin, but small enough to load into the trunk of a car."

"So why go through all this? Why not just smuggle the heroin instead of morphine?"

"Well, morphine is half the cost of heroin. Maybe that's all the smuggler could afford. Might also be what he or she could acquire at the time."

"Thanks," Santana said.

"Tell me where you—"

Santana disconnected, turned off the light switch, shut the door, and hooked the latch with the broken padlock. Then he trudged through the snow to his SUV.

Duran wouldn't confess that he had a stash of heroin. Santana would have to figure out another way to get the drugs and chemicals and arrest Duran in the process.

Chapter 29

That evening Santana met DEA Special Agent in Charge Scott Weston. As head of the Omaha Division, one of twenty-three DEA divisions in the US, Weston directed operations in North and South Dakota, Nebraska, Iowa, and Minnesota. With his short blond hair, his blue suit and striped tie, and freshly pressed button-down white shirt, Weston fit his ex-military and by-the-book reputation.

Santana met Weston at Runyon's, a five-minute walk from the DEA office in the Washington Square building in the Warehouse District of Minneapolis. Santana was already seated at a table for two in the high-ceilinged tavern, across from the bar and against a wall lined with celebrity photos and plaques with pithy sayings. One in particular caught his eye.

**Your toughest competitors are
Always ready to teach you a lesson.**

Weston made no apology for being twenty minutes late, and Santana hadn't expected one. He had more important concerns on his mind.

"Don't get across the river much, huh?" Weston said.

"Try not to. But these Buffalo wings are worth it." Santana pushed an extra plate and the basket of wings toward the middle of the table. "Have one."

"I've had 'em before." Weston glanced at his watch. "I'm in a hurry. What's so urgent that we had to meet?"

Santana sipped his beer and wiped his mouth with a napkin. "Joel Ryker."

Weston's eyes narrowed. "Ryker's dead."

"But not forgotten."

"What's that supposed to mean?"

"Ryker was a rogue agent. He tried to steal a half-million dollars in drug money."

"Yeah. And he got himself killed over it."

"That's not the story that ran in the media."

Weston started to answer and then paused, putting it together. "Easy now, Detective. Threatening the DEA is not a good career move."

"I'm more worried about Ana Soriano. You remember her."

"I do."

Santana waited for a more complete accounting of Ana's contributions to the DEA. When nothing more was forthcoming, he said, "She helped put away drug dealers and sex traffickers."

"And we helped her."

"How exactly?"

Weston let out a frustrated breath. "All right. Lay it out for me, Santana. What do you want?"

"Ana's mother and sister are missing in El Salvador."

"Sorry to hear that."

"I need your agents there to find out where they are."

Weston let out a laugh that sounded more like a cough. "You're shitting me."

Santana stared at him without responding.

"Who said we have any agents in El Salvador?"

"My turn to laugh," Santana said.

Weston set his elbows on the table. "Even if we did have agents there—and I'm not saying we do—they wouldn't have time to look for a woman and her child."

"I'm not bluffing, Weston."

"You run this by your commander?"

"I did."

"I haven't heard anything from her."

"You both need an attitude adjustment."

"No way I'm gonna run this by my supervisor."

"Then don't." Santana finished his beer and pushed the basket of remaining Buffalo wings closer to Weston. "My treat," he said, standing.

"You leak anything about Joel Ryker to the media, Detective, and you can kiss your career goodbye."

"It'd be worth it. But here's an incentive for you, Weston. I'll let you in on a four-kilo, half-million-dollar China White drug bust. When that's cut for the street, we're talking somewhere in the neighborhood of two and a half million dollars. Big drug bust for the DEA and your career."

Weston remained silent for a time as his eyes focused inward. Santana imagined the promotional wheels turning in Weston's head.

"How do I know you're not bullshitting me?"

"Because I'm dealing with Ana Soriano's life and the lives of her mother and sister."

Weston nodded as if he understood. "Where are the drugs?"

"You know I won't tell you that till you convince me you've located Ana's family and, if need be, are getting them out of El Salvador."

Santana stood and slipped on his coat. Then he put both hands on the table and leaned in close to Weston. "The woman and child have been missing for two weeks. You need to get on it now because this drug bust is going down soon."

He removed an envelope from his coat pocket and laid it on the table in front of Weston. "Their last address and phone number are in the envelope. I'll be waiting for your call."

"I can only do so much."

"Better do more than that," Santana said, heading for the door and the cold once more.

*　　*　　*

Later that night Santana sat on the couch in his living room with Ana Soriano. Gitana lay sleeping on her back on the couch between them while Ana rubbed Gitana's belly.

"Have you spoken to the DEA about my mother and sister?" she asked.

Santana had hoped she wouldn't inquire about her mother and sister's situation in El Salvador till Weston agreed to his demand. He was sure Weston would complain to Janet Kendrick. She, in turn, would threaten him with suspension—or worse. But he was in no mood to negotiate or back off. He couldn't let Ana go to El Salvador. And going with her would be a fool's errand as well.

He had no knowledge of the country or even where to begin looking, though he had read that the El Salvadoran government had cracked down on the gangs after eighty-seven people were killed in a three-day period. Referred to in El Salvador as the *Régimen de Excepción,* or State of Exception, and the *Guerra Contra las Pandillas,* or War Against the Gangs, over 53,000 people accused of having gang affiliations had been arrested. Seven of the fifteen board members of the Mara Salvatrucha, or MS-13, known as the *"Ranfla Nacional,"* had been arrested. The rest of the leaders had purportedly fled to Mexico to evade arrest.

Domestically, the crackdown was popular among Salvadorans weary of gang violence, but the *"mano dura,"* or "iron-fist" policies, had led to a doubling of the prison population and massive overcrowding. In response the government had built the "Terrorism Confinement Center," a gigantic prison to lock up the thousands of gang members arrested.

"I spoke to Scott Weston," Santana said.

"I remember him from the trial. What's he going to do?"

"We need to wait and see."

Ana released a frustrated breath but didn't reply.

"Did you try calling your mother again?"

"Yes. But the call keeps going to voicemail."

"You have to trust me on this."

"It's the DEA I don't trust."

Her Caribbean blue eyes shimmered in the light as she looked at him. Without makeup and with her long black hair worn up in a high bun, Ana looked closer to her age. She was still beautiful and mature beyond her years, but Santana knew because of her experiences she could be overconfident.

"I have some leverage," he said. "The DEA will come around."

He kept the doubt out of his voice. He'd placed his bet with the DEA, and now he'd either have to fold or play his hand. If Weston believed Santana was bluffing, then he'd call him on it. That would leave him no choice but to follow through with his threat and probably tank his career. He hoped it wouldn't come to that.

"I won't wait much longer," Ana said.

"I know."

Chapter 30

As Santana finished his breakfast on Wednesday morning, he received a call from Dana Monroe. She'd completed a computer portrait of the skull Santana had dropped off at her house.

On the drive to Monroe's house, Santana called Del Taggart at the Washington County Sheriff's Department.

"Arrested the guy who shot Angel Duran yet?" Taggart asked when he answered the phone.

No mistaking the sarcasm in his voice.

"Getting close," Santana said.

"Want to fill me in?"

"Not that close."

"I figured. What's up?"

"Did you search Angel Duran's place?"

"Why would we do that?"

"Maybe find a clue. You know. Like who tried to kill him."

"Yeah, smart guy. We searched it. Came up empty."

"How did you leave the place?"

"By the door."

"Not what I meant."

"I knew that. But I can be a smartass, too."

"Good to know. You going to answer the question, or do I have to guess?"

"Well, we didn't tear the place apart, I can tell you that. Didn't find anything related to the shooting either."

Forty minutes later, Santana sat on the rattan couch in Dana Monroe's living room among the kilim pillows and rugs, tapestries, macramé wall hangings, candles, and green plants, as he had on his first visit. She occupied the same rocker opposite the couch and nearer the logs burning in the fireplace.

Dana Monroe still wore her gray-blond hair twisted into a single braid that hung down her back to her waist, but bright red lipstick had replaced the black shade on her full lips, and a pair of black jeans and hushpuppies, and a turtleneck and headband that matched her lipstick, had supplanted the tie-dye dress, headband, and open-toed sandals.

Her calico cat ambled across the living room and curled up in front of the fireplace.

"Have you found the answers you're looking for, Detective?" she asked.

As he looked into her gray eyes, he thought for a moment that her question had a deeper meaning.

"Not all of them," he said.

She offered a hint of a smile and handed him the 8 1/2" x 11" computerized portrait she'd created from the skull he'd given her. "Perhaps this will help."

One look at the portrait and Santana knew the scattered bones found around the city belonged to Taimur Khalil.

"I use a computer program to create three-dimensional reconstructions. My computer approximations are usually more effective in victim identification because they don't appear too artificial."

"They certainly don't," Santana said. He compared the iPhone photo he'd taken in Tara Easton's bedroom with the portrait Dana Monroe had generated, then handed his cell phone to Dana Monroe. "The first bearded man wearing a tunic shirt and pants and a turban to the right of the woman is Taimur Khalil."

Dana Monroe nodded her head as she peered at the photo. Looking at Santana again she said, "It's him."

"Good work," he said.

She handed his cell phone back to him. "Thank you. I didn't want this face to look like a digital sculpture, so when it came to the muscles I sculpted them in wax and then 3-D scanned them the same way that the skull was scanned. I added photographic textures to made it look like a person."

"What exactly is that?"

"It's a process of selecting photographs of several different people that look similar to the 3-D model and then projecting it onto the skull. Here's a few others I've done of missing people."

Unlike the police sketches Santana had seen, what struck him as he looked at each of the portraits she'd created was the soulfulness in the eyes and ebullience in the features. Whatever death had done to the people Dana Monroe portrayed—even if it had reduced them to skeletons—she could give them life.

* * *

The Minnesota Bureau of Criminal Apprehension is located in a two-story brick and glass building on Maryland Avenue in East St. Paul. Usually an eight-minute drive from the LEC, it took Santana and Cruz twice as long due to the freezing rain that iced windshields and slicked roads.

Yellow lights on MNDOT trucks flashed against the low, gray sky as they spread sodium chloride along Phalen Boulevard. Santana turned the defrost fan on high and the wipers on intermittent to keep any lingering sleet and black ice off the windshield.

Santana had showed Cruz the computerized portrait of Taimur Khalil that Dana Monroe had created.

"Easton, Khalil, and Beckham are dead," Cruz said. "Someone nearly killed Angel Duran, which leads to Abdul Rahim."

"You find any info on his whereabouts?" Santana asked as he kept his eyes glued on the slick road ahead.

"Got a possible address from Accurint."

Accurint was a locate-and-research tool within the Lexis-Nexis system.

"We'll check it out after we talk with Dennis Crane."

Crane's white lab coat hung from narrow shoulders that reminded Santana of a wire coat hanger.

On the long lab table beside Crane, Santana saw Blaine Beckham's chainsaw and a femur bone he now knew belonged to Taimur Khalil. A small dish next to the femur contained a gray powder. The side cover at the base of the chainsaw's guide bar had been removed.

Santana introduced Cruz. Then he looked at Crane. "Been waiting to hear from you."

Holding his palms out in a stopping position, Crane said, "I was going to call, Detective. Just been really busy here."

"What do you have?"

Crane sat on a stool beside the table and shook his head in frustration. "No identifiable prints on the shell casings found at the Duran shooting and no hits on the casings from NIBIN."

The information disappointed Santana but didn't surprise him. He figured whoever had shot Duran had worn gloves. But he still thought looking for possible prints on the shell casings was worth the effort.

"Shell casings didn't come from Beckham's AR-15 either."

"Shit," Cruz said, looking at Santana. "Then where did they come from?"

Santana shook his head. "Don't know now. Any hits from NamUs?"

"Nope," Crane said. "But I've got better news for you gentlemen regarding the DNA on Blaine Beckham's chainsaw."

He explained that Khalil's femur bone had been cut at the proximal anterior shaft below the lesser trochanter. Crane had used the femur because, along with the teeth, tibia, and fibula, it delivered the best success rate for DNA detection.

After cleaning a skeletal sample, Crane had inserted it into a grinding vial. Then he'd placed the vial into a small box-like machine on the counter filled with liquid nitrogen called a Freezer Mil 6750.

"Your suspected perp cleaned the chainsaw with lye. But . . ." Crane said with a sly smile, "I found a small tissue sample inside the side cover. Used it for comparison with the DNA from the femur."

"And?" Santana said.

"Blaine Beckham used this chainsaw to dismember Taimur Khalil."

"You're sure."

Crane stiffened his back. "Of course I'm sure."

"And you'd testify in court if it comes to that?"

"Absolutely."

"Good work," Santana said, patting him on his bony shoulder.

Crane grinned, showing off his yellow stained teeth. "Any time."

Santana knew Crane loved the limelight. Stroking his fragile ego with compliments and putting him on the stand in a courtroom, if he had to, would serve two purposes. First, it would help prove that Blaine Beckham's chainsaw was used to cut up Taimur Khalil's body. Second, testifying in court would feed Crane's love of the limelight and his need to be called an expert. He would also owe Santana the next time Santana came asking for a favor.

"What about the comparison between the DNA vaginal swab from Tara Easton and Blaine Beckham's DNA sample Tanabe took after the gun shop shooting?"

"No match," Crane said. "But . . ." he paused again.

Santana waited, knowing Crane enjoyed creating the suspense.

"Tara Easton had sex with someone else."

"Well," Cruz said, tapping his hand on the counter. "Let's hear it."

"Tara Easton had sex with none other than Matt Easton before she died."

* * *

Santana recalled from last week's interview with Matt Easton that Easton had to work on January 31st. Checking the online SPFD work schedule, he determined that Easton was off today.

"Surprise is the best option," Santana said to Cruz as they walked up the sidewalk toward Easton's house. "Gives him less of a chance to come up with a reason why the ME found his DNA on his estranged wife's body."

"You have news about Tara's death?" Easton said, holding open the front door.

"We do," Santana said.

Easton invited them in and they sat in the living room.

"What can you tell me?" Easton asked.

"More like what you can tell us," Santana said.

"What do you mean?"

Santana opened the briefcase in his lap and removed a manila folder. Then he closed it and set the file on top of it.

"What's that?" Easton asked.

"Your wife's autopsy report from the medical examiner."

"She didn't kill herself?"

"Why would you say that?"

"Well," Easton said with a shrug, "I never believed she would. What else could this be about?"

"You told us in our first interview that the last time you saw your wife was Christmas Eve when she brought presents to the house."

"That's right."

"Then why did the medical examiner find your DNA in your wife's body?"

Easton's complexion reddened.

Santana pressed his advantage. "You lied to us, Mr. Easton."

Easton's eyes glazed over as he shook his head slowly. "No."

"And you're lying now."

"I . . ." He paused to reconsider his response.

"You went to see your wife the night she died. You had an argument. Things got out of hand. You forced yourself on her. She resisted."

"No! You've got it all wrong."

"What have we gotten wrong?"

"Okay. I did see her the night she died. But I didn't kill her."

"You raped her."

"No! No, I didn't." He wrung his hands as he paused again. "We talked about getting back together. Yeah, we had sex. You have to understand . . ."

"Understand what?"

"Tara liked it . . . rough sometimes. We hadn't had sex for months. We kinda got carried away. But I didn't hurt her. And I certainly didn't kill her. I loved her."

"Why did you lie to us?" Cruz asked, looking up from his notebook.

"When you told me her throat had been cut, I thought someone had killed her."

"Why did you think that?" Santana asked.

"Because I never believed Tara would kill herself. We had our disagreements, sure. But I found the letters she wrote to Jamie and me. You must've read them. Tara never would've intentionally left Jamie."

"Doesn't tell us why you lied."

He threw up his hands. "Who do the police automatically suspect when someone's wife is murdered?"

"What time did you leave your wife's apartment?"

"Around nine or nine-thirty."

"Did anyone see you leaving?"

"I don't know."

Santana remembered watching the security video from Tara Easton's apartment.

"What were you wearing that night?"

"I guess my parka."

"With the hood up or down?"

"Up."

Santana looked at Cruz, who nodded. They both recalled the hooded figure they'd seen coming and going in the security footage.

"Did you see anyone else in the building that night?" Santana asked.

Easton shook his head.

"What about Hannah Thatcher, the woman across the hall?"

"No. Never saw her."

Santana had watched Matt Easton's body language, looking for any tells that he was lying. He hadn't caught any inconsistencies between Easton's words and facial expressions. That didn't mean Easton wasn't lying.

"Are you going to arrest me?"

"Should we?" Santana asked.

"No way. Only thing I'm guilty of is telling you a little white lie."

"Any lies in a murder investigation are not little, Mr. Easton."

"Then you do believe Tara was murdered."

"We find any more 'white lies,' Mr. Easton, and we'll be back."

"Everything else I've told you is the truth."

"For your sake, it better be."

As they returned to their detective ride, Cruz said, "You believe Easton?"

"I'm leaning in that direction."

"It could've gone down the way Easton said it did."

"No way to prove it didn't right now."

Chapter 31

Later that morning Santana drove to Megan McKenna's Craftsman on Churchill Street. He wanted to speak to Jadyn Hartley, who'd been released from the hospital two days ago. Santana figured McKenna would be at work.

He rang the doorbell twice before Hartley answered.

"We need to talk, Jadyn."

"About what?"

"Blaine Beckham."

Hartley's hand rested on the door handle as his eyes flitted from Santana, to the shoes on his feet, and back to Santana. Finally, he said, "I don't know him."

"You were in his gun shop last Thursday."

Hartley hesitated.

"I've got video evidence."

Hartley's shoulders sagged as he nodded, turned, and headed for the living room, leaving the door open.

Santana entered and closed it behind him.

Dressed in sweat socks, jeans, and a black turtleneck, Hartley plopped himself down on the couch.

Santana sat in a lounge chair across from him. "How are you feeling?"

He shrugged. "I've been better."

Haven't we all, Santana thought.

"Tell me about Blaine Beckham."

"I went to his gun shop. So what?"

"You can't purchase a gun with your record. What were you doing there?"

Hartley shrugged again.

"That's not an answer."

"Best I have."

"We know who the bones belong to," Santana said. "And we know that Blaine Beckham was involved in the victim's death. That clears you. But I need to know what you were doing in Beckham's gun shop four days before he was shot dead."

Hartley's gaze wandered around the room for a few beats, his eyes never settling on Santana. Then he said, "I don't sleep well at night. Worse since I . . ." His voice trailed off and his gaze turned inward.

Trying to encourage him, Santana said, "You can trust me."

"That's funny. You thought I buried the bones."

"We had to investigate everyone connected with them. Doesn't mean I thought you were guilty. And you did find them."

"No, I didn't."

"What do you mean?"

"I was up before sunrise on Thursday. Walked over to Lake Como. Saw Beckham park his car and carry a skull to the water. I looked inside his car. Saw a stack of Combat Zone posters in the back seat."

"You're sure it was Beckham you saw? Could've been one of his employees driving the car."

"Later that day I drove to the gun shop and went inside."

"And you ID'd him."

"Introduced himself. Asked me what I was interested in. I looked at a few handguns so he wouldn't be suspicious. Then I left."

Just then the front door flew open and Megan McKenna stormed in, her eyes blazing at Santana. "What the hell are you doing here?" she asked, slamming the door behind her.

Santana looked at Hartley. "You call her?"

He shook his head. "She comes home for lunch to check on me."

"And I'm damn glad I did. You have no business here, Detective."

"I believe I do."

She jabbed her index finger toward the front door. "You need to leave. Now!"

Santana's gaze slid to Hartley. "You want to tell her or should I?"

"Tell me what?" McKenna said, her voice leaden with anger.

Jadyn looked down at his hands.

"Jadyn saw the man who buried the bones," Santana said, his eyes locked on McKenna's.

The color drained from McKenna's complexion. She stood perfectly still for a time, her mouth partly open, as if she couldn't find the words. Then she made her way to the couch and sat down beside Jadyn.

She tried to take his hand, but he pulled it away. She let out a breath and said, "Why didn't you tell me?"

"I was afraid."

"Of what?"

"I think he saw me."

"Who saw you?"

"Blaine Beckham," Santana said.

"The man involved in the shootout at the gun shop?"

"That one. Jadyn went to his gun shop."

McKenna stared wide-eyed at Hartley. "Why would you do that?"

Averting her gaze, Hartley said, "I wanted to make sure it was him."

"Do you think he recognized you?" Santana said.

Hartley nodded. "When I came home from school the next day, his car was parked on the street in front of the house."

"How did he know where you lived?" McKenna said.

"Jadyn's name and photo were in the *Pioneer Press*," Santana said.

McKenna's eyes blazed with anger. "Thanks to you and that damn reporter."

"Did Beckham get out of the car?" Santana said, moving on.

"No. But the car sat there for an hour." He paused for a moment before continuing. "I read about Beckham in the paper after he was killed. Scary dude. I could see it in his eyes."

McKenna looked at Santana. "Many of the soldiers who come back from war are psychologically damaged, like Blaine Beckham."

Likely Beckham had some psychological issues before he enlisted, Santana thought. But Beckham's plan to intimidate Hartley had worked. Santana wondered if the intimidation had also played a part in Jadyn's suicide attempt.

"I understand that some of these Afghani soldiers, and some from the US, have been accused of war crimes and other human rights abuses," McKenna said. "We should not give all of these people a free pass. We should carefully screen them and look into any accusations of human rights violations. Don't you agree, Detective?"

Santana focused on Jadyn. "Should've come to me for help."

McKenna gently touched Hartley's shoulder. "Or me, Jadyn."

"Like anyone would've believed me."

"I would've," she said. "You can always talk to me about anything."

Jadyn glanced at her, his eyes wide, his brows rising in an expression of disbelief.

"No need to worry about Beckham now," Santana said.

McKenna glared at him. "And no need to bother Jadyn anymore."

Santana stood, his eyes finding Hartley again. "I'm glad you're still here."

Hartley offered a half-smile and held his eyes on Santana for a moment. "Me, too," he said.

*   *   *

Santana and Cruz sat cross-legged on the Afghan cushions on the floor of Nasrin Khalil's apartment as they had when they had first met her.

She wore jeans and sneakers as before, but her loosely tied headscarf and sweater were both rose-colored. She wore no lipstick and did not offer them tea.

"You have found my father."

"I'm afraid we have," Santana said.

Her green eyes filmed. "I have known he was dead for a long time. I could feel it here," she said, placing a hand over her heart. "Where did you find the body?"

Santana knew she would ask the question, but he had no good answer. "We haven't found all of his body . . . yet."

Nasrin opened her mouth to speak and then hesitated as a flame of anger replaced the film in her eyes. "Someone dismembered his body."

Santana nodded.

"Who?"

"We can't share that information at this time."

"Can't or won't?"

"Both," Santana said.

Nasrin went silent for a time. Then she said, "It is one of the men in the photo you showed me on your first visit."

He could feel Cruz's eyes on him as he held his gaze on Nasrin.

"I have read about two shootings involving the names of two of the men in the photograph," she said. "Angel Duran and Blaine Beckham. Someone wounded Duran, and your fellow police officer killed Beckham and paid for it with his life."

"Once we close the case, I promise I will tell you everything."

"Will those responsible be punished?"

"Yes," Santana said.

He saw the doubt in her eyes along with something else, but recognition eluded him.

"They will be punished," Cruz assured her.

In Blaine Beckham's case, Santana thought, he already had.

"We'll need a DNA sample from you," he said. "In order to make a positive ID."

Nasrin gave a reluctant nod.

Cruz, looking embarrassed, gently took a buccal mouth cavity swab.

When he'd finished, Nasrin said, "Did you send the other man to see me?"

"What man is that?" Cruz asked.

"Tall man. Bald. He asked about the unnamed Afghan in the photo you showed me."

"Was his name Crawford?" Santana said.

"Yes. A very rude man."

"What did you tell him?" Cruz asked.

"The same as I told you. I do not know this man or his name."

"Abdul Rahim," Cruz said.

Santana gave him a hard look, indicating his displeasure with Cruz's reveal.

Cruz shrugged in his defense.

Picking up on the body language, Nasrin said, "His name means nothing to me."

But it could mean everything to the investigation, Santana thought.

*   *   *

Santana and Cruz were returning to the LEC after leaving Nasrin Khalil's apartment when Lynn Pierce called.

"Blaine Beckham turned off his cell phone on January twenty-ninth."

Not a surprise, Santana thought.

"You find any of the bone poems written on his computer?"

"'Fraid not."

"Okay. Thanks, Lynn."

Santana knew he and Cruz had to update Janet Kendrick.

In her office that afternoon, Santana told her about the DNA match Dennis Crane had found on Blaine Beckham's chainsaw.

"Then Beckham killed Taimur Khalil."

"We believe he murdered Tara Easton as well. Choked her out. Then injected her with heroin before cutting her throat."

"And he did this because?"

"Beckham, Duran, Khalil, Easton, and an Afghan named Abdul Rahim smuggled heroin out of Afghanistan and were trying to sell it here. Beckham wanted the money from the sale."

Had Santana said morphine instead of heroin, Kendrick would've asked more questions. Questions that Santana didn't want to answer—yet.

"Was the BCA able to match the shell casings from the Duran shooting to Beckham's AR-15?"

"No."

"Then who tried to kill Duran?"

"We're working on it."

"Where's the heroin?"

"My guess is Duran has it," Santana said with a straight face.

"But you have no proof."

"My CRI told us someone was looking to unload the heroin. But it'll be expensive. Only one man in town might have the cash on hand to make the buy."

"And who is that?"

"Montez Dixon."

"Dixon? Doesn't he run a successful outreach program for former drug offenders?"

"That's what I heard."

Kendrick tented her fingers and fixed her gaze on Santana. "I think the mayor is a big fan of Dixon."

"Gave him some civic award," Cruz said.

Kendrick nodded in agreement. "That's right. Big ceremony at City Hall."

"Narco/Vice thinks he's still dirty," Santana said.

"You talk to Briggs?" Kendrick asked, referring to Jim Briggs, the Narco/Vice commander.

"Got the information on Dixon from an undercover narc."

"And who is that?"

Santana preferred to keep Thornton's name out of the discussion but had little choice. "Luke Thornton," he said.

Kendrick leaned back in her chair and considered the source. "Thornton's usually reliable."

Santana felt relieved. "He is."

"Let's back up for a minute," Kendrick said. "Beckham, Khalil, and Easton are dead. Duran is still in the hospital. Beckham dismembered Khalil's body. Why would Beckham write the poems to lead us to the bones?"

"Lynn Pierce couldn't find anything on his computer. Though he could've used another computer we're not aware of. My guess is he or Duran wanted to throw us off. Make it look like we were dealing with a serial killer. Not US soldiers smuggling heroin."

"Well, that should wrap everything up," Kendrick said. "Let Narco/Vice handle Angel Duran and the heroin."

"What if the shootout between Tatum and Beckham was staged?" Santana said.

"We're back to that again."

"Someone erased the video surveillance tape in Beckham's gun shop."

"You're sure?"

"Why would only that time span be erased and nothing else?"

"Then who was the shooter?"

Santana showed Kendrick his phone copy of the photo found in Tara Easton's bedroom. "It could be Abdul Rahim."

"Perhaps he's the one who tried to kill Duran."

"We think so," Cruz said.

Santana clicked off the photo app. "A former SIGAR agent, Wade Crawford, is looking for Rahim as well."

"What's SIGAR?"

Santana explained.

Kendrick thought about it. "You both realize the media is all over this bone case. We know Blaine Beckham is likely responsible for killing Taimur Khalil and for dismembering his body. If your theory about the heroin is correct, Detective, then it goes to motive. As for this Abdul Rahim, we have no idea where he is, or if he's responsible for any of the murders."

Santana could see where Kendrick was headed, and he didn't like it. It would be politically expedient to let Blaine Beckham take the fall for the murder of Tara Easton, Taimur Khalil, and Art Tatum. And for the attempted murder of Angel Duran. But the erased security videotape still troubled Santana. Plus, the shell casings found at Duran's cabin didn't come from Beckham's AR-15. Abdul Rahim could be responsible for Beckham and Tatum's deaths, as well as the attempted murder of Angel Duran. Until Abdul Rahim was in custody, Santana believed the case remained unsolved.

"Thanks for the update," Kendrick said, letting them know the meeting had ended.

Santana and Cruz stood.

Kendrick pointed an index finger at Santana. "I'd like you to stay, Detective."

Cruz glanced at Santana as he exited the office.

Santana sat down again. He could see the hard glint in Kendrick's eyes and knew immediately what she had on her mind.

"You actually threatened Scott Weston?" she said, her eyes wide with amazement.

"I wouldn't call it a threat."

"Telling Weston you would go to the media about Joel Ryker if the DEA refused to look for Ana Soriano's mother and sister in El Salvador is not a threat?"

"More of a *quid pro quo.*"

"Oh, so you're doing Weston a favor."

"They buried the truth about Ryker."

"Yes. And we cut the DEA some slack because the DA agreed not to prosecute Ana Soriano for her role in the stolen drug money."

"Then we're even."

Kendrick nodded vigorously. "Exactly. We're even."

"And now I'm offering Weston another deal."

Santana chose to not tell Kendrick about the potential drug bust he'd promised Weston. If the bust didn't happen soon, he would have to let the press know about the DEA's cover-up involving rogue-agent Joel Ryker's death, which would probably lead to his dismissal.

"No, Detective," Kendrick said. "You're not offering Weston a deal. The DEA is too busy in El Salvador to spend time looking for Ana Soriano's family. If you leak anything to the press about Joel Ryker, your career here is over. Am I making myself clear?"

"Perfectly. But understand this. I'm willing to lose my badge to save Ana Soriano. Make that clear to Scott Weston. Either he does what I asked, or the DEA will have to deal with the fallout when the media learns that Ryker attempted to steal a half-million dollars in drug money and was responsible for two murders. Their hero story goes up in smoke."

"Don't do this, Detective."

"I already have." Santana stood. "Tell Weston he better get back to me soon. Otherwise, I go to the press."

Chapter 32

Montez Dixon operated out of his West Side Boxing Club located in an old warehouse on Water Street overlooking Harriet Island and the Mississippi River.

Dixon grew up in the violent West Garfield area of Chicago. Kilos of drugs moved through the streets in the 1980s and 1990s like water through a sewer pipe as gangs fought wars over turf and supply. As drugs and prostitution ran rampant, so did urban blight and heavy deterioration, and the community became one of the more devastated neighborhoods in Chicago.

Dixon joined the Gangster Disciples at age fifteen after the death of his father. He soon became addicted to heroin, and at the age of eighteen he went down on a drug possession charge and served three years.

While in prison he took up boxing. After his release he continued training at the Sam Colonna gym in Chicago. Dixon later won an Illinois State Golden Gloves light-heavyweight title before losing in the finals of the National Golden Glove championship. He fought the last round with a broken right hand and lost on a decision after leading for much of the fight.

After his mother's death, Dixon moved to St. Paul to live with an older brother. He trained and fought professionally, climbing up the ranks of the light-heavyweight division before being accused of throwing a fight for $20,000 cash to pad the victory record of a former Olympian and up-and-coming light-heavyweight being groomed for big money matches. Wanting to avoid becoming a "labeled man," or someone that opponents could pay to lose a fight, Dixon notified the FBI. He then recorded a secret tape of his manager offering him another twenty grand to throw a second fight.

It didn't surprise Santana that some fights were thrown. He recalled reading a quote by Jimmy Cannon, the legendary boxing journalist, who once described boxing as "the redlight district of sports."

Dixon's manager was arrested along with the promoter. Though Dixon was never charged, the four major boxing associations blackballed him from fighting again. He took his earnings and became a successful promoter. Santana wondered if Dixon supplemented his now considerable earnings with drug sale profits.

Having been a fan of boxing since his teenage years, Santana had visited a number of boxing clubs. He recognized the key furnishings present in all of them as surely as he'd recognize an altar in a church.

Red and black banners bearing the club logo of a boxer raising a gloved right hand in victory decorated the white walls. Punching bags of different sizes and shapes ranging from heavy punching bags hanging from low overhead girders, freestanding bags on round bases, reflex balls, maize bags, and uppercut mini-bags and speed bags attached to the walls gave fighters an opportunity to work on a variety of equipment.

A young woman dressed in a hooded sweatshirt, trunks, and boxing shoes shadowboxed near the ring, working through the angles of her punches.

Trophies won in boxing tournaments and title matches filled a large glass case along the back wall.

A raised ring with four ropes sat in the center of the gym, empty now, one of thousands of boxing rings in thousands of boxing clubs across the world, a space waiting to be filled by two combatants.

A customary photo of Muhammad Ali graced the wall outside Dixon's office.

Through the open office door Santana could see Dixon seated behind a big metal desk with his large Nike shoes resting on a corner, his shaved black head gleaming under the lights. He wore bright orange sweatpants with zippers on the ankles and a tight black Under Armour T-shirt. He rubbed the chin patch and mustache that circled his lips as he read a copy of the *Pioneer Press*. He still looked like he could go ten rounds with no problem.

A guy sitting in a cushioned chair to the left of Dixon's desk had a head full of long dreadlocks and a dark horseshoe mustache. He wore Nike shoes and sweatpants as well, but his were yellow.

Santana knocked on the open office door as he stood at the entrance.

Dixon looked up from the newspaper.

The guy to his left stood up, like he was ready for trouble.

After a few beats, Dixon grinned and stood up. "What can I do for you . . . Detective?"

"That obvious, huh?"

"I've met a few in my lifetime. Might as well wear your badge on your chest."

Santana approached the desk and held out his badge wallet.

Dixon peered at it and then set the newspaper on his desktop. "Pull up a chair," Dixon said. "Make yourself scarce, Reggie," Dixon said to the other man.

Reggie nodded and walked past Santana without looking at him.

Santana retrieved one of the two metal folding chairs against the wall and sat down in front of Dixon's desk.

Along with the two folding chairs, Dixon had a desk and office chair. A framed article about his outreach program and boxing club hung on the wall, along with a handful of framed photos taken with city and state politicians and local celebrities. A tattooed Dixon was an up-and-coming light-heavyweight in the framed photo on the desk.

"Like your club," Santana said.

Dixon eased himself down in his chair and folded his hands on the desktop. "Training some good young fighters. Getting them out of the gang life. Got a tattoo artist who works with us. Cleans them up."

Santana noted that the tattoos that had once sleeved both of Dixon's arms had been lasered off.

"It's a clean place to get a workout, learn some boxing moves, get in shape," he continued. "Been in a lot of boxing clubs. Each one, like a person, has a soul and a body. Didn't want this to be a spit and sawdust club, if you know what I mean."

"I do."

"We're here for everyone, from the boxer hoping to be the next Ali to the casual gym-goer avoiding a left hook. We keep it real, but not too real," Dixon said with a chuckle.

Dixon didn't sound like or act like a gangbanger just off the streets. Santana guessed Dixon could switch his persona depending on what crowd he was speaking to as easily as he changed shirts.

"Majority of people who call say they're fed up with the mainstream gyms," he continued. "Don't want the identical Starbucks-and-Subway experience, the theater showing the fifth superhero film of the year. They want something different. Same for women. The ladies love the workout. Put 'women friendly' on our website. Been adding more classes for women every year. Damn near have more women members than men now."

Santana remained silent as his eyes lingered on Dixon.

"You look like a guy who can handle himself, Detective. Ever put on the gloves?"

"Not professionally."

"Maybe some amateur fights?"

"You could call it that."

Dixon chuckled again. "Yeah. Man in your profession need to know how to handle hisself."

"Comes in handy sometimes."

"Bet it does." Dixon's eyes stayed on Santana's for a few moments more before he said, "What brings you here?"

"I'm looking for someone who wants to unload four kilos of China White."

Dixon sat perfectly still with his dark brown eyes fixed on Santana. "Why come to me?"

"Some people say you're the man to see. Only guy who could afford the sale."

"Shit," he said. "You been talkin' to the DEA or your homies in Narco/Vice? They ain't never gonna let it go, no matter what good I done."

Dixon had unconsciously slipped back into his street lingo.

"I'm telling you what I hear. Not what I know."

"And I'm tellin' you I ain't gangbanging on the job. I gave that life up a long time ago. You lookin' for someone who's doing the nation's work, you've come to the wrong place."

Santana understood that "doing the nation's work" was gang slang for working for the gang to which you belonged. Typically, selling illegal drugs or in some other way aiding and assisting in the distribution of unlawful narcotics.

He also understood that lying had once been a learned and practiced art in Dixon's gang life, as it was with most gangbangers Santana had dealings with. He couldn't tell if Dixon now lived a more truthful and honest life, or if everything he'd built was nothing but trappings that concealed his true purpose.

"You say you're out of the life."

"Been out for a long time."

"Maybe you hear things."

"If I was paying attention."

"Then you'd contact me if you heard about something going down."

"Leave me your card. You'll be the first to know."

Santana took a business card out of his wallet and laid it on the desktop.

Dixon gazed at it for a time before engaging Santana again. "You're homicide, not Narco/Vice. We talking about someone's murder here?"

"We are."

"Drug dealing and death go hand and hand."

"Let's see if we can prevent both," Santana said.

* * *

That evening after dinner at home, Santana received a phone call on his department cell phone from DEA Special Agent in Charge Scott Weston.

Santana clicked the speaker icon on his cell phone. He, Ana, and Gitana were all sitting on the living room couch.

"We've located Ana Soriano's mother and sister."

Ana grinned as her hands went to her mouth, as if to suppress a scream.

"I'm impressed," Santana said.

"You should be. Ana's mother was accused of being an activist and arrested."

Ana gasped.

Weston must've heard her because he said, "Take it easy. We got her out."

"How?" Santana asked.

"Tipped them off about a handful of bangers hiding in a neighborhood in exchange for her release."

"What about my sister?" Ana asked.

"A neighbor looked after her. She's fine."

"What's the plan?"

"Up to you," Weston said. "They appear safe for now. Don't know if they want to leave El Salvador."

"Have the mother call Ana."

Santana looked at her.

She nodded in agreement.

"If they want to come here, you get them out, Weston. That's the deal."

"And in return?"

Santana knew that Luke Thornton and the Narco/Vice unit wouldn't be happy with the DEA bigfooting the drug bust. But Santana had to give Weston something in return. And he'd given his word.

"I'll let you know when the China White drug bust is going down. Be ready. Got a feeling it'll be soon."

Chapter 33

On Thursday morning, Santana and Cruz, along with several thousand people, including hundreds of police officers from across the upper Midwest, attended Art Tatum's funeral service and burial.

Under a clear blue sky with temperatures in the upper 30s, police cruisers, police motorcycles, and other emergency vehicles flashed their red, white, and blue lights to honor Tatum.

A procession of St. Paul police officers dressed in uniform blouse coats with white shirts and gloves marched down the street as Santana, Cruz, and hundreds of other officers saluted. Similarly dressed members of the honor guard also wore Sam Browne-style belts, including a shoulder strap and a black mourning band across the badge.

After the church service, Art Tatum's burial took place at Elmhurst Cemetery, a one-hundred-acre site in the North End, just east of Como Park, and the third oldest cemetery in St. Paul.

A horse-drawn carriage brought Tatum's casket from the church to the cemetery.

Uniformed personnel formed an aisle extending from the hearse to the grave. Standing near the grave beside Gabriel Cruz, Santana watched as pallbearers removed the casket from the hearse.

His thoughts shifted for a moment to the death of one of his first partners, Rick Anderson, and Anderson's plea to him as he lay dying.

"Listen, John, if I don't make it, I want you to promise me you won't blame yourself."

"You're going to make it."

"It was my idea to cover your back. Not yours. Promise me, John."

"All right," Santana had said.

As in Tatum's case, Santana's reluctant decision to give in to a request had cost a man his life. It was the kind of weight no cop wanted. Santana had had no reason to believe Tatum would be walking into a dangerous situation. Still, despite attempts to reason away blame for Tatum's death, guilt again seeped into his consciousness, like a cold winter wind through an imperfect window seal.

Had he gotten Tatum killed?

Santana glanced at Cruz, trying to read his emotions, but his partner appeared lost in his own thoughts.

The pallbearers carried Tatum's casket between the ranks and honor guard to the gravesite before setting it on the lowering device.

Santana could see the firing party approximately fifty yards away, positioned so that it wouldn't fire directly over the mourners but over the grave. A bugler stood near the firing party and in view of Tatum's wife seated at the gravesite.

A replica oak-and-forged-steel Civil War cannon caisson holding a bell and cradle rested on a rise beside the firing party. A trailer had transported the eleven-hundred-pound, eight-and-a-half-foot-long bell and cradle to the cemetery. A replica of the St. Paul police star badge, created in 1854, was attached to the carriage, along with the gold eagle atop the bell.

Each year at the department's Memorial Day ceremony honoring all those killed in the line of duty, officers rang the bell. When not in use, the bell and caisson resided in the lobby of the Western District, which housed the SPPD police museum.

After the pastor's benediction, the firing party fired three volleys of blank ammunition and then assumed the position of present arms. They remained in this position as the bugler sounded taps. The end-of-tour was called and the bell rung fifteen times to honor Tatum's years of service.

The pallbearers folded the American flag into the shape of a cocker hat and passed it to the Honor Guard commander, who placed it in the hands of Thomas Murdoch, the chief of police. Murdoch then presented the flag to Tatum's wife, Halle.

Santana had remembered her name because it was the same as the Hollywood actress. He'd expressed his condolences to her before the church service began, as had Cruz. He didn't know her well, having seen and briefly talked to her only a few times at SPPD functions.

But when he'd bent over to speak softly to her as she sat in the church's front pew, she'd looked up at him with bloodshot eyes, clutched his sleeve in her small hands, and asked, "You sure this is how my Artie died?"

Santana hadn't known how to respond, or why she suspected her husband hadn't died the way the department and press had reported it.

"'Cause if it isn't, John, you make sure whoever killed him pays for it."

He'd been surprised by the use of his first name as well, given that they weren't close.

"You have my word," he'd blurted, without thinking.

She'd offered a thin smile and patted his sleeve. "Artie always spoke highly of you. I know you'll do the right thing."

With that her eyes returned to the Bible passage she'd been reading.

To Santana's surprise, it was Ezekiel 37, 1-2, the same passage Professor Xavier Dryer had asked him to read when he'd visited the professor at the University of Minnesota.

*   *   *

The address Cruz had found on LexisNexis for Abdul Rahim indicated he lived in a one-and-one-half-story Craftsman on Bush Avenue in Hazel Park on St. Paul's East Side. The neighborhood consisted of small-to-medium-sized single-family homes and high-rise apartments built in the mid-twentieth century and occupied by a mixture of owners and renters.

Santana had once read that the Hazel Park neighborhood had more Finnish and Asian ancestry people living in it than nearly any neighborhood in America. It also had one of the highest percentages of French-speaking residents in the States. He wondered how many Afghans lived here now and if one of them was Abdul Rahim.

Cruz hadn't spoken about Art Tatum's funeral on the drive to Hazel Park. Now, as they pulled to the curb in front of the house, Cruz asked, "What did Tatum's widow say to you at the funeral service?"

Santana recalled the Bible passage Tatum's widow was reading when she spoke to him. He considered telling Cruz and then realized he had no logical explanation for it.

"She wanted my assurance that if Art hadn't died the way it was reported I'd find her husband's killer," Santana said.

"Why would she think that?"

Santana shook his head. "I don't know."

"But you're not sure that Tatum and Beckham killed each other."

"I'm not."

"Couldn't be Duran. He was still in the hospital."

Santana nodded.

"Then it has to be Abdul Rahim."

"We won't know that till we find him," Santana said.

"What did Luke Thornton have to say?"

"Only guy in town Thornton thinks could handle four kilos of China White is Montez Dixon."

"Never heard of him."

"He's a former Chicago gangbanger turned pro fighter and boxing promoter. Owns a boxing club near Harriet Island. Does really well financially."

"You think drugs are his sideline?"

"Didn't get that impression yesterday, but Dixon is an accomplished liar."

"You spoke with him."

"I did."

"Were you planning on telling me?"

"I just did."

Cruz let out a frustrated breath.

"I haven't worked with a partner for a while. Takes some getting used to again."

"Not much of an excuse."

"Best I have," Santana said.

As he and Cruz were about to exit their detective squad, Santana glanced in the rearview mirror and noticed that a dark SUV with an Ohio license plate had pulled up behind them.

"Wait," he cautioned Cruz.

A moment later Wade Crawford, wearing his heavy overcoat, rubber boots, and a fedora, stepped out of the SUV and walked up to Santana's driver's side window.

Santana opened the window. "You following us, Crawford?"

"Brilliant deduction, Sherlock."

"What do you want?"

"Never got a chance to talk to you at the funeral."

"That your reason for being there?"

"And to pay my respects."

"So, what's so important?"

"Mind opening the back door so I can slide in? Haven't gotten used to freezing my ass off here in balmy Minnesota."

"This is a warm spell."

"I heard. Guess I spent too much time roasting in the Middle East." He gestured with a hand toward the back door.

Santana clicked open the door locks and Crawford slid in and closed the door.

"Keep the car running, will ya?" he said, blowing on his bare hands.

"Get to it," Santana said, half-turning in the front seat so he could see Crawford. "We're busy."

"What're you doing here?"

"None of your concern."

"I think it is. Maybe I'll just tag along."

"And maybe you won't."

"Come on, Santana. I know you're closing in on Abdul Rahim."

"Says who?"

"I did. Extra backup couldn't hurt."

"We don't need backup."

"Like the guy you just buried."

Santana grabbed Crawford with one hand by the front of his coat and pulled him forward.

"Easy, John," Cruz said.

"Unlike Art Tatum, you have no jurisdiction here, Crawford. Stay out of our way."

Crawford held up his hands in a surrender gesture. "Take it easy, Santana. I meant no disrespect."

"Could've fooled me."

"Look. We all want the same thing."

"What's that?"

"To figure out what was smuggled out of Afghanistan and who has it. Not to mention Rahim's location and who's responsible for the body parts showing up all over town."

Santana let go of the big man's coat. He figured he already knew the answers to Crawford's questions, except for Rahim's whereabouts. But he wasn't ready to share.

"Maybe Crawford could cover the back door," Cruz said.

Santana shot him a look. He didn't appreciate Cruz's suggestion.

"You are hunting for Rahim," Crawford said, adjusting his coat.

Santana shifted his eyes to Crawford. "You speak Dari?"

"Some."

As reluctant as he was to involve Crawford, he figured he could use him to translate while Cruz covered the back door.

"You have a piece?"

Crawford opened his coat, revealing a shoulder holster filled with a Glock.

"Leave it here."

"Come on, Santana. We don't know if Rahim is in there. I can't go in unarmed."

"Your choice. Leave the gun or stay here."

Crawford shook his head in frustration as he slid the Glock out of its holster and set it on the back seat.

"I'll do the talking, Crawford. You keep your mouth shut."

"Roger that."

Glaring at Cruz, Santana said, "Cover the back. I'm not letting Crawford out of my sight."

Chapter 34

Santana opened his overcoat for easier access to his Glock as he, Cruz, and Wade Crawford walked along the shoveled sidewalk toward the house where Abdul Rahim supposedly lived.

Thick drops of melting snow fell from the gutters as Cruz stepped into the ankle-deep snow blanketing the yard and headed for the back door.

A minute later he used his two-way to let Santana know he was in position.

Santana opened the storm door and fisted the solid wood entry door. "Police! Open up!"

A bearded man Santana made for his mid-fifties or early sixties opened the entry door. He wore a black loose-fitting tunic shirt and pants, sandals with colorful socks, and a black turban with a tail that fell over his shoulder.

Though Abdul Rahim had had a similar look in the photo in Tara Easton's bedroom, Santana could tell by the man's age that he wasn't Rahim.

"Do you speak English?" Santana asked.

The man shook his head. A moment later a teenager with shaggy black hair and a slight two-inch-long purple scar across his left cheek came to the door. He wore white socks, blue jeans, and a gold and purple sweatshirt with a Minnesota Vikings emblem on the front.

"I speak some English," he said.

Santana showed him his badge. "What's your name?"

The young man didn't answer at first, seemingly reluctant to reveal it.

"Your name," Santana said with more force.

"Omar."

"Omar what?"

"Omar Rahim."

Crawford nudged Santana.

Santana gestured at the older man. "Who is this?"

"My grandfather."

"What's your grandfather's name?"

"Ali."

"Where's your father?"

"He's dead."

Omar's answer confused Santana. "What's your father's name?"

"Saad. Killed by an IED in Afghanistan working for you."

Santana assumed "for you" meant Americans, but Omar spoke matter-of-factly, with no evident anger or bitterness, as if it were a fact of Afghani life. Santana imagined it was.

"Sorry to hear about your father. I lost mine when I was about your age. It's never easy."

Appearing surprised by Santana's comment, Omar gave him a slow nod.

"Mind if we step inside, Omar? No sense in heating the outdoors."

The young man said something to his grandfather in what Santana assumed was either Dari or Pashto.

The grandfather nodded his head as Omar waved Santana and Crawford inside.

"Did you understand that?" Santana said to Crawford.

"They're speaking Dari."

Santana closed the door behind him and stood in front of the two men in a short hallway that led into the living room. "I'm looking for Abdul Rahim."

Omar's eyes drifted to his grandfather, who shook his head.

"You do know him," Santana said.

The old man shook his head again.

"If your grandfather doesn't understand English, how did he know what I said?"

Omar's dark eyes jittered as he considered an answer. "He speaks a little English. But he does not know this man."

"What about you?"

The young man shook his head, but his unwillingness to make eye contact said just the opposite. It was a tell Santana often saw when someone was lying.

"He's lying," Crawford said, stepping forward.

Santana put a hand in Crawford's chest. "Remember what I said."

Crawford gave a reluctant nod and stepped back.

"Can you translate?" Santana asked Crawford.

"My Dari isn't great."

"Do the best you can."

"I can translate," Omar said.

Santana wanted Omar on his side but didn't trust the kid to tell him the truth as long as his grandfather was in the same room. He pulled out his iPhone and clicked on the photos app till he found the picture of Abdul Rahim with Tara Easton, Blaine Beckham, Angel Duran, and Taimur Khalil.

Turning the phone toward the two men, Santana pointed to Rahim and said, "This is the man we're looking for. This is his last known address."

Omar and then Ali stared blankly at the photo and then at Santana.

Crawford stepped forward and got in the old man's face. He spoke forcefully in Dari.

Ali nodded his head quickly and answered Crawford.

"I told you to keep your mouth shut," Santana said to Crawford.

"You want answers, Santana, then let me do my job."

"Your job is translating. Nothing else."

"You want to know what the old man said or not?"

Santana backed off. "What did you tell him?"

"That we'd send him and his family back to Afghanistan if we found out he was lying."

"And what did Ali say?"

"Abdul Rahim is Omar's uncle. He lived here for a while, but left a few months ago. The old man said he doesn't know where Abdul is."

"What about you?" Santana said to Omar.

"My grandfather speaks the truth."

Crawford said something else in Dari. Then he said to Santana, "Let's go sit down. See who else is here and what they can tell us."

Santana used his two-way to contact Cruz. "I need you in front."

Thirty seconds later, Cruz knocked on the front door.

Santana opened it.

Cruz stomped the snow off his boots and stepped inside, closing both doors behind him.

The furniture in the living room was worn but comfortable, something that might be found in a secondhand store. The unframed prints on the walls depicting various winter scenes gave no indication that an Afghani family lived here. Santana concluded that the Afghan Cultural Society had acquired the house merely for rental purposes to house some of the fleeing refugees.

Santana turned to Crawford. "Tell the grandfather we'd like to look around. Ask if he minds."

Crawford spoke in Dari to the old man.

"Hey," Cruz said, "that's not what Santana asked."

"What'd Crawford say?" Santana asked Cruz.

"He told the old man we were going to look around, and if he got in the way he'd be in handcuffs."

"You speak some Dari," Crawford said with a crooked smile to Cruz.

"Damn right. So don't screw around."

Santana thought he should've let Cruz do the translating. But then he would've had to let Crawford keep his gun and cover the back door.

Cruz said something in Dari to the grandfather, who answered.

Cruz nodded and spoke to Santana. "The grandfather said there are women upstairs. He does not want us to go up there."

"Tell him the women have to come down. Then we'll take a look."

Cruz repeated the instructions to Ali.

The old man spoke to Omar, who went upstairs to relay the message to the women.

The four of them sat down to wait.

A few minutes later three women dressed in black hijabs came down the stairs. Two of them appeared to be Omar's age. Santana figured the older third woman was the girls' and Omar's mother.

"Wait here while Cruz and I check upstairs," Santana said to Crawford. "And don't stir up any trouble."

Crawford placed an open hand over his heart. "You have my pledge, Detective."

"Right," Santana said. Nodding at Cruz, the two of them ascended the stairs.

When they got to the landing at the top of the stairs and out of sight of Ali, Omar, and the women downstairs, Santana drew his Glock.

"You think Rahim is up here?" Cruz said, drawing his gun.

"We'll see."

The hallway seemed unusually dark for this time of the day. Santana figured curtains covered the windows in the rooms off the hallway. He flicked on the hallway light switch but no overhead light came on.

"Not a good sign," Cruz said.

"I'll go first," Santana said. "You cover."

"Copy that."

Before entering a room with an open door, Santana placed the bezel of his mini-Maglite between the door and the doorframe. The last thing he wanted was someone ending up behind him after he entered the room.

Then he and Cruz used the leapfrog technique as they worked their way down the hallway. While Santana entered a room, Cruz covered the unexplored portion of the hallway. When the room was cleared, Santana returned to the hallway and advanced past Cruz till he came to the next room to be searched. Then he took the cover position while Cruz searched the room. They repeated this technique till they arrived at the last room on the right that faced the backyard and alley.

"Door's closed," Cruz said, looking back at Santana. His eyes were lit with energy, but Santana saw no fear in them.

"Ready?"

Cruz gave a quick nod, turned the door handle, and shoved the door hard, making sure it slammed against the wall or anyone standing there.

They remained covered behind the wall on each side of the door, waiting till the last possible moment before revealing themselves.

Peering around the doorjamb, a quick scan revealed an unmade bed and men's clothes scattered around the floor and on a hardback chair to Santana's right. Another closed door directly ahead likely opened into a bathroom.

Santana followed Cruz and his Glock into the room and double-checked behind the bedroom door.

Seeing no one, they hurried across the room and stood on each side of the second door.

Santana pounded on the door. "If anyone is in there, come out now with your hands up!" He looked at Cruz. "Crawford told me Rahim speaks English. But if it isn't him in there, can you translate?"

"I've had some practice." Cruz translated the order into Dari.
Silence.

Cruz tried the door handle and shook his head.

Santana stepped in front of the door and slammed the bottom of his foot against it. The door swung open as the latch and spring bolt broke away.

Straight ahead they saw an open bathroom window.

They hurried to the window just in time to see a late model beige Toyota race out of the alley.

"You get the license?" Santana asked as he holstered his Glock.

Cruz shook his head. "I'll get the car."

"Don't bother. He's in the wind now."

"You figure it was Rahim?"

"Who else?"

"But we didn't see him."

"Omar and Ali don't know that."

Cruz holstered his Glock as they headed downstairs.

"What's going on?" Crawford said.

"Rahim went out the back bathroom window."

Crawford stood.

"Sit down," Santana said. "We won't catch him now."

Santana squatted in front of Omar. "Where did your uncle go?"

Omar kept his eyes lowered as he shook his head.

"Tell me."

"Let me deal with him," Crawford said.

"Shut up," Santana said without looking at him.

Omar raised his eyes and said, "I don't know where he went."

"How long has he been staying here?"

"A few months. But sometimes he goes and does not return for days."

"And you don't know where he goes or stays when he's not here?"

Omar shook his head.

"He's lying," Crawford said.

Omar glared at Crawford. "I am not lying. I tell the truth to this detective. Not to you."

Santana stood and looked at Cruz.

Cruz nodded as if to confirm Omar's statement.

Santana took out a business card and handed it to Omar. "We need to speak to your uncle. He must call me if he returns. Otherwise, all of you here will be in a great deal of trouble. Do you understand?"

Omar peered up at Santana and nodded. "I understand."

*   *   *

Santana and Cruz were seated at their desk chairs in the Homicide and Robbery Unit. A BOLO had been issued for Abdul Rahim, listing his description and a description of the Toyota they saw him driving.

"What now?" Cruz asked.

"I'm going to sit on Angel Duran for a while," Santana said. "See if anything shakes loose."

"Why Duran?"

Santana knew he had to level with Cruz.

"Duran has four kilos of heroin."

"How do you know that?"

"I know."

Cruz stared at him. "You were in his house."

"Didn't want you involved, Gabriel."

"I'm your partner."

"That's why I'm leveling with you now."

"It's a little late."

"But not too late."

"What else haven't you told me?"

"You know what I know."

Cruz sat quietly for a time. Then he stood and grabbed his overcoat off the coat tree beside his cubicle. "You're not going alone."

"All right. I'll notify Kendrick. Then I'm going home to get some cold weather gear. Never know when we might need it. I'll meet you back here in three hours."

* * *

Janet Kendrick was straightening the files on her desk, getting ready to leave for the day, when Santana knocked on her open office door.

"What's up, Detective?"

"Angel Duran is out of the hospital."

"Okay."

"I believe he has four kilos of heroin he wants to unload."

"And how do you know that Duran has the kilos?"

"Luke Thornton heard it from his CRI."

If Kendrick went to Thornton, Santana figured the narc would support his story, especially if he brought him in on the bust.

"You think he'll make a move soon?" Kendrick asked.

"I do."

Particularly after Duran sees that someone has ransacked his place, Santana thought.

"I'd like to sit on him tonight," he said.

"Cruz, too?"

Santana nodded.

Since the department faced staffing shortages, overtime had become a hot issue, something Santana assumed Kendrick was contemplating as she considered his request.

During his years in Homicide, Santana had often worked on his own time, as had all the detectives in the unit. They treated investigations as more of a calling than a job. You couldn't be a good homicide detective if you were always watching the clock.

He saw it as his mission. He spoke for the dead who had no voice.

"All right," Kendrick said at last. "But bring me something, Detective."

Santana hoped he could.

Chapter 35

Dusk settled over the landscape as Santana parked his SUV in the garage and entered the back door of his house on the St. Croix.

As he walked into the dining room, he saw Ana Soriano seated at the dining room table, holding Gitana by the collar. A clean-shaven, black-haired man dressed in jeans, a sweatshirt, and a leather bomber jacket sat to her right at the far end of the table. Santana didn't recognize him till he looked into the man's dead eyes.

Abdul Rahim.

Santana went for the gun on his hip, but Rahim was quicker.

Gesturing with the barrel of his Glock 19, Rahim said, "This can go one of two ways, Detective."

Santana considered his limited options. Seeing no fear in Ana's eyes worried him. Her experiences and ability to survive dangerous situations could lead to overconfidence. He wondered now if she knew about the Glock in the holster attached to the underside of the table. He wished it was at his end of the table instead of Rahim's. When this was over, he'd attach a second holstered Glock there—if he lived.

He let his hand fall away from his gun.

"You made the right decision," Rahim said. "Keep making them and nothing will happen to you or the young lady here."

Rahim's deep voice held a slight accent and conveyed authority.

"Nothing better happen to her."

"I admire your confidence, Detective. But do not get careless. Now, take off your coat. Set your holster and gun on the middle of the table, and sit down at the other end."

Santana did as ordered.

Gitana whimpered and Ana let her go to Santana. She put her head in his lap and licked his hand. He patted her head and said, "Everything is all right, girl."

"It is all right," Rahim said.

Ana's eyes narrowed. "You didn't fool me. I never believed you were John's friend."

"I am his friend. He just doesn't know it yet." Looking at Santana, Rahim said, "And I will make it better for you and your woman."

"I am not his woman," Ana said.

Rahim glanced at her and shrugged. "Then perhaps you can be mine."

"When hell freezes over."

Rahim gave her a crooked grin.

As Santana studied Rahim, he noted that without the beard Rahim looked ten years younger. He had a hard jawline and a jumble of dark wavy hair cut short around the ears. Santana made him for his early thirties.

"*Puedo alcanzar el arma debajo de la mesa,*" Ana said.

"Speak English," Rahim said.

"It's okay, Ana. I'll handle this."

So she does know about the gun under the table, Santana thought.

"What did the woman say?"

"She said she wasn't afraid."

"That is a mistake."

"What do you want?" Santana said.

Rahim laid his gun on the table, near his right hand. "The right question is, what do *you* want, Detective?"

"I want answers."

"Then ask your questions."

When first looking at the photo of Tara Easton and the four men taken in Kandahar, Santana had thought Rahim's dark eyes were as depthless as a snake's. Now as he looked into the man's eyes, he thought he might as well be looking for emotion in a cup of black coffee.

Despite this, experience had taught him that most humans, except sociopaths and psychopaths, had an innate desire to confess. He needed to ensure that Rahim had space to do so. Patience was key. Like a hunter waiting till his prey was in sight, vulnerable and unthreatened, Santana had to lay the groundwork. Rahim had to trust him.

Santana wanted to start with non-threatening questions first, questions to which he already knew the correct answers. This would establish a baseline for how Rahim responded when telling the truth. But first he wanted Ana out of danger.

"Ana isn't part of this."

"Unfortunately, she is."

Ana started to stand but Rahim clamped down on her arm.

"Ow! That hurt."

Santana felt the heat of anger, followed by frustration that he could do nothing.

"I apologize," Rahim said, looking at her. "Please. Sit down."

Ana hesitated and then sat.

Rahim shifted his gaze back to Santana. "Ask your questions, Detective."

Santana released a calming breath. "What's your name?"

"Why ask what you already know?"

"What I think and what I know are not always the same."

"My name is Abdul Rahim."

"Where do you live?"

"Where you found me."

In the silence that followed, Rahim stared at Santana, his dark eyes fixed on him, his thick eyebrows lowered and pulled close together.

Santana had often used mirroring to build rapport during interviews and interrogations. But he knew the technique had to be employed subtly. Given Rahim's highly skilled training, he figured Rahim had been taught interrogation techniques and was familiar with non-verbal communication. If Rahim thought that Santana was copying his behavior and mannerisms, it could be detrimental to establishing rapport.

"What did you do before you became a soldier?"

"I taught at Kabul University."

"What was your field?"

"Engineering. Now I am here. And you want to persecute me."

"That's not what I'm doing."

"Then why were you chasing me?"

"Why did you run?"

"In my country you know not to trust the police."

"You're not in your country now."

"So, all the police here can be trusted?"

Santana wished that were the case. Experience, unfortunately, had taught him otherwise.

"I can be trusted."

Rahim's head tilted back slightly as a corner of his lip curled in a sneer. "Then you will not lie to me."

"I will not."

Santana understood he could lie to Rahim about certain things in order to get him to confess truthfully. Courts had upheld the tactic. But that could be a two-edged sword. If Rahim caught him in a blatant lie, it would be a game-changer. He might never be able to establish or restore any level of trust.

He'd once watched a young detective tell a suspect that his prints were found inside the crime scene. Since the suspect knew he'd worn gloves, the lie cost him all credibility.

"Then tell me why you are pursuing me," Rahim said.

"Let me reach inside my sport coat pocket."

Rahim placed his hand on his Glock and nodded.

Santana took out his phone, found the photo he'd taken in Tara Easton's bedroom, and pushed the phone toward Rahim. "Who are the people in this photo with you?"

Rahim leaned forward and peered at the phone.

"The jingle man. Taimur Khalil."

"What's your relationship to Khalil?"

"We had no relationship. I knew he worked for the Americans."

"Who's the woman?"

Rahim looked up. "I do not remember her name."

"Yet you posed for the photo."

"Crawford asked me to."

Santana felt a jolt of adrenaline. "Wade Crawford?"

Rahim sat back in the chair again. "Yes. That was his name."

"He took this photo?"

Rahim nodded.

"How did you know Crawford?"

"I did not know him. I saw him around the base in Kandahar."

"So why pose for the photo?"

"Beckham and I went on missions together."

"Blaine Beckham."

"That is right."

"You served in the Afghan paramilitary in what US forces called 'ghost units.'"

"A stupid American term."

"Did you know the other American in the photo?"

Rahim shook his head.

Santana pointed to the phone. "I believe the woman in this photo, Tara Easton, was murdered. So were Taimur Khalil and, possibly, Blaine Beckham. Someone tried to kill Angel Duran, the other American in the photo."

Santana paused, letting the silence hang in the air, giving Rahim a chance to respond.

His mentor, Wendell Hudson, had once told him that during any moment of silence in an interview or interrogation, the first one to break the silence loses the round. Listening was the most important skill.

"So that is why I am here?" Rahim said. "Because of these people," he gestured at the phone.

"Where were you on the evening of Sunday, January twenty-ninth?"

"I do not remember. But if I had murdered someone that evening, I would remember."

"Curious, isn't it, that nearly everyone in this photo—but you—has been killed or wounded?"

"It is not so curious, as you say."

"And why is that?"

"These people were, how do you say . . . smugglers."

Santana felt another rush of adrenaline. He let Rahim continue.

"Beckham wanted me to help."

"In what way?"

"He wanted morphine and my help to buy it."

"You just pointed Beckham in the right direction. You weren't involved in smuggling morphine."

"That is not what I am saying. I did not provide a source for Beckham. I did not help him smuggle morphine."

"Then how did Beckham get the morphine?"

"Taimur Khalil had many connections."

"That included the Taliban."

"Certainly."

"How did they smuggle it out of the country?"

"Beckham showed me the false bottom in his AWOL bag." Seeing the question on Santana's face, he continued, "Like a gym bag."

In that moment, while Rahim's eyes were focused on Santana, Ana pulled the Glock from the holster underneath the table and pointed it at Rahim's head.

"Reach for your gun and you're dead," she said, her voice leaden with threat.

Rahim lifted his hands. "I believe you are serious."

Santana moved quickly out of his chair, secured Rahim's gun on the table, and took a set of handcuffs from his coat pocket. "Stand up and turn around."

Rahim complied.

Santana cuffed him and looked at Ana. "Thank you. I'm sorry this happened here. In our home."

Ana lowered the gun and stood. "You'll explain everything."

"Yes."

"I am afraid you do not understand the situation," Rahim said.

"What situation is that?"

He turned and faced Santana. "I fought for America for many years. I lost my home, the life I had, and all my hopes and dreams."

"You don't want the same thing to happen here."

"Your government will not allow it."

"What does that mean?"

"Arrest me and see."

"Fleeing a police officer in a motor vehicle. You're looking at imprisonment for up to three years and a day and a fine of five thousand dollars, Abdul."

"None of that will happen."

"I wouldn't be too confident of that if I were you."

*   *   *

After booking Abdul Rahim on charges of fleeing a police officer, Santana met Cruz in the Homicide and Robbery unit and told him what had happened.

"He could've killed you and Ana," Cruz said.

"That's just it. He *could've* killed us both. But he didn't come to my house to do that. What I'm reading is not what I thought we'd get."

"You think he's telling the truth?"

317

"About Crawford, yes."

Despite Rahim's denials, Santana wasn't convinced the man was innocent. But experience had taught him that innocent people rarely moved off denials. And Rahim had likely been trained in how to withstand torture, so credible denials in a police interrogation setting would be nothing to him.

"We need to brace Crawford," Santana said.

"You think he's in on the morphine smuggling."

"Or knew about it and provided the source," Santana said. "Maybe SIGAR suspected Crawford was dirty and let him go."

"If Beckham killed Easton and Khalil, then Crawford could've killed Beckham and tried to take out Duran."

"And Art Tatum happened to be in the wrong place at the wrong time."

"Gave Crawford a perfect setup," Cruz said. "Made it look like Beckham and Tatum shot each other. Then erased the tape."

Santana thought about it. "We've got thirty-six hours beginning tomorrow before we have to charge Rahim or let him go. For now, let's change into our winter gear and stake out Duran's place."

Chapter 36

Angel Duran's cabin was lit and smoke drifted from the chimney as Santana and Cruz passed by. After a quarter-mile, Santana made a U-turn and parked at the beginning of a curve fifty yards away, where Duran would have difficulty spotting his Ford SUV. Since the entrance to I-94 and the fastest route to the city were the other way, Santana figured Duran wouldn't turn in their direction if he left his place.

Santana's repeated calls to Wade Crawford went unanswered.

"Not surprising if Crawford is involved in morphine smuggling," Cruz said.

"Hot chocolate?" he said to Cruz, sitting on the passenger side of the SUV.

"Sure. But keep the SUV and heater running. What's the temp anyway?"

"Fifteen degrees, last I heard."

"Feels colder," Cruz said.

"Always does at night."

Santana cracked a window open to let in fresh air. Every winter stories appeared in the local media outlets about someone found dead from carbon monoxide poisoning while sitting in a running vehicle, usually in an enclosed garage. Some were accidents, most were suicides. But even sitting in an idling car in the open air could be dangerous.

Better to let some air in even if it was ice cold.

Cruz held two plastic cups that Santana filled with hot chocolate. He took a cup from Cruz, leaned back against the heated seat, and focused his eyes on Duran's cabin.

Black clouds slid across a rising full moon that resembled the end of a bone. Long shadows shaded white snowdrifts, and snow glistened in the pale light.

"You think Duran will contact Montez Dixon?" Cruz asked.

"I do."

"And he'll do it soon."

"Given his cabin was ransacked, Duran has to figure some-one was searching for the four kilos even if they didn't find them. The longer he waits, the greater the risk that someone will take them, and he'll get shot again in the process. If it were me, I'd sell them as soon as I could."

"Why not just sell the heroin in smaller quantities?"

"I don't think Beckham or Duran saw themselves as small-time dealers. More likely to get busted. They wanted one big score. Set them up for life and get out of the drug business."

Santana paused and sipped some hot chocolate. Duran had to be wondering who had ransacked his place. He might have called the Washington County Sheriff's Department and com-plained to Del Taggart. But since Taggart didn't know about the hidden heroin, he had no reason to leave Duran's place in a mess.

"You think Wade Crawford ransacked Duran's place?" Cruz asked.

"According to Abdul Rahim, Crawford took the photo at the Kandahar airbase. That puts him much closer to the five people in that photo."

"And maybe in on the drug smuggling."

"No reason for Rahim to lie about Crawford."

"Which might be why Crawford has suddenly gone off the grid."

"And after we were growing so close."

"That's supposed to be sarcastic, right?" Cruz said.

"Yes."

"Ought to try that more often."

"I'm working on it."

From where they were located, Santana could hear the dis-tant hum of traffic along I-94 and the call of a coyote.

"Duran hasn't cleaned the snow and ice off his Range Rover," Santana said. "Would likely do that if he planned on going somewhere."

As he continued looking out the windshield, Santana spotted a late model sedan slowly approaching, as if the driver were searching for an address.

"We've got company," Cruz said.

"It's Luke Thornton. I called him."

Santana flicked his headlights on and off.

The sedan did the same.

Thornton drove past Santana's SUV, made a U-turn, and pulled up fifteen yards behind them.

A few moments later Thornton slid into the backseat behind Santana and eased the door closed.

"Glad you could make it," Santana said.

"Appreciate the invite."

"You wearing your vest?"

"Feel naked without it."

Cruz poured some hot chocolate into another plastic cup and handed it to Thornton.

Thornton slid the hood on his parka back. "Coffee?"

"Hot chocolate," Cruz said.

"Guess it'll have to do. Anything shakin' yet?"

"Not yet," Santana said.

"How about bringing me up to speed?"

Santana did.

"I'm betting Montez Dixon is in on this," Thornton said when Santana finished.

Santana turned toward him and settled his back against the driver's-side door. "Still waiting for the proof."

"Hope we don't have to wait too long."

A half-hour passed with no movement.

Then Santana spotted a dark Hummer with blacked-out windows turning into Duran's driveway.

"Montez Dixon," Santana said. "I recognize the Hummer."

"I knew he was dirty," Thornton said, ratcheting a round into the chamber of his Glock. "Deal's going down."

Two men got out of the Hummer and headed toward the cabin's front door. One carried a briefcase.

"Can't make them out, but it's likely Dixon and Reggie," Santana said.

"Reggie King. Dixon's older half-brother," Thornton said. "Dixon's enforcer and one mean son-of-a-bitch. Did time in Stillwater for assault and carjacking. No recent charges or convictions. But that doesn't mean he's clean."

"What's the plan?" Cruz asked Santana.

"Easier to take them down when they come out."

"Except we won't know for sure if Dixon has the kilos," Thornton said.

"Maybe in the briefcase. You have your two-way?" Santana asked, indicating Thornton's handheld radio.

"Yeah."

"Cover the back door. Cruz and I will take the front. There are sidelights on each side of the front door. We'll be able to see what's going on inside."

"Copy that," Thornton said.

Three minutes later Santana said, "Let's go."

Small clouds of condensation formed in the frosty night air as they crept through the icy snow in the driveway with their Glocks drawn. A dead calm couldn't mask their movements, and each crunch of the snow beneath their feet sounded like a gunshot.

Santana wished they had a new moon instead of a full one, but he could do nothing about that.

Once in position near the front door, Santana could hear voices inside the cabin. He moved just enough to peer through a sidelight window.

Angel Duran and Montez Dixon sat across from each other at the dining room table, Duran to Santana's left, Dixon to his right. Reggie King sat at the far end facing the front door. Each man had a bottle of Budweiser in front of him.

Four glassine-wrapped kilos of heroin sat in the middle of the table beside an open aluminum briefcase with stacks of bound cash inside.

"They've got the kilos and the cash," Santana whispered into his two-way to Thornton. Cruz, who had set up on the opposite side of the door, nodded.

Santana keyed his two-way. "We're going in," he said to Thornton as he motioned toward Cruz.

Moving slightly to his left, Santana peered one more time into the sidelight.

Reggie King no longer sat at the head of the table.

Santana jerked his head toward Cruz. "Wait!" he said softly.

But Cruz had already pulled down on the lever. The door swung open and Cruz went inside behind his gun.

Santana followed, staying to Cruz's left.

"Freeze!" Cruz yelled at Duran and Montez Dixon. "Hands on the table!"

Neither Duran nor Dixon moved.

Santana heard the crash of the back door breaking open. *Thornton.*

Out of the corner of his eye, he glimpsed Reggie King standing near the roaring fireplace.

Everything unfolded in slow motion now as King drew his gun and lifted it into shooting position.

Santana dove at Cruz, driving his shoulder into him just as King fired. Santana tried to aim a shot as he and Cruz were going down, but he couldn't get a bead on King.

Thornton fired two quick rounds. Both found King. Center mass. He went down. Thornton swept his gun to his right. "Don't move!" he yelled at Duran and Dixon.

Santana scrambled to his feet. "You okay?"

Cruz picked up his Glock and got to his feet. "I'm good. Thanks."

Santana trained his Glock on Duran and Dixon and motioned to Thornton. "Cuff 'em."

Thornton holstered his Glock. "Stand up," he said to Duran. "Hands behind your back."

"I've got a bad leg."

"Tough. Stand up."

Duran wobbled slightly as he stood.

His left pants leg had been cut off above the knee in order to accommodate the heavy bandage around his leg. A thick cane hung on the back of his chair.

Thornton cuffed Duran and pushed him back in the chair and looked at Santana. "Got an extra set?"

Santana tossed him a pair of cuffs.

Cruz had gone over to Reggie King to check his pulse. He shook his head, indicating he'd found no heartbeat. Then he stood and holstered his gun.

Dixon said, "You shot my brother, motherfucker."

"I'll shoot you, too," Thornton said, "you don't get your ass up out of that chair."

Santana was about to call the Washington County Sheriff when he felt the hard metal of a gun barrel press against the back of his skull.

"Steady now," the voice behind him said. "No one else has to get hurt. Drop the gun."

Santana recognized the voice.

"Do it, Santana."

He stooped and set his Glock on the floor.

"Who's the asshole?" Dixon said.

"I'm the ghost of Christmas past."

"Wade Crawford," Duran said, spitting out the words, as if he had something sour in his mouth.

"Thought you wouldn't remember your old friend."

"We were never friends, Crawford."

"You can't count on anyone nowadays. Lose your gun, Cruz. Same goes for the bearded narc."

"Don't do it," Santana said. "He shoots me, he's a dead man."

"Well," Crawford said, pushing the barrel of his gun harder into the back of Santana's head, "aren't we the brave one."

Crawford shot Cruz and then Thornton.

Santana went for his gun on the floor, but Crawford grabbed him by the collar, stuck the barrel against the back of his head again and said, "Don't!"

Santana slowly rose to his feet, his fists clenched in anger.

"Your partners are wearing vests. Right? They'll be fine. All I want is the money and the kilos. Then I'm out of your hair. Pick up the cuffs and use 'em on our African-American friend."

Santana hesitated, his mind visualizing the possible outcomes while hoping Cruz and Thornton hadn't been injured too seriously.

"You ever been shot in the vest, Crawford? It hurts."

"Never have and don't plan to. Now move!" Crawford said, pushing the gun barrel into Santana's back.

Santana edged forward and picked up the handcuffs Luke Thornton had dropped when he was shot. As he pivoted towards Montez Dixon, still seated in the dining chair, Dixon spun around, a gun in his hand, and fired at Crawford. The bullet pierced Crawford's throat, severing a carotid artery, resulting in a fountain of blood. Crawford retaliated with one shot before he crumpled to the ground. The bullet struck Dixon in the head.

Santana dropped to his knees beside Crawford and applied direct pressure on the artery.

Angel Duran, who had thrown himself to the ground, sat up.

"Stay there," Santana cautioned.

"Get the cuffs off me."

"Shut up and stay down."

Holding his phone with one hand and attempting to stanch Crawford's bleeding with the other, Santana called 911 and requested assistance.

Crawford muttered something.

Santana leaned closer, but the jumble of words made no sense.

"Save that thought," he said.

Two minutes later, Crawford died.

Chapter 37

As Santana sat in Janet Kendrick's office, waiting for her to close the door, he popped the tab on his can of Coke and drank until it was empty. The caffeine would curb his exhaustion and help him stay alert during the interview. He listened to the crack of his own body as he shifted his weight. His watch read 8:15 a.m. It felt much later.

Washington County deputies and forensic techs from the BCA had quickly moved in to work the crime scene, their flashlights casting eerie beams of light that illuminated the surrounding woods till the high intensity LED tripod floods had been set up.

Gabriel Cruz and Luke Thornton had been taken to Lakewood Hospital in Stillwater. Thankfully, their bullet-proof vests had prevented any major damage, though the impact of the bullet each of them had taken had caused bruising and possible broken ribs.

Angel Duran had been taken to the Washington County jail, where he lawyered up. Wade Crawford, Montez Dixon, and Reggie King had been transported to the Ramsey County morgue.

Santana had notified Scott Weston, and DEA agents had quickly arrived.

Deputies and investigators from the BCA had debriefed Santana. Now it was Kendrick's turn.

She closed the door, then took a seat at her desk. She set a white legal-sized pad in front of her.

"How are you feeling?"

"I've been better. You hear anything more about Cruz and Thornton?"

"Chest x-rays came back negative on both. They'll likely be released later today. But they'll be sore for a while."

"That's good news."

"Yes. Could've been much worse. I know you'll write a report on what exactly happened at Duran's cabin, but give me the CliffsNotes version now."

"Angel Duran, Tara Easton, Blaine Beckham, and Taimur Khalil smuggled morphine out of Afghanistan at the end of the war."

"I thought it was heroin."

"I did too. Let me explain."

Kendrick nodded.

"Beckham killed Tara Easton and Taimur Khalil. He cut up Khalil and soaked the body in lye. I think he planned to dissolve the bones as well, but that takes a lot of time, and his mother was moving in with him. So he buried the bones in Como Park and Lake Como. When the Winter Carnival medallion hunt began, and Jadyn Hartley discovered the first set of bones, Duran and Beckham decided to send us in the direction of a serial killer. Duran likely wrote the poems we received."

"And the morphine?"

"Once they returned to the States, Duran had the Sinaloa Cartel ship acetic anhydride to him."

"Duran had connections to the Sinaloa Cartel?"

"Through his brother, Enrique."

"Meanwhile, Duran purchased the rest of the chemicals needed to convert morphine to heroin. Took some time to make it. When they were ready, Duran and Beckham arranged to sell the four kilos to Montez Dixon."

"Would Duran be willing to talk to you?"

Santana shook his head. "He's got a lawyer. If he didn't do the killings, he'll go down on the drug charges. Hard to beat those."

"I got a call from Jim Briggs, the Narco/Vice commander, wanting to know how the DEA got involved in our drug bust."

"I tipped off Weston."

Kendrick nodded her head slowly as she processed Santana's reply. "You cut a deal with Weston."

"I did."

"Without telling me."

"It worked out. The DEA located Ana's mother and sister. And the cover story about their rogue agent, Joel Ryker, is safe."

"And Narco/Vice got screwed in the process."

"Nearly two and a half million dollars in drug sales got taken off the street. Only ones who got screwed were Angel Duran and Montez Dixon and the street dealers they'd sell it to."

"I don't appreciate you going behind my back."

"I asked you to approve the stakeout."

"And I told you before what I thought of you threatening Weston and the DEA."

Santana decided no response was the best way to go.

Kendrick wrote a note on her legal pad.

Santana wondered what she'd written. He sensed it wasn't something good.

"How does Wade Crawford fit in?" Kendrick asked, switching subjects.

"He knew the four of them in Afghanistan when he worked for SIGAR and took the photo we found in Tara Easton's apartment. Crawford suspected they'd smuggled the morphine. The mistake he made—and I did, too—was thinking the fifth person in the photo, Abdul Rahim, was part of the smuggling operation. That's why Crawford tailed me. He figured Rahim had the morphine."

"And you'd find it."

Santana nodded.

"We need to charge Rahim with fleeing a police officer," Kendrick said.

"If I go to the DA with this and Rahim is charged, he could go to prison and be deported back to Afghanistan. That's a death sentence."

"He committed a felony."

"He did. But he can also be a cooperating witness for the DA."

"You think he will?"

"Given the alternative, yes. Duran is the one that needs to do time."

Kendrick considered it. "All right. I'll talk to the DA." She wrote a note on her legal-size pad. Then she looked at Santana again. "You think Beckham attempted to kill Duran? Keep the drugs and money all to himself?"

"The shell casings at the scene don't match Blaine Beckham's AR-15."

"Beckham owned a gun shop. Could've been any of the AR-15s there."

"Doubt he would use a rifle he wasn't familiar with."

"Might be the motive for Duran killing Beckham and Art Tatum," Kendrick said.

"Duran couldn't have killed them. He was in the hospital when Beckham and Art Tatum were shot and killed."

Kendrick shook her head. "Then they must've shot each other."

"I don't know that."

"What's triggering your doubt?"

"The video system in Beckham's office was blank during the time the shooting occurred."

"Could be a malfunction."

"Awfully convenient."

"Crawford could've killed Beckham and Tatum," Kendrick said.

"I'd be good with that idea if we had some proof."

"Well, if the scenario we just described is correct, that wraps up everything."

"Is that the way you want to roll, *Commander*?"

Santana might have put a little too much emphasis on the word "commander."

There was a long beat of silence before Kendrick spoke again.

"Why don't you head home, take a shower, and get some rest, Detective. When you're thinking more clearly, type up your report. I'll sign off and take it to the chief."

She ended the sentence with a tight smile.

Santana stood and exited Kendrick's office, leaving the door open as he left.

*   *   *

Shrugging off his exhaustion, Santana signed out a department ride and headed for the Holiday Inn downtown at the corner of Kellogg Boulevard and W. 7th Street, adjacent to the Xcel Energy Center. He wanted to check out the room Wade Crawford had stayed in.

While he drove, he called Rita Gamboni, who'd left text and voice messages on his personal cell phone.

"Sorry I didn't get back to you sooner, Rita. I've been in debriefing meetings since early this morning."

"All I'm concerned about is if you're okay."

"Tired but otherwise fine."

"What the hell happened?"

Santana gave her a quick summary.

"You're lucky to be alive," she said.

"Can't argue with that."

"Thank goodness Cruz and Thornton are all right."

"I'll run up to the hospital later."

"Get some rest. We'll see each other soon."

"We will," Santana said.

Like all homicide detectives, he hated loose ends. No matter whether Crawford was alive or dead, he had to know if Crawford had killed Beckham and Tatum. The Washington County Sheriff's Department would be responsible for notifying any next of kin. But, like Santana, family members and the sheriff's department would be looking for answers.

According to the autopsy reports, the bullet tracks in Blaine Beckham and Art Tatum were at a downward angle, indicating that the shooter was tall. If Santana found a security camera jammer in Crawford's hotel room, it would definitely link Crawford to the Combat Zone gun shop and the two men's deaths.

After parking in front of the hotel and entering the building under the canopied entrance, Santana explained to the desk clerk that Wade Crawford had been killed the previous evening, and he needed to search his room.

Santana believed that Crawford's hotel room could be searched immediately without a warrant under the exigent circumstances section of the Fourth Amendment because evidence of a crime would be lost or destroyed. He'd record the search to cover all his bases.

The desk clerk contacted the manager, who met Santana on the fifth floor. A Holiday Inn name badge on her left lapel identified her as Jessica.

Crawford had left a DO NOT DISTURB sign on the door. Santana instructed Jessica to ignore it.

The window curtains were partially open, and Santana had a clear view of the Landmark Center from inside the room. Dirty clothes were scattered on the unmade king-size bed. Two used paper cups on the desk stood beside a Keurig coffeemaker.

Pulling out his cell phone, he turned on the video camera, handed it to Jessica, and asked her to record his search.

"Chain of custody," he said.

"I've heard of it on all those crime shows, but I'm not sure what it means."

"It shows who had possession of certain items and when. Once it's collected, it's kept in police control."

Santana gloved up and first searched the closet, then the pockets of the two sport coats and pants hanging there. After switching to the drawers, he began at the top and worked his way down.

Under a heavy cable sweater in the bottom drawer, he found a plastic bag containing Crawford's passport, three thousand in cash, and a handheld jammer.

Santana figured Crawford had planned to flee the country at some point after unloading the drugs.

"Make sure you get a video of this," he said to Jessica.

After Jessica videoed the passport, cash, and jammer, Santana placed them in separate evidence bags. Then he wrote his name, badge number, the date, time, and a description of the item and the place where the evidence was found.

He checked under the mattress and box spring as well as the nightstand drawers, but found no more incriminating evidence.

* * *

After leaving the Holiday Inn hotel, Santana headed for the Combat Zone gun shop, satisfied that he'd tied up one loose end. More evidence would be helpful in proving that Wade Crawford had murdered Blaine Beckham and Art Tatum, such as Crawford's cell phone location on the evening of the murder. But Crawford had likely deactivated its functions, including wireless communication and Google location. Only his last location displayed before the device was turned off could be determined.

Santana still had to establish who had tried to kill Angel Duran. Wade Crawford wouldn't have tried to kill Duran till he had the kilos of heroin in hand.

Blaine Beckham was the most likely suspect. He'd killed Tara Easton and Taimur Khalil, so why not take out Duran and keep all of the money from the heroin sale? Except the shell casings Santana had found outside Duran's cabin hadn't come from Beckham's AR-15.

Janet Kendrick had suggested that Beckham could have used another AR-15 from his gun shop. Short of test firing each one in Beckham's shop, forensics couldn't conclusively prove that he hadn't. But Gabriel Cruz had a point: Beckham owned a Daniel Defense DDM4 V7, a much more expensive rifle than the average or low-cost AR-15. If Beckham had intended to shoot and kill Duran, he would have used his own pricier weapon, one he was used to using and relied on.

That left one other obvious suspect.

The heavy-set man with a few days' growth of stubble and a fade haircut stood behind the counter in the Combat Zone gun shop. He wore a red flannel shirt with the sleeves rolled up to his forearms, exposing the sleeve tattoos depicting a wolf's head.

"Help you?" he asked

Santana badged him. "Your name."

"Gus," he said.

"You managing the shop now?"

He shook his head. "I'm the RSO," he said, meaning the Range Safety Officer. "Working for Renee now."

"Renee Beckham?"

"Yeah. She took over for her son."

"She in?"

Gus nodded and went to the open office door. "Cop here to see you, Ms. Beckham."

Renee Beckham stepped out of the office and looked at Santana without expression. "Detective Santana, isn't it?"

"That's right. Got a few minutes to talk?"

She waved him in. "Have a seat."

The office looked the same as it did the night Blaine Beckham was killed.

Santana sat in the canvas director's chair. She sat in the desk chair.

"How are you doing?" he asked.

"Good days and bad."

Santana understood. He'd never truly gotten over his mother's murder.

"Gus said you're taking over the shop."

"Gonna try to. Know a little bit about guns. But nothing about why my son was killed."

The question of how much to tell a grieving mother about her son's death was like walking on thin ice. The further Santana ventured from the safety of the shore—or the more information he offered—the more perilous it became. He was certain that Angel Duran and Blaine Beckham had smuggled morphine out of Afghanistan, and it had eventually led to Beckham's death. He also believed that Wade Crawford—and not Art Tatum—had killed Beckham. Revealing this to Beckham's mother would only increase her suffering.

"When I know everything about your son's death, I will come and tell you. But I need your help first."

She looked into his eyes for a long moment, as if weighing the truth of his statement. "What can I do?"

"First, I need Gus to show me the range."

"All right."

Renee Beckham monitored the counter while Gus took Santana downstairs to the shooting range, which was empty.

"Slow day?" Santana said.

"Yeah. Business has dropped off some since Blaine's death. Lots of regulars don't know that we've reopened for business. We're getting the word out. Should pick up again soon."

Santana noted the sticky mats at the exit of the live fire area, which caught the lead dust from customers' shoe soles, and the sinks used to wash lead off hands and faces. He always took a long shower after shooting at a range and made sure he washed his clothes when he got home. Never a good idea to mess with lead.

Gus made a sweeping gesture indicating the shooting lanes.

"Got a dozen shooting lanes with state-of-the-art, digitally-controlled target area systems," he began. "All of our lanes are twenty-five yards long. We can handle pistols and rifles up to fifty caliber. Also have a top-notch air filtration system that ex-changes air every ninety seconds."

Santana scanned the shooting stalls separated by wide wood dividers. The stalls had benches and angled screens so that any casings that bounced forward would roll back to the shooter.

"See you looking at the screens," Gus said.

"Good idea."

Gus hiked up his jeans. "Yeah. I've seen shooters do all sorts of stupid things like bending over in front of someone with a gun. That's how people get their fool heads shot off. A few years ago, we put wooden beams under our shooting benches 'cause some idiot crawled out under the bench to retrieve his brass during live fire. Move ahead of the firing line to pick up brass, you're out of here. Why we have a no-brass-pickup policy. Started that a few years ago. Occasionally someone will steal the brass in the collection bucket left behind by other shooters. That's disrespectful and outright theft. We recycle the brass. Began about the same time that we started requiring shooters to buy their ammo at the range. All about the extra cash. Blaine made no apologies for it."

"You take reservations?"

"Members only. We'll take the lane reservation up to two weeks in advance."

"You allow shooters to use steel-cased bullets?"

Gus shook his head. "No way. Gotta shoot brass."

"Thanks for the tour and information, Gus," Santana said, heading for the stairs.

Once he and Renee Beckham had returned to her office, Santana said, "I need you, or Gus, or whoever's on duty, to call me when Hannah Thatcher comes in to shoot."

"You sure she comes here?"

"She's a member. All I need is a phone call. Anyone else working here besides you and Gus?"

"I have two other employees."

He took four business cards out of his badge wallet and handed them to Renee Beckham.

"Keep one card for yourself. Give the others to your employees. And the bucket of brass from Thatcher's AR-15 needs to be saved."

"I'm sure you have your reasons, Detective. So, I won't ask you why."

"Better that you don't," he said.

Chapter 38

Santana got a few extra hours of sleep on Saturday morning. Upon waking, he was relieved to hear that Ana had taken Gitana for a morning jog and had already fed her. He'd made sure to call Regions Hospital yesterday after leaving the gun shop to check on Gabriel Cruz and Luke Thornton, but both men had already been discharged. Thornton hadn't answered his cell phone, so Santana had left him a voicemail. Cruz had answered his cell phone and had assured Santana that he was all right, despite his sore ribs and labored breathing.

Santana told him to take as much time as he needed to recover.

"I think we have everything sorted out," Cruz had said.

"Seems like it," Santana said, suppressing any hint of irony.

Santana drove to the LEC later on Saturday morning and logged into the department computer in the Homicide and Robbery unit. He updated the chronological record and typed up crime scene notes for Janet Kendrick. Washington County and BCA investigators and forensic analysts would create their own reports, as the crime had occurred in their jurisdiction.

Santana received a call from Luke Thornton as he finished up his reports.

"You cut me out when you contacted the DEA," Thornton said.

"You heard."

"Would've liked to hear it from you. Now I want an explanation."

Santana told him about the deal he'd made with Weston to find Ana's mother and sister in El Salvador.

Thornton listened without interrupting and then stayed quiet for a time.

"Still pisses me off," he said at last. "But I get it. Got to take care of Ana."

"I do," Santana said.

That evening Santana took Rita Gamboni out to dinner at The Dock in Stillwater. The restaurant on the shore of the St. Croix looked upriver to the historic Stillwater Lift Bridge and downriver to the new St. Croix Crossing Bridge.

They sat at a table near the crackling fireplace and a large window that looked out onto the frozen river while sharing a bottle of Chardonnay. For dinner Rita ordered salmon. Santana chose walleye.

As usual, Rita looked great in a slim, dark blue, long-sleeved, mid-calf dress with a brown double ring belt and matching knee-high boots.

Santana recounted more details about what steps he'd taken before the stakeout and how the shooting had played out.

"How are Cruz and Thornton doing?" she asked.

"They're both sore but okay. Thornton wasn't happy about my contacting the DEA."

"Not surprising."

"But he understood why I did it."

"What about Kendrick?"

"Not so much."

"Blackmailing Weston could get you fired," Rita said.

"More of a *quid pro quo*."

"Semantics."

"Have you heard anything from Kendrick?" he asked.

"She'll likely go to the chief with her complaint. Best case scenario is a likely suspension."

"You won't have any say in the matter?"

Rita cocked her head. "You think?"

"Probably not," he said.

"By the way, Abdul Rahim was released."

"Kendrick must've convinced the DA to let him go."

Rita shook her head. "Feds came and got him."

"You mean the FBI?"

"I'm guessing CIA or NSA."

"What the hell?"

"Afghani special forces, right?"

Santana nodded.

"He's a valued asset."

"Rahim told me the government would never allow his arrest."

"You wanted him released anyway. He wasn't involved in the drug smuggling or murders."

"Just bothers me when the Feds bigfoot a case I'm working. Nothing against your former colleagues at the FBI," he quickly added.

"Sure," Rita said with a little smile. "Well, regardless, you and Cruz solved the case and the DEA had a major drug bust. That's good publicity for the department and for the Winter Carnival. No more bone hunters."

"Likely some bones still out there, as well as the person who shot Angel Duran."

"I don't get it."

Santana explained.

"You have a suspect?"

"Hannah Thatcher. Has the apartment across the hall from Tara Easton."

*   *   *

On Monday morning, Santana received a call from Renee Beckham at the Combat Zone gun shop. Hannah Thatcher had been in shooting her AR-15. Gus had collected her shell casings.

At the gun shop, Santana gloved up, turned on his video app and gave Gus his iPhone.

"Video everything I'm doing," Santana said.

He picked out two brass casings from the bucket Gus had used to collect Hannah Thatcher's brass. He asked Gus to verify that the brass casings came from Hannah Thatcher's AR-15. Then he placed the casings in separate evidence envelopes. When Gus stopped the video, Santana picked up a third casing and put it in his coat pocket.

He took the evidence envelopes to Dennis Crane in the forensic lab at the BCA.

Crane sat at his neat desk in the lab, eating a sandwich he'd taken out of a black insulated lunch bag. The lettering on the side of the bag read:

Sorry I Am Late
I Was at A Crime Scene

Santana said, "I need you to compare the markings on these brass shell casings with the markings on the steel casings I found at Angel Duran's cabin."

"You know I need to examine the particular rifle first to set the standard. See what similar marks, if any, the rifle is consistently reproducing. Then I can compare the evidence cartridge cases to the standards to see if they're similarly marked."

"If the steel and brass shell casings have the same markings, I'll get you the AR-15 in question."

Crane took his time considering Santana's request.

Probably looking for another excuse, Santana thought.

"Figured the case was all wrapped up after the shootout at the OK Corral."

Crane grinned, enjoying his joke.

Santana set the two evidence envelopes containing the casings on the desk in front of Crane. "I'll wait."

The grin faded. "Come on, Santana. I can't jump every time you show up."

"I'll be doing media interviews after I break this case open. I'll be sure to mention your name and excellent work."

"You think I care what you tell the media."

"Actually, I do."

Crane frowned and took a bite of his sandwich while he chewed on Santana's response.

After a long pause he said, "Can I finish my sandwich first?"

*   *   *

Later that afternoon, Santana drove to Hannah Thatcher's apartment building.

"What brings you here, Detective?"

He sat in the chair across from her in the living room.

"Your AR-15."

Santana could see the confused look in her eyes.

"Why are you interested in my rifle?"

"You always keep it in your bedroom?"

She nodded. "Case any asshole breaks in."

"You were shooting at the Combat Zone gun shop today."

"Yeah. So?"

Santana took the shell casing out of his sport coat pocket and held it up. "Tell me why your AR-15 shell casing matches the shell casings found at the Angel Duran shooting."

"What?"

"You heard me. This brass casing has the same striated chamber marks as the steel casings found at the crime scene. Also has the same impressed ejector marks. Just so we're clear, ejector marks can only be reproduced when cartridge cases are fired and not by simply hand chambering and ejecting a live cartridge."

"This doesn't make any sense."

"Oh, it makes perfect sense. Tara Easton told you she and Duran, Blaine Beckham, and Taimur Khalil had smuggled morphine out of Afghanistan and were planning on converting it into heroin to sell. Easton told you Khalil was already missing and presumed dead. She was concerned that Beckham would take her out as well. After he killed her, you decided to take Duran and Beckham off the board and collect the heroin for yourself. You only wounded Duran, and someone else took out Beckham for you."

"You're crazy."

Santana held up the cartridge again. "Then explain this."

Thatcher shook her head. "I can't. There must be some mistake."

Santana checked his notebook. "Where were you on Wednesday, February first?"

"What time?"

"Late afternoon."

"Probably working."

"Uh, uh. I checked with Tinucci's. You had the day off."

Thatcher took out her cell phone and used facial recognition to log in.

"Look at February first on your calendar app," he said.

She did.

"You were at Angel Duran's cabin on the first, trying to take him out."

She glared at Santana. "If I'd tried to take Duran out, he'd be dead and buried by now. Believe me. I don't miss. On the day someone shot Duran, I went ice fishing."

"Where?"

"Drove up to Duluth and Lake Superior. Returned late that night. Saw you when I was running along the river the next day."

"Anyone see you or talk to you up North?"

"A few anglers. But I don't know their names. So, unless you've got something else, get the hell out of my apartment."

"You tell anyone you were going out of town?"

She shrugged. "Might have. I don't remember."

"Ever use steel-cased ammo in your AR?"

She let out a scornful laugh. "I would never shoot that shit."

"You always keep your AR-15 here in the apartment?"

"Yeah. Sometimes I even sleep with it. I like the feel of cold steel against my body. Gets me all hot. Know what I mean?"

She saw the skeptical look on Santana's face and laughed. "Just jerking your chain, Detective. But my AR is more trustworthy than any man I've ever known."

"And it's never been missing."

"How the fuck could I lose my AR?"

"Ever let someone else use it?"

"Never."

"Ever have it repaired?"

"Recently. My fired brass was getting stuck in the receiver instead of cleanly ejecting. Turns out the extractor had a slight crack."

Santana knew that once worn, the extractor couldn't grab the rim of the spent casing and remove it from the receiver. And that steel brass could cause the problem. It would also explain the ejector markings.

"Where'd you take it?"

"Combat Zone."

"Blaine Beckham's place."

"Yeah."

"What was the date?"

She opened the calendar on her iPhone again. "Took it in on Thursday, February second."

The day after someone tried to kill Angel Duran, Santana thought.

"When did you pick it up?"

"A week later on the ninth. Shop closed for a few days after Beckham's death. Heard his mother is running it now."

"I'll need your AR."

"Like hell. Get a warrant."

Santana stood and put on his overcoat.

"You think someone used my AR to shoot Angel Duran, don't you?"

"Haven't ruled you out yet," Santana said.

*   *   *

Santana needed solid evidence that Hannah Thatcher had attempted to kill Angel Duran. She certainly had the skill set and a possible motive if Tara Easton had told her about the heroin shipment. Given the positive shell casing comparison, a judge would likely sign a warrant for her AR-15. But Thatcher's demeanor and response to his questions had created doubt, as had her expletive regarding steel-cased ammunition. Considering Thatcher's experience and knowledge of weaponry, Santana questioned whether she'd use cheap ammunition in her prized AR-15.

He drove back to the LEC and updated the chronological record. As he finished, Gabriel Cruz called.

"How you doing?" Santana asked.

"Feeling great. Long as I don't have to move too much."

"Want me to pick up groceries or anything else for you?"

"Uh . . . no. I'm good."

The hesitation in Cruz's voice had tweaked Santana's curiosity.

"Nasrin taking care of you?"

"Yeah, she . . ." His voice trailed off.

"Thought so," Santana said.

"What's the big deal?"

"Not a big deal. Glad she's helping you out."

"Nasrin has been a big help. She's a good woman. First one I've cared about for a long time."

Santana couldn't come up with a quick response.

"You're invited for dinner tonight. She's cooking Kabuli Palau. It's a traditional national rice dish made with raisins, carrots, nuts, and lamb. You'll love it."

"You at her place?"

"Yeah. Come over in a couple hours."

"Looking forward to it," Santana said.

*   *   *

When Santana got to the lobby, Nasrin buzzed him in. Santana took the stairs to the third floor and then paused outside her apartment door.

The shoes, boots, and slippers were spread out on a large mat, as they had been before. But one pair of light brown leather boots caught his eye now. They were about nine inches high with two-inch black rubber heels.

Santana picked up one boot and turned it over.

Adrenaline rushed through his body as he peered at the yellow Vibram logo.

He recalled how he'd seen it all in his dream—the bones, the gold bug, the polygon shape on the horizon—he hadn't understood the most crucial part till now. *The darkness.* Unable to see what was right in front of him the whole time.

He knocked on the apartment door.

Nasrin Khalil opened it with a big smile. But as she looked at his face, her smile faded, like a ray of sunlight behind a dark, ominous cloud.

"Your father's boots?" Santana said.

"Yes. They were."

Chapter 39

Santana set the boot on the mat, entered the apartment, and closed the door behind him. He remained standing there while Nasrin stood beside Gabriel Cruz, who sat on a cushion on the floor.

Nasrin kept her eyes on Santana, as if she were reading his mind.

"Dinner is ready, John," Cruz said, indicating a cushion beside him. "Come and sit down."

"You want to tell him or should I?" Santana said.

"Tell me what?" Cruz said, looking up at her.

Nasrin shook her head as she cast her eyes down.

"I showed you the photo of your father with Tara Easton, Angel Duran, and Blaine Beckham. You wore your father's boots when you shot Angel Duran. You planned to kill them all."

"What?" Cruz said, his eyes locked on Santana.

"Ask her," Santana said.

Cruz shifted his gaze to her. "Nasrin?"

She raised her head and focused on Santana, as if Cruz wasn't present.

"Those men murdered my father and cut him to pieces."

"Beckham did. But that's a matter for us to solve and for the courts to punish."

"Jesus," Cruz said, shaking his head. "You used me."

"No, I did not, Gabriel," she said, glaring at him. Then, as her expression softened, she said, "I love you."

Santana could see the vertical furrows between Cruz's eyebrows, what Charles Darwin called the "grief muscle," indicating distress and sadness.

"You knew Thatcher was heading up north and that she had an AR-15," Santana continued. "You picked her apartment lock. Got the rifle. I wondered why you took the shot when I was with Duran. The more I thought about it, I realized you only had a limited amount of time before Thatcher returned home and found her AR missing. Plus, you figured if things ever went sideways, we'd pin the shooting on Thatcher. But you bought your own cheap, steel-cased ammunition to shoot Duran. Thatcher would never use it in her own weapon."

Fixing her eyes on Santana, Nasrin said, "I learned many skills from Major Thatcher and your armed forces."

"That you did."

"Now the promise I made to myself has been fulfilled."

"Except for Duran."

"He will face the punishment of your courts for smuggling drugs. Prison may be a worse punishment than a bullet's quick and painless death. And you cannot prove I did anything. It is all speculation."

Cruz's gaze locked on Santana's. "She's right, John. The case is thin. We go to the DA with this, he'll laugh us out of his office."

Santana recalled his own act of vengeance now. How he'd taken the lives of the two cartel members who had murdered his mother.

As he stared at Nasrin Khalil, saw the pleading look in her eyes, he said, "I'm sure we could find out where you purchased the ammunition, if we looked."

"*If* we looked?" Cruz said, expectation in his voice.

Nasrin stood perfectly still for a time before she said, "You are honorable men. Honor is . . . unusual in my country, especially when it comes to men and women. It is unfortunate that your friend and colleague Tatum got killed. I have learned much about collateral damage and the unfortunate deaths of the innocent."

"Don't know if it matters to you," Santana said, "but I believe the other Afghani in the photo, Abdul Rahim, had nothing to do with your father's murder."

She nodded her head slowly. "That is good news. But I will not be sent back to my country."

She opened the drawer of the small round table beside her and pulled out a what appeared to be a 9mm, Springfield 911.

Santana took a step toward her.

"Stay where you are, Detective. I am familiar with this weapon."

She spoke in a firm but calm voice.

As her eyes found Cruz again, Santana inched forward.

"I am so sorry, Gabriel."

"It doesn't have to end this way," Cruz said. In obvious pain, he pushed off the cushion and got unsteadily to his feet.

"If you plan to pursue charges against me, there is no choice."

Santana saw the tears in her eyes when she smiled at Cruz.

Then, as she raised the gun barrel towards her temple, Cruz cried out and leapt forward, grabbing her wrist and twisting the gun away from her head as she pulled the trigger.

Epilogue

Lynn Pierce in forensics found the poems sent to Santana on Angel Duran's computer. The DA charged Duran with a controlled substance crime in the first degree. Minnesota sentencing guidelines ranged from sixty-five months to forty years. Santana had urged the DA not to offer any plea deal in hopes that the judge would sentence Duran to a long prison term.

Abdul Rahim had disappeared. Santana figured government agents had moved him somewhere else in the country and had likely given him a new name—or they had taken him permanently off the grid. Whatever Rahim knew about the Taliban and the US operations in Afghanistan would never see the light of day.

Though the medallion had been found a day before the Winter Carnival ended, some city residents continued to search, believing more bones were out there somewhere.

Santana wondered if some would surface after the snow melt in spring.

Instead of going through Nasrin Khalil's head, the bullet she'd fired had gone through the apartment ceiling and rooftop, thanks to Gabriel Cruz's quick action.

In the weeks that followed, Cruz had sought help in dealing with his PTSD from Karen Wong, the department's psychologist. It was in Santana's hands to determine the future of Nasrin Khalil, and he'd chosen to leave it up to his partner. He knew that convincing the DA to charge her with second-degree attempted murder and second-degree assault with a dangerous weapon for shooting Angel Duran was a long shot at best, and he had not pursued it.

Santana felt conflicted about punishing her for what was essentially an act of retribution, something he himself had committed as a sixteen-year-old in Colombia after his mother's murder. And, in Nasrin's defense, Angel Duran had survived, only to face years in prison for his crimes.

His belief in justice remained constant, but he understood that the way in which it was achieved could differ, depending on the time and place. Justice had been and would be served for the men who had taken the lives of Taimur Khalil, Tara Easton, and Art Tatum.

Cruz's counseling sessions helped him deal with his PTSD and his deteriorating relationship with Nasrin, and they had gradually drifted apart. Santana understood that trust was the cord that held two people together in a relationship, and when it was severed, disconnection often occurred.

Chief Thomas Murdoch had publicly praised Santana and Cruz for their work in solving what had the media had dubbed the "Medallion Bones Case." Murdoch and Kendrick had then suspended Santana for five days for "coercing" DEA Special Agent in Charge Scott Weston.

Santana hadn't fought the suspension.

Three days into his suspension, Ana Soriano sat beside him on the couch in front of a crackling fire in the living room. Gitana was snoring lightly as she slept at his feet.

"Can we talk?"

"Absolutely," he said, putting aside his newspaper.

Santana had previously explained what had led to their threatening encounter with Abdul Rahim. Santana admired the maturity and confidence Ana had shown in the tense and dangerous situation while expressing his concern that she could have lost her life.

"It wasn't the first time that my life was in danger," she'd said.

"Hopefully," Santana had said, "it will be the last."

Now, as she sat beside him she said, "First, I want to thank you again for locating my mother and sister. I know that's why you are sitting here and not working. How you risked your career to help me."

"I wasn't really risking—"

She held up a hand to stop him in mid-sentence.

"I understand it's hard for you to accept credit for anything. But I know what you did."

Santana wondered if Rita Gamboni had talked with Ana.

"But there is something else we need to talk about."

"Okay."

Even though Santana knew what was coming, he felt the heavy weight of disappointment.

"I want the DEA to get my mother and sister out of El Salvador."

"I'll talk to Weston."

"Thank you. But we all can't stay here. I need to get an apartment for the three of us. So, I'll need access to the money I made . . . working."

Ana had managed to put away a large sum, though the madam she'd worked for had planned to steal it.

"Your money won't last forever."

"I know," she said with a nod.

Gitana got up, walked over to Ana, and laid her head in Ana's lap.

"It'll take a while before the DEA gets your family out. No need to rush off."

Ana smiled as she gently petted Gitana. "Perhaps if I could stay here a bit longer, with you and Gitana, I could . . . figure things out."

"I would like that," Santana said.

Reward

I offer you, the reader, the opportunity to redeem a cash award for introducing this novel, or another of the author's novels, to any producer who offers an acceptable contract [to the author] for his work. The reward offered is 10% of any initial option contract for film up to a maximum of $10,000.00.

Our mutual goal is to introduce this work to producers. Many of you are familiar with the term "six degrees of separation," the theory that anyone on the planet can be connected to any other person on the planet through a chain of acquaintances that has no more than five intermediaries. This is what I aim to accomplish here with your help.

- Think about whom you know and whom they might know.
- Think about whom you know that reads and would enjoy this book.

Send any leads, opportunities, or introductions via email to www.christophervalen.com.

Thank you in advance for your help.

Acknowledgments

The author gratefully acknowledges the help of many in the research, writing, and editing of this book. They include:

Abigail Davis, Linda Donaldson, Lorrie Holmgren, Chuck Logan, Peg Wangensteen, and Jennifer Adkins, my editor, for your time, insightful reads, edits, and suggestions of the work in progress. Thanks also to Rebecca Treadway for another terrific cover.

Special thanks to Tim Lynch, Homicide Commander, St. Paul Police Department (Ret.), for once again answering my procedural questions, and for Ed Steenberg, Senior Commander, St. Paul Police Department (Ret.), for his knowledge and help regarding SPPD funeral services and memorials for officers lost in the line of duty.

As always, thanks to my wonderfully supportive wife, Martha, without whose inspiration and experiences John Santana would not exist.